The Heart Chasers

The Heart Chasers

A Tale of Twin Flames

William and Emma Moore

Sirius Publishing Partners

The Heart Chasers: A Tale of Twin Flames

Cover Art by Jennet Inglis
Interior Design by Day to Day Enterprises

ISBN: 0-9748616-2-6
Printed in the United States of America
10 9 8 7 6 5 4 3 2 1

LCCN: 2004111571

Published by Sirius Publishing Partners ✵ Bozeman, Montana

This book is dedicated to all heart chasers everywhere.

Acknowledgements

Meant to inspire others, this work of fiction was born of the inspiration and support given to us by others. As we are all one, the good done on our behalf is passed on to those who are now in need of a story that enlivens the longing to fulfill the heart's dream, to build a new reality, to bank the warm and tender moments before it seems too late.

We give my thanks to Margaret Paul, Ph.D. for her spiritual maturity and wisdom that encouraged us to become whole while tapping into the Divine. Her profound good judgment gave life to the story's character, Francis, the psychologist. His words are her words.

Appreciation goes to Christine and Norman Arens who taught Emma the spiritual purpose of Astrology, to Joanne Thordardson who opened Emma's eyes to the miracle of Health Kinesiology, to Marilyn C. Barrick, Ph.D. who coached Emma through the EMDR method of handling trauma and to the New Warriors who teach and enable men to connect with their true feelings. Each played a part in the progress of this tale of twin flames.

We thank our friends Susan and Arturo Carvajal, Maureen Frances, Clara Gillard, Ragnar Johansen, Lydia Erja and Debbie Smoker for reading the manuscript and giving us their much needed feedback. This offering of their time and energy, freely given, moves us to feel honored to have their friendship.

Many thanks to our publicists, Mari Selby and Javier Perez for leading us through the maze of the marketing/publicity world. We are very grateful to Jennet Inglis whose beautiful cover art perfectly captured the essence of this story and to MyLinda Butterworth whose interior design continued the beauty from without to within.

Our appreciation also goes to my publisher, Therese Emmanuel Grey, for her vision and drive and to Marcia Yudkin and Bob Spear for coaching and editing excellence.

Finally, we express our appreciation and love to those forces of Light who quietly guide us, teach us and guard us each day.

Table of Contents

One

The Why in the Road

MEG SLEPT WELL most nights. Her regular bedtime was 10:30 and she usually got up at 6:00. That night was different. She was awakened at 2:00 a.m. by a dream. A beautiful being of Light was standing over her. She couldn't tell if it was a man or woman. No matter. Light radiated from all sides of the being. The luminous face was full of love and it wore robes that were as brilliant as sunshine mirrored on snow. The voice was calm and soothing, but the words it spoke were a command. "You must wake up. Go downstairs. Look in his briefcase."

Right then Meg awakened feeling completely rested. She bounded out of bed and ran to the door. The lock was noisy, so she had to move it slowly. The last thing she wanted to do was wake up Nick, who lay sleeping in the guest bedroom. Each night he kept his door open so that he could eavesdrop and be aware of everyone's whereabouts and doings.

The lock slid open quietly and Meg's next challenge was the stairs. They were old and creaked reliably. Carefully and slowly tiptoeing on the part of the treads that squeaked the least, she clung to the railing and put most of her weight on it. Once she got to the bottom, she sprinted into the dining room and turned on the light. His briefcase was on one of the side chairs. She had to move quickly.

"What am I looking for," she whispered, "financial stuff, legal stuff?"

It was customary for Nick to lie about their finances, so Meg expected to have to question his numbers. Feathering through his papers, she looked for financial stuff. Then she froze. She saw an envelope with the name and address of a well-known deprogrammer on it, a man who made his living kidnapping people who were involved in alternative religious groups. His wide definition of "cult" enabled him to bring in big bucks.

"Oh you bastard, you won't get away with this!" she whispered, and flew up the stairs with envelope in hand.

She lay in bed thinking about how low Nick was prepared to go. Living in the same house with the man she was divorcing did not make for a tranquil mode of life. She knew he was going through her private papers and correspondence each time she left the house. That alone showed what a rodent he was. Because of that, Meg didn't feel guilty about flipping through his briefcase.

She still wasn't tired or sleepy. Her mind raced as she realized how easy it would be for Nick to have her deprogrammed. He could simply open the front door and let the guy at her. She would be hauled away against her will and not one neighbor would lift a finger to help her.

A friend had carefully revealed to Meg that Nick had carried out a brilliant smear campaign against her while she was on a spiritual retreat that summer, a retreat that Nick had planned and insisted she take. Should any neighbor intervene, Nick could simply say that Meg was crazy and that he was having her taken away to a hospital for help. According to her friend, Nick had made certain that all of their neighbors believed that she was a cult member. They would all nod approvingly at his caring decision and return to their elegant suburban homes.

Hearing Nick's footsteps outside her door changed her train of thought. She held her breath. He walked down the creaky stairs quickly and came back up seconds later. *Surely,* she thought, *he knows I have the letter.* Passing by her door, he went back to the guest bedroom.

Her breathing came rapidly as she panicked and whispered, "I don't know if I can go toe to toe with this man. Is this divorce worth it?"

"What are your choices, Meg?" she questioned herself. "Think back. Breathe slowly. Calm down." Her heart rate slowed as she pressed her hand into her solar plexus.

"Yes," she reminded herself, "I have reasons. I do have reasons."

Her mind went back to 1959. She was nine years old and saw her grandmother's intense face in front of hers. Grandma Donlon lived with them after Meg's dad had died. Meg's Mom was terribly depressed, and Grandma had come to help. She sat on the living room rug and looked up at her Grandma, who sat on the edge of her chair. Grandma wore a navy and white polka dot dress covered by a well-worn apron that hung down between her knees. She wore stockings held up at the knees by pieces of elastic, black oxfords with square heels and a hair net over her bun, just like all of the other old ladies.

"Always follow your heart, Meggie. It connects you to the Divine," her Grandma whispered as her arthritic hands gripped Meg's shoulders. "Always listen to your heart, and you are sure to end up where you're supposed to be." The pain from the arthritis made Grandma grouchy a lot, but Meg loved to hear about her dreams that warned of what was to come.

"But Grandma," Meg said with a giggle, "my heart doesn't have a mouth. It can't talk."

"Oh yes it does, dearie. It talks to you with feelings, thoughts. Promptings, I call 'em. Right here," she said as she tapped Meg's heart. "Always listen. If you don't, your connection will end and your promptings will stop, and oh, what a terrible day that would be."

"Why, Grandma?"

"Because if you lose that connection, you are lost. You forget who you are. So always follow your heart, Meggie. Do you understand?"

Meg nodded. "But, Grandma, I'm Meg Walsh. How could I ever forget that?"

"No, dearie. Not your name. You'll forget who you really are, a beautiful spirit, a spark that's connected to the Divine. Oh, so many people have forgotten who they are. 'Tis a shame. Don't let that happen to you, Meggie." Meg sat looking at her grandmother with wide eyes and mouth ajar as the advice continued. "Understand, too, that when you follow your heart some people will criticize you. Condemn you."

"Why?"

"Because the heart isn't always logical or practical. People may find it hard to understand your decisions. They may even say you're crazy. You may feel as if you're on a lonely road. But it doesn't matter what they think. If you follow your heart, you will always end up where your soul needs to be, and that's more important than what anyone thinks."

"Is that what you did when you came to America?"

Her Grandma looked surprised. "Why yes, dearie, the promptings told me that I was meant to leave my home in Dublin. Your Grandpa's soul was calling me here. Oh, I will always regret breaking my Da's heart. He never did forgive me for leaving, you know. But sometimes you have to give up everyone else to find yourself."

Meg lay in bed as she remembered her Grandma's advice. "I've seen too much of Nick's shadow," she said quietly. "There's way too much control. He wants me to stay the same, but I want to move up higher. If I stay with him, my soul will dry up and blow away." Tears formed and hurried onto her pillow. "I need to follow my heart. I want a man who still has the capacity to feel, to evolve, to face the truth. I want a man with whom I can have a heart-tie. I need a new reality." She repeated, "I do have reasons. I do have reasons."

It was the fall of 1993. Meg had filed for divorce six weeks before. She was a young 43. Her dark brown hair hadn't grayed much at all. She was five foot seven and still thin. Her eyes were large, blue and pretty like her mother's, and her smile, friends had told her, put the jump start in every one of their parties.

Her thoughts went back to the spring of 1971, when she had first met Nick at a party in college. They were both in their senior year. With his hazel eyes, dark brown hair, modified mutton chops, mustache, and large, dull nose, she had found him handsome in an Eastern European way. At a little over six foot three, his slender frame could best be described as a basketball body.

The room was very dark. Those dancing looked herky-jerky as the black light, which was de rigeur for the age of rage, flickered mindlessly, never varying. Weird, acid-dropping music played in the background at a volume that vibrated the floor and walls of the dorm. Meg was seated on a couch that one of the guys had, no doubt, retrieved from a local dumpster. A sheet was thrown over it to hide the grimy, cheap fabric, but the look of it was a lot worse after the effects of the black light. She stood up to get away from its luminescent purple glow and strolled over to the stereo. The volume had finally gotten to her. Before her hand had the chance to touch the volume knob, the oscillating figure of a male approached her from her right. "Hey, you bitch. Get your hands off my stereo," he shouted as he bent over into her face.

"I know how to work this stereo," she said defiantly. "My brother has one that's a lot more challenging than this."

Meg was stunned by his coarse ways. She had seen him dancing from the other side of the room and wondered why, although drunk, he had the courage to get out on the dance floor. His whole act resembled that of a frog leaping about in a purple flowered bongo shirt. "Hey stupid," she bantered as she fingered the puffed sleeves, "did you steal that shirt from Ricky Ricardo?"

"No," he said, "my mother sent it to me." He didn't seem to catch her drift.

"Well, with a shirt like that, I bet you're just the envy of every guy in this room."

Her tone was pointed and sarcastic. Her dislike for him was immediate, but she could definitely feel a strong, sexual pull between them. "What a loser," she mumbled to herself as the fates inserted a psychedelic Nick Banacek into her circle of life. As she turned to walk away she heard him say, "Would I like to get inside of that pair of jeans!"

"Oh yeah?" she quipped over her shoulder. "Make that your mantra."

"Hey, you can't get rid of me that easy," he slurred as he clung to his beer. His buddies laughed as they watched them interact. "I like a fox with a smart mouth."

When Meg got back to her dorm that night, she found out from her roommate that Nick's fraternity brothers referred to him as "Ragdog," a tribute to his moody and critical personality. He was well known around the frat house as a malcontent, and for his birthday they had given him a box of tampons with "Ragdog" printed on it in red sparkles. "He's also known to be quite the stud," whispered Meg's roommate while she raised her eyebrows.

The next day, as she was studying for finals, Meg's phone rang.

"Hello," she said.

"Hi, this is Nick. We met at the party last night."

"Oh yeah, Nick! I remember you. Are you using that mantra, Ragdog?"

"Does everybody on this campus know that I'm the Ragdog?"

"Yeah, that's some Nick-name," Meg said, putting the emphasis on "Nick."

"Ya know, I was pretty drunk last night, and I can get obnoxious when I'm that far gone."

"Is this an apology, Nick?"

"Yes, but it won't be complete until I take you out for an apology dinner. Afterwards, we can go dancing at Bobkowski's."

Nick must have been reading Meg's mind, because she hated the campus cafeteria, and loved to polka. Besides, she told herself, there were only two more weeks to go until graduation, and if she didn't like the guy, she could escape and go back home to New York. "I'll go with you on one condition," she said.

"O.K. What's that?" Nick asked.

"You can't wear that bongo shirt!"

"You're on. How 'bout I pick you up around five?"

Meg had a great time that night. She taught Nick how to polka, and after he got the hang of it, they danced until well after one a.m., which was still early for Bobkowski's.

"Nick, there is something I have to tell you," Meg said as they sat down for a breather.

"Spill it," he said.

"All during my freshman, sophomore, and junior year, I dated a guy named Rob. He graduated last year, and he's back in New York. When I go home this summer, I'll be dating him again."

Nick was quiet for a moment. "I really had a good time tonight, Meg."

"I've had a really good time too, Nick, but I have to be honest. I have to be up front about Rob."

"Are you in love with him?" Nick asked.

"I was in love with him, and now I have to go back and find out if the flame is still there."

After graduation, Meg and Nick went their separate ways. Meg and Rob dated for almost three years, but Rob was the type of guy who had a permanent case of wanderlust. He left New York for good, and Meg had to get on with her life. She spent her days teaching behaviorally disturbed kids in a Brooklyn public school, and she arrived home each evening feeling drained. Her dream was to go to law school. One evening as she lay on her couch reading a book about the LSAT, her phone rang.

"Hello," Meg said.

"Meg, is that you?"

"Yes, this is Meg. Who is this?"

"It's Nick."

Meg was stunned. "Nick! How in the world are you? Where are you?"

"I'm here in New York on business, and I couldn't resist calling you. I heard you and Rob split up."

"Ahh! Good detective work, Nick."

"Yes, New York is crawling with my spies."

"Where are you working now?"

"I'm working with a firm in Chicago. I'm a lawyer. How about you? Where did you land? My spies tell me you've been teaching."

"I'm working with disturbed kids at a public school in Brooklyn. I'm hoping to take the LSAT and eventually go to law school."

"That's a wonderful dream. The legal profession needs more women to compensate for guys like me," he joked. "You could make a difference."

Meg ignored the quip. As the conversation continued, she remembered that there had been a sexual attraction between them, and she could feel the tug once more.

"Would you like to take a ride on the Staten Island Ferry?" he asked. "I've heard about a charming Italian restaurant on the other side."

"I'd love to!"

The Ferry was one of her favorite things to do. It fulfilled her need to be away from the city's frenetic pace. New York had a different feel down in Battery Park. It was wide open and windy. Facing the Narrows, the skyscrapers seemed a world away. The water there had the feel of the ocean instead of the dirty, clogged rivers that surrounded Manhattan. Riding toward Staten Island made her feel as if she was going back in time, back to the country, back to where she really wanted to be.

Nick drove onto the ferry and squeezed in as close as he could to the car in front of him. Meg jumped out of the car, excited to feel the wind and spray on her face. She ran over to Nick's side, grabbed his arm, and pulled him away with her. "Let's go over to the rail!"

The seagulls were everywhere, appearing to hang motionless as they kept time with the Ferry. "This is wonderful, Nick! I'm so glad you came! I've been cooped up in my little apartment all week. This is just what I needed."

"The city's beautiful to look at from out here, but it doesn't compare to your face," Nick said, getting closer to her.

Meg looked up at him. "I like you better without those mutton chops and that mustache. You're quite handsome, Nick Banacek."

They laughed, and Nick put his arm around her waist. "I've thought about you ever since graduation," he said, looking into her eyes.

"Have you been practicing your polka as I showed you?" Meg teased.

"We've got to go dancing while I'm in town," he insisted. "I can't wait to impress you with all my new moves!"

"You're on," she said, "but not tonight. I've got someplace special I want to take you after dinner!"

They chatted romantically until the ferry docked, and Nick drove them to the restaurant. It was a charming place with a casual atmosphere, and they reminisced throughout dinner.

"Meg, is there a new man in your life?" Nick asked, changing the subject and taking her by surprise.

Meg kept her composure. "No. How about you?"

"There's definitely not a man in my life," Nick said, grinning widely.

Meg laughed. "How about a woman?"

"No, but I've been thinking about a certain woman for quite some time now."

"Really?" Meg asked, feigning disinterest.

"I've been thinking about her ever since she told me to 'Make that your mantra.'"

Meg looked down for a moment, feeling a surge of energy between them. She looked back at Nick and met his gaze. "Nick, we are free now. There's nobody to get in our way anymore."

They lingered over dinner for hours, and Meg felt the world change all around her. They finally had to leave when the head waiter told them he was closing down, and when they got back to Manhattan, they went over to Morningside Park and looked out at the moon shining over the Hudson River.

"I love this park," Meg said. "When you come for your next visit, I want to take you to the Cloisters. It's not far from here. It's part of the Metropolitan Museum, and it has parts of five real medieval cloisters that were shipped over from France and reassembled, brick by brick."

"Are you inviting me back?"

"Yes, Nick. Please don't stay away too long."

"There is no way that I could," he replied, pulling her to him and kissing her at last.

For six months they endured a telephone romance and took turns flying the distance between New York and Chicago. By Christmas they were engaged. Nick came to New York to give her a ring, and later that day as they skated in Rockefeller Center, he impressed her with his considerable skating ability. She watched him skate backwards, do turns and stop abruptly without ever losing his balance. It was a magical scene, with Christmas lights blinking around the rink and snowflakes falling.

"How can you stop on a dime like that?" she asked as she skated tamely from one end of the rink to the other, her arms outstretched ever so slightly in anticipation of losing her balance. For Meg, to stop on a dime was not within the realm of possibility. Her method of stopping was to slam into the wall.

"Well," he said, "I learned to skate at the local rink when I was in high school. It was a great place to pick up girls. You had to be able to stop next to the right girl. If you couldn't be precise, you might end up with a real dog."

They married in early August of '75. Nick was unyielding in his refusal to transfer to his firm's New York office, so Meg quit her teaching position and moved to Chicago's north shore. There was a glut of teachers on the market, and as she searched for a position she also applied to law schools. When she finally found a job, she paid her tuition with her salary and matriculated as a law student in the University's evening division. Life seemed good and full of promise.

With that recollection in mind, Meg got out of bed. She walked over to the window, brushed aside the petit point curtains and looked up at the stars. "I do have reasons," she whispered as she recalled the first year of their marriage.

Her underpants had gotten holes in them. She purchased some replacements, and without thinking, left the boxes on the bed. Arriving home from work, Nick saw the purchase and shot her an angry glance. "Why did you buy these?" he said, incredulous. Meg explained about her old underpants. Both she and Nick were working full time; what was the problem? It made no impression on him. His goal was to be a millionaire or better by the time he was forty, and he only had fifteen years in which to do it. For days, he silently fumed behind a cold exterior. He did not speak to or look at her. She pleaded with him to discuss the reason for his anger. With each entreaty, he held back even more. She missed the warmth there had been between them. Living without his love was too painful for her, so she bowed to his will and avoided spending "his" money. Nick made it very clear that their money was his money.

The change in Meg's behavior was not lost on Nick. She noticed that he enjoyed having her under his thumb, that her submissive behavior did not tweak his conscience in the least and that he didn't seem to need either love or affection. He preferred to interact with her as little as possible.

His job was demanding. An "eighty hour plus" work week was expected. He gave his all to his superiors and had nothing left to give when he got home. Meg was alone most of the time. After he arrived home, it was her job to pick up his empties and bottletops and throw them in the trash. Depending upon the time of year and the hour at night when he returned home, she could count on at least a six pack or more of empties. He'd chug a few Black Russians right before he fell into bed.

After their marriage, Meg had discovered that Nick's parents were both alcoholics. That explained his heavy drinking. He never acted drunk when he was drunk, so his problem was a well-hidden secret. He never missed a day of work, like his parents before him. Because theirs had been a long distance romance, the drinking, the long hours, and the differences in their ideals had not come out. Feeling very much alone, she mused, "Had we lived in the same city while we dated, I would have seen it all. I could have made a quick exit from his life."

Before their marriage, Nick had admitted to Meg that the higher degrees and sensible manner of her family impressed him. "You'll add class to my climb up the career ladder, Meg," he said. This she did willingly at first, but soon changed her mind. She hated the kiss-ass way he acted when he was around the partners in his firm and noticed too frequently that when he came in the back door at the end of the day, his eyes had no light in them. "The money's not worth it. You're selling your soul," she told him. "I don't want this kind of life. You're never home." He ignored her. Her wants didn't matter. She was left with the choice of accepting his lifestyle or getting out.

There were times when she needed to talk. She was lonely. Adjusting to to the north shore was a big change for her. Opportunities to make local friends were slow to arise. Calling her old friends in New York was out of the question. Nick would turn even icier over the long distance bills. At first, he was her only contact. She made a habit of listening to his problems, which he laid out in great detail, but if she began to talk about herself, he would turn around and walk out of the room. One night she decided to force the issue. He wasn't working under a deadline, so he would probably get home by 10:00 p.m. She never knew when he would call to say he was on his way. *He won't want to talk. He never does,* she thought. *But if I set up an appointment with him, maybe that will work.* She dialed his work number.

Nick answered with his business voice, "Nick Banacek."

God, I hate that phony voice, she thought as she visualized him swaggering around the house, shoulders back, nose in the air, too important to talk to her.

"Hi Nick, it's Meg," she said, realizing that she'd better talk fast because there wasn't room for her on his time report. He responded tersely, confirming that there wasn't room for her on his time report. "Listen, there are some things I'd like to talk to you about. Will you meet me in the kitchen at 10:00 p.m. so we can talk?"

"Sorry. I can't," he said. "I'll be watching the news at 10:00 p.m."

She began to discern that Nick perceived himself as his own god. He submitted his will to no one. Growing used to his daily rejections, Meg found married life the loneliest of conditions. Over time, she found that he lied even when he didn't have to, that he was brooding by nature, rarely smiled, and was charming only when he wanted his way. His power games and intrigue left their malicious mark on her soul way down at levels that she could not even fathom. Behind closed doors, she lived a life of quiet grief.

Snow clouds moved across the night sky. Meg looked out at her neighborhood, lit up by a small number of street lights. "The fewer the streetlights, the more exclusive the suburb," one of her neighbors who cared about such things had told her. Barnstable was an older suburb on Chicago's north side. Each block had two street lights, enough to be a suburb but not enough to be really ritzy, her neighbor had concluded.

Meg thought about the kind of people she had for neighbors. Everyone was friendly, happy and nice, but there seemed to be little depth to it. "A monochromatic lot," she reflected. "Zero tolerance for variety. Success and money are sought after with a vengeance. I don't fit in."

As she watched the snow clouds moving across the night sky, she whispered, "Feelings and intuition cause you to get too close to people. Closeness kills the ruthlessness so necessary for success." Meg was feeling angry. The old rage was coming back again. She knew that Nick couldn't tolerate the discomfort that feelings and intuition can bring. Self-observation was strictly taboo, reserved for those who were too weak to find a convincing scapegoat. For years, she had observed his need to be aloof so that he could climb over the competition without disturbing what conscience he had. Each day he went off to work as if he was a soldier going to war, but why did she too have to be the enemy?

"Because he hated your intuitive nature. Your ethical questions made him squirm," she responded quietly, thinking back. He had seemed uptight one night, and in a vulnerable moment revealed his fears to her. One of his clients was shredding evidence. The partner told him to look the other way. He looked pale as he told Meg that he was present when the partner "bought" a witness. "Obstruction of Justice. This is how people get disbarred, Nick," whispered a shaken Meg. "Get outta that firm. Why go along with this?"

"Because we want our fee!" he quipped. Sounding irritated, he shot her a look of disbelief and said, "We don't want to lose the client. Look, I may not be as smart as some of the guys that I work for, but I make up for that with long hours and allegiance. No matter what they do is just fine by me. I'm gonna be a partner someday and that's how I'm gonna get there."

He made her feel stupid. Did he really expect her to believe that it was okay to lie as long as you get your money? Surely he could earn a living without engaging in such deceit. She watched him seethe and retreat into denial each time she exposed his shadow. The years revealed to her that she was superior to him in ethics and smarts, but his ego needed to be better than her. Casting a critical eye on her every move, exaggerating her smallest mistakes, denouncing her as he nitpicked and reproved her demeanor, he seemed to convince himself, despite his admitted lack of brilliance, that she was beneath him and worthy only of scorn.

Meg wasn't ready to go back to bed. A lovely snow had begun to fall. Its contrast to her ugly memories was disquieting. "Nick will be up early this morning," she said to herself. "He'll need a lot of time to blow the neighbors' sidewalks." They all believed that Nick was a great guy. He had to be. Who else but a great guy would blow his neighbor's sidewalk? But Meg knew that his real motives were carefully concealed. Snowblowing was a great time waster, and Nick would do just about anything to avoid his family, especially Meg.

Blowing your neighbor's sidewalk is also a great way to enhance your public image. Image was everything to Nick. "He lacks the motivation to be nice, but his craving to seem nice is potent," she whispered.

Eyeing his furrowed brow, as he worried about what others thought of him and as he furiously picked his cuticles when trying to impress or deceive, Meg wondered what his real motivation was. "Is he deceiving them or just himself?"

Nick dressed well with Meg's guidance, got to work seven days a week an hour early, paid his taxes fashionably late after only one extension and cheating only a little bit, went to Mass each Sunday, and outwardly seemed to live a life that was above reproach. Perfection governed his self-image, which was craftily contrived. He wanted everyone to think that he was a great guy. Meg knew it was all a lie.

"I should have divorced him after that first year," she mused. "I was such a dumb little Catholic girl, always worried about what my family would think, never doing what was best for me." She had told herself that she could make the marriage work, that if she gave him enough love, he'd have to respond in kind. "No more dumb little Catholic girl," she swore.

Two

One Way Trip

It was the summer of 1968, and the Volkswagen bus chugged its way up Independence Pass toward Aspen, Colorado, heavily laden with camping gear. Busby, Hills, Stash, and Long were blasting away on the bus's custom-installed tape deck, and two young couples were grooving on their radical sound.

"This is so far out!" Michael shouted. He had never before seen the Rockies, and he was stoked. "I've never been this high before!"

"What about last night?" his girlfriend Amelie asked.

"Come on baby, take me higher," Michael sang, doing his best imitation of their current rock idol.

"I've got a surprise for all of you tonight. Especially you, Michael!" she said, opening her hand and showing him the LSD she was carrying for this special occasion. "We're going to find out how high we can go!"

Michael was the only one of them who hadn't dropped acid yet. "I'm supposed to start at Berkeley next semester," he said. "I don't want to fry my brains."

"Why Michael, what would people think?" Jean asked, turning around from her front window seat. "You don't think you're better than us, do you? We're all in this together. We are the Love Generation."

"How many times have you dropped, Amelie?" Bob asked, looking at her in the rear-view mirror.

"I stopped counting," she said defiantly, looking back at Michael. "Don't worry, baby. I'll follow you all the way up." She stroked the back of Michael's neck, and he felt sexual excitement surge through him.

"You're on," he said.

They laughed and sang the rest of the way to Aspen, and as they pulled into town, Michael sensed a glow and a presence to his left, and glanced over at two men walking into town after a morning hike in the mountains. One was carrying a gnarly walking stick, and as Michael looked in his direction, he turned and met Michael's gaze. The man smiled, and Michael felt his entire soul ignite. Such a smile! Not a trace of vanity or pride. Light and serenity poured from his face.

Michael turned back to focus on the road, and he and his little group continued on until they reached a park in the middle of town. They parked the bus, got their sack lunches, and sauntered over to a shady spot.

"Let's go get some pop," Amelie said. "We can walk around a little and check out the scene."

"You guys go ahead," Michael said. "I just want to cool it here for a while."

"See ya later," Amelie countered as her eyes lingered just a little too long on Michael's, as her hips swayed just a little too hard. She and the others walked off, and Michael fixed his gaze on her well-defined hips made all the more alluring in her hip hugger bellbottoms. A few moments went by, and then suddenly Michael felt the same glow and presence come over him that he had felt when he first entered the town. As he turned around, the two men he had seen earlier were sitting down next to him. They had an air of dignity and quiet athleticism about them, and they were definitely not the type to indulge in drugs. The one with the walking stick was opening up his back pack. He withdrew a journal, opened it up to the page he wanted without even looking at it, and placed it on the ground in front of him. Michael looked into his eyes. They seemed to focus on everything at once, yet when they looked directly at Michael, they were aware of his entire being. Michael looked down at the page in front of him and beheld an exquisite drawing of a sprout bursting out of the ground into the sunlight.

"Where did you get that gnarly walking stick?" Michael asked, not really getting directly to the point.

"It is a gift from the infinite storehouse of the Creator," the man explained.

"What is that drawing all about?" Michael asked, this time asking him the question he really wanted the answer for.

"Man is like this seed, growing up into the sunlight."

"May I see your journal?"

"Certainly."

Michael perused the pages, astonished at what he saw. The handwritten pages and hand-drawn pictures were flawless and totally without corrections. He continued to read and stopped when he came to the sentence, "As above, so below."

Michael looked up. "What does this sentence mean?"

"It is your quest!"

The man then gently took the book and returned it to his backpack. Rising softly without effort, he and his companion turned and walked away.

Michael sat there in complete amazement, the entire scene indelibly printed on his mind. Eventually, Bob, Jean and Amelie returned.

"What kind of a trip are you on?" Amelie asked. "Can I come, too?"

Michael recovered his hip image, but he didn't want to share what had just happened with anyone. "I'm just groovin' on this mountain scenery," he said.

They stayed in the park all day, and when night came, they passed the LSD around. Against his better judgement, Michael swallowed the little tablet Amelie gave him, but he didn't have the experience she had promised. Perhaps his LSD was contaminated, perhaps not.

As he looked over at Amelie, he watched in horror as her face appeared to melt away. Uncontrollable energy was pulsing through him, and it left him in a frazzle when he came down off the acid. He had made a terrible mistake, and now it was too late to change it.

"Amelie," he said, a feeling of dread and fear coming over him. "You don't seem real."

"You're freaking me out, Michael. You're putting out really bad vibes."

"I can't help it," he explained. "Something went wrong. Something is not right with me."

"If something went wrong, you made it go wrong. You just didn't go with the flow," she said. "The rest of us are just fine."

The next morning, Michael awoke with a sense of pure despair. He had hoped a good night's sleep would return him to where he had been before he took the LSD, but it didn't. He could converse, and nothing looked wrong on the surface, but inside the circuitry was damaged. His soul had retreated somewhere, and Michael couldn't get it back into alignment with his body. He kept repeating, "You don't seem real, you don't seem real," over and over again to Amelie, and after a while he began to repulse her. Michael felt scared and helpless, and as Jean and Bill started to realize this, they didn't want anything to do with him either. They were on their summer vacation, and they were only interested in having fun. Michael had become a liability, and they didn't want to be seen with him. What's more, they didn't want to take any of the blame for what had happened to him. They had all met casually, and they could split up just as casually. When Michael awoke in their little hotel room the next morning, he discovered Amelie had left town with Jean and Bill. The tears ran down his face as he read Amelie's farewell letter.

"Please understand, Michael. We all came out here to have a good time, and since we took the LSD, it has really been a bummer to be around you. You are bringing everybody down. You used to be a lot of fun, but now there is nothing there. How can I love you when there is nothing there? Peace and Love, Amelie." It was the last he ever saw of her.

Michael found a job washing dishes in Aspen, and saved enough money for a bus ride home to Houston, his home town. He flunked out of Berkeley the next semester because he just couldn't concentrate, and things got worse from there. All through his early twenties, he was a street person with nowhere to go. He would work out of the temporary labor pools with winos and other street people. He knew he didn't belong there, but he realized that they really didn't belong there either. He was no different. He was not special anymore. He was walking around in tattered clothes. He was nameless and unknown.

Gradually, Michael was able to painstakingly reconstruct his identity. He got a job driving taxis, then at last a job waiting tables. The stress and the fear of failure or looking stupid were enormous, but he had no choice. He enrolled in the local college a few times, but he flunked out. The records remained on his college transcript. The years passed, and he got better in little increments.

At last he enrolled in school at the local college again. He managed to keep a reasonably good grade point average, but he made a "D" in physics. He took the class over again, and actually made an "A." He was ecstatic. That same semester he made an "A" in Calculus, and a "B" in Differential Equations. It was his only "B," and everything else was an "A." He made the Dean's list. He had recovered physiologically, but not psychologically or emotionally. He felt as if he had a scarlet "A" for acid on his forehead, and he felt a deep stigma. He was aware of it every moment of every day. When the time came for him to announce his major, he went before the dean to explain why he should be admitted into the college of electrical engineering.

Michael remembered the contempt and disgust in the dean's eyes as he looked over his transcripts. The dean told him that if he could make a "B" or higher in the two hardest classes on the engineering curriculum, he would allow him to continue in electrical engineering.

"If you can't make at least a 'B' in these two classes," the dean said with an arrogant sneer, "don't ever darken our door again."

The pressure the dean put on Michael was too much for him, because his self-esteem and confidence just weren't there yet. He felt as if people wanted him to fail more than they wanted him to succeed, but in most cases, they didn't care one way or the other. Michael made a "C" in both classes, and changed his major to Computer Science. Working all day and going to school at night was taking its toll on him. Eight years passed, and finally, he graduated.

After a long job search, Michael interviewed with a man who put aside the records and looked deeper. Unlike all the others, the guy had a heart. As Michael left the interview, he took a long, deep breath. His new job with NASA started the following week in Houston. He had to accept a lower pay grade than the hardware engineers. Software engineers were considered to be somewhat lower on the totem pole, but at least, he was back on track.

As the years progressed, people kept looking at his title, and not at his essence. He was categorized, and he felt locked in, unable to move up. He saw people who had every credential in the book, who looked perfect on paper, and who were completely incompetent. They were the ones who moved up. They knew the right people. They could maneuver others into doing the real work. In many cases, they had all of the power, and none of the skill.

It had been more than twenty years since that night in Aspen, and during those years, Michael determined to himself he was going to shun every substance that was even remotely unhealthy for him. He didn't drink, he didn't smoke, he didn't eat sugar, he didn't eat chocolate, he didn't eat meat, and most of all, he didn't associate with anyone who did drugs. He never went to bars, and he got a good night's sleep every night. He worked out constantly, and he rode his bicycle over 150 miles a week. He had gotten into cycling almost ten years before, and it had become a way for him to boost his self-esteem. He was lean and muscular, over six feet tall, with long wavy dark hair and a radiant smile, looking much younger than his years. He had been playing catch-up, and there was no quit in him. He knew he still had a long way to go. He had to reconnect what was below with what was above.

It's going to be a fun bike ride tonight, Michael thought one Saturday evening as he sat in his townhouse, practicing his classical guitar. *"I've been looking forward to this Midnight Ramble for a long time."*

The phone rang, and he reached over and picked it up. "This is Michael," he said.

"Michael, I'm so glad you're home!" It was Mindy, a girl his biking buddies had fixed him up with a week earlier.

"What's wrong, Mindy?"

"Michael, can I please come stay with you tonight?" Mindy pleaded.

"What happened?" Michael asked.

"Someone tried to break into my apartment last night, and I'm scared."

"What time was it? Were you there?"

"It was around 2:00 a.m. I turned on the light when I heard someone try to open the patio slider, and whoever it was ran away."

"Not good," Michael said.

"Can I come over tonight?" Mindy asked, sounding like a frightened little girl.

"I'm going to the Midnight Ramble, but I can leave you a key under the doormat."

"I'll be waiting up for you," Mindy said seductively as she hung up the phone.

Three

Don't Ever Change

THE WIND WAS BEGINNING to pick up speed, and the cold air slipped through the windows in their 90-year-old home. Meg hugged herself, rubbing her arms with her chilly hands. Climbing back into bed, she propped up her pillow and pulled the covers over her arms. She recalled the morning their younger daughter, Amy, was born. It was March, 1983. The weather was similar. There had been a terrible ice storm the night before. The trees were encased in ice down to the tiniest twigs. It was a beautiful sight. The cars were in the same condition. Meg heard the familiar sound of a scraper on a windshield multiplied by many households. Her labor pains were coming, she was three days overdue and she told Nick before he left for work, "I think the baby's coming. I'm going to have it this morning."

Nick responded, "Oh, you always think it's coming." With that, he walked out the door and drove to work. He had a lot of meetings.

Their neighbor, Harry, didn't hesitate to come to Meg's rescue. A baby was too important. He'd tell his boss his neighbor was in labor, and that's why he was late. After leaving a message with Nick's secretary about the significant event, he scraped a little hole in his icy windshield and drove Meg to the hospital. He even offered to be her Lamaze coach until Nick arrived. As Meg politely refused his offer, she wondered about the beauty of Harry's nature and envied his wife.

The entire birthing took only three hours, but it involved intense back labor. She had wished that Nick had been there to rub the tennis ball on her back. There was no time for the nurses to give her a pain-killer. They all looked overworked and told Meg that the ice storm was to blame. There were twice as many babies being delivered as there were beds. Full moons and atmospheric events bring on the births in big numbers, they said. There were moms in labor out in the hallway.

As Amy crowned, Nick arrived. He casually walked alongside the bed as Meg was wheeled into the delivery room, carrying the cigars he had stopped to purchase on his way to the hospital. Amy was born minutes later at 9:45 a.m.

Meg's exhilaration at the sight of Amy was dashed when she heard Nick say with disgust, "Ugh, it's another girl." The Doctor shot a worried glance in Nick's direction, then looked at Meg.

The windows shook, and Meg could hear the air vents for the whole-house fan flip-flopping in the attic window. The storm outside had worsened. "I do have reasons," she vowed as she recalled that her world had been going on as mechanically as ever when Nick made a troublesome disclosure one night at the dinner table. The year was 1985.

Nick's parents and sister were over for dinner. Meg had felt a kinship of sorts with his sister, Helena. She was an avid reader, as Meg was, and although she never really acted interested in Meg or her life, she demonstrated by her fine conversation that she had the ability to engage in higher philosophical thinking. Meg never saw the rest of the Banaceks come close to achieving this. "There's a density about them that they choose to be proud of, claiming money is more important than anything, except maybe the booze," a frustrated Helena confided. "Never stopping to think about how much money is enough, they live the most obtuse of lifestyles." Meg knew she felt hurt because her parents had never really accepted her and her lifestyle. Nick was the star of the family.

He started to brag about having had three summer jobs when he was in college. "I thought that you had two jobs," Meg commented casually while scraping the plates.

"No, I had three. I drove a cab, waited tables and made shells."

Meg thought, *Shells? What does he mean, shells? I hope he's talking about pasta.*

Helena rose a few inches out of her chair and asked. "You don't mean shells for Viet Nam, do you?"

"Yeah," said Nick defiantly as he glanced over at his approving parents, their smiles making him even cockier. Meg wondered at the pride they showed for their arrogant son, who was a workaholic from a very young age. They never asked about how he earned his money as long as he earned it. They enjoyed, no admired, his greed. As immigrants to this country, they wanted the American dream with a lust that made Meg squirm. Helena, on the other hand, was given almost no respect by them. She didn't make much money as an artist, but Helena had more of a conscience than all of them and had confessed to Meg years before that she chose to live outside Santa Fe to get away from their ignorance.

As her mind raced to absorb the awkward scene before her, Meg recalled that Nick had gotten a high number in the lottery. He knew he didn't have to go to Viet Nam, so why not make shells? Meg knew Nick better than Nick knew Nick, and she could almost hear his thoughts, "I'm not going to Nam, so these shells won't kill me. They'll kill some other poor bastard."

"I can't believe you did that," Helena, the older sister, hollered. She had already moved to New York City when Nick had left for college. Wrapped up in her craft, she knew little of Nick and his jobs during those years. "You made shells during the Viet Nam War?"

"Yeah," laughed Nick. "And I made great money doing it!"

The conversation continued between the two siblings as Meg observed a stubbornness in Nick that had taken over his greed and pride. There was little Helena could say to encourage any kind of repentance or regret. It appeared to Meg that in his heart, Nick considered himself to be above reproach. Since Helena questioned the ethics of his making shells, she had to be scapegoated. Anyone who implied that Nick was bad had to be sacrificed. To deny his own wrongdoing, he had to conclude it was Helena who was bad. To Meg's mind, he had lost the capacity to feel and the ability to be empathic.

From that day forward, his projection was complete. Helena was treated no better than Meg. He regularly spoke of her with scorn. "She makes no money as an artist because she has no talent for it. She's lazy, poor, and an impractical space head." Nick would not look at Helena or respond to her favorably when she was in his presence. She was never to be forgiven.

The windows in Meg's bedroom were beginning to ice up as the memories kept on coming. She thought of Helena and how different from Nick she was. It was Christmas of '87. While running to her car in the airport's parking lot, Meg's feet became entangled in an old, rusty coat hanger that lay on the asphalt. She fell face down with such force that she rammed her chin into the ground. Her ribs ached, and she worried that they were broken.

Helena insisted that she go to the emergency room. "If you break a rib, it can puncture a lung. You'd better check it out," she said. So Meg brought Helena and the kids home and then drove herself to the hospital. It took all afternoon and evening to get through the maze of paperwork and the crowds of people who needed X-rays.

Nick came to the hospital after work, but silently avoided all eye contact with Meg. With a tightly locked jaw he approached the cashier. Their insurance deductible was jacked up high because he disliked paying big premiums. His body stiffened when he realized that their deductible was greater than the bill. The walk to the car was a silent one. Her fall had inconvenienced him and his wallet.

For weeks, she couldn't sleep at night without a whole load of painkillers. Nick never asked how she was or how bad the pain was. Her vulnerable state seemed to make him all the more scornful.

"I have reasons," she assured herself. "The pain will all be worth it when the divorce is over. I did all I could do to make it work, and I endured that dimwit of a therapist." The resentment returned as she thought about it. He was so sincere when he talked to their therapist, telling her that he wanted the marriage to work. But when he was away from her office, he was the same old Nick.

"He went to therapy to maintain his image of the great guy, but he feared even the smallest change to his personality, as an ordinary man dreads death," Meg whispered. He walked the razor's edge of speaking sincerely while changing none of the behaviors that were so destructive to the marriage.

"I'm telling you nothing has changed," Meg told the therapist. "He brings me bouquets of daisies that are wilted, clinically dead. For months he's done this. Then he brings me a bouquet of beautiful, fresh, white roses, and as he hands them to me he tells me that they're for the girls. Don't you think there's a message there?"

Nick claimed he didn't know that Meg's flowers were dead. The therapist sided with him, referring to his sincerity. "It's the thought that counts, Meg," she said.

"I thought therapists were supposed to be perceptive," Meg wondered. Finally, after a year, she gave up, thanked the therapist and withdrew from future sessions. The therapist was happy. "Isn't it wonderful when a marriage is saved?" she gloated. Nick beamed. He had won. No more performances for the therapist, and he hadn't internalized a thing. Meg was even more convinced that no one would believe the truth about him. If the therapist couldn't see through his mask, who would?

The kids suffered from Nick's mind games because their mother spent too much time trying to fathom his motives and intrigue. She received his undeclared messages while wondering if she was imagining it all. She felt his hatred while he declared undying love. She submitted to his stinginess while he lavished his money on charitable causes and the kids' every wish. She winced at seeing his congenial public image while he shunned her company in their home. She was no longer able to be there for Heather and Amy. All of her energy had to be dedicated to the survival of her soul. The craziness of the relationship made her irritable, edgy and afraid. The well was running dry, as she gave more than she got. She found herself exploding at the least provocation. It seemed to Meg that her misery gave him a reason for being, that he was crushing her with an unseen hand.

Meg slid down under the covers and could hear the icy snow scratching against the window. As her head dropped onto the pillow, she thought about how the big salary had affected Nick and how Nick had affected the kids.

When she had married Nick, he had had some humility. Not much, but some. With each year he had earned more and more money, but became less and less likable. The measure of his wallet was the measure of his ego. Judging people by their money and sometimes by their job title, he had become smug and superior around the house. Meg's part-time job wasn't impressive enough for him to refrain from making her the main object of his scorn.

"Why don't we go running together?" she asked him. "You could teach me to get started the way you did. Remember how you would walk for a while and then run until you were able to run a whole mile?" Creating something that they could have in common was important to her. It might save the marriage. She was sitting at the kitchen table.

"I'm not gonna run with you. You're too slow," he said with a sneer while he gazed out the window.

A few days later Nick went running with their older daughter, Heather. She had just turned fourteen. Meg watched as he patiently taught her how to warm up and alternate walking with running until she passed her first mile. With each improvement, the two celebrated together and formed a cozy clique.

As the marriage wore on, she felt more and more like the housekeeper and got less and less respect from the kids. They saw how Nick treated their Mom. Their allegiance was with him. That pleased him. He was very generous when he was pleased. Theirs was a survival tactic that Meg had seen as early as the playground. The betrayal stung.

The night moved on, and Meg thought about her own Mom. Mrs. Walsh had passed away in '91 and Meg had missed her every day since. She recalled the Christmas of '89 when her Mom had come for the holiday.

Meg and the kids had driven to the airport to pick her up. "O.K. guys, it's time to start praying to the parking angels for a good space. Grandma Walsh says that there are parking angels who have only one job, and that's to help us get parking spaces. Tell them we need a good spot that's near the entrance, so grandma doesn't have to walk too far." From behind her, she could hear their voices whispering to the angels.

The stellar parking space appeared as requested, and Meg said, "O.K., now we have to thank the angels for this spot. Let's hear it for the parking angels."

"Thank you, angels," the kids screamed as they ran for the crosswalk.

Mrs. Walsh alighted from the airplane as spryly as a 50-year-old. Although she was almost 80, her mind was quick, and she chatted happily about Meg's brothers and her grandkids all the way home.

Happily settling into the guest room, she unpacked while Amy talked incessantly. Heather was the shy one. She watched her grandmother and said little. Meg knew from her Mom's stooped shoulders that she was exhausted, yet she patiently listened to Amy's chatter.

Hunger pain jogged thoughts of dinner to the fore of her mind. She was inspecting the defrosting chicken when the phone rang. Surprisingly, it was Nick's voice on the other end. "I need you to pick me up at the train station. There's a bad storm in the works, and I don't want to drive home. I'm gonna leave the car down here. I'll call you when I get to the station." At the conclusion she almost expected to hear, "This tape will self-destruct..."

Almost two hours later, he called from the train station. Meg put on her boots, coat, hat and gloves to head out into the best of Chicago's winter. The flakes were big and wet, like sloppy kisses landing on her face. The driveway was slippery, and she was sweating it as she pulled out. "Don't hit the house," she warned herself, "or you'll be in deep doo doo even though you're doing him a favor. It won't matter." The five-minute trip to their train station took fifteen minutes that night. There was lots of ice under the snow, so she crawled along while in a reverie. The snow was unusually beautiful that night. Every branch and twig on the trees and bushes was holding inches of the heavy powder. The street lamps haloed thousands of flakes traveling sideways. It was the kind of night that made you believe in Santa Claus.

The downtown of their village was decorated for Christmas, and it was easy to spot Nick illumined by all of the twinkly lights. Standing next to him in the same doorway was a street person, a skinny, wobbling, elderly man in a thin, dirty coat who looked weak and very ill. He had no hat or scarf. His hands were shoved into his pockets, and his shoulders were raised up to his ears as he tried to keep warm. *How sad,* she thought. *What kind of Christmas is he going to have?*

Meg stopped in front of the store, and Nick hopped in. Looking forward to going home, Meg began to turn right at the next corner, but was forced to a sudden halt by the same street person she had seen standing next to Nick. He was crossing the street in front of the car. He struggled through the snow without any boots and turned his head straight down to keep the snow out of his face. His gloveless hand was pulling his coat up around his neck. His shoes were full of snow as his strength gave out and he fell to the asphalt. Cars were coming in both directions. Meg reacted without thinking, opening her car door, reaching for the man and picking him up. She was surprised at how light he was and was able to lift him without strain. She put him in the back seat of her car and asked, "Where do you live?" hoping that he had some place to call home. He responded, "At the 'Y.'" The YMCA was not too far away, and Meg headed in that direction. She didn't care what Nick thought as he sat next to her in silence. He offered the old man no help when Meg stopped in front of the "Y."

"Would you like me to help you walk to the front door?" Meg offered.

"No," he said. "I'll be O.K."

Meg waited until he walked the 50 feet to the front door to see if he could make it. He was unsteady the whole way, but reached the door without falling.

Meg and Nick drove home in stony silence. She knew he was angry with her for picking up the old man, but she didn't care. When they pulled into the driveway, Nick got out of the car and walked around to the rear seat where the old man had been.

"What are you doing?" she asked as he brushed the upholstery with his expensive leather glove.

"I'm just making sure that he didn't stain the upholstery."

His words cut deeply into her soul. She turned to Nick and spoke with a fury that shocked both of them. "You big jackass. All you ever think about is your precious car and the things that you own. Things don't matter, Nick. People matter. That man is worth a thousand cars, but you look down on him because he has no money. You disgust me."

Nick's face showed no change in expression. She turned and walked into the house.

Recalling that scene made Meg's body go rigid. She lay in bed and thought once again of her Mom and the part she had played in Meg's decision to file for divorce. It was the day before Thanksgiving in 1990, and Mrs. Walsh sat at their kitchen table as Meg prepared their dinner. The familiar squeak of their back porch door interrupted the conversation between mother and daughter. Meg turned, smiled and said "Hi" as Nick opened the back door.

Meg was going to call the girls into the kitchen to greet him when she noticed that despite her mother's presence, Nick wasn't putting on an act. There was none of the expected charm. He was acting as if Mrs. Walsh wasn't there.

With briefcase in hand, he slowly walked across the kitchen with his eyes cast down at the floor. He said "Hello" to neither Meg nor Mrs. Walsh. There was no light in his eyes. He didn't look depressed, just arrogant and cold. He passed out of the kitchen, hung up his coat and went up to the master bedroom. Mrs. Walsh looked disturbed by Nick's behavior, but she said nothing.

Meg turned to the sink to peel some potatoes for dinner. *Nick behaves that way every night when he gets home from work,* she thought. *He always looks like that.* She had gotten used to his strange ways, convincing herself that his behavior wasn't odd. Dissociating from the weirdness of their relationship helped her to deal with the pain. She had denied what was true for years rather than deal with the fact that she was married to a man whose soul was not O.K. She had daily doubted her sanity, but seeing her mother's reaction to Nick's behavior confirmed in her own mind that she wasn't crazy. The truth was there to be faced. There was a strange and dark side to Nick that Meg could no longer deny.

"Mom," Meg said as she sat down at the kitchen table, potato peeler in hand. Her eyes were riveted on her mother's. The disturbed look still hadn't left Mrs. Walsh's face. "Remember how you used to give my old boyfriends the 'intractable' test?"

"Oh, yes," laughed Mrs. Walsh. "Well, I wanted to make sure that you married someone who could keep up with you and your brothers. I wanted you to be equally yoked," she added.

"Equally yoked?" asked Meg.

"Yes. A woman will never be happy if she marries a man who is her inferior."

"You mean, if he's dumber."

"Well, yes. Inferior mentally. That goes without saying, but also spiritually, ethically, morally, however you want to say it. The marriage won't work if you have different ideals, standards. You have to have the same dream, the same purpose."

"How come you never gave Nick the 'intractable' test?"

Mrs. Walsh froze. She stared at Meg in disbelief. "Well, honey, I... don't know. I...don't remember," she stammered.

"Oh, come on, Mom, tell me the truth."

Mrs. Walsh looked around to see if the kids were listening, and then averted her eyes. "Well, he was doing such a good job of taking you by storm. He was a little slow, maybe boring's the word, but he seemed nice. There was little to no intellectual curiosity in him. He certainly wasn't much of a reader. And my Lord, he didn't even know how to buy a decent suit for work. I know you had to teach him how to dress, but he was very attentive. You seemed to like that. The relationship had quickly taken on a life of its own. I didn't want to upset the apple cart."

"So you mean you didn't think that he'd pass the 'intractable' test?"

"Well, now, I didn't say that. Meg, what good is it to talk about this now? You've had two children with him."

"Mom, please tell me the truth."

"I used to use the word 'sinecure' too. Remember? That word really stumped Charles Punt from the Jesuit high school," said Mrs. Walsh, laughing and enjoying the memories. "What an arrogant young man he was. Your grandmother would have called him 'His Nibs.'"

"Mom," said Meg, touching her mother's hand to bring her back to the present, "do you think I'm equally yoked?"

"Honey, I can't answer that."

"Mom, please, I need to know what you think."

"Meg, this is so confidential."

"I know. I know. But am I equally yoked?"

Mrs. Walsh looked pained as she spoke. "No, dear. No."

Meg got out of bed again and began to pace. It wasn't long after that conversation that Mrs. Walsh passed on from a stroke. Dealing with the loss of her Mom and the daily rejection she felt from her less than successful partnership with Nick brought Meg to her knees. There had to be something more to life than living in the suburbs with a man who fancied her as his serf. "No more dumb little Catholic girl," she swore. She began a spiritual search.

She didn't do this in an ordinary way. Meg wasn't interested in learning anything else that the Catholic Church had to offer. Hinduism, Buddhism, Islam, Jewish mysticism and the Kabbalah were all on her "to do" list. There had to be something out there that could help her find God, or at least feel closer to Him. She branched out and included some channelers and occult stuff too. She wanted to make the leap from religion to spirituality. Eventually, Meg ended up learning with a small group of spiritual seekers in Barnstable who were well versed in all of the above and then some.

It did not take long for Meg to notice Nick's disapproval of the changes in her. Engaging him in a conversation or getting him to do things with her was no longer one of her goals. She wasn't under his thumb any more. She had found her own interests. He couldn't hurt her. She didn't care. He didn't matter to her anymore. She told him he could work as much as he wanted, learn how to play golf and stay out on the course as long as he wanted. The kids would live without a father as she had, and that was that. It was their lot in life.

Meg thought he would be relieved to hear that she didn't care about his absence from the home. Wasn't that what he had wanted all along? But Nick seemed annoyed that he couldn't jerk her around any more.

To Meg's mind, he sensed that this new-found spiritual search meant a lot to her, so he began to block her search. He questioned all of the books that she was reading, the meditations and chanting that she was experimenting with. He even objected to the Catholic rosary that she was saying. The peace that Meg had found from her spiritual quest seemed to threaten him. Instead of relishing the harmony that it brought into the home, Nick stepped up his private war against her.

"What are you reading?" he demanded as she sat, opened book in hand, with foot draped over the couch.

"It's one of my metaphysical books. This one's on reincarnation," Meg responded.

"Don't you know only idiots believe in reincarnation?"

"No, I didn't know that, Nick. Perhaps you should inform all of the world's Hindus and Buddhists about that helpful fact."

"And what's that chanting that you're doing?"

"Some of them are Hindu chants, and some are decrees, prayers, or affirmations. Don't worry, Nick, they won't hurt you," replied Meg.

"But what are they?" hassled Nick.

Meg explained, but Nick didn't listen. "Why do you ask me a question when you don't intend to listen to the answer?" she asked.

He was a Catholic who wasn't a Catholic. Meg could see that he belonged to the church because his parents had enlisted him when he was a few weeks old, but he really didn't believe in anything that the church taught. She didn't understand why he went to Mass at all, except to be seen and enhance his public image.

Each time Meg chanted, Nick demanded that she stop. She began to whisper the chants and prayers in the bathroom in order to get away from him. Then he'd bang on the bathroom door. "What are you doing in there?" he'd yell. "Are you doing those chants? Stop it right now. I don't like these changes and I don't want you saying that stuff. Do you hear me?"

Nick hated change. Any kind of change. He wanted everything to stay the same forever, and that especially applied to people.

Four

New Digs

THE STORM OUTSIDE had worsened as Meg paced back and forth. She heaved a cleansing breath as she sat down into her armchair with head in hands and recalled Nick's news that came shortly after her Mom's death. He had gotten fired by his firm. Even though he was a partner, they fired him, or "asked him to leave," as they said, because he hadn't brought in any new clients. After eight years in the partnership, he was no longer doing the work of the drones and one of his main duties was to go out, socialize with the big wallets in the community and lure them in as clients. They had given him the very important message, "bring in the clients," for his final five years with the firm. Meg had watched Nick as he told her this after each of his last five annual reviews. To her surprise, he never really did anything about it. Whenever the subject of joining a country club or rubbing elbows with the big boys came up, Nick left the room. So Meg figured that he knew what he was doing and left him alone.

When the ax finally fell, Nick flew into a rage. "They can't get rid of me," he bellowed. "I've been with the firm for 20 years. I won't leave." Unchecked arrogance rose to the surface. Here was his dark side, his shadow, his Mr. Hyde. She had jousted with Nick's shadow almost daily, but never before had she seen such an ugly display. The shadow she was familiar with had been cold, covert, deceptive and very much in control. This loud, incensed, rebellious version of Nick was quite a spectacle. The freeze-dried executive, the one willing to give them his allegiance no matter what, molted before her very eyes.

Nick defied his fellow partners for the better part of a year, arriving at his office every day as if he had never been given notice. He brought in no new clients and the blame for his expulsion from the partnership was laid on every other partner's doorstep. At home, he strutted back and forth, all puffed up like Mussolini in an old newsreel, repeating over and over, "They can't get rid of me. I won't leave."

Meg began to realize that Nick wasn't able to bring in new clients. His overblown ego needed to be seen as preeminent. He felt comfortable only when he was around people to whom he could feel superior. The big wallets intimidated him because they had more money and talent than he had. He had to avoid them in order to feel superior. How could he recruit those whom his ego needed to avoid?

To keep up the facade of normalcy, he insisted that they continue to go to the firm's social functions, so the couple silently drove to the next partner's reception in their carefully polished luxury car. Meg had a feeling of foreboding as she stepped out of the car. "We shouldn't be here. This will prove embarrassing, Nick," she predicted.

Upon their arrival at the country club, the tuxedoed waiters were handing out the hors d'oeuvres and champagne. The harpist was playing etheric music, and each one of Nick's fellow partners slowly turned his back as he felt Nick's approach. Each and every one snubbed him, the wives too. It was a joint effort of the most subtle kind. For once, Nick was forced to stay with Meg all night instead of leaving her alone while he ran around to kiss up to the partners who mattered. She actually felt sorry for him. He had made the mistake of complacency and become smug. His naiveté prevented him from knowing that he was working in a snake pit. He thought he had it made.

Finally, the head of Nick's division told him that the firm had found him another job. The interview was with an insurance company that was a client of the firm's. Meg wondered if they had reduced the client's fees to get the interview set up. That night an angry Nick arrived home to say that he had gotten the job. His $400,000 salary was reduced to $275,000 or so depending on the size of the bonuses. Meg was thrilled. Nick was not. He complained that he had been denied the opportunity to network while jobhunting.

Friends and neighbors were told the insurance company had given Nick an opportunity he couldn't refuse. That way his enormous ego stayed intact, and he learned nothing from one of life's most important lessons. "His whole life takes place in a state of denial," Meg whispered.

She watched out the window as the snow grew in height. It was four in the morning and she was frazzled from the memories. Her confidence came back as she recalled the morning she had told Nick she wanted a divorce. Telling herself that she'd need a decent amount of child support, she waited to be certain that Nick's new job worked out. "It wouldn't be smart to divorce an unemployed man. You've become somewhat calculating, Meg," she self-observed.

She woke on a Sunday morning in January of '93 and looked over at Nick in the bed next to her. *Oh God, it's now or never,* she thought. *I'd better talk now before he leaves for work.*

"Nick," she said firmly, "I've got to talk to you before you leave. You know we've talked about this before. I want a divorce. It's not working, Nick, and the kids are older now. I can work without putting them in daycare. We've tried counseling. That was a joke. Neither one of us is happy, so let's end it. We can be friends instead."

Meg waited for Nick's response. He gave no reaction at first and sat with his head down, feverishly picking at his cuticles. She figured he'd acknowledge the joyless, loveless union. He raised his head and looked out the window. "No," he said, "I don't want a divorce. I took a vow and I'm gonna stick with it."

"What?" screamed Meg, "You took a vow to love, honor and cherish me. How many years has it been since you've done that? You won't look at me, talk to me, do anything with me. You block whatever is important to me. You can't be serious!"

Meg was furious. She had wasted too many years of her life on the jerk, and now he wanted to drag it out. Realizing that Nick was tossing out more confusion, her mind raced. *What's he doing?* she thought. *It's a setup, Meg,* the little voice inside her said.

"Why don't you go on that summer retreat that you've talked about?" he said. "You know, the one where you learn all about the world's religions, Buddhism and that Aquarian stuff. I'll arrange for a housekeeper. I'll do all of this as a demonstration of my commitment to the marriage, Meg. I'll change, Meg. I promise." Nick spoke sincerely, oozing humility, all the while picking his cuticles.

Meg thought about it. She had dreamed of going on a retreat. Nick held his breath. She thought some more. "I can't do that," she said, still in shock. "I'm not willing to leave the girls. When Amy's in high school I'll do that. Thank you, but the timing's not right."

"Oh no, it'll work," Nick said, sounding a little desperate. "The kids will be fine. The housekeeper will be there for them. I know this means a lot to you. It's my peace offering." He picked at his cuticles a little harder.

"But how will we find a housekeeper for two months? Housekeepers always want longer arrangements and..."

"We'll find somebody. It'll give you a break, and things will be better when you come home in August. It'll be a whole new start for us."

Meg wasn't buying it, although she wanted to. "Nick, I've heard this all before. I've warned you about my filing for divorce for years. You've made promises like this in the past, and it lasts for a few days. You just don't have it in you. You don't know how to have a relationship. We keep going through the same one-act play. You make promises that things will get better. It takes up all of your energy to look at me and talk to me. It's actually hard work for you. You run out of steam. After a few days, you start ignoring me again. We're back to having no connection, no flow, and then we start the act all over again. I wanna get off this stage and outta this play. I've had it."

"Look, just go on the retreat and we'll make a new start when you get back," Nick pleaded.

Meg thought about it. *Is he really sincere? Or is this another one of his crazymaking games?* She put her cards on the table. "O.K., Nick, I'll go on the retreat, but I'm not making any promises. While I'm away I'll think about things, and when I get back, if this 'new start' lasts, then great. If it doesn't, I'll definitely file for divorce, and that's that." Nick looked satisfied—not happy or relieved, just satisfied.

There was one thing that Meg could say on Nick's behalf, and that was that he was consistent. His sins were never done at the level that would require his going to jail, but they were done stubbornly, covertly and consistently. She had watched him play his games and felt his intrigue all around her. A broken promise is a lie, but to Nick, a lie was just another game. He connected with her for two days, but once again, he withdrew. For five months he barely spoke to her. Connecting with him was not of interest to her. She privately made up her mind that she would file for divorce when she got back in August.

Meg began to pace again. Back and forth across her bedroom, her slippers brushed against the carpet. She thought about her summer away from home. It was late June of '93. O'Hare Airport was crazy and loud as usual when Nick dropped her off at the curb. He didn't walk her to the gate. "I think I'll save money on parking," he said. He looked angry, and Meg didn't care. She was so sick of his act. She'd miss the kids, though, and with that sad thought worried about whether she was making a mistake.

"Lady, this ain't no duffle. This is a body bag," whined the skycap.

"I'm gonna be gone for several weeks, so I need a lot of clothes," Meg offered absentmindedly. She was surprised at how good it felt to know that she wouldn't see Nick for the summer. She felt bubbly, lighter and happier than she had felt in years. Nick had grown to be a piano on her back, and now the piano was gone.

The weeks flew by quickly while Meg was on her retreat. She learned about Buddhism, Hinduism, Taoism, Zoroastrianism, the Kabbalah, the Christian mystics and the Saints from East and West, the Gnostics, the Essenes, the Nag Hammadhi texts and some of the more recent occult teachings. She spent her days and evenings studying and speaking with people from all around the world, while she spent nights in quiet meditation.

Meg was amazed at what she learned. The teachers tied in the ancient teachings with the modern. The soul gets as many lifetimes as it sincerely needs to return to the Creator. Earth is a schoolroom where we are given tests. Shakespeare was right; the world is nothing more than a stage. People with whom we have karma are put in our face to test us. When we have balanced our karma, we get off the "wheel of karma" and ascend or return to the Divine, never having to embody on earth again.

To get rid of karma, you can do good works, serve others, pray, decree, or say special mantras while meditating. The prayers and decrees bring down a special energy or Divine Light that balanced out the darkness on the earth. That was the whole point of prayer, to get rid of karma and raise the vibration of the world with Light. That way we can live in golden ages instead of dark ages.

Absorbing all of this was challenging for Meg. She forced herself to lengthen, widen and deepen her thinking. When it was all put together for her, it made sense. All of the questions she had ever had about spirituality were finally answered.

Becky, Meg's roommate from England, summed it up one day as they walked back to their room. "When you mix all of the religions, teachings and paths together things begin to make sense."

On the last day of the retreat, the teacher said, "Strive to always be in touch with your Higher Self. Meditate and imagine yourself sending a flower of love to it. It will return more love to you, 'As above, so below.' As you do this, you'll get closer and closer to it and assume its Christly consciousness. You'll be one step closer to your return to the Divine. When you send love to the forces of Light, they will respond in kind. But sending love or Light to the dark ones will not benefit you. They'll steal your gift and never reciprocate."

While Meg was in her world of spiritual bliss, Nick was back in Barnstable laying out the treachery. Meg found out about all of it from a distant friend who demanded the strictest confidentiality from her. "Look," said the friend, "what he has said about you is so out of keeping with who you are, that I have to say something. You've kept to yourself a lot, Meg. But he's always outside befriending everyone. I don't know you well. But I don't believe that you are what he says you are. It's only fair that you know this."

Apparently, Nick oozed his way around the neighborhood looking forlorn so that the neighbors would ask him what was going on, whereupon he cranked out his award-winning performance.

"Meg's gone," he said, pouting. "She's abandoned the kids and me so she could join a cult. I really don't know what to do about it. I've tried to be a good husband. I mean, I know I've made mistakes, but this is really a blow. I'm trying to hold the family together as best I can. She wants a divorce and I don't. I love her and I want us to continue to be a family. I think it's what's best for the kids, you know. I really want us to start over and save the marriage. What would you do if you were in my shoes?"

One by one, Nick had earned the sympathy of the neighbors and friends, but especially, he had won over the children. Heather believed all of the distortions that he had laid out while her mother was gone. Over the years, Heather had gotten nothing but conditional love from her father. All at once, he was Superdad, and she liked it. She finally had his complete approval.

Amy, on the other hand, was able to see through some of the deception. She was too young to stand up to her Dad, but she knew he had trashed her Mom, and she didn't like it.

When Meg arrived at the airport that August, Nick told her that she was moving out and he was getting custody of the children. Meg informed Nick that she wasn't moving out and that if Nick wasn't moving out, then he was to sleep in the guest room. Nick refused, but Meg threw his clothes out in the hallway, and the scene was ugly. She had decided that Nick was leaving and she was getting custody of the kids.

The storm was over, and the desire to sleep had returned. Meg got into bed once again. Nick would be up in an hour or so. "It's best to not be up and about when he's snooping around," she whispered. The grim job of calling Lynn, her attorney, in the morning was best put out of her mind so she could relax into forgotten dreams.

First thing in the morning, Meg called her friend, Jane. Their friendship had developed when Meg had joined the circle of spiritual seekers in Barnstable. Jane, a beautiful African-American woman who taught second grade, headed the group, and Meg wanted her input before she called Lynn.

"I found a letter in Nick's briefcase addressed to that deprogrammer who's always in the papers," Meg reported. "Jane, it's actually quite brilliant. Diabolical, but brilliant. It's the perfect way for him to get me out of here so he gets custody and the house. He could have me deprogrammed and put in a mental hospital. There are doctors who would cooperate, for the right price. What do I do?"

"Well, I don't know," Jane admitted. "God, what nerve! This guy really is a bastard. I guess you have two choices. You can be submissive and pray he won't carry it out, or you can take the offensive and go after him. My choice would be the latter, but that's my personality. You have to decide which way suits you."

The aggressive route sounded better to Meg. She had been scared during the night, but with the light of day, she was feeling pretty confident. The very next phone call she made was to her attorney, Lynn. After Meg's quick summation of the facts, Lynn became outraged.

"Oh," she said in her usual feisty way, "Don't worry about this. I'll talk to Sol. Sol is such an idiot. I bet he put Nick up to this. I'll let him know that this is totally unacceptable, and if you disappear, Nick will be the first person we have arrested. In fact, we won't just arrest Nick, we'll make sure we arrest him at work in front of all of his co-workers and to make sure he's sufficiently humiliated, we'll have the sheriff handcuff him in front of everyone. You need to communicate this to Nick in no uncertain terms, and I'll handle his stupid attorney."

Wow, I'm glad I hired her, Meg thought while she began to relax. *She's more pissed off than I am.* Lynn worked for Matt Mirenda, one of the ten best divorce attorneys in Illinois. Nick's attorney, Sol, was just as weird as Nick. He kept insulting Lynn's performance from the beginning of the matter, saying that she was a woman and that women make lousy attorneys. Meg was fighting with Nick, and Lynn was fighting with Sol. It was a war within a war.

That evening, Nick came home and stood in front of the fireplace. He picked his cuticles as Meg approached him. She spoke with a voice that was so firm that she even surprised herself. "Nick, you know I found the letter in your briefcase. If you have me kidnapped, I swear to God I'll return like Napoleon from Elba and make your life hell. When I'm done with you, you won't know which side of you your pecker is on. Not to mention the fact you'll lose the $16,000 that scumbag deprogrammer is charging you. Back off, Nick. If I disappear, Lynn will have you arrested and handcuffed at work in front of everybody in your office. And wouldn't that do wonders for your perfect public image?"

Nick looked surprisingly sheepish. "All right," he said. "I only have one question. What made you look in my briefcase?"

The weeks progressed, and the divorce dragged on. It was December, 1993. The level of stress in their home had reached the point of explosion. Heather had taken a Christmas ornament and heaved it against the wall of her bedroom.

"Do you see what you've done to them by filing for divorce? They're totally stressed out," Nick hissed.

"If you had been a decent husband, I wouldn't have filed. If you had moved out, there would be no stress," she retorted.

Meg looked at the soup she had cooked for dinner. Nick was sitting at the table like the master of the plantation. He was waiting for Meg to serve him.

"This house is a mess. What do you do all day? What about those curtains that you were gonna make for the basement windows? The material is just sitting there, and you're such a lazy bitch, you'll never make them. Your attorney costs too much. Why don't you get out and get a decent paying job? I don't know anyone with more education than you, and you do nothing with it." Nick was skilled in the art of reproach. He whispered so that the kids couldn't hear. That way, when Meg got angry and defended herself, Heather and Amy would think that their Mom was the only one who yelled and got angry.

Meg interrupted the whispered tirade. "Nothing? You think that raising the kids is nothing? You want me to get a full-time job? What for? So both of us can never be home? Why did we have these kids if neither one of us ever sees them? Divorcing you is a full-time job. We could do this in a much more civilized way, but you always have to turn everything into a struggle."

"I'm going to stay here and make you love me again. You can't get rid of me. I won't move out," he hissed.

"You tried this tactic with your old firm. It didn't work. They got rid of you by finding you a new job. Am I gonna have to get you a new woman?"

"Good idea. Get me one. It doesn't matter who she is. Anybody would be better than you."

Nick turned away and continued to squawk. Meg looked at the soup she had just cooked. She filled the bowl and walked slowly toward him. She didn't want to spill one drop. She stood behind him. He was looking straight ahead as she lifted the bowl over him and dumped it on his head. He looked really silly with green beans inside his collar.

"You bitch, you bitch. I'll get you!!" he screamed as he jumped up.

Meg turned tail and ran up the stairs. She locked the door behind her as Nick stood in the hallway screaming and swearing. This time, the kids heard him. Meg stood on the other side of the bed, waiting to see if he'd kick the door down. He chose not to. *He doesn't want to pay for the repair,* she thought.

Then Meg laughed. She sat in her armchair and she laughed with her hand over her mouth. Seeing Nick with a necklace of green beans was such a joy. He took himself so seriously, and this was like watching the king slip on a banana.

It wasn't always so funny. As the stress had risen over the past few weeks, she got her share of bruises on her arms and neck. Nick wasn't always so tame. She hid in her room most nights to get away from him. She felt like a slave more than ever before. She was outnumbered and was seething inside. She fixed dinner for Nick every night and still did his laundry. To refuse to do so meant that the kids would get angry with her. He definitely had their sympathy. She couldn't deal with their anger coupled with Nick's, so she waited on him with resentment. She needed her daughters' support, and it wasn't there.

"I can't believe this," she told Jane. "I stayed in this lousy marriage eight years longer than I wanted to so that they wouldn't have to be in daycare. Instead of getting some appreciation, they turn on me whenever I refuse to cook and clean for him. It's easier to just cook for him and do his laundry than to take their lip."

It was a Friday in March of '94. Meg jumped in the car to pick up Amy at school. It was a big day for the sixth grader as fifteen of her friends were coming over for her birthday party. Heather was a freshman in a local high school, and she'd come home on the bus.

As Meg sat in the car waiting for Amy to come out, she noticed the Assistant Principal, Mrs. Dufo, coming out of the side door.

There she is, thought Meg as she studied the woman. *Could she wear that skirt any tighter? She acts so sassy and she's as cold as Nick. No, colder.*

Meg had had a bad experience with Mrs. Dufo years before. She had asked her if she could keep an eye on Heather during kindergarten recess because some of the older kids were bullying her. Heather was an abnormally shy child. The teacher had recently told Meg that she was operating on the periphery of the class. To have her bullied during recess could cause even more adjustment problems. Meg elicited the help of Mrs. Dufo, who was on duty during recess.

"What do you want me to do?" asked Mrs. Dufo, her eyes filled with defiance. She was a tall woman, close to six feet with thick black hair and definitely well-endowed.

"Would you keep an eye on her just in case she needs help?" asked Meg, wondering why she felt such hostile energy coming from Mrs. Dufo.

Mrs. Dufo's eyes squinted as she looked down at Meg, and her widespread nostrils flared even more. The left side of her mouth curled as she locked her jaw and said, "No. I don't think so. She has to learn to fend for herself. Excuse me."

She left Meg standing in the middle of the courtyard in a state of shock. *How can someone that callous work with children?* she thought. *She seems to hate me, but I've never had contact with her before.*

Meg sat with her right hand on the steering wheel and her left hand propped up under her jaw. It didn't add up. There was nothing soft about her. She was an intense competitor, unlike most people who work with kids. There was an edge to her that didn't jive with the work that she did. Her face was hard and intense, sort of like a female grinch. Her calculated sexiness didn't conform with a grammar school setting. The school personnel were usually careful and professional when they spoke to parents. Mrs. Dufo was too big for her britches. What gave her the confidence to be so brazen and rude? Or did she simply overestimate herself?

The night of their encounter, Meg had told Nick about Mrs. Dufo's behavior.

"Well, I had a conversation, if you want to call it that, with Mrs. Dufo today," said Meg.

Nick said nothing, but looked at Meg suddenly. He went to put some coins on the top of the dresser, missed and dropped them on the floor.

"What a witch," said Meg as she helped him pick up the coins. "I asked her to keep an eye on Heather during recess. Some of the first graders have been bothering her. She's scared of them. So the woman sent me daggers of hatred with her dirty looks and then she refused to do it. Heather's in kindergarten. Is that too much to ask? What are we paying this private school tuition for if we have to put up with such brazen, rude people?"

Nick was silent. He kept his back to her.

"Well, you're on the Board. Have you heard anyone else make comments about her attitude?"

"No," he said quickly as he closed the bathroom door behind him.

Meg's reverie was interrupted as Amy ran to the car. "Hi Mom," she said. As usual, Amy ran down the list of the day's events, eager to share her life with her Mom. As they pulled into the driveway she asked, "Are you ready for my big night?"

Meg felt trepidation. At any minute the doorbell would ring and the house would be filled with fifteen pre-teen girls who were just beginning to learn the meaning of the term "vicious gossip." Decibel levels were not their concern. The main goal was to consume as much sugar and make as much noise as possible in the allotted two and a half hours.

Meg wondered if she had enough candy and hoped the crafts Amy had chosen would hold their attention. Amy had decided she wanted to make earrings at the party, so they bought those little hangy wire things and beads of assorted colors and textures to do the job. Of course, there was also the required video to watch, which would give Meg a breather after the earrings were made, as well as cake, ice cream, special bags in which each girl would carry her booty home and soda, commonly known as "pop" in Chicagoland.

After two incredibly noisy hours the doorbell rang. Pat Mulgrew, Sheila's Mom, stood on the front porch. Meg invited her in out of the cold and asked, "Is something wrong?"

Exhaustion was written all over Pat's face as she walked into the kitchen and said, "Well, you know I'm divorced, and Sheila's father is always angry. We've been divorced for four years, and he still sends me doses of hatred no matter what I do. Today was a particularly bad day. I don't know why he can't just get on with his life. He found out that I'm going out on a date tomorrow night and he blew up at Kathleen, my oldest, who told him."

There was a bit of a lull in the conversation. Meg wondered if she should confide in Pat.

"Nick and I are getting a divorce," Meg said.

"I am sorry for you," Pat said. "Divorce isn't easy. But it will be better when it's over. At least it was for me. I have bad days with him now and then, but at least I don't have to live with a man that I have no heart-tie to."

"Is that the whole reason that you got a divorce?" Meg asked quietly. She was excited to meet this kindred spirit.

Pat didn't hesitate with her answer. "I got a divorce because I wasn't happy. We never talked or had any fun, and I thought that if I'm going to be married, I want to be married to someone that I can talk to and laugh with. I need that give and take. Someone who looks me in the eye and tells me what he's thinking, tells me that I'm beautiful, tells me that he loves me. Someone who I can look in the eye and say, 'I love you. I love to be with you and do things with you.' We never had that give and take, that beautiful back and forth. He drank a lot and the Guinness was his mistress. I wanted a man who thought of me at the same time as he thought of himself. With my ex, I was always an afterthought.

"It was about freedom, too. I wanted to be free to find a life that made me happy. I knew that I would never be happy with him. There was a density I couldn't get through. He wouldn't change, so my only alternative was divorce." Pat looked off into the distance as she spoke passionately. "But, you know, when I told my Aunt why I was getting a divorce, she said, 'So who says that you have the right to be happy? Marriage is an obligation.'" Pat sighed, "Needless to say, I don't talk to her any more. Don't expect to get much support from family and friends. They really don't care that much about your happiness. They just don't want things to change. It's an inconvenience to them, and they worry about your kids. They also think that divorce is contagious, and they don't want it to infect them. They're scared. Expect them to be angry with you. In fact, get ready for it."

Pat was a beautiful, tall redhead with an aristocratic nose. Meg wondered why she hadn't remarried. Pat must have read her mind. After the girls ran into the dining room for cake and ice cream, she revealed, "I won't remarry until I find a man that I can have that heart-tie with, a beautiful give and take flow of love. A loving quid pro quo."

"I totally understand," Meg said as she nodded her approval. "A quid pro flow."

The next night Meg had to go to work. Her lecture was all prepared, but she needed an old file of handouts she kept up in the attic. The door to the attic creaked, and as she entered the neglected room, a triangle of light shone on its contents. A reflection on the upper shelf caught her eye. It had been many years since she had noticed the old humidifier. Covered with dust and crusted inside and out with hard water deposits, she pulled it down from the shelf. A dull pain filled her chest and her eyes watered over. How many times had she filled it with water? How many times had she approached Heather's crib to see if she was breathing easily? Her asthma weakened her ability to fight off the colds and flus that the other kids shook off with ease.

It was 1980. Meg had just graduated, passed the Bar Exam, and was working in the Trust Department of a bank. Guilt ruled her work days as Heather lay in bed at home with bronchitis and pneumonia. The sitters complained. They didn't want to take care of a child who was so frequently sick with fever.

"Momma, no go," Heather cried as she grabbed Meg's ankles. "Momma, no go. Please, you read me," she begged each morning as Meg was about to walk out the door for work. She held a stack of story books. Meg loved to read stories to her. Heather screamed and cried as the sitter, Dee Dee, pulled her hands off her Mom's ankles. Meg looked into Dee Dee's eyes and saw pity.

For several months, Heather began to get up after midnight to visit the working Mom she missed so much. "Heather, it's time to sleep. Momma needs to sleep. I have to go to work in the morning," said Meg as she lifted Heather back into her crib.

"Please, you read me, Momma."

After a year, the combination of a lack of sleep and babysitting woes moved Meg to give up her full time job to stay home with Heather and the soon-to-be-born Amy. A teaching job at a local university was the perfect solution to her career challenges. Giving lectures on estates, trusts and wills kept her in touch with the law and it solved all of her babysitting difficulties. It was easier to hire a sitter at night, and she could be with her girls during the day.

Nick made it clear Heather and Amy were Meg's responsibility. He refused to help in any way.

Meg wiped her eyes and returned the old humidifier to its shelf. It was time to go. As she walked down the stairs, she heard the TV weatherman's alert of dangerously cold conditions. Twenty-three below zero with a wind-chill factor in the minus sixties. People were warned to stay home except for emergencies. Street people were urged to go into the shelters and old people were told not to go outside under any circumstances. "The flesh can freeze in a matter of minutes, and hypothermia results..." The words entered her mind in sort of a dream state, kind of like "blah, blah, blah." She had lived in Chicago's burbs for too many years to worry about 20 below zero. It happened too often to give it much notice.

She jumped into her car and headed for work. The Northwest Tollway was approaching, and Meg had to merge. That road at night spooked her. There were many miles between each exit, and the surrounding area was more rural than suburban. The sky was black and starless. Meg was several miles away from the next exit when she suddenly noticed that the car felt different; it was quieter. She pressed the accelerator and nothing happened. The car slowly began to decelerate.

Meg said under her breath, "Oh God, please help me. I could die out here tonight." The realization that she could freeze to death was not something she could ignore, although she had trouble believing it, because Meg almost always was helped out of bad situations by lucky circumstances. The car slowed down to 65, 55, then 45 m.p.h. She moved from the far left lane to the middle lane.

The thought of walking to the next exit was out of the question. She was wearing heels and didn't have a hat. The wind beat against her car, reminding her of the TV weather report and something about a wind-chill factor. What did that weatherman say? Sixty below? She'd have frostbite in less than five minutes.

It was too cold to stand out in the wind to flag down a car. There weren't many cars anyway. Rush hour was over. Staying in her car until another car came by was her only option, and she prayed that the Highway Patrol would come by before she became hypothermic, or even worse, before she became as cold-blooded as Nick. "If I freeze to death, I'll look just like Nick!" she whispered, trying to add a little levity to the situation.

Gradually she could make out something shiny up ahead. It was a pair of taillights parked over on the shoulder. "Oh God, please give me a little more momentum," she prayed. Her car inched on at 35, 25 and 15 m.p.h. from the middle lane to the right lane until it stopped 20 feet in front of the vehicle, which, to Meg's amazement, was a tow truck. She laughed and said to herself, "If my mother were here, she'd say, 'Meg Walsh, the angels love your dirty drawers.'"

It didn't take long for Meg to jump out of her car and run to the passenger side of the truck. The door handle was cold even with her gloves on, and she felt instantly grateful to find that it was unlocked so that she wouldn't have to beg the driver to let her in. In pressured situations, Meg could be a very pushy double Aries. As she opened the door and jumped in, the driver looked more than a little surprised. "Excuse me, please," Meg said wryly, "The bad weather causes me to forget my good manners. I am Meg Banacek, and, as you can see, I need a ride."

The driver was short as tow truck drivers go. His shoulders were lower than hers. The lecture was paramount in her mind, and because of that, she had asked for a ride to her classroom. The car could be dealt with later. He smiled and said happily, "Sure. I'm Steve. Where's your classroom?" Meg gave him the directions and began to relax.

As they pulled up in front of the classroom building, she spoke firmly. "I want to give you some money for this, Steve. You really helped me out."

His response was just as firm. "No. I don't want your money. It's O.K."

Meg was struck by his firmness, and said jokingly, "Well then, I'll just have to say a prayer for you."

He smiled a bit, nodded and said, "Sounds good."

The door was heavy to open, and even heavier to close. She made a point of remembering the name of the tow truck company and its phone number painted on the door. After reaching the warmth of her classroom, she wrote down the name and number in her planner and made a note to call him. With that approach, maybe she could persuade him to accept the money. Meg had a tendency to be a little relentless. When she had a goal, she didn't let go of it easily. It meant a lot to her to pay him back for his good deed. *Good Samaritans should be appreciated,* she thought.

In May, Nick announced that he was moving out. It took him a while to find a place that was worthy of him. An apartment wasn't good enough. "Apartments are for losers," he said. He finally ended up in a condo about five blocks north of the house.

For the first time in nine months, Meg left her bedroom door open. Her almost 19-year prison term was over. The divorce wasn't final yet. She would still have to struggle with the guy until then, but she was free to walk around her own home without dealing with his hatred and criticism. Sitting in front of the fireplace, she put her head in her hands and cried.

A week later, Meg went out to lunch with Jane. "You look great," said Jane enthusiastically, "except for that pocketbook. Girl, with all of your money, why don't you buy yourself a decent pocketbook? I swear I've seen women in the welfare lines with better looking pocketbooks than yours."

"My God, Jane, it's a good thing I have reasonably high self-esteem, or I wouldn't be able to survive around you."

Jane laughed, "I know, I know, but honestly, get yourself a bag. You've got on a nice suit and shoes but the bag..." She raised an eyebrow and cocked her head.

The mall wasn't far away. With Nick gone, Meg had her own checking account now. He was no longer breathing down her neck over every purchase. There was a friendly-looking lady at the pocketbook counter.

"Hi," Meg said, "I'm in the middle of a divorce, and I've decided to treat myself. I'm gonna buy a nice leather bag."

"Well," said the saleslady with a chuckle, "That's probably a good idea—for both of us. How long have you been going through the divorce?"

"Oh, about nine months. He just moved out."

"Oh my. You mean you lived with him while you were divorcing him?"

"Yeah. It was hell, and I'm exhausted," Meg said. "I've been married to him for 18 years, and I've never owned a leather bag. He would have squawked too much about the price, so I always bought canvas or nylon bags to avoid an argument." Meg picked out a beautiful cream-colored Mooney & Rourke for the summer. "I'll take that one. I've always wanted one of those."

"That's a beauty. You've got good taste," she said as she put the bag in its box and started to wrap it up.

She looked at Meg closely and said, "Don't ever regret the divorce. Just get through it. I used to be married to one like that and I got rid of him. I haven't regretted it a single day. Here I am working as a shopgirl, and I still don't regret it. I've got my freedom, and that's all that matters. I see women who stay in marriages so they'll have financial security, but they aren't happy. Some of them look like the walking dead. A woman like that is living a lie. She hasn't followed her heart."

It had been several months since Meg had thought of Steve, the tow truck driver. In June, a prompting reminded her of him. "Where is that number?" she mumbled as she dug through her planner.

"West Side Towing," a cheerful woman answered.

"Hello," said Meg. "This is Meg Walsh. I'd like to speak with one of your drivers. I believe his name is Steve."

"We don't have a driver named Steve," the lady said.

"Have you ever had a driver named Steve?"

"Nope."

"Are you sure? He was about five foot eight with sandy colored hair that was kind of curly," said Meg.

"Honey, I've owned this company with my husband for twenty years, and we've never had a driver named Steve."

"Well, maybe I have the wrong name. He was about five foot eight with sandy colored hair that was curly. Do you have a driver that looks like that?"

"No. We really don't have a driver that fits that description. Are you sure you have the right towing company?"

"Well, yeah, I'm sure. I copied the name and phone number right off your truck."

"Well, sorry," the woman replied, rushing the conversation. "All of our drivers are big. Well over six foot. They do heavy work and they're all big, and none of them are called Steve. I have to go now. Bye."

Meg stared at the phone and slowly dropped it into its cradle. A breeze blew aside the curtains in the kitchen. Her nose caught the scent of a warm June rain as it dribbled on her unmowed lawn. "Who could that man have been?" she whispered.

Five

Moonlight Lady

MICHAEL SAT THERE, trying to realize what had just happened.

It's only for one night, he thought. Michael was thinking with the little head, totally disconnected from above.

He thought back to his first date with Mindy. When he got to her apartment to pick her up, there was a note on her door. He took it down, and there were directions to her friend's house. He took note of the penmanship and remembered thinking that she must be a graphic artist. The letters were all painstakingly printed, and the directions were precise and extremely accurate, taking into account each tenth of a mile. The note explained how she had found a wounded bird next to her front porch, and she didn't have the heart to leave it there to die. She had found a shoe box, cut out some holes in it, and put the bird inside. She explained how she had stuffed some twigs and leaves inside with it to make it feel at home. She explained that she would have waited for him, but she had to get it to her friend right away, because she was a veterinarian. Then she explained that the friend wasn't really a veterinarian, but that she knew a veterinarian, or at least knew someone at the humane society who could help.

Michael followed the directions to her friend's house, thinking that he wanted to see the bird as much as he wanted to meet Mindy. Thanks to Mindy's precise directions, he got to her friend's house without taking any wrong turns. As he walked up to the front porch, he imagined the bird had already bitten the dust, and that it was lying belly up in Mindy's little box with its legs sticking straight up in the air. They were probably giving it a little burial ceremony out in the back yard. He chuckled to himself as he rang the front doorbell.

"Yes, can I help you?" a lady asked, opening the door halfway.

"I'm here to pick up the bird lady!" Michael said.

The lady looked confused for a moment, as if he was there to pick up the bird. Finally, she came around. "Oh!" she said, smiling. "You mean Mindy. Come on in!"

She led him to the kitchen where a girl with blue eyes, freckles and long wavy red hair down to her waist was putting a little wooden cross made of popsicle sticks on a shoe box. One could only assume the bird had expired, a funeral procession would be forthcoming, and it was Mindy who was fashioning the little cross. She was somewhat of a tomboy, and it looked as if she spent a lot of time at the gym. There was a distinct lack of refinement about her, a kind of roughness that came from the drudgery of a life filled with one laborious task after another. There was nothing frilly about her, and Michael thought that she was the type who might enjoy giving his car an overhaul.

"Hi Michael," she smiled, looking him up and down like a cattleman at an auction. "We'll be outta here in no time. I've just got to bury this little sucker in the back yard."

"No problem!" Michael said, "We can catch the late show. I already called in and canceled our dinner reservations, though, so we'll have to come up with a plan there."

"I'm dying for some nachos and burgers!" Mindy exclaimed.

"You're on!" Michael replied, realizing that this wasn't going to be a white tablecloth and five-star restaurant kind of a relationship. Right there, he had settled. He wasn't going to look out for himself, for what he really wanted. His life had taken so many crazy turns already that he just didn't seem to know which way to go sometimes.

What a night, Michael thought as he continued to reminisce. *That was the first girl I ever took to a junkyard.*

It was true. Mindy loved cars, and since she needed some spare parts, she begged Michael to take her junkyard hunting.

"Whoa," Michael said, breaking his reverie. He glanced down at his watch. "I'd better get downtown to the start of the Ramble." He went out to the garage, got in his car, and blasted off down the road.

As Michael drove down familiar streets, he felt a loneliness surround him. This was his home town, but he had become a guest in it. Gone were the days when you could walk to a friend's house unannounced, or walk down the street and talk to neighbors as they went about their lives. Gone was the girl next door, leaning out of her window and smiling at him. People had closed their doors and windows to block out the deafening noise of the city, the police sirens wailing in the night, the homeless victim begging on the corner.

"I need to get out of this place," he said with conviction. "I don't belong here anymore. How I'd love to run off to the Rocky Mountains."

Michael arrived at the Ramble and actually found a decent parking spot. He could see his cycling buds riding around and warming up, and he began to psych himself up. They were all scientists, except for Butch, who was a lineman for the power company. Michael was always going to new extremes to impress them and to keep up with them, because his dream of getting that engineering degree had been thwarted.

"I should get an Oscar for the act I put on with these guys," he said to himself. He mounted his bike and pedaled over to where everyone was warming up.

"They're not getting this thing started on time!" said Don. "This is inefficient."

"Don," Butch said, "it's close enough."

It was a mild October night in Houston. The moon was full, and it was bathing the men with its ethereal light. Several thousand crazed cyclists were getting impatient, waiting official word to start rambling. This was not a race, just an opportunity to wake up in the wee hours of the morning and ride your bike in the light of the full moon. Most of the group was there, with the exception of wives and girlfriends. This was male bonding night and "the boys" meant to tie it real tight. Don, Roger, Butch, George, Rufus and Michael were going to be back to back, belly to belly. Figuratively speaking, of course.

They had their mountain bikes, because Don had decreed it. Roger agreed. He and Don were casting a critical eye over the crowd.

"Pedestrians!" Roger analyzed. "Give these guys lots of room." He loved that word "pedestrians." It stuck with him after he read an article about an English rider who was doing sub-four-hour centuries and calling the people who were finishing in four hours "pedestrians."

Michael actually agreed with Roger, though. True, he was an engineer, but he was also very astute. They had all been in their share of road crashes caused by careless or naive cyclists. Even though they weren't going to be jammin', people would be all over the road.

A voice next to Michael said, "Head 'em up, move 'em out!" Someone had given the signal to start, and suddenly you could hear the sound of thousands of cleats clicking into their pedals. The air crackled with excitement. The guys had gotten up at the front of the group, because they didn't want to get stuck behind a bunch of "pedestrians." They were all psyched for this, and couldn't stop themselves from howling at the moon.

"Aaaaaaaoooooooooo!" they all howled. That's the special howl for a full moon. When it's only a half moon, you have to cut it short, something like, "Aaaaaooooo."

Michael was free now. He was cycling. The energy of the group was infectious. He wanted it to surge through him. There was a police escort, and traffic was being directed around the route. There were no cars to contend with.

"Roger," Don shouted. "How does it go?"

"There's a hole, there's a hole, there's a hole in the middle of the road."

"No, not the hole song!" George shouted. He had been quiet all night, but this got him going. He was usually the quiet man, steady and dependable.

"There's a log, there's a log, there's a log in the middle of the road. There's a log in the middle of the hole in the middle of the road." Roger could keep adding on all night.

"We need a theme song," Don proclaimed. "Where's the minstrel?"

"Over here," Michael said. "What might the nature of this theme song be, sire?"

"Methinks cycling. Dost thou agree?"

"Splendid, splendid. Does John Boulder offend?"

"Not at all. A likeable lad."

"All right guys. Here it is, "Thank God I'm a Biker Boy."

"Yeeehaaa!" they all shouted.

"Well I'd ride down the middle of the road if I could,
But the law and my wife wouldn't take it very good,
So I pedal down the side, yield when I should,
Thank God I'm a Biker Boy!"

The group liked it, and performed several more verses for the crowd as they rambled along. They were the wild and crazy Biker Boys!

When the song came to an end, Michael receded back into his own world. The singing was fun, but something was missing. Whatever it was gnawed at him. As he pedaled along, he noticed that there were damsels everywhere, and as he was the only single man in the group, this affected him more than the others. His was a romantic nature, and although it was satisfying to bond with the boys, his mind sought beauty, his heart sought love, and his soul sought for its twin flame. This made it somewhat awkward for him, because he couldn't go up to a girl and say, "Excuse me, are you my twin flame?" The response would not be, "Why yes, I think I must be!"

So he rambled through the moonlight, not knowing if she were in his midst. Casual conversation was always safe, but it left a gaping hole into which he kept falling, and sometimes the effort seemed so futile. As he passed a girl, he wondered if she noticed, or if his feelings were just locked in his own world, never to be shared. The moon's moody energies tugged at him, cresting in their fullness.

Suddenly, as Michael rode on, alone yet surrounded by his closest friends, an image burst into his mind. It startled him so that he almost hooked Don's wheel.

"Yo, dude, you need to back off just a bit!" Don exclaimed.

"I feel like a blind man on wheels, dude!" Michael said, giving his head that side to side motion. Don laughed and Michael dropped back a few feet. He was still reeling from the image that had appeared to him. It was beautiful, angelic. A lovely moon goddess, whose face he couldn't really make out, and who vanished as quickly as she appeared. But no matter, for she had left a permanent impression that could very well alter his life. She wore a beautiful amethyst necklace, and the power of its radiance rocked him. She imparted so many things to him in that brief instant. He felt as if he knew her, as if she was calling to him; waiting for him to return to her. He felt unlimited love and light coming from her, and complete acceptance and understanding. He wanted to turn around and pedal back to where he had seen her, but he realized that would attract way too much attention. Here he was, doing his best macho act, being pulled in two opposite directions at the same time. He had to somehow tuck her away in the back of his mind, get back into the swing of the ride, try to cover up his shock and resume his poker face. "Did you see something in the road?" Don asked. "A broken bottle or something?"

"It wasn't in the road," Michael explained. "It was up there!" he said, pointing up. Michael had let it slip before he could get a grip.

"A broken bottle, up in the air?" Don asked.

"A woman. I saw a woman. She was up in the air. I had a vision!" If Michael had had more time he could have made up a story, but now it was out in the open, and he knew he would be the brunt of a great number of tasteless jokes.

"You need to get laid!" Butch said.

"Do you know what a vision is, Butch?" Michael asked.

"Sure," Butch replied. "I have these yellow lenses for night vision. I live in a subdi-vision, where I watch my tele-vision. I don't need super-vision, because anything I want, I can en-vision."

"But have you ever had an actual vision? Something that comes to you from a source that is not physical?" Michael asked.

"I thought I was having a vision once, but I was passed out. It was my dog licking my face."

"Butch is a man of rare vision," George explained.

"Without vision, the people perish!" Rufus said.

The guys continued bantering back and forth about vision amongst themselves, and Michael reflected back on what he had just seen. The woman was standing next to a waterfall that splashed down from a steep mountain slope. There was a pink glow all around her, and it seemed to him as if she was surrounded by roses that glistened in the mist of the waterfall as the sun's rays caressed them. Her eyes of fiery blue peered out at him through the tresses of her dark wavy hair that fell gently around her shoulders, and she was standing in pink petals that fell all around as the mountain breeze blew gently.

"So what did this girl look like?" Roger asked, bringing Michael back into the flow of the conversation.

"Was she scantily clad?" Butch asked. "Was this an erotic vision?"

"No," Michael said patiently. "It was an etheric vision," he explained, wishing the subject had never been broached.

"Where's the fun in that?" Roger asked.

"Is anything sacred to you guys?" Michael scoffed.

"O.K.," Don said. "What did her face look like? Did you recognize her?"

"The face wasn't real clear," Michael explained, getting impatient. "The features weren't well defined."

"Sounds like one of those suspects they interview on television where they block out the face," Butch said.

"It was somewhat loftier than that," Michael said. 'Come on guys, that's enough."

"Look," George shouted. "In the distance. It ain't no vision. It looks like Mount West Park."

Butch strained his eyes for confirmation. Yes, it was the West Park bridge, beckoning to the flatlanders. Butch got out of the saddle, sprinting like a madman. He had to take them by surprise, because in the mountains, he was "large and NOT in charge." One by one, the group got by him, and Butch gave each guy a special profanity as he passed. Don edged George and Michael out at the top, with Rufus and Roger right behind. Butch got to the top and raised both arms, pretending to be the winner.

They cruised down the other side of the bridge, passing the "pedestrians" in their way.

"Bon soir, mes amis," Michael shouted to them as he came by. They all perked up, thinking he was an elite French cyclist gracing their presence. "Je suis le plus vite du monde," Michael continued. "Au revoir, au revoir." They didn't understand a word of it, but it sounded good.

"We're American," some guy shouted back, grinning broadly.

"Take that guy out of the gene pool," Don said.

Michael winced inside to hear Don say that. It sounded cruel, insensitive. He knew Don really well, and he knew he would help anyone. Don just had the attitude that in order to be a good cyclist, you had to choose your parents wisely. He was a walking encyclopedia of anatomical information, and he would size up a person's cycling future with one quick glance. Michael would never argue with him, because Don knew all the latest theories and went purely by scientific evidence and the scientific method.

It was idealist versus realist, and Michael never could get him to look past the veil of the physical world. His style was to ask Don's opinion. He would throw out some ethereal concept, mainly with the intent for Don to hear it and absorb it into his subconscious, as if planting a seed.

Michael would say, "Did you hear about that woman who lifted a car off her little boy?" Don would say, "Did you hear about the baby that was born inside a watermelon?"

Michael would just laugh, because Don had a quick wit and Michael loved his perspective on things. Don could fix anything, and Michael felt foolish trying to bring home some point while at the same time depending on Don's mechanical expertise. He admired Don's skill and dexterity. Still, Michael always wanted to push the borders of their conversation a little further away from the practical and the empirical. He also wanted to beat Don in a sprint, and work on his own bike the way Don did.

The thrill of the hill subsided, and the image of the woman came back into Michael's mind. She didn't say anything to him; she just let the impact of her presence speak for her. Michael felt excited, realizing that she might be real, and that he might meet her some day.

"So this was a blurred vision," Roger said. "You couldn't make out the face."

"She could be a real dog," Butch said.

She could look any way she wanted, Michael thought, not attempting to explain that concept to Butch. "Like one of your old girlfriends?" he chided.

"Oh no!" George said.

"A scary vision," Roger said.

Fear can't exist where this vision came from, Michael thought. *The vibration is too high.*

"If she looks like one of Butch's old girlfriends, then Micheal needs corrected vision," George said.

"If he had 20/20 vision, he'd have better night vision," Rufus said.

"Tunnel vision would do the trick," Don said. "Keep it straight ahead."

"But then he'd have narrow vision," George said.

"He should be a man of broad vision," Roger said.

"Global vision!" they all shouted.

The guys kept the vision game going, and began to work up a fresh batch of testosterone. The pace was picking up. It had gone beyond brisk to some undefined category. They had formed a disciplined double pace line, each group of two taking a timed pull at the front to break the wind.

"Hole," someone shouted at the front. The whole group moved over as one body and mind.

"Rider up," Don shouted, and everyone moved left.

"Dirt alert," Michael yelled out.

Michael and Don were carrying on a normal conversation in the middle of all of this, just as if they were sitting in the living room. You weren't supposed to act as if you were working hard. Keep that poker face on. They stopped talking about the vision for a moment just long enough to discuss fast twitch fiber, that particular characteristic of certain muscles which enables one to sprint like a champion.

"You've got to choose your parents," Don stated emphatically. He thought your limits were determined by your genetics.

Michael jumped over a pipe, which kept him from doing a face plant and getting a core sample down his throat. He heard what Don was saying, but he didn't like to think that you had to hang it up if you didn't get it from your parents.

"I don't know, Don. I've seen guys do things I didn't think they were capable of doing. I think we have the power to become what we think about."

"Who's this 'we'?" Don asked, as he and Michael peeled off and faded to the back. Don hopped up on the curb to avoid a grate.

"'Female Units' on the right!" Roger exclaimed. There was a whole bevy of them, probably doing the female bonding thing. The guys took up the speed about five or six more notches, and made it look effortless as they blasted by the F. U.s.

"WWombats," Butch said. He recognized one of them.

Rufus, Mr. Formal, looked at Butch in a most quizzical way. "Butch," Rufus asked. "Were you referring to those women as wombats? I don't understand."

"Wild Women's Mountain Biking and Tea Society," Butch explained. "That's wwombats with a double 'w'. They ride hard, and they party hard."

"Oh, of course." Rufus smiled politely. "The formality of a tea party contrasting nicely with the lower beastly nature that comes out while cycling."

The group was approaching two riders, and Rufus was studying their riding form.

"I don't like what I see here guys, let's move way left." The very moment they moved left, one of the two guys in front of them ran right over a four-by-four and took a rather nasty header. The group blasted by him, avoiding a pile-up.

"Rufus, how did you do that?" Michael asked in awe and reverence.

"I'm a safety engineer," Rufus replied. Michael grinned at him.

"You must have chosen your parents!" Don said. "That was crystal ball stuff, Ruf."

"Remember when Butch's old girlfriend crashed?" George asked.

"Oh man, she was still ridin' when she was eight and one half months pregnant," Michael said, happy that they were off the subject of his vision for awhile.

"I heard she rode her bike to the delivery room," Rufus added.

"That's right," George said. "And she changed a flat tire along the way."

"Excuuuuse me," Roger said. "Before we develop an urban legend here, tell the crash story."

"Tell us a story, story guy!" the group insisted.

"She was on her mountain bike on Ho Chi Min Trail," George began.

"In Viet Nam?" Rufus asked. George looked at him sideways.

"In Memorial Park," George explained. "She came up a little roller hill so fast that she left the ground and got stuck in a tree. She was hangin' upside down, held in by her cleats."

"Say not so!" Butch said.

"So," George said. "When we got her down, all she did was grin. She had a great big piece of bark between her two front teeth."

"Was this on the way to the delivery room?" Roger asked.

"No," Butch said. "This was on the way home from the delivery room. The baby was in her back pack."

"Right out of the manly man survival manual," Don said.

All this talk about crashes was beginning to disturb Roger.

"I don't know if I trust all of these pedestrians, Don," Roger said. "Let's slow it down." Roger was right, they were all over the road, and besides, this was a ramble, not a race. What's more, the group was on their mountain bikes, which weren't designed for road racing. The fat tires made high-pitched whirring sounds, sucking up energy as they spun against their own inertia.

"Hey Roger," Michael yelled, "Tell us about being Flattened at the Flatland." It was a good tactic to steer the guys away from the vision.

"Refresh my memory, Michael," Roger asked.

"You were trying to take a picture of everyone, and you went up ahead of the pace line. You were looking back at the group, holding the camera, and you were drifting into the oncoming lane, just as a car was coming down the road."

"Oh," said Roger.

"Everyone was yelling at you to turn around. If you had gotten that picture off, it would have been your last."

"It would have been a great picture, though," Roger reflected. "Everyone with their mouths open, shouting my name and waving."

"Wow," George said. "That was just after we passed that rattlesnake."

Everybody cringed. They were riding in a double pace line over a narrow back road that had high weeds on either side. They rounded a corner, and the rattler was right in the middle of the road, sunning himself. He uncoiled the top half of his body until it was upright and tried to figure out who to bite. His mouth was wide open and his fangs were exposed and ready, but he just kept turning his head back and forth as each guy passed him.

"I could feel my whole leg tingling, expecting him to bite into my ankle," Don said.

"Can you imagine cycling down the road, spinning at 100 r.p.m. with a rattler going round and round with you?" Michael asked.

"Is that rattlers per minute?" Roger asked.

"If that rattler had bitten me," Don said, "it would have died of lactic acid."

"Man, it was so hot that day. I almost got dehydrated," George said.

"You know how to tell when you're dehydrated, don't you?" Butch asked.

"Is the doctor in?" George asked.

"Yes, but there is no charge for mystical knowledge."

"Then tell it, tell it."

Butch looked over at him with a sly grin. "When you get off your bike to take a natural, nothin' but smoke comes out."

The group roared with laughter. Butch had imparted his wisdom.

The cyclists were stretched out for miles now, and the guys had put some distance between themselves and the main pack. "Rambling" and "testosterone," two more words which didn't usually go together. The tall trees cast endless shadows along the road, and the moon ducked in and out.

Michael rode out of the shadows and into its pale light, and thoughts of his startling vision returned. He felt transparent, lost in the images he saw. They would come of their own accord, and if he tried to capture them, they would vanish. But they were there now, flooding into him, wonderful pastoral settings of pure light. He was looking out from a lovely cottage, and there she was, sitting in a mid-air windowsill, smiling. Her silence shouted at him, inviting him to come through the window into the world beyond. She reached out her hand toward him, and then Butch came blasting by.

"Hey," Butch shouted, pointing to a jogger. "There is always someone running at Memorial Park."

Michael thought, *What a rude way to ruin a vision*.

"Get a bicycle, dude!" Butch pleaded as the group glided by.

Michael used to jog at Memorial in the mornings, before they resurfaced the three-mile trail. It had been all mulch, with lots of tree roots swarming through it. He was blasting along the path at 5:30 a.m. in the dark, and suddenly went airborne when his foot struck a root. It was the only time he had ever experienced a runner's high. He bounced right up, embarrassed and pretending that he was O.K. Just to prove it, he ran the rest of the way back to his car and then spent the next few weeks on crutches with a sprained ankle. When he was able to walk again, he went out and got a bicycle.

"That's right where I fell," Michael said. "I was exactly halfway around the trail."

The guys talked about their injuries for a while, keeping the conversation channelled into acceptable areas. Michael went along, relieved that they weren't talking about the vision, because he knew he could not express his thoughts openly. His ridin' buddies were not his confidants, so he conformed to the norm. Deep inside himself, there was a valiant orator, but Michael wouldn't let him say much more than the most common vernacular. He compromised his real worth, letting it be sabotaged. He would make a joke out of his life so that others could laugh. He realized that he was being controlled in this way, and he was struggling to find faith in his inner light before it could be methodically drained out of him. He needed friends more than the glory of a victorious sprint. He preferred the closeness of nature to the lure of a 60 m.p.h. mountain descent. He would do these things and enjoy them afterwards, but they scared him silly while he was doing them. His mind was not the calm, clear stream he wanted it to be. Au contraire. His head was channel surfin' like a crazed movie junkie. There was the healthy spirit of trying to transcend yourself, and then there was the outer edge, the extreme. That place where even your manly man manual wouldn't save you.

Michael marveled at all the versions of himself he had invented in order to fit in. Would the real Michael please stand up? He realized each man had the power to define his own world, and that would be his reality. It was an awesome power each one of them could wield, but Michael felt the point would be lost if he suggested they imposed their own limitations upon themselves with these fallen fiats. On inner levels he knew this, yet he continued to be silent about these basics and follow the manly man manual instead. So the tangled web wove on, each man relegating himself to the cycling order of things.

Michael felt uneasy. He felt the need for action, but what kind of action he could not for the life of him figure out. It was easy for him to get "spaced out" when he pondered these matters, and he wasn't sure if he really had control of his own mind or if someone was projecting their thoughts into him.

He imagined a conversation with Don on the matter. Don, Mr. Practical, Mr. Logical. Michael would say, "Don, I think my mind is being controlled by psychotronic projections from enemy psychics." Don wouldn't even consider the possibility. He would think that Michael was a genuine goofball. Don only had time to entertain thoughts that would give him an edge over the competition. Such things as the number of grams of weight he could save if he used titanium hubs, or how much less the moment of inertia would be if he used a radial 28-spoke front wheel. Michael had a great fear of being considered a goofball, especially by his manly peers. The horror! The degradation!

Then Michael imagined telling Butch about the law of capillary action, whereby your thoughts were like seeds that had the power to draw everything they needed for their fulfillment to them. Butch would grab his manhood and say, "I got yer capillary action right here!" Michael wanted to explain that the law of capillary action transcended statistics, and that we become what we think about. Don would never go for it. He talked about pro cyclists as if they were gods, made from another mold. Don's life was a horizontal circle, completely ruled by the laws of physics and the material world. Michael knew which way Don was going before he went there. Competition for Don was a process of eliminating the wimps. If you lost, it was more than just game over, man. It was a statement that you were doomed to inferiority. That prospect created incredible tension in the ranks, much like a hopeless desperation.

Michael didn't want to think in terms of scarcity, as if there were only a limited amount of energy that was parceled out by random and impersonal laws. He didn't want to think that laws of chance determined who got the good genes and who got the bad ones. He wanted to think in terms of abundance, as if there was an unlimited supply of everything. People were reaping the results of their abuse of free will over who knew how many lifetimes. It seemed so clear; you reap a little, and then you sow a little. You keep coming back until you get it right. Sow what then?

Michael felt that he dared not tell anyone what he thought the possibilities were when they did finally get it right. The endorphins were flooding his mind and body, and he couldn't stay too serious.

"Where's the beer can house?" Butch asked, jarring Michael out of his thoughts.

"Next left," George said. "Let's ramble over there."

The boys turned left, some of them wondering what Butch was talking about.

"There it is!" Butch said. "Solid beer cans and pop tops. Now that's a man with vision."

"He's probably so drunk, he has double vision," Roger said.

Michael cringed.

The hedge was made of beer cans, and beer cans were imbedded in the sidewalk. It was not a bar, but an actual residence. The guy had covered the entire facade with beer cans, until nothing of the original house showed through except the roof and the windows. The sound of thousands of pop tops which were hung like mobiles filled the air.

"How can anyone sleep with that noise?" Rufus asked.

"They're passed out," Butch said.

"It's kinda like the Ginger Bread house, only with a different theme," George commented.

"I wonder if he increased the resale value?" Don asked.

"I think that would depend on what kind of beer the guy drinks," Rufus said.

"He could recycle his whole house and make a fortune," Michael said.

A Volkswagen bus, the kind that looks like a roving art mobile, was parked out front. Someone had painted, "Forgive me, Jimmy boy, for my mind has gone astray," on both sides. The guys gawked awhile longer, and then returned to the main stream of the ramble.

"You know, if we had been on a training ride, we would have missed that place," Roger said.

"Yeah," Don said. "I come through here all the time, and I never noticed that place. All I remember is the wheel in front of me."

The guys pedaled back to the main road, and the neighborhood was becoming quite exclusive. The houses were elegant and expensive, but the guys couldn't have cared less about all of that. All that matters when you cycle is being in shape. Energy is the legal tender, your ticket to ride. You can't pretend to have it when you don't. You ante up with your training, and you earn your right to be with the group. It had become a positive addiction for each guy there. The highs they had experienced from cycling were far greater than those they had reached through alcohol and other stimulants. All of them had dabbled with these in some form or another when they were growing up, and now they had made a choice. They would sometimes take on a positive arrogance about it, because they knew how good they felt after a hard, fast ride in the country. There was no hangover, no aching head. It was the feeling of being the very wind itself, of being motion itself. It was knowing that they could feel this way while they were getting in the best shape of their lives that made them feel as if they had discovered some special secret, some magic elixir.

"Hey look, it's Turbo!" Don cried.

"Hey, Turbo, is that you?" Rufus asked.

They all swarmed about him. There he was, all of seven years old, riding tandem with his Dad. His Dad had nicknamed him Turbo, because when his Dad would get into a sprint, Turbo would kick in just in time for that extra power boost.

Don asked Turbo, "When are you gonna get your own bike?"

"My Dad promised me one for my next birthday. It's gonna say Turbo on it!"

"All right. What are you eatin'?"

"Atomic fire balls," Turbo explained. "It's my secret weapon. Same thing as a jaw breaker."

"Oh."

It made Michael want to lecture Turbo about eating sugar. It was like putting gasoline on a fire, one quick burst and no lasting good effects. Ask any macrobiotics counselor. He hoped his Dad would set down some guidelines for him. They wished Turbo well with his new bicycle and rambled on.

"Those atomic fire balls just aren't going to provide any lightning for his tree energy," Michael said aloud to himself. Butch looked at him in disbelief.

"I've been listening to macrobiotic tapes!" Michael said. "Really far out stuff."

"That's girl food," Butch said. "Tofu has no taste." Whenever Butch got hungry, he would back the cow up to the table and cut off a piece.

"It's a question of balance. Your body has seven chakras that act as energy transformers that step down your crystal cord energy and distribute it throughout your body to 144,000 distribution points. The energy travels over your body's meridians. According to Chinese medicine, all energy is either expanding or contracting. These two basic characteristics are the yin and yang of creation."

Michael had said it, he had really said it. He didn't want to sound as if he had invented any of these ideas, and sometimes he wasn't sure if he was explaining it right, but there was a yearning in his heart to know and to share with his friends. It was a real challenge for him to say what he thought and felt, because peer pressure was a very powerful influence over him. He half expected Butch to make fun of what he said, but to his surprise, he could tell Butch was really thinking about what he'd said. Michael liked Butch just as he was, because the things he would say were so perfect and uncensored. Butch didn't appear to have a lot of inner conflict about just being Butch, and his masculine bravado appealed to the alpha flame blazing within all of the guys there.

"I've heard of blow it out yer yin yang," Butch said.

"Yeah, that's the ticket!" Michael said, smiling.

They were coming back into town, having completed the short ramble. The majestic Houston skyline towered over them. They made their way through town and back to the convention center. The ramble was over, and Michael could feel the sudden drop of energy and excitement. The guys all wanted to get home quickly, so everyone said their good-byes and split up to get back to their cars. Michael got his bike on the car rack, and then did a quick change back into some dry clothes. He put a towel around himself for modesty's sake and got his cycling jersey and shorts off while keeping the towel in place. It was the magic towel act. Once dressed, he slid into the driver's seat and sped away. After relying on his body for power on the bike, he was amazed at how effortless it was to go so fast in a car.

"Hole!" he shouted, pointing out the hole's location and pulling the car around it. He laughed at himself, realizing he was still mentally out there on the bike. He put the moon roof down and turned off the radio.

He was glad to be by himself again, free from the stress of putting on such a macho facade. Michael lived in three rooms, yet the third room called to him now most fervently. The outer room was for the boys. He felt that to keep their friendship he had to have this room tidy at all times. The white glove passed upon the windowsill must not be soiled, and the coin tossed upon the bed cover had to bounce, and bounce high. A hidden door, known only to an intimate circle, led to the middle room. This room held many confidences, and they could not leave the confines of their guardian walls. Yet neither of these two rooms would be there if it weren't for the third one. Ahh, the third room. It was for the Moonlight Lady, wherever she was. It was an architectural masterpiece, a collection of all his private treasures existing only to be pleasing in her sight.

The cool night breeze rushed in, and Michael could see her radiant image, etched forever on the canvas of his mind. It had been planted there, sending its roots deep into the soil of his soul. It was a deep, rich soil, made fertile by the mighty torrents of his lifestream.

"I'll find her," he said softly.

He reached his street and turned into his drive, almost crashing into Mindy's van.

"Oh my gosh! I forgot about Mindy!"

Six

A Higher Appointment

MEG WAS AMAZED a grown man would care about such petty junk. "You can lay them all out in the street and drive your car over them for all I care," she said to Nick. "I'll tell the girls to divide them up and you can come over and see if it meets with your approval. I don't want to have anything to do with this. I don't care about any of those bulbs."

Heather was in charge of dividing up the dated Christmas ornaments and told her Mom when she and Amy had finished the selection. Nick had called to say that he wanted his share of them. He arrived, took his bulbs and departed without a problem. Later, Meg got a call.

"I didn't get my fair share of the ornaments," he whined. In her mind's eye she saw him with a baby bonnet on his head and a rattle in his hand.

"What do you mean you didn't get your fair share?" she asked, puzzled. "The girls said you left the house happily."

"I didn't get my fair share. I didn't get half. They shorted me," he insisted.

"Why don't you talk to the girls about this?" she asked.

"I didn't get my fair share. I didn't get half. They shorted me," he repeated.

"Well, tell them that they shorted you. I am not involved in this."

"I'm coming over and I want my fair share," he said as he hung up.

The dated ornaments were on a table in the basement. He walked around the table with a predator's eye, checking out the ornaments. He picked at his cuticles as he nervously surveyed the goods. He clearly wanted them all and didn't want to share with his kids. Meg watched him in horror, wondering how she could have lived with such a miserly toad for all of those years. If she had stepped aside, he would have manipulated the girls into giving him all of them. Heather would have felt sorry for him as he plied his forlorn and lonely act. Amy, outnumbered by Nick and Heather, would have been forced to accept the decision. No, Meg would not back away from this one. She would not let him take advantage of her girls.

"These aren't all of the ornaments," he said.

"What are you saying?" Meg replied. She didn't want to waste her time with such trivialities. "You know, Christmas is for kids. Have you thought about being magnanimous about this? If they shorted you, it's because they're kids. You're the adult. Let it go."

"You told them to short me," Nick fumed at Meg, nostrils expanding and contracting. They looked like big caves in his head.

"I did not! O.K., so it's another power struggle between you and me. Here we go again. This is another setup, isn't it? You know I'll defend the kids. I always do. I won't let you manipulate them into giving you their share of the ornaments. I know they really want them. They're kids. I told you I don't give a damn about those bulbs. What's really going on here? You are using these stupid Christmas bulbs to create another power struggle so that you can fight with me. You hate me so much that you love to fight with me!

"I don't give a flip about these bulbs. In fact, if I had my druthers, you could have them all. I don't want them under my roof because they will remind me of you," she said.

"You bitch. I don't have to listen to you. I don't have to be generous if I don't want to. I don't have to listen to you. You're just a bitch," he yelled as he stomped back and forth.

Meg was stunned. She looked down at her feet in embarrassment.

Her reaction was not wasted on Nick. Suddenly, he stopped charging back and forth, and a metamorphosis took place. He stopped dead in his tracks and stared at Meg. He pulled his body up to its greatest height, sucked in his gut, lifted his chin and did a mountain pose that would have made a yogi proud. The voice dropped an octave into business mode and he said, "You're going to tell everyone about this, aren't you?" He seemed scared.

Meg didn't respond to Nick, but she thought, *You can bet your greedy little ass, I will.*

Suddenly, he flew past her and ran up the basement stairs up to the first floor. She wasn't able to stop his approach into the living room. There he slowed his gait, head swaying rhythmically left and right, as he surveyed all of the items that were left in the living room. Meg knew his avaricious mind was deciding whether he had gotten screwed regarding the value of the remaining furniture.

He paused at the front door with his successful Corporate Counsel demeanor back in place, shot Meg a look of hate and left.

Sighing, she turned to walk back into the kitchen, relieved that such a memorable scene was over. Amy stood before her.

"Thank you, Mom," she said, looking as if she was about to cry. "Thanks for not letting him take our bulbs."

Meg thought about all of the times that she had defended the girls against Nick. They had no idea of all of the times she had squared off against him to fight for what was best for them. "Oh, it's O.K., honey. Did you hear all of that?" she asked.

Amy looked distraught and said, "Yes, Mom. You were so brave. Thank you." She hugged Meg, and Meg hugged back. It was a rare moment. Nick had screwed up. He had forgotten to ask whether the girls were home, and Amy got to see her Dad minus the mask.

The issue was still not finished as far as Nick was concerned. The next weekend he rang the front doorbell with a brown paper bag in his hands. Meg walked out onto the porch and thought, *Oh, God, no, not again*.

She opened the door in as light-hearted a manner as she was able to muster, but couldn't bring herself to even say hello. She looked at Nick as if to say, "Now what?"

He opened the brown bag that he was clutching and said, "I just want you to know that I have counted these ornaments, and I have less than half. They hid some of them. We have an ornament for each year of the marriage and I didn't get half." His lower lip was pouting as he turned and walked down the path to his little, red, luxury convertible.

"Hey, girl, you've gotta get motivated," prodded Jane as she sat in Meg's living room. "The divorce is final. Now get yourself up and going."

It was the day before Thanksgiving, 1994, and Meg hadn't bargained for the post-divorce letdown. Victory had been anticipated, but an unqualified weariness and desire for seclusion ruled her mind. Nick's smear campaign had turned her friends, neighbors and even some family against her. The only contact she had had was from Jane.

"You know, Jane, I'm really grateful that you're here with me. None of my friends or even family have called, and I doubt they will," she said sadly.

"You can't be serious!" said a shocked Jane. "I swear, I can't figure white people. When a black person goes through a divorce, the whole community gives support. That's how we survive the hard times. Are you sure they know that you've been getting a divorce?" she asked.

"Of course they know. Nick told them that I abandoned my children to join a cult. Remember?" Meg recalled. She leaned forward, putting her head in her hands.

"Oh yeah, that's right," Jane recalled as she looked off into the distance. "Well, you ought to start calling them. Why should you sit at home waiting for them to call? Let them know you're still alive." She slumped back on Meg's couch and was quiet for a while. Her thoughts drifted and then she asked pointedly, "He hates blacks, doesn't he?" Jane's eyes were filled with pain. It lasted only a second.

"Yes," Meg said. After a moment of silence, she asked guardedly, without hiding her surprise, "How did you know? That was Nick's most carefully kept secret. Only I know, or maybe Helena."

"Girl, I've been in a black body for 45 years now, and I can feel that vibration a mile away." Meg remembered how Nick had hated Jane from the instant he met her. At first Meg was perplexed, because Jane was kind and dignified when she met him. Then Meg remembered that Nick hated black people. The first time he spoke about them was when he and Meg were first married. He complained that blacks were no good, dishonest and lazy.

"Why do you hate black people?" Meg asked.

"Because, when I was fifteen, a black kid stole my car. He drove it all around the city and had it painted a different color and destroyed the thing. By the time the cops found it, it was abandoned and worthless."

"So, because one black guy stole your car, you hate all blacks."

"Yeah," said Nick defiantly as he glared at Meg to let her know that he had no intention of changing his ways.

Meg took a deep breath and whispered, "I'm in deep trouble."

Years later, Meg met Nick's Uncle Bob and his daughter, Louise, at a family function. Louise had married a black man named Warren five years before. Warren was a Vice-President of a bank and a really nice guy who supported Louise and her children emotionally and financially. But Uncle Bob refused to speak to or look at Warren during the entire afternoon. Helena confided in Meg that Uncle Bob hated black people and that's why he snubbed Warren. "This has been going on for five years," said Helena as she rolled her eyes.

Meg was devastated. *How did I get myself into a family like this?* she thought. It certainly explained Nick's ability to be callous for long periods of time. With a role model like Uncle Bob, how could she expect better behavior from Nick?

Meg was taught by her Dad that color and religion didn't matter and that you should treat all people with the same respect. She recalled the memory from 1957.

"We are all one," Mr. Walsh grunted and shook his head one summer day. Meg sat on the floor and watched him read the *New York Times.*

"What do you mean, Daddy?" she questioned.

"It means if one person in this world is enslaved, we are all enslaved. It means if one person in this world is treated unjustly, we are all treated unjustly. You must fight to the death to ensure other people have their freedoms and are treated fairly. Don't ever think that you don't have to worry about an injustice done to someone else. If you look the other way when your fellow man is suffering, it's only a matter of time before you will be suffering the same fate. And that, squirt, is truth. We are all one. Don't ever forget it." Mr. Walsh pinched Meg's chin and grinned.

Jane got up to leave and said quietly, "I don't know how you lived with him for so long, Meg. His poison was so subtle. Those white neighbors of yours will never figure it out. They're all too self-absorbed. You gotta get out of here. You're not like them. You'll never be happy here." Jane got up to leave as Amy and Heather came pounding down the stairs looking for food.

"Hi Jane, are you staying for dinner?" Amy asked.

"No, honey. I've gotta get going." Jane lifted her coat as if it weighed a hundred pounds and walked toward the porch. The girls ran into the kitchen, and Meg walked Jane to the door.

Talking over her shoulder as she stepped down onto the front path, Jane mused philosophically, "Well, that man is a reptile, but I've gotta give credit where it's due. At least he didn't turn your kids against me."

"He would have if he could have done it without looking bad." Meg closed the door slowly behind her.

"What's wrong with Jane?" Amy asked as her Mom walked back to the kitchen.

"Oh some painful memories, honey. She'll be O.K."

Amy always noticed when the adults around her were sad. It was as if she was trying to understand the intricacies of adulthood far in advance of her arrival. "Adults can do whatever they want. Why would they ever be sad?" she asked.

Meg and her daughters were adjusting to their new life without Nick. During their meals together, Heather sat at the table in silence, and Meg grew weary of trying to get her to engage. She had a hard time not returning Heather's anger. To Meg, Heather was nothing but a spoiled ingrate, and she felt guilty thinking such unattractive thoughts about her own flesh and blood. Heather was still in Nick's court, and Meg was running out of patience.

A few days later, Heather bought some 100 percent cotton blouses for school. She said, "Mom, I don't have any blouses. Who's gonna iron these blouses?"

Meg thought, *I wonder how fast your father would iron your blouses. If you think he's so wonderful, why don't you ask him?* Instead she said, "Well, you're fifteen years old. You're more than capable of ironing your own blouses."

"You mean you're not going to iron my blouses?" Heather said. She looked outraged.

"That's right," said Meg. "I'll be happy to teach you how to do it, but I'm no longer doing it for you. You have to learn how to iron a blouse. When you go to college you'll have to take care of your own clothes. Now's as good a time as any to learn." Meg turned to walk away but read Heather's thoughts. "Don't bother complaining about me to your father. I don't care what he thinks."

"Well, I know he wonders why a woman with a law degree doesn't even have a job. You certainly have time to iron my blouses. What else do you have to do?"

Heather's words stung Meg's soul. It was obvious that Heather and Nick had been criticizing her behind her back. Nick had portrayed Meg to Heather as a "lazy bitch." Words he had used frequently to run Meg down.

"You ungrateful little brat. How dare you speak to me with such disrespect?" Meg was breathing quickly. There was murder in her eyes. She was yelling. "Do you want to know how hard I've worked to find a job? Do you want to know why I haven't found a job? Because I've wasted my life raising you. They won't hire me because my law degree is old. The law is a very unforgiving profession, Heather. Almost as unforgiving as you are! Working part-time all of those years didn't make a damn bit of difference. I'm afraid that I've made a terrible mistake. I spent too much time serving you. I made my children a priority and where has it gotten me?" Heather backed into her room and closed the door.

"Don't close the door in my face, you little brat. You've turned against me, and you believe all of his lies. You refuse to see my side of the story. Didn't you ever notice, Heather, how he treats me? Would you like to be treated that way? Or is that why you side with him? Because you're afraid that, if you don't, he might treat you as badly as he treats me? So you've betrayed your mother for your own stinking safety.

"Did he ever stay home from work because you had bronchitis umpteen times? Did he give up his career for you? Fat chance. But I did. When you were two years old, you begged me to stay home with you and now you condemn me because I don't have a career. He didn't give a damn about you until I announced I wanted a divorce. Then, overnight, he turned into Superdad and you fell for it. I took care of you for all those years because I loved you. But now, Heather, you're on your own. You can iron your own damn blouses."

Meg slammed the door on her way out. She knew she had said too much. She knew that a mother isn't supposed to say things like that even if they are true. But how else would her truth be told?

Meg knew her law degree was old and no firm would want to hire her. She had gone on a number of unsuccessful interviews, and finally an old friend from law school had bluntly told her, "I wouldn't hire you now. You'd have to get an LL.M. before I'd even consider it." Meg tried hard to not be bitter. So she began to look for alternatives. Mediation was an area that seemed promising. Only a minor amount of training was required, and she liked the idea of helping people to resolve their differences in a respectful and benign way.

After attending a week-long mediation seminar in Chicago she decided that she wanted to do an internship that was to be held in a town north of Milwaukee. She had approached one of the seminar's teachers and asked, "Are people able to earn $40,000 a year or so as mediators?" Meg figured that $40,000 added to what she was getting in alimony and child support would give her enough money to pay the monthly mortgage of $3,300 plus the rest of the bills. Taking money out of the bank every month to pay the mortgage was scary. After doing a little math, she figured that if she wasn't able to earn at least $40,000, she'd have to sell the house, which would be traumatic for the kids.

The teacher was in the process of moving on when Meg asked the question. She answered over her shoulder, "Oh yes, of course," but she seemed a little anxious to get away. Meg filed that answer in her long-term memory and made plans to go to the week long internship. She arranged to stay in Milwaukee with Rhonda, an acquaintance she had made while at her spiritual retreat the summer before. During her conversation with Rhonda, she unloaded. It was funny that she did so. She hadn't talked to anyone about her health problems. She was so wrapped up in getting her life back in order that she had ignored those issues. "I'm so tired all of the time. I never really feel well. I had bronchitis after Christmas and took antibiotics. Ever since then, I've felt completely wiped out."

"Well, let me make an appointment for you with Howard," Rhonda suggested.

"Who's Howard?" Meg asked.

"Oh, Howard Peak. Oh...well...it's hard to explain. He's sort of a medical intuitive but he's really an acupuncturist. He's, like, got a gift. I'll make the appointment, and you can see for yourself."

The trip was scheduled for February. About three hours of driving were ahead of her, but that didn't faze Meg. She planned to listen to different lectures on Zoroastrianism and Buddhism while she drove. If it snowed, it snowed, and she would deal with it.

Nick acted very put out as he agreed to take the kids for the week. "Certainly, a week with Heather will make him happy," she whispered. There was a vibration of a kind of passive incest between them. Meg believed that nothing physical had ever happened between them, but Nick had successfully placed his daughter on the pedestal that Meg had expected for herself. He treated his daughter as an honorable man would treat his wife and treated his wife as a dishonorable man would treat the hired hand.

Since Meg was going to Milwaukee to get her career jumpstarted, she thought he would be happy. Instead he asked, "Are you going up there to party for a week with your spiritual friends?"

After she arrived in Milwaukee, the internship went well. Meg was as fired up about mediation as she could be, considering her health issues. But the highlight of the trip was her appointment with Howard Peak.

On the whole, Meg liked Milwaukee. She followed the map and soon found herself in front of an older house in what seemed to be a mostly residential neighborhood. She entered the front door and waited politely in the waiting area. There was no receptionist or bell she could ring to announce her arrival. "How's he gonna know I'm here?" she wondered. Within a few minutes Howard Peak descended the house's narrow stairs.

"Hi," he said as he held out his hand. "I'm Howard."

"Hi," Meg replied. "I guess you heard me come in."

"No, not really. This is an old house. Noise doesn't carry very well. Too much plaster in the walls," Howard said simply. He had a very quiet, calm voice. A tall, muscular man with a wide face, brown kinky hair, olive skin and large, brown eyes, Howard appeared to be Lebanese or at least from the Middle East. There was a mysterious quality about him. He was confident, with a dollop of humility that Meg found refreshing. "My office is upstairs. Just follow me," he said softly.

His office was very small, with a massage table in the middle of it. A window on the west side of the room made things bright and inviting. There was no wallpaper or decorations of any kind, so that it was strictly a man's office. All along the walls were oriental and homeopathic medications and instruments that she had never seen before. His certificate from an acupuncture school on the East Coast hung on the beige walls.

"Please lie down," Howard said, "and then tell me how you would like me to help you."

"Well, I have been losing weight to the point where I now weigh 106 pounds when I used to weigh 126. I spent most of last year getting a divorce, which was final in November, and I lost maybe 10 pounds during that time. I had bronchitis in December and I took some antibiotics. Since then, I've lost another 10 and I'm still losing. I can't seem to control it. It's as if an unseen hand is trying to kill me. The more I eat, the more I lose. It's crazy, and I'm afraid that I'm gonna die."

"O.K., you say you've taken antibiotics lately. Did you take any acidophilus during or after that time?"

"No," said Meg. "The doctor said nothing about that. All he said to me was, 'Hum, you seem to have lost some weight. Women are supposed to have curves. I read that in a book.'"

Howard grabbed a copper tube with a diameter of about two inches. He had Meg hold a probe that had a wire extending to a brass tray placed before him on his desk. He held a disk containing some colored materials that he waved inward and outward from the side of Meg's ear. She thought that this was a little weird but lay quietly to take in the show.

Suddenly, he stepped back from the table and put down the copper tube. "Do you often get headaches?" he asked.

"No. Usually only when I'm under a lot of stress."

"I have to tell you something that you may think is strange," he said sincerely. "Do you believe in God, or angels or spirits of any kind?"

"Yes, very much so."

"Good," he said. "I am not able to work on you until I make some calls."

He then called out loud to the angels, angel devas, saints and some beings that Meg hadn't heard of before. He approached Meg again and picked up the copper tube. His hand waved back and forth once or twice, and then he squinted his eyes and stopped again.

"I'm sorry, but I must also pray a little," he said apologetically.

He called to a spiritual being whose name she had never heard before. The prayer had a poetic rhythm to it. After three repetitions, Howard stopped. He walked toward Meg, picked up the copper tube and waved his arm back and forth over her once again.

"It's O.K. Now I can work on you. Their energy has been blocked."

"Whose energy?" asked Meg.

"You see, there aren't just positive spiritual forces," Howard began. "There are also negative. It would take a long time for me to explain. I would recommend that you read the Book of Enoch. It tells the story of the dark forces. It happened a long time ago, but the story still goes on. Most people think that it's just a fairy tale, but it isn't. The dark ones hate the Creator because His law required that they leave the etheric realms. They had misused so much of their energy with pride that their vibration had become very low, too low to remain in the higher vibrational planes, or heaven as we know it." His voice trailed off as he examined Meg.

"Yeah, and....," said Meg, hoping he would continue.

"They were forced to go somewhere with a denser vibration and that place is what we know as Earth. Since they hate the Creator, they attack His children. What better way to hurt someone or get revenge than to hurt your enemy's child? You may not realize that you are a child of the Light, and so they will do anything to hurt you. You have three assigned to you."

"Wait a minute," said Meg in disbelief. "Who is assigned to me?"

"Three dark ones. Yes. Their greatest achievement is that no one believes that they exist. Their job is to prevent you from returning to the Divine at the end of this life. They often work through others, your friends and even your family, not just through enemies. They will do anything to prevent your upward spiritual spiral and they'd like to find a way to end your life prematurely. But by God's grace and love you will be protected. They are sending you harmful energy that can make you sick. It's like voodoo. Somehow you've been directed here. Now you can realize what's going on and be spiritually accelerated and protected by the guardian presences who cherish you."

"Wait, I don't understand. If these spiritual beings love me, why have I not been protected before?"

"You see," Howard explained patiently, "we, meaning the children of God, usually have a natural immunity from attack when our auras are bright, when we're full of devotion to the Light, cherishing ourselves and those around us and fulfilling our divine mission. But when we worry about things, our energy weakens. Trust and worry can't coexist at the same time. It's like static that blocks the inner voice. If we look to the outer world, to our fellow man for satisfaction and acknowledgment, rather than to the Divine, we create chinks in our armor and are open to attack.

"Can anger lower your vibration and weaken your aura?"

"Yeah, anger lowers your vibration and blocks you from moving upward on your spiritual path, not to mention the negative effect it has on your physical heart," Howard commented. "All the negative emotions lower your vibration...jealousy, hatred, greed...Even using your energy to dominate or manipulate others to do what you want or what you think is best for them can lower your vibration."

"So if you raise your vibration, it helps you to move upwards on your path?"

"Yeah. You get closer to God and closer to the possibility of returning permanently to the etheric or heaven world. Our Hindu friends call it getting off the wheel of karma or attaining moksha," said Howard. "But even then, many choose to stick around and continue to help out from the other side. They don't feel their mission is complete until everyone is free."

"And you raise your vibration by feeling the positive emotions?"

"Yeah," he said, "like love, kindness, appreciation, compassion and so on."

Howard continued, "You can sit up if you like. Right now you have an overabundance of candida albacans in your intestines. They are a type of yeast or fungus that are O.K. to have in your body in small numbers, but when the numbers get out of control, they can drain you of your energy and nourishment and even make you crave sugar. The antibiotics killed off the good bacteria in your intestines that usually hold the candida in check. Without the good bacteria, the candida multiplies quickly. Thus, you are losing weight rapidly and feel exhausted. I'll give you some homeopathic remedies to take, and I recommend a change in your diet that will starve off the candida."

"So I don't just take yogurt?" Meg asked.

"When the candida is out of control, taking yogurt, especially the commercially available kind, isn't enough. Besides, dairy products, in general, should be used sparingly. We'll use the beneficial bacteria in capsule form to start with."

Howard looked at Meg and continued, "You have to remember that there's a whole other world besides the physical one. You must pray to your Higher Self, the angels, Masters and others who serve the God in you and ask for protection from these dark ones every day. It's obvious that you're a lightbearer. You have a lovely aura and pray a lot I see. You're surrounded by a beautiful violet and white light. Please take what I've said seriously and call for protection each day. Anyone on a spiritual path should do this. Prayer is part of it, but service to others is the other key. As you become God in action, the joy of your spirit flows through you more abundantly. Who would dare attack someone like that?"

Howard outlined the diet and gave her the necessary homeopathics. "Your body would really benefit from a shiatsu massage," he said clinically.

"It would?" asked Meg, who didn't have a clue as to what her body would benefit from.

"Yes," said Howard, "I'm feeling that you need one. You've been in flight and fright mode for so long that it needs to be soothed and opened up a bit. Also, your adrenals are exhausted from all of the stress that you've been under."

He massaged along all of the body's meridians and tsubos according to oriental medicine. As he worked on the meridians in Meg's back, she had a prompting, "You'll be leaving Chicago in two years, February, '97."

As she lay there quietly, her rational mind began to assert itself. *"That can't be. My girls are in Chicago. I can't leave there until Amy leaves for college,"* she thought.

On the street outside, she heard little children giggling as they walked home from school. Her heart grew warm as she remembered her daughters when they were young; their innocence and high-pitched voices sounded so sweet even when they argued. All of this had to be cherished. She slipped into a vibration of love and connected with her Higher Self. Then came another prompting, "A man will soon enter your life."

At that very moment Howard spoke softly, "Do you have a man in your life, a boyfriend maybe?"

"No," answered Meg, surprised by the seeming coincidence.

"Be careful. As you become more spiritual and get closer to your Higher Self you are given opportunities. An outer man or your twin flame may appear."

"Do you mean a husband?" Meg asked.

Howard took a deep breath and continued. "When you come to a certain stage of spiritual devotion, you feel joy not so much from what you get but from what you can give. You rely on your oneness with the Divine within, your Higher Self. That special intimacy can mirror itself in the physical as a marriage partner. By loving and supporting each other as partners you can do more good than each of you could do separately. But always remember it's your relationship with the Divine that you must rely on. The marriage must support that relationship, not replace it.

"When you're ready for that kind of union they may send your twin flame to you. But be very careful because the dark ones may send in an imposter, one with whom you have heavy karma, to muddy the waters."

"*A twin flame,*" she thought. She knew that it was significant, but didn't have a clear explanation of what it was. "How will I know which is which?" she asked.

"By staying connected to your Higher Self," he said.

"Right. I believe my Higher Self speaks to me through my promptings. I was stranded one night on the highway. It was way below zero..." She relayed the rest of the story of Steve, the tow truck driver. "My promptings tell me Steve was a spiritual presence, but my rational mind moves in and insists that it was merely a coincidence, that there's a more mundane explanation. I struggle each day between believing my promptings and following the logic of the world."

Howard looked toward the window for a few seconds. "I think," he said softly, "that Steve was sent to save your life. The forces of Light needed you to stay in the physical. Steve was their solution."

Meg didn't have a chance to comment, because as Howard massaged her feet she felt a sudden pain. "Sorry," he said, "that was a bit deep. This is the point for the kidney and the adrenals. It's painful because they are exhausted. The candida is putting stress on the kidneys. This point won't be so tender as you get the candida under control and your kidneys and adrenals get stronger. You'll sleep well tonight, I promise, but take a salt bath first for fifteen minutes. A warm tub with about two pounds of salt. Call me if you want to talk about the Book of Enoch or anything else, for that matter."

Meg felt as if she had just landed from another cosmos. Opening up Rhonda's back door, she found Rhonda in the kitchen looking through the mail. She looked up when Meg opened the door and said, "Hi, how was it? Oh, you look the way we all look when we get back from Howard."

"Well," said Meg, "that was a thoroughly joyful and interesting visit, to say the least."

"I know," Rhonda said, "he seems to have some real spiritual sensitivity. I'm grateful that people like Howard are out there to help us on the path. So what's wrong with you?"

"Well," continued Meg, as she leaned against the wall, "the long and the short of it is that I've got candida, there are three dark ones assigned to me to prevent me from attaining 'moksha,' my kidneys are weak, my adrenals are run down and I think I might be moving from Chicago in two years."

"Oh, my God!" said Rhonda.

"Look, I'm sorry I'm not better company, but I feel so wiped out. I've gotta take a hot salt bath and go to bed. I'll see you in the morning. O.K?" she said, excusing herself.

Meg went to bed at 7:00 that evening and woke up the next morning at 9:00. It was a sleep of the deepest kind and she had a recollection of a beautiful dream that she couldn't wait to tell someone. After searching the house from basement to attic, she found herself completely alone. Disappointed, she packed her stuff, loaded the car, left a little "thank you" note on the kitchen table and headed toward the highway.

Seven

Fruits I Have Known

A FEW DAYS LATER, Meg drove up in front of Jane's little brick house with blue awnings and shutters. Her dog, Jake, patrolled the quaint side yard. Barking regularly, he was making Jane crazy.

"Hi," Jane said as she opened the door. "I'm gonna kill that dog. He's been barking all morning, and I can't get him to shut up." She opened the window in the kitchen and screamed, "Shut up Jake," then closed the window.

"Why don't you bring him inside for a while? Then I want to tell you about my dream."

Jane opened the door and in came Jake. He got a loud lecture on the evils of barking too much as he stared blankly. He was a large, not too bright collie with a long thin snout.

"O.K.," said Jane, "I'm ready. What's this about a dream?"

Meg got comfortable and shifted into raconteur mode. "I dreamt I was in a beautiful university. It was sunny, and the sky was a gorgeous blue with a few bright, white clouds. It was so sunny the white sidewalks were almost too bright to look at. There were blond brick buildings that had pretty tops to them, peaky looking. Anyway, I was sitting outside at a picnic table that was on the lawn. There were sidewalks going straight and some that were diagonal, and there were pine trees, maple trees, oak trees, all kinds of trees and lots of bushes. It was beautiful. I had a book in front of me and I was studying."

"What were you studying?" Jane asked.

"I dunno," said Meg. "But it was weird. I'd stare at the book and then look up, and I noticed that at the end of the quad there was a man who was looking at me. I didn't recognize him, so I looked back down at the book and read some more. Then I looked up again and he was closer, about a third of the way up the quad, and he was still looking at me. He acted as if he didn't want me to know that he was watching me. I felt a little nervous, so I looked back down at my book and read some more. Then I looked up a third time and he was very close, about ten feet away, but he was hiding behind a big bush that was behind me and to my right. Then I woke up."

"Huh," said Jane. "So, do you think that this was symbolic or something?"

"No," responded Meg, "I don't think it was one of those symbolic dreams. It wasn't weird as dreams usually are. It seemed real. I mean really real. It was as if I was awake and there."

"Well, then maybe you've seen a little bit of the future, or maybe you were at an etheric retreat or school. I've read some of them look like places on the earth, but they are above the earth, at etheric levels you can reach only during sleep," explained Jane. "There are Masters who have vowed to help us return to God and they school us at those retreats while we sleep."

"Where are these schools?" Meg asked.

"They're all over the place. I think there are lots of them. The point is this is a special dream that you ought to write down. Come on. Let's get some food."

Meg and Jane went to lunch at Grandma Angela's. They loved to eat lunch there because they could chow down on waffles, scrambled eggs, toast and fruit. She was grateful for Jane's friendship. Jane loved to think, to ruminate about the higher meaning of most everything.

"The appearance is never the reality" was one of her favorite sayings. "God tells us not to judge others. Every time I judge somebody, I find out later that I was wrong because the appearance is never the reality. So I've got to learn to just shut my big mouth and not judge."

At the end of their meal Meg looked at Jane and had an unexpected prompting. "She's leaving Barnstable. She won't be here much longer."

Before Meg could speak, Jane blurted out, "I'm thinking of moving to Denver."

"Denver?" asked Meg in shock. Jane had never mentioned Denver before. She had no family or friends there. They were all back East. "Why Denver?"

"I don't know. I just feel as if I'm supposed to go there. People tell me that there are no ghettos in Denver. That would be a nice experience."

"But do you know anyone there?" asked Meg. "If you go there, you'll be all alone. Who will you stay with? What about a job? What about your house?"

"I don't know. I'm just thinking about it. I might not go."

Within two weeks, Jane was gone. One of her friends bought the house and she resigned as president of their study group. Another friend adopted Jake.

Jane had been Meg's crutch during the divorce. She was like an eagle who soared high above the earth and flew down only to help people in need. It took Meg a while to accept the void in her life that Jane's departure had made. She was lonely but especially regretted the effect it had on the study center.

Despite an aversion to leadership, two years earlier Meg had been elected as an officer of her study center. Some of the group's members thought the neighborhood in which they rented space was unsafe. Meg didn't think it was so bad. She had seen worse neighborhoods while growing up in New York.

At one of their officers' meetings, she listened to the complaints of Hazel Janus, a fellow officer. Hazel lived out in Kingston, a wealthy suburb north of the city, and had a lot of foo-foo friends. She wanted to be able to bring them to the study center but was too ashamed of the neighborhood. It was Hazel's mission to move the group out to the suburbs so that she wouldn't be embarrassed to bring her snobby friends there.

Hazel's constancy in her criticism of their rental space had left the group with an unduly negative attitude about their situation. Meg was sick of listening to Hazel's whining and said, "What are you complaining about? There are no street people around here, no pimps, no whores. I see families. There's always hope for a neighborhood when you see families." By speaking out, Meg had crossed Hazel, an act which caused the other officers to hold their breath. Meg noticed their reaction and wondered why everyone was so afraid of Hazel. After the meeting, Helspeth approached Meg.

"Meg," she said, "I'm impressed with your courage, but do you know what happens to people who cross Hazel?"

"No."

"Well, you're treading on thin ice. Hazel is ruthless. Be careful."

"Are you sure? She seems so goofy," said Meg. "And besides, I didn't cross her. I just said that I didn't think the neighborhood was that bad."

"If you don't agree with her, she makes note of it and gets you back. You'll see. I'm just warning you. She loves to destroy people to the point where she's actually happy when they leave the group. It's sick, but doing that makes her feel powerful, and she gets a rush when she feels powerful. I can't tell you how many people have left the group because of her. Be careful." Helspeth spoke in a low voice so that the others wouldn't hear.

"How does she get revenge?"

"If you cross her, she gets one or two of her 'lieutenants' to join her in condemning you. She loves to rip people apart and accuse them of doing things that aren't true. Just be prepared for the lies. She lies even when she doesn't have to lie. She's got the sickest psychology I've ever run into. You'll soon learn that Hazel always gets her way one way or another. She doesn't care who she injures or who she forces out of the group. She believes the end justifies the means. She's actually proud of herself when she stomps on someone and then gets her way. It confirms in her mind that she is superior."

"Then why do people come here if they have to put up with her?"

"To learn about the different mystical paths and to have a spiritual path of their own," said Helspeth. "We have occult information here that you can't find easily. Look, the darkness will come to wherever there is Divine Light. It's easy to be an angel when you're surrounded by angels. She's here to give us our tests."

"I thought that 'the end justifies the means' is the logic of the dark ones?" Meg asked.

"It is."

"While you live in Chicago, honey, you'll never see a spring," Meg's aunt had told her when she first arrived from New York as a newlywed. To Meg's great disappointment, the warning had proven to be only a slight exaggeration. She sat in her favorite spot at the mall. A park bench had been placed under three crab apple trees heavily laden with baby pink and white blossoms forming a kind of floral canopy.

Pink, purple and white tulips covered the grounds around the bench. This pleasing natural display lasted maybe a week or two each year before Chicago's winter stepped aside to let the typical hot and humid summer drop like a rock on its residents. Each year, Meg kept watch as the crabapples slowly began to bloom, not wanting to miss the best that the fleeting season had to offer. "I need peace," she whispered as she admired the tulips. "I am changing my life so that I have peace."

For the rest of that spring, summer and fall, Meg spent every free moment seeking peace. She found it always at the Lighthouse beach and often at the Art Institute when there weren't hordes of people buffeting her about. She strolled the aisles of the Art Institute admiring the Impressionists. The vivid colors soothed her soul. She walked along the beach and sat on the boulders at the University's edge. She counted the waves as they slapped the rocks. To her left, near the ivy covered buildings, a single redbud stood out from the crowd, purple and vibrant, different from all of the others. Somewhere along the line the redbud had decided to follow its heart.

"Are you crazy?" too many people had asked her. "You're set for life. Why would you divorce a rich man?" Her grandmother's words were never far away, "They may even say you're crazy. You may feel as if you're on a lonely road..." Art and nature brought peace to her life still fraught with unpleasant issues as she followed her heart. *Issues like Hazel Janus*, she thought.

The quintessential used car saleswoman, Hazel always had a forced smile on her face which, unfortunately for her, accentuated a rather large pointy nose. She was very thin, to the point where her hands looked like talons. Her clothes hung from her bones and she never failed to be overdressed. Blouses splashed with rhinestones and fake pearls were her trademark. She accessorized with gold lamé heels, scarves and purses.

Hazel's gaudy taste served her purpose of making everyone else think that she was richer than she was. Armed with a high-pitched, nasal voice that would raise the hair on anyone's neck, her "Hi," which she shrieked upon entering any room, could make all present think that a cat-fight had just broken out.

After Helspeth's warning, Meg began to observe Hazel and realized that Helspeth's comments were more accurate than she had expected. It seemed that having grown up poor on Chicago's West Side, Hazel took pleasure in looking down on the people she left behind after she moved to Kingston. Determined to get her way, she had the personality of a steamroller and rejoiced in squashing others. If she couldn't get it overtly, she switched to covert means. That was when her gift for intrigue and treachery came to the fore. Less fortunate souls were manipulated by half truths to do her dirty work. Some of the poorer people in the group wanted to get in the rich lady's good graces, so they did her bidding. It was difficult to trace the dirty deeds back to Hazel because she demanded total allegiance from her foot soldiers, who never dared betray her for fear that she would turn on them. Those who saw through her act were consistently frustrated, because Hazel never left any fingerprints. It didn't really matter, though, because if confronted, Hazel would just lie her way out of the situation or simply say, "Oh, I'm so sorry. There must have been a misunderstanding."

Keeping others confused was one of Hazel's greatest weapons. With her enemies confused, she was in control, and Meg noticed Hazel liked it that way. Her greatest fear was to not be in control of everyone and everything around her. Concluding that Hazel's scorpionic psychology was the source of most of the trouble within the study group, Meg wondered how a person with such flagrant disregard for the Ten Commandments could possibly be on a spiritual path.

Having sized up Hazel, Meg was reminded of her experiences as a child with the nuns and priests in her grammar school. The nuns were pretty brutal to the kids in her class. They never touched Meg because Mrs. Walsh had visited the Pastor after one of the priests had hit Meg's older brother. A scrappy woman for her size and for the times, Mrs. Walsh told the Pastor that if one of her children was struck again, she would report the incident to the Cardinal. From then on, the Walsh kids were off limits. But Meg suffered when she saw her friends get beaten, and she reported to her Mom that she didn't want to have anything more to do with Jesus. If the nuns worked for Jesus, then Jesus must be just as bad as they are. To Meg's surprise, Mrs. Walsh laughed and related a story from her own childhood.

"When I was almost your age I came to the same conclusion. That day, I walked home from school and went down to your Grandpa's shop in our basement. I told him the same thing that you've just told me. He was an electrical engineer, do you remember?"

"Yes, Mom," said Meg.

"He slowly put the makings of his next invention down on the shop table and climbed the basement stairs. He looked very grim and weary, while he ran his fingers through his gray hair. He took a beer out of the ice box and poured it into his favorite salted and frosty mug. With anger in his eyes, he lowered himself into one of the kitchen chairs. I sat across from him. I thought maybe I was in trouble. He looked at me, slammed his mug onto the table and said, 'Anna, don't let those bastards get in between you and your God.'"

Mrs. Walsh touched Meg's hand and said. "What he taught me, Meggy, was that you go around people like this and have a direct relationship with God. That's what prayer and meditation are for, and you don't have to go into a church to pray. You can pray anywhere.

"Look at Jesus' life. Remember the Bible phrase, 'By their fruits you will know them'? Well, he would never have struck a child. He was kind and good.

"Don't reject Jesus because those people who claim to be devoted to him are not living his teachings. Meggy, we don't need those nuns and priests. They have far too many of us convinced that we need them to get to God. The truth is they need us. Without us, they'd be out of a job."

Eight

Mindy's Moves

MICHAEL GOT OUT of the car and took in a curbside view of his home. The house was dark except for the bedroom lights upstairs, and he could see Mindy's silhouette moving slowly across the room.

"I'm up here!" Mindy called as she heard him come in. "Come on up!"

Michael walked up, rounded the corner, and there was Mindy. She was standing on the other side of the room, combing her waist length hair, completely naked.

"Hello, Michael," she said.

The next weekend Mindy moved in all her stuff, and Michael was assuring her that she would be much safer with him than in her old apartment. He started taking her on bike rides each weekend, short ones at first, which gradually increased in speed and duration. She was a natural on the bike. Her riding style was different from Michael's, though. She rode to win, to be the fastest woman on two wheels. Michael could see her ambition getting stronger each weekend, and he was impressed with Mindy's strength and power. The months passed quickly, and when Mindy was strong enough, she joined a local bicycle racing club. The annual L150 ride for Leukemia was coming up, and Mindy's racing club was sponsoring a training ride to Utah. They both signed up for the training ride and put in for some vacation time at work.

"I'm going to drive in by myself today, Mindy," Michael said as he crunched on some corn flakes. "I want to get in extra early. We've gotta get ready to go to Utah tomorrow, and I have a lot of loose ends to take care of at the office." They usually rode to work together, because Mindy had a job with a local advertising agency that was near NASA, and her office was right on the way.

"O.K.," Mindy said. "How about meeting me for lunch in our favorite park?"

"You're on," Michael said. "I'll be there around noon."

Soon he was off, and his commute down to NASA was in full swing. It was a madhouse on the freeway, but Michael had learned to take it in stride. He loved driving his sports car, and the rush hour traffic provided plenty of challenges. Michael maneuvered through the traffic with the mastery that comes from the daily grind of repetition. He arrived at the office at 7:00 a.m., giving him plenty of time to take part in the morning bull session in the coffee room.

"We should never have lost the Challenger!" Mel said. "Management didn't listen to engineering. They should never have launched."

"What's-'er-name was such a fox!" Ted said. "What a tragedy!"

"Yeah, right. Ole what's-'er-name. To say nothing of the rest of the crew," Tammy reminded him.

"Let's change the subject," Michael pleaded. "This is way too grim for this hour." He remembered that day only too well, and the shock of hearing his manager say, "We lost the shuttle!"

"I agree," Mel said.

"So many of the astronauts have really inspired me," Tammy said. "They talked about having a higher state of awareness while out in space and made me realize that spirituality and science are like twin pillars. Science goes after the truth from the external side, and spirituality goes after it from the internal side. When you get them to meet up, you've really got something."

They all nodded in agreement.

"There are some wonderful scientists who have come and gone, and who we should pay more attention to. Men like John Keely, to name just one," Michael said. "He lived in the 1800's, yet he invented a dynasphere that scientists today are just beginning to understand. Keely understood the concept of the neutral center, and he formed a circuit which had a neutral center. Given an initial impulse of a few pounds, his dynasphere could keep rotating indefinitely."

"It's incredible that Keely could do all that work in sympathetic vibratory physics without the use of computers," Tammy said.

"He didn't use fractions," Michael explained. "He used only whole numbers, a quantum arithmetic that was probably used by Pythagoras and even by people before him. Keely understood what a wave really is, and how quantum arithmetic precisely describes a wave. If you understand one wave, you understand them all, you understand nature. He understood the push, pull and balance of forces, which in spiritual circles is called the "trinity." His forty laws of sympathetic vibratory physics are worth studying. I mean, we live in a musical universe. Everything vibrates, and the laws of harmony are key."

"Right," Ted said. "Keely understood the real musical scale, the music of the spheres."

"The coolest thing," Mel said, "is that the formula for the volume of the torus is the same as the volume for the hypersphere.

"Hey!" Mel said. "Shouldn't we be getting to work? What are we, a bunch of government workers?"

"What are you working on today, Tammy?" Ted asked.

"The shuttle's Hal compiler. We're looking at porting it to a Unix machine."

"How about you, Michael?" Ted asked, casting a clinical eye in Michael's direction.

"I've got a meeting today over at Mission Control," Michael said. "They want to go over the pre-launch check points, and I think they want to do a zap right before the shuttle launch."

"A zap? What's that?" Mel asked.

"They don't have time for a testing cycle, and they want to change some computer instructions based on last minute requirements. They call it a zap because they put the object code into memory without compiling," Michael explained.

"I'm glad I'm not doing the flying!" Mel said.

"They're using a very primitive computer system," Michael said. "All the onboard computers, even the back-up computer, still use magnetic iron core memory. That's because when they started planning the system, they didn't have the technology we have today. By the time the planning was complete, it was too late to change. They have to manually load a tape for launch, load another tape for orbit, and load another tape for re-entry. I mean, they could do a better job with a PC."

"They should use strange attractors to figure out what's coming before it happens," Mel said.

Michael gave him a "what are you talking about" look, and each one ambled off to his office.

The morning passed quickly, and Michael was off for his rendezvous with Mindy. As he was driving, a strange and wonderful thing happened. He began to feel an altered state of consciousness come over him, and as he looked at the road ahead, a towering, angelic figure appeared before him. Just for an instant, time seemed to stand still, and there was the angel, as tall as the trees, standing in the middle of the road. His waist was at road level, as if earth and sky had no meaning for him. He disappeared just as suddenly as he had appeared. Michael had no idea why he had come, but he felt the same way he had felt in Aspen all those many years before when he saw the beautiful smile of the man with the walking stick. He pulled into the park entrance, and when he spotted Mindy's van, he pulled alongside. He just sat there for a moment, completely dazed. Mindy rolled down her window. "Michael, come on over. I have a surprise for you!"

Michael got out of the car and walked around to the passenger side of the van. He opened the door, and when he looked over at Mindy, he got his second big shock in a row. Mindy was naked from the waist down, and she was facing him.

"Come on, big boy!" she said. "It's just a simple in and out procedure. Quick and dirty. Let's get down and do it!"

"Mindy," he said, looking quite frustrated. "I can't do this right now. I just..."

"All right, Michael, I get the message. Some romantic you are turning out to be. I'm beginning to wonder about this relationship," she said, slamming the door and laying a peel out of the parking lot.

"...saw an angel," he said softly, watching her ride away.

Michael felt as if he was operating on remote control. He drove through the back gate at NASA, blasted past the Saturn V rocket and went into the Mission Control parking lot completely oblivious to his surroundings.

"Look at all these talented men and women," he said to himself. "Which one of them understands how that angel appeared like that? Which one of them can do what that angel just did?"

The meeting lasted the rest of the afternoon, and when it was over Michael felt relieved. He bolted out the door, eager to get up to Utah and do some cycling in the mountains. He put his vision in the back of his mind, and wondered how things with Mindy were going to work out.

I don't want to commit to her, he thought as he drove back home on the freeway. *She's been trying to get me to marry her ever since she moved in, before she even knew anything about me! This is really getting awkward. Where does she get off telling me I'm not romantic? Sex with her is lewd, it's anything but romantic. She talks about sex with all her girlfriends in the crudest way possible. When I overheard her on the phone last week, I was shocked. Nothing but how many times we did it recently, how big this guy is compared to that guy, and which position she prefers. Sex is supposed to be a sacred exchange of energy.*

In spite of the scene at the park that afternoon, Mindy was reasonably amicable as she and Michael packed up for the big trip to Utah. They met up with the riders from the racing team the next morning at the airport, and Michael's biking buddies Don and George were there too, both of them with their wives. Everyone had shipped his bike to Utah a couple of days earlier via Greyhound bus, because Don had explained that it was more efficient. They all flew to Vegas, and then rented a couple of vans for the drive to Brian Head, Utah. When they arrived in Brian Head, they picked up their bikes and wasted no time getting to the condos for a good night's sleep. There were two condos, one for the racers and one for the "pedestrians."

As the sun came over the mountains the next morning, they all pedaled off down the road. The racers, with the exception of James, a tall, muscular cyclist from a nationally known racing team, took their road bikes the first day, and everyone else went mountain biking. James had not taken his eyes off Mindy since the trip started.

As the morning progressed, Michael had only fallen over twice, and he was feeling pretty good about himself. The first time he fell, it was because he ran right over a huge rock. He had been looking at it before he hit it, knowing he wanted to avoid it, and then he hit it dead center. It was almost as if the thought of hitting it guided him into it. His second fall was caused by a falcon hurtling toward its prey at over fifty miles an hour. Michael was riding along the edge of a bluff, and the falcon was using him for cover. The bird, while circling overhead, had spotted a mouse on the other side of the bluff from Michael, and when it went into its dive, Michael was between it and the mouse. Michael didn't hear a sound until the bird flew right over his head, and then the rush of wind sounded like a miniature sonic boom.

Mindy hadn't paid much attention to Michael's falls, because she had become quite enthralled with James and his racing stories.

"I'll never forget the time I was racing down El Grande in West Texas," James said. "All of the sudden, my bike started to wobble wildly from side to side."

"Something must have caused it to hit its resonant frequency," Don said.

James gave him a confused look and ignored him.

"What did you do?" Mindy asked.

"I had to think fast. I went into a tuck and pressed both my knees in hard against the top tube."

"Wow," Mindy gushed. "How awesome. Did the bike stop wobbling?"

"I had it under control in no time."

"Michael, did you know that you could stop your bike from wobbling by doing that?" Mindy asked.

"That's the first time I've heard of it," Michael said.

Mindy gave Michael a haughty look, and then gazed longingly at James. "Tell me more, James!"

Michael did his best to ignore them and enjoy the ride, which was starting to get more challenging as the road got steeper.

"I have to focus here," George said, "I've got to carry my big schlong all the way up this mountain!"

Eventually, they came to a high ridge, looking down into a valley. At the edge of the valley was a very dense forest, and just beyond that was the highway that led back to the condo.

Don and George wanted to go down into the valley, cross through the dense forest, get on the highway, and pedal back to the condo. Michael was thinking, *Don't give up the high ground, guys.* Michelle and Winnie were talking about the latest cycling fashions, content to leave the navigating to the men. James was telling Mindy about his latest sub-four-hour century.

"We could retrace our steps and get back to the condo that way," Michael suggested.

"Been there, done that," Don said. Michael had been discounted and dismissed. Don and George were making the important decisions here. Michael marveled at how cohesive they had become, but he told himself not to get into the "me against them" thing. Michelle decided to head back and retrace her steps, but the rest of the group decided to go forward.

Don and George mounted up and started down, and the rest of the group followed. The road was a winding, rocky single track all the way down, and then it widened out at the bottom into a series of roller coaster ups and downs. It was a lot of fun, and the predominant direction was always down. Eventually they came to the edge of the forest and started in. The road was very sandy and rocky with overhanging trees on each side, and Michael only fell over once! As they rode on, they kept getting lower and lower, and it kept getting hotter and hotter. The road didn't even look like a road anymore, and they had to carry their bikes over all sorts of obstacles and brush back the branches as they went. The air was still and dry, and the dust caught in their throats. A barbed wire fence presented itself, and they hoisted their bikes over and continued on.

"The highway should be just ahead," George predicted.

"Did you guys see Deliverance?" Winnie asked.

"They were on a rafting trip," George replied.

"What else?" Winnie goaded.

"Well, they met a really good banjo player along the way," Michael said.

"What else?" Winnie asked with more urgency.

"Most of them made it out!" Don reassured her.

"Some of them didn't make it out," Winnie reminded him.

"They didn't deserve to live," Don said. "That's natural selection!"

Winnie gave him an unnatural look that said it all, and they continued in silence, brushing off the horse flies as they went.

"Look! A satellite dish!" Michael shouted. "Must be a resort!"

They pushed their bikes a little faster in the excitement, and came to the edge of a clearing. There was the satellite dish, surrounded by empty beer cans and whisky bottles. Scrawny looking sheep and goats were bunched together here and there, and a little hut stood precariously on gray construction bricks next to a dilapidated well. Empty ammunition boxes were scattered everywhere, and an old swaybacked mare stood over on one side, brushing flies off with her tail. Sitting on a rock next to her, holding her reins in his hand, sat a leathery skinned sheepherder. He was staring at the ground, not even acknowledging the presence of the gaily clad mountain bikers with all their high tech cycling gear.

The group paused politely, waiting for the sheepherder to introduce himself. All was still, except for the sound of the horse flies buzzing around and the swishing of the old mare's tail. The stench of neglect filled their nostrils. Don was the first one to break the silence.

"May we fill our water bottles from your well?"

Without looking up, the sheepherder nodded, "yes."

Michael was eyeing the rifle that was propped up against the little hut within easy reach of the sheepherder.

"George," he said, "Remember that pistol you used to carry in your saddle bag?"

"It's at home."

Michael thought, *It's time for some protection!* He knew he couldn't call to the hierarchy out loud, so he quietly whispered.

Don brought out his charcoal filter pump and began drawing water from the well.

"Ask him where the highway is, George," Winnie whispered.

"Do you know where the highway is?" George inquired.

The sheepherder had a strained look on his face, as if he was searching for the "mot juste," just the right phrase.

"To the right?" Michael asked.

"Yeah."

"To the left?" Michael asked, testing for comprehension.

"Sure." One of his eyes wondered off independently of the other.

"He's a monosyllabic moron!" Don exclaimed.

"Yeah," Michael confirmed. "Of course, maybe we are surrounded by highway."

"Wait here a minute," George said. "I'll check it out."

He wandered off to the right, leaving everybody else to get acquainted.

The sheepherder kept staring at the ground, so Don went over and made some drawings in the sand right in front of him so that he could point to where they were.

Instead of pointing, he gave them a toothless grin and shrugged his shoulders.

After a few minutes, George came back, not looking too hopeful.

"There's a huge ravine between us and the highway," he said. "We'll have to climb back up the mountain and retrace our path."

That was fine with everyone except Winnie, who had almost reached her limit. She was not going to be able to keep up.

"Don," Michael suggested, "why don't you guys head back, and Winnie and I will follow you at her pace. When you guys get back to the condo, you can get the van and start back after us. What do you think, George?"

Don and George both agreed, so they all started back up. It wasn't long before they disappeared into the undergrowth ahead as Michael and Winnie followed more slowly behind them.

"You know, Winnie, we were never in any danger. It was just our imaginations running wild. All we have to do is follow the same trail back out, and we can stop and rest whenever you want."

Winnie was actually a superb athlete, but this trek would have challenged anyone.

"You're probably right. Don thinks he's Magellan, though. We should have made a group decision before coming down here."

They were pushing their bikes up a steep, sandy slope, and as he looked over to Winnie to reply, he could see the sheepherder on his horse behind them, carrying his rifle. The sheepherder's eyes were deadlocked on Winnie's buns, which were all the more tantalizing underneath her lycra shorts.

"Sheepherder, six o'clock!" Michael whispered.

"What's he doing?"

"He and his horse are just sauntering up the trail for no apparent reason."

"Let's just ignore him and keep pushing!"

As the sheepherder came up to them, he didn't say a word. He just kept moseying along past them, as if they weren't even there. After a while he was out of sight, and they never saw him again.

"I think he was just out making his rounds, Winnie," Michael surmised.

"Probably so."

They pushed further up the trail, and Winnie broke the silence once more.

"Remember when we were back there at the sheepherder's place?"

"Yes, charming. That must be his summer residence."

Winnie laughed through the strain of the climb. "What were you whispering to yourself about?"

"Oh, that was nothing."

"Come on, Michael."

Michael looked at her. It was always a risk to discuss these types of subjects, because people could react in so many different ways. Should he pour it on full strength? Should he give her a diluted dose? Was he being arrogant? Perhaps she was just playing along and just looking interested, and when she got back to the condo, she would tell everyone how weird Michael was. The worst possibility of all, though, was that she was gleaning information and developing a dossier on Michael. What if she considered these truths dangerous?

"You're going to think I'm extremely weird."

"I already know you're extremely weird!"

"Oh, well, in that case, I'll tell you. I was calling for protection," Michael confessed.

"Protection?" Winnie asked.

"If you make the call to the spiritual beings who are all around you, they will respond," Michael explained.

"Well, I knew you were weird, but I had you at a lower level of weirdness. You just moved up a couple of notches," Winnie chided.

"If you ever see one of them, it will blow you away," Michael countered.

"Have you ever seen any of them?"

"Yes!"

"Where?"

"Just last week, at lunch."

"You had lunch together? Who paid?"

"He didn't invite me to lunch. I was driving to the park to meet Mindy, and there he was, right in the middle of the road."

"I hate it when that happens."

"This guy was huge. He was as high as the trees, and he was waist level with where the road was before he made it disappear."

"He made it disappear?"

"That's not a good way to describe it. My take on it is that he was there all the time, and the freeway was there all the time, but he is in a different octave that we normally can't see or detect."

"Why do you call it an octave? I thought that was a musical term," Winnie said.

Luckily, the ground had smoothed out, and they were back on their bikes, breathing normally. It made it much easier to converse.

"Seven is the primary harmonic quantity of the universe, so people use the word octave to describe higher levels of reality. By higher, they mean at a higher frequency. My theory is that everything consists of concentrated and coagulated patterns of sound waves."

"Cool!"

"Also, you have seven bodies," Michael went on.

"How so?"

"Your I AM presence, your causal body, your Higher Self, which some people call your Christ Self, and your etheric, mental, emotional, and physical bodies."

"Wow. Seven bodies. I'm working as hard I can to keep this physical one in shape!" Winnie smiled to herself, and then looked serious again. "So why did this being appear to you?"

"I'm still working on that one!" he said. "He could have appeared to you just as easily as he appeared to me!"

"Oh yeah?" Winnie looked encouraged.

"Yeah. Take my big sister, for example. She was riding along in the car with my niece, Elsa, and they were passing through a fairly sleazy neighborhood. Taylor started to get a little nervous, so she called for protection. She called silently, because she didn't know what our little niece, who was only seven at the time, would think if she heard her. They kept cruisin' along, and suddenly Elsa got a huge grin on her face, looked over at Taylor, and told her there were angels all around the car."

"That's incredible," Winnie said.

They talked and talked as they sometimes pushed, sometimes rode their mountain bikes back up to where they had originally come down. Eventually, as the sun started to set, they began to hope that they would meet up with Don and George real soon.

"I hope there aren't any wolves out here. I mean, it's almost dark," Michael said.

"If we're out here overnight, you and I are going to get a lot better acquainted!"

Michael looked down, not wanting to go there. He knew they would be O.K. if they just stayed on the trail. They finally made it back to the main dirt road, which was a double track, big enough for a four-wheeled vehicle. As they pedaled along, a cloud of dust started coming toward them.

"Looks like a Tasmanian devil!" Michael mused.

Out of the dust cloud came Don and George in the van, screeching to a halt. George got out, rubbing his abused head, which had been bouncing off the ceiling as they raced through the countryside. He gave Winnie a big, relieved hug, and everyone climbed in for the ride back to civilization.

"Now I see why they say, 'Don't ever give up the high ground!'" Michael said.

"We had to give it up," Don said. "Otherwise, we wouldn't have met the sheepherder!"

"Yeah," George said. "It gave him the opportunity to socialize and get out a little."

George seemed to always go along with Don, and Michael wondered what George really thought. Michael loved harmony, though. It was the Libra in him. Rather than explain that things could have gotten really serious, he went with the flow.

"We caught him by surprise, though. It was kind of rude to pop in unannounced," Michael commented.

"Next time," Winnie said, "Let's call first."

When they got back to the condo, Michelle was glad to see them.

"Sorry I left early," she said. "Don told me you guys made a new friend."

"Why didn't you stay with us?" Winnie asked.

"Never give up the high ground!" Michelle confirmed, giving Don the look of authority.

Don started to make his rebuttal, but thought better of it. Instead, he shot her a boyish grin that said he could do no wrong.

"I've got dinner ready!" Michelle announced. She definitely got everyone's attention. A hungry cyclist can eat an obscene amount of food, and Michelle, being a cyclist herself, had put an obscene amount on the table.

"Where's Mindy?" Michael asked.

"She's over at the other condo," Michelle said, avoiding Michael's eyes.

Michael made normal conversation at dinner, and dismissed himself politely when the meal was over. He went upstairs to the loft, unfolded the sleeper sofa, got into bed, and gazed up through the skylight at the starry night sky.

I'm glad she's getting interested in James, he thought to himself, *but this is a cruel way to do it. She wants to flaunt James at me, and use him to hurt me. I must say, it does hurt, but why should it hurt this much? We aren't right for each other, and I don't want to commit to her.*

Michael turned on the night light and looked through the books he brought from home. *Reading will take my mind off of her*, he thought.

Even so, he couldn't bring himself to pick up a book. As his body relaxed into the cushions his mind moved slowly as if carried by a current and absorbed the sacredness of the stars. He thought of St. Germain, a Master who explained the nature of matter. He said that God's love is the heart and source of all things physical. Every electron is comprised of Spirit or the Divine essence of the Creator. It radiates its own Light and brilliance, obeying the directing activity of love. Electrons respond to each person's conscious will and thoughts. An individual has conscious control over the electrons in his or her own body simply by thinking or feeling positively or negatively. We literally will our bodies into healthy or unhealthy manifestation!

He turned off the light and gazed up again through the skylight at the starry sky. It was absolutely luminous. He could feel its life pulsing through and around him. It wasn't dark and mysterious. The image of the girl who appeared to him at the Midnight Ramble came to the fore. Was she real?

If I ever meet her, he thought, *things here below will be the way they are above.*

Nine

Portents

Meg ran out the door and slid into her car. She was on her way to her astrology class. Astrology was a subject that she was interested in from the time that she was a little girl standing next to her Mom in the grocery store checkout line. There were little books next to the cash register with strange names like Aries, Sagittarius, Pisces and funny pictures of animals on the covers. There was an inner knowing. That still, small voice told her that someday she must learn about those books. Today Meg was stepping back into the world of astrology. She had taught herself quite a bit about the subject over the years when Nick wasn't around, but it had been twenty years since her last course. She needed to do the things she was meant to do, the things that Nick had stopped her from doing.

Meg remembered back to 1975. She and Nick had just been married. She signed up for an astrology class with one of her friends. Nick was curious about what she was doing in the class, so Meg invited him to come. Back in '75 there were no personal computers, so Meg learned to cast a chart by hand. The students struggled with the spherical trigonometry that the teacher patiently outlined on her blackboard. Meg and Nick finished their charts. Nick was enjoying himself until the teacher came over to their table and picked up his unnamed chart. Most of the people in the class were taking it for fun. The teacher followed suit with a very lighthearted approach to the subject.

In silence, she looked at the chart and then delineated it carefully. "This person is very dedicated to his work and could easily be a workaholic if he isn't careful. He has a great love of detail regarding the law, and with Mars in Libra he could use this talent to fight for justice. He'd make a good litigator. With Venus in Virgo as part of a stellium in the sixth house, he must guard against being unfeeling with loved ones and having an exaggerated allegiance to his job."

Nick froze and his face grew pale. The teacher held up the chart and said, "Whose chart is this?"

Nick didn't answer, but Meg said, "It's Nick's chart."

"Oh," said the teacher, "So, tell me, Nick, what do you do for a living?"

Nick never went back to Meg's astrology class and never lost an opportunity to make fun of her teacher. He was terribly threatened by the woman who blew away his stunted concept of the world. Showering her with scorn meant that he wouldn't have to take her seriously or worse, change. From that time on, Meg had to read about and study astrology only in Nick's absence. She put her books and charts under the bed and stifled that part of her soul to keep the peace.

As Meg drove north from Barnstable, she entered Richmond Park and followed the directions to the Church of the One. It was a pretty building in a pretty neighborhood. She descended the basement stairs to the classroom and was greeted by an elderly gentleman who was gracious and calm. He took Meg's hand in his and looked directly into her eyes. His eyes were full of kindness. "Hello, my dear," he said. "My name is Bernard and up in front is my lovely wife, Jeanne. We are to be your teachers. Please tell me your name."

"My name is Meg. Meg, uh, Banacek," she said, hesitating on the Banacek. She wanted to go back to her maiden name, but wasn't sure if that name suited her any more than Banacek did. The confusion regarding her name reflected the confusion regarding her identity.

"Well, Meg Banacek, we're pleased to meet you. Please take a seat anywhere you like, and tonight I'm going to cover a short introduction to the Divine Science of Astrology," he spoke gallantly.

Meg walked toward the tables and chairs and chose a seat in the last row. Whether choosing a seat in a theater or a classroom, Meg always sat in the back. There was a dull, ancient memory of being attacked from behind and sitting in the last row assuaged her fear.

When Bernard was ready to speak, he walked toward the front of the room with Jeanne. Meg was soon to find out that Bernard and Jeanne had practiced Astrology for a total of over 75 years. Their astrological knowledge was impressive. They were happy people, especially Bernard, who enjoyed everyone he met.

He started the class by saying, "Astrology is a divine science. It's a gift to us from our Creator. Those who study it and enjoy its benefits are mocked and ridiculed, but only because there are those on the earth who want to keep the Creator's children from its helpful knowledge. It is meant to help us to prepare for our tests.

"As you probably know, the earth is a schoolroom and we come here in our different embodiments to learn our lessons and evolve upward to a higher consciousness so that we may return permanently to our Creator. When we pass our tests, we have used our energy properly. We earn what some people refer to as 'good karma.' When we fail our tests we bring sorrow into our lives by using our energy for erroneous thinking and wrong actions. Some people refer to these errors as 'sins.' Others just call it 'bad karma.'

"When we use the divine science of astrology to our advantage as the Creator intends, we are warned ahead of time of the tests that are coming, and we are meant to prepare ourselves for them. It is like standing in the ocean and facing the waves. We can decide to jump over the little ones and dive through the big ones. We strategize our way around and through those waves so that we aren't injured by them.

"If we don't take advantage of the knowledge of our astrology because we are afraid that others will make fun of us or because we refuse to believe that the energies of the planets can have an effect on us, then we are like a person standing in the ocean and facing the shore. The waves come from behind and knock us down because we didn't see them coming. Life is filled with disruptions and surprises.

"As this course proceeds, we will be learning about how to interpret your natal chart and to anticipate the waves that are coming to knock you down, as well as the waves that are coming to assist you."

After class, Bernard approached Meg and said, "Would you like me to look at your chart now or some other night?"

"Oh, now would be great," she said, remembering that a consultation on the student's natal chart was paid for as part of the course's fee.

"You have a copy of your natal, don't you?"

"Yes, but it's done by hand. I did it twenty years ago in my first astrology course."

"Well, this is wonderful. I'm an old-timer and I don't trust computers. Oh, Jeanne is always singing the praises of computers, but I think astrology is too important to trust to a computer.

"What if it makes a mistake? You're giving a client life-changing advice that could cause him to go down the wrong road. Ohhh, I shudder to think about it."

Bernard glanced at Meg's chart and did a double take. He looked serious. Astrologers have to have poker faces. Their clients listen to their words, but give their body language an equal amount of credence. Surely, after so many years of practice Bernard knew this, but he was not able to hide his concern.

"Oh, my dear," he said, looking with compassion at Meg, "you have had a very difficult time for the last several years. Oh, you've had changes, upheavals and now there's confusion. Neptune will surely improve your spiritual life, but it will do so by bringing you to your knees. You will suffer confusion with your career and you have been divorced recently, I assume. It probably happened somewhere around the Fall of '93?" he asked.

"Yeah, well," said Meg. "That's when I filed in court."

"Ah," he said. "Then it was probably final in November/December of '94. But just wait a minute and let me talk to Jeanne. I'll be back, and we'll find some good stuff to balance out the bad. Remember, my dear, there's always something good going on to balance out the challenges."

Bernard smiled at Meg, patted her on the shoulder and strolled calmly into the kitchen, where Jeanne was laughing with some of the other students. Bernard began to speak in what he thought was a whisper. "Oh my God, Jeanne, you wouldn't believe her chart. What a mess! It's so awful. I don't know what to say to her. Uranus and Neptune are square to her Sun, Moon AND Ascendant, Pluto's inconjunct to them, Saturn is conjoined her Venus and the upcoming eclipse is directly conjoined with her Sun, Moon and Ascendant! Oh, the poor woman."

Meg heard every word and saw his silhouette formed by the overhead light. He was holding his head in his hands. Jeanne really was whispering, so that Meg couldn't hear her comments. Soon Jeanne came out of the kitchen and walked toward Meg with a forced smile on her face. Bernard followed.

"Hi," she said cheerfully. "Bernard's been telling me about your chart. Can I see it?"

"Sure," said Meg. She handed Jeanne the chart, pretending that she had not heard Bernard's comments in the kitchen.

"O.K.," said Jeanne as she scanned the chart. "Look, Bernard, there's the possibility of a marriage coming when her progressed Venus hits her Sun, Moon and Ascendant. That's a wonderful thing. Tell her about the marriage, dear," she said, smiling, and ran outside to say goodbye to the other students.

Bernard looked relieved. He composed himself. "All right," he said, ruminating over the chart. "Yes, there is the possibility of a marriage. Oh, wait, it looks as if there will be two marriages."

"TWO marriages?" said Meg. "Oh, that can't be. No, not possible."

"Well, what I see is that the second marriage will be a quick one, and the third one will be long lasting and happy. Bernard smiled at Meg and then asked, "But why so glum? Aren't you looking forward to a little romance in your life after feeling so rejected for so long?"

"How did you know I've been rejected?"

"Oh, my dear, it's in your chart. Venus opposed Saturn in the fifth. You came into this embodiment with that momentum. It involves your kids. Your relationship with them will be your greatest challenge in this lifetime. But what about the marriage, huh? Let's concentrate on that."

"Oh, I am definitely looking forward to it. It's just that I don't know how my girls will react to my having two more marriages."

"Let me see your ex's chart," he said.

Meg gave him the chart and he looked at it sternly. "His Midheaven is several degrees before yours. Uranus conjoined his Midheaven before it conjoined yours. It squared his Sun before it squared yours. What this means, my dear, is that your husband wanted the divorce long before you did. Did he file or did you?"

"I filed."

"I don't have time now to explain, Jeanne is waiting for me, but from looking quickly at his chart I can see a lot of deceit, games playing, manipulation, and power plays from a stellium in Scorpio in his progressed chart and a desire to divorce long before you filed. He drove you to it and set you up as the fall guy. There was probably another woman, and he sabotaged the marriage in a very covert way. You have nothing to feel guilty about. You were honest; he wasn't. You do need to be careful, though. He's watching you and could have others watching you. Have you noticed anyone following you?"

"I don't think so," said Meg .

"Well, he wants to take the children from you. It's a matter of hatred. He's looking for a way to do it. He's plotting and scheming. He wants to destroy you, to break your heart, and what better way to destroy a woman than to sever her from her children. He doesn't really want the children; he's too wrapped up in his work and himself. But he thinks it would be better for him financially if he had custody. He'll sweet-talk his girlfriend into taking care of them so that he doesn't have to. This will all be done covertly because he doesn't want to look bad in front of the children. My guess is that he will turn them against you, if he hasn't already done so, by manipulation and twisted facts. He wants them to feel sorry for him, so he can manipulate them more easily. It's good that you got rid of him. He's a nasty fellow with a lovely facade. He's going to become worse as Pluto conjoins his Mars in the eighth. Be glad about the upcoming marriages, and I'll see you next week. Will you be joining us?"

"Yes," said Meg. "I'll definitely be here."

For the next few days, Meg interviewed realtors. The time had come for her to sell her house. After taxes, the alimony and child support barely covered the mortgage payment. The money earned from mediation was a far cry from the $40,000 she needed. Each month she had to take out thousands from her account to pay the bills. Money was going fast, and Meg was very nervous.

It seemed a bit risky to put the house on the market, because she expected Nick to put a bid in to buy it. He would schmooze Amy and Heather into staying in the house after he bought it, and Meg could lose custody, the child support and maintenance. It would mean another legal battle, and Meg fully expected Nick, who always fought dirty, to do it. His hold over Heather was almost eerie, and Amy would follow her big sister's decision. But Meg had no choice, given the financial situation, and she hired a dynamo lady named Fran DiSimone, the town's realtor who never slept.

Fran arrived with her assistant, Donna, who took notes and helped her measure the rooms. Fran knew her stuff, and when Meg asked her if she could sell the house without putting a sign on the front lawn so that Nick wouldn't know that the house was for sale Fran said, "Well, we can try it for a while. But I really wouldn't advise it. It'll still be listed, but since he's not a realtor he won't be checking the lists unless he's looking for a house of his own. Is he looking to buy a house at this time?"

"I'm not sure. He's got a condo now," said Meg, "He'll probably buy a house soon, and if he doesn't try to buy this house he'll probably buy a Tudor in Indigo Falls."

"Why a Tudor in Indigo Falls?" asked Donna, while Fran looked doubly quizzical.

"Well, he hates me, so he'll try to spite me. The last time we looked for a house I wanted to move to Indigo Falls because I thought it was a pretty little town right on the commuter line. At that time we weren't able to find the kind of home we wanted in Indigo Falls, so we didn't move there. More importantly, we didn't move there because Nick was opposed to Indigo Falls."

"Why?" asked Fran.

"Because I liked Indigo Falls. It was spite. Nick always tries his damndest to block my dreams."

"So back then he spited you by blocking Indigo Falls and now he'll spite you by choosing Indigo Falls?" suggested Donna.

"Exactly. Nick likes to get revenge in a way that no one discerns but me. That way he preserves his perfect public image," explained Meg matter-of-factly.

"And," said Fran, "it probably follows that he'll buy a Tudor because he knows you like Tudors."

"Yup," said Meg. "Well, he thinks I like Tudors. Actually, my tastes have changed. If he bought a log home, I'd be filled with envy."

"Well, I don't think he'll find one of those in Indigo Falls," said Fran. "But just to be on the safe side, we'll keep that confidential." Looking over at Donna, she smiled and said, "This one's gonna be fun. Who says selling residential real estate is boring?"

Fran advised Meg to put the side lot on the market separately from the house. She said that Meg would get more money if she sold them separately. This was good news for Meg, who figured she could use the money from the sale of the side lot to pay the mortgage on the house until the house sold. Cash was the need of the hour.

When the sign went up on the side lot, it didn't take long for a builder to put in a respectable bid. "My only problem is my neighbor, Nicoletta. She lives to the south of me on the other side of the lot," said Meg. "I told her several months ago that I'd let her know if there was a bid on it. She said that she and her husband would like to bid also."

"Well, that's stupid. Why didn't they just make an offer months ago? You always pay more when you're in a bidding war," Fran commented, knowing that this would delay things. Meg was listening with one ear as she gazed out her kitchen window at her other neighbor, the one who lived to the north.

Nancy Macy had been Meg's neighbor to the north for some five years. With each year the woman got crazier and crazier. The latest scoop on Nancy was that she had been arrested the Friday before in a local bar for attacking a cop. Wild-haired and wild-eyed, Nancy ranted and raved on a regular basis at the fence Meg put up between their properties. She vandalized Meg's house and garage whenever she was pissed off. When Nick brought home their luxury car from the dealer, Nancy punctured their front porch screen with a piece of scaffolding. When Meg bought a used mink coat to celebrate the signing of the divorce papers, Nancy pitched a potato through the garage window. It was all done under the stealth of nightfall. No one ever saw her, but everyone knew it was her. Most of her neighbors joked about Nancy's insanity, but Meg viewed Nancy in a more serious light. She saw her as a woman who had gone slowly nuts from motherhood, marriage and the suburbs. Nancy was on the same road as she but only slightly ahead of her. *If I don't get my freedom soon, I'll end up just as crazy as she is,* Meg thought.

Fran was jabbering on and on in sales talk as Meg looked out of her kitchen window and right into Nancy's eyes. A disquieting smile crossed Nancy's face. Whenever Meg was at home, Nancy always knew what room Meg was in. She had an eerie psychic edge to her. She just knew that Meg was in the kitchen and so stared right through the kitchen window until Meg came into view.

"Hello. Are you there?" asked Fran, exasperated with Meg's woolgathering.

"Yes, yes. I'm with you. Sorry, I'm watching my crazy neighbor act crazy," replied Meg.

"The one you want to sell to?"

"No, the one to the north of me. I have two neighbors. To the south is Nicolletta Hundarp and to the north is Nancy Macy. The poor woman is almost totally out of her mind."

"Woman, I don't know anyone who's surrounded by more lunatics than you. The vengeful ex with the perfect public image, the crazy neighbor who attacks off-duty cops...O.K., look, I'll call your neighbor, what's her name? Nicolletta Dunharp? I'll tell her there's a bid on the lot."

"No, no, her name is Nicoletta Hundarp," said Meg.

"Does it suit her?" asked Fran.

"Definitely. She's the queen. Actually, most of the time she's been pretty nice to me. That is, until I filed for divorce. She's mad at me now because my yard doesn't look as good as it did when Nick lived here. She's a woman who lives in a very small world. People are getting blown up in the Middle East, they're dying of AIDS in Africa, the Dalai Lama has been driven out of Tibet and Nicoletta is pissed because my yard is no longer manicured. If my Mom were here, she'd comment that Nicoletta is 'vapid.'"

"Vapid. Now there's a great word. I've got a lot of people I could use that one on." Fran let out a hearty laugh as she and Donna stepped out onto the back porch. "I want to check around the outside now. I'll call you, lady, as soon as I've got some news."

Meg closed the door behind them. One look out the kitchen window revealed that Nancy Macy had disappeared into the shadows of her house.

That Sunday, Meg went back to her Astrology class and Bernard lectured on the Ephemeris and Table of Houses as well as the different interpretations of the signs of the Zodiac. After class he approached Meg and said, "I am so sorry that I had to depart quickly during our last meeting. Please forgive me. Something has been bothering me about your chart during this past week. May I see it again?"

"Sure," said Meg, as she dug the chart out of her backpack.

"There is a very quick transit coming up. Lasts maybe a week at most. It involves Mars, Neptune, your natal Moon, Pluto and Mercury. You'll be under a very painful attack soon," he said quietly. "It will change your entire approach to higher philosophical or spiritual thinking."

"An attack?" asked Meg.

"Yes, a verbal attack. There is a lot of hatred behind it. It comes from a woman who is angry with you. There is a lot of deceit and revenge as part of it. You'll have to steel yourself and be prepared to defend yourself as a lawyer in court. My dear, you are going through a lot of tests right now. But your astrology is showing a big wave is coming. If you prepare yourself, you will survive the test. I look forward to seeing you next week." Bernard walked out the back door to once again meet Jeanne, and Meg contemplated his words.

Ten

I Do

A FEW DAYS LATER, Meg got a phone call from Margie Virtue, a former president of the study group who had always seemed to Meg to be very benign. A meeting had been scheduled, and she wanted to know if Meg would come. "No," said Meg. "I resigned recently. Haven't you heard?"

Margie assured Meg she wanted her to be there because she valued her input, the meeting would be no more than a half an hour long, and she only meant to discuss the role and responsibilities of the officers. Based upon Margie's promises, Meg agreed to attend.

She arrived at the meeting two nights later and sat down calmly. With day planner in hand, she sat next to Daniel with Hazel and Glenda across from her. The last three members, Henry, Helspeth and Peter, arrived last. Meg looked at her watch and hoped the meeting would go fast. Margie Virtue arrived, sat down to the right of Daniel and said, "O.K., let's get things started. This meeting is for the purpose of getting the truth out into the open. We need to get to the bottom of Meg's resignation. I want everyone to lay their complaints out on the table. Hazel, let's start with you."

Meg looked over at Helspeth with a confused expression. Helspeth looked scared. Meg looked at Margie and thought, *The witch lied to me to get me in here.*

Meg realized at that point that Margie Virtue was nothing but Hazel's pawn. She was a liar, and the whole meeting was a setup. The purpose of the meeting was to see that Meg was sufficiently humbled and that Hazel got the revenge that Helspeth had warned her about.

Hazel, Daniel and Glenda together dreamed up lies and false accusations against Meg. They came so fast and furious that Meg couldn't even recognize the time or situations that they were referring to. At that point, Meg summarized each of their accusations in her day planner. She thought about walking out but didn't want to look weak. Hazel and Daniel were given plenty of time to criticize Meg, but Meg was denied the time to respond. She began to interrupt, and answered each accusation one by one. This clearly irritated Margie, but Meg didn't care. Then she remembered Bernard's words, 'You'll have to defend yourself as a lawyer in court.'"

From that point on she responded to the rest of their accusations, which were mostly deliberate misinterpretations of petty stuff, in a mechanical way. The only one who spoke in her defense was Helspeth. The rest of the night was a blur that lasted three and one-half hours, as opposed to the half hour that Margie had promised. When the meeting was over, Hazel, Glenda and Daniel all shook hands and smiled and celebrated. They seemed to think the meeting was their victory and looked, to Meg, as if they were savoring the low frequency of revenge.

After the meeting, Margie asked Meg if she had anything to say. Meg looked at Margie as if she was out of her mind. "I thought I'd give you a chance to say something on your behalf," said Margie.

"Now that the meeting is over and no one will hear what I say?" asked Meg.

When Meg got home, she called Helspeth. "Helspeth," asked Meg, "remember when we were talking at the center and you told me that darkness always follows the Light? What did you mean?"

"Well, that's why many churches and spiritual groups have such unlikely people at the helm. The spiritual activity of the organization brings down a lot of God's Light through prayer and chanting, singing hymns, or whatever, and the dark ones want the Light. With intrigue and treachery, they work their way up through the ranks of the organization. They very often end up in the most powerful positions within the group and see to it no one else has any rights or authority whatsoever."

Meg wondered out loud, "Helspeth, how could I have had such a lack of discernment? Those people are no different than the nuns and priests that I knew years ago. Total control freaks. There is no understanding of justice or even a desire to carry it out. In the name of God, they can be as tyrannical as they want."

The shock of experiencing such intrigue in a spiritual group took its toll on Meg. There was a loss of innocence that required an effort to be far more discerning in the future. Most of the plots and schemes had been detected but not the depth of the problems. Next time, she would be wiser. Her grandfather's words prevented her from turning away from spirituality altogether. The feistiness within her brought forth the determination to not let the bastards get in between her and her God.

The next day, Fran called to report to Meg about her conversations with Nicoletta. "Well," she said, "I've talked to your neighbor every day for the last three days and I tell ya, she's a peach."

"What do you mean?" asked Meg.

"Well, she is truly an immovable object. I have practically begged her to make you an offer, and she has more excuses than I've got listings."

"What are her excuses? She told me they wanted to buy it before anyone else."

"Well, she could have fooled me. First, she said that her husband is out of town and that she has to wait until he returns. So I told her we could draw up an offer and fax it to him to sign. So then she said that she would not bother him at work. I told her that you could lose the builder's offer if we waited until her husband got back next week, but she still refused to fax him. This woman is like, living in the nineteenth century. She won't use her telephone to call the guy. She won't use the fax to get him to sign an offer. I can't believe it. Can you tell I'm frustrated?"

Meg chuckled. "Listen, I'd like to give her a couple of days."

"Well, O.K.," said Fran, "but it's not smart to hold out for too long, Meg, because you could lose the builder's offer. Three days is already plenty of time. Real estate moves fast around here. If I were you, I'd look out for myself. Maybe they're holding out on you, hoping the builder will withdraw his offer so they have no competition. Think about it. I'll call you tomorrow."

Meg couldn't argue. Fran was making a lot of sense, but she also was certain that Fran wanted her commission.

As 1995 was about to close, some unusual events were drawing Meg closer to Helspeth and her husband, Doug. After defending Meg, they had been thrown out of the study center by Hazel and Margie for a year. With the study group now officially off limits to them, Helspeth and Doug were angry at Hazel Janus, Margie Virtue and, especially, God. It all seemed so unjust and Meg got hooked into it. After all, Helspeth was the only one brave enough to speak on her behalf during Margie Virtue's so-called meeting that felt more like a lynching.

Doug was trying to use some of his political connections to help Meg get a mediation job down at the Domestic Relations Court in Chicago. It was the perfect job for her. The pay was $45,000 a year, and the hours were nine to five. That meant her commute would get her home in time to fix dinner for the kids, and the salary, after taxes, would cover the cost of the mortgage. Meg went on several interviews over the course of the summer and fall and was told she was one of the two final contenders when unexpectedly, a new Chief Judge was appointed to the Court and, to her utter disappointment, he brought all of his own mediators with him. Her ideal job disappeared overnight, and melancholia set in.

Soon another mediation job came to her attention, only this time she was successful. After two interviews, she was hired to mediate divorces at a community center affiliated with one of Chicago's prominent hospitals in the northwest suburbs. The pay was hourly, because it was only a part-time job. She had already begun a mediation business from home. The pay from both positions didn't even come close to matching the income the Court job would have paid. Still forced to withdraw money from the bank each month to pay her bills, Meg stayed on a low emotional level after the loss of her dream job at the Court.

Two days later Meg got another call from Fran. "Look," she said, "I've talked to Nicolletta two more times, and she still is jerking me around. I think that you're going to have to make a decision about the builder's offer. Do you want it or not? He's called me several times, and he may withdraw it if you don't accept soon. There are plenty of other lots he can buy out there. Yours isn't the only one. Nicoletta would be very happy to get rid of that bid. Then you'd be at her mercy, stuck with her lowball offer."

Meg thought about the cash she needed and how she had lost her dream job that would have solved all of her money problems. Feeling dejected, she really didn't trust Nicolletta or her husband, Stan.

"O.K., Fran," said Meg. "I've given them five days to make an offer. They haven't committed in any way. Let's get this over with. Bring over the builder's contract and I'll sign it."

Even though it was their screwup, Nicolletta and Stan were furious with Meg for selling the lot to a builder. They criticized her to all of her neighbors and demanded a hearing with the village administration. They trashed the builder and said that he had a reputation for building inferior homes. The sale went through as planned, and Meg survived another battle. But she wished that her Mom was still alive so that she could cry on her shoulder. Mrs. Walsh would have said, "Honey, some people can't live without a scapegoat. Just go around them."

During the last week in December of '95, Meg received a phone call from Doug, Helspeth's husband. "I'm calling to talk to you about a financial opportunity. My partner in Arkansas has just informed me of an investment that has a phenomenal return. They don't usually let small investors into opportunities like this, and so that's why I'm calling you." Doug was talking fast.

"What do you mean by a phenomenal return?" she asked.

"Well, all we have to do is come up with $10,000, and when the deal comes in we'll get $600,000," Doug replied.

He and Helspeth were short on liquidity but long on opportunity. He promised Meg that he would split the $600,000 with her if she put up the $10,000. When Meg informed him that she wasn't interested, he promised that he'd forward a prospectus to her.

A few days later Doug called again, and a few days after that Doug called again. Each time Meg refused his "offer," even though each time he tried to sweeten the pot. Meg had received and read the prospectus that he had sent her. It was poorly written, and she knew as soon as she had read a few paragraphs that it was not written by a lawyer.

"Doug, I think you should know that this is a schlock operation. The prospectus isn't even written by a lawyer. You shouldn't be wasting your time with this," warned Meg.

"Oh no, I know these men and they're all really experienced investors with lots of success stories behind them. This is the opportunity of a lifetime," he said forcefully. Doug was really giving Meg the hard sell, but her answer was still "No. I can't afford to lose $10,000."

Finally, days later, Meg got a call from Helspeth. She said, "Meg, if you put up the $10,000, Doug and I will split the $600,000 with you if the deal comes in. If it doesn't come in, we'll pay you back your $10,000 in full. If the deal falls through, all you will lose is the interest you would have earned on your $10,000. I'm willing to promise this to you. That's how sure I am of this deal. It should come through in a few months."

Meg figured that a few months of interest was not too much to lose to help out a friend. She felt a certain allegience to Helspeth because she was the only one who defended her in front of Hazel Janus. She thought about how Doug had tried so hard to help her get the mediation job at the Court. She felt a little beholden to him. "O.K.," said Meg, figuring that she had only a little at risk.

By the following summer the deal still hadn't come through. Every time Meg asked Helspeth about it, she had an excuse as to why things were delayed. Meg had figured the deal would fall through but wasn't worried because she knew she'd get her money back. She trusted Helspeth, who was downright ingratiating towards Meg for most of those months, making certain that they had lunch at least twice a month and being about as supportive of Meg as a body could be.

In June, Helspeth suggested that they go on a vacation out to Yellowstone. "We could camp out and go white water rafting. It would be so much fun. Doug won't be able to make it, but that's O.K.," she said.

Meg was in need of some peace. Heather was giving her a hard time about not having a full-time job, and Meg was still grieving about losing her dream mediation position down at the Court. Getting away for a week or so sounded like a great idea. "Sure," she said. "I'd like that."

So Heather and Amy went to their Dad's, and Meg and Helspeth piled into Meg's car and drove west. Helspeth had some friends living near the West Yellowstone entrance to the Park, so they stayed there in a hotel for two nights and camped out in the Park for the remaining nights. Meg was enjoying the waterfalls, Yellowstone Lake, the geysers and of course the big selection of pastel paint pots. The night sky was a far cry from Chicago's and that, along with the relaxing scent of pine, was a feast for the two urbanites.

Nature was the only thing on Meg's mind when one day she went to the bathroom and on her way out of the door she bumped into a man just leaving the men's room. She instantly recognized him. Her mind was racing as she tried to place where she had met him before. He was tan, jovial and he flashed a radiant smile as they stepped back from the mutual collision. Meg noticed that he was maybe six feet tall with big shoulders, big blue eyes and blonde hair. He had what she would call a fairly well-preserved swimmer's body for a man in his forties. She realized that she was staring at him for a time that was too long to be considered appropriate and so she said, "I'm sorry, but are you from Chicago?"

"Oh Lord, no," he replied with a laugh.

"Are you from New York, then?" she asked, clearly perplexed.

"No," he said with a big grin, clearly enjoying the interchange.

Meg was embarrassed, because at that point she knew that he thought she was trying to pick him up.

"Oh well, never mind. Excuse me," she said and started to walk up the trail back to her tent.

He walked a few paces behind her up the same trail and finally spoke, "Are you from around here?"

She spun around. "Me? Oh no, I'm from Chicago. That's why I asked you if you were from Chicago. Because you looked so familiar," replied Meg nervously, not realizing that he had been behind her.

"Well, have you ever lived in California? That's where I'm from. Cielo, actually," he asked.

"No, I haven't...but I...I have been to California, but only the wine country and San Francisco. I've never been to Cielo," she said, a little ruffled, "but, to answer your question, I've never lived in California."

"I just came to this area a few months ago," he offered. "It's a new territory for me. I'm in sales, computer hardware, and my territory is Montana, Wyoming and Idaho." He held out his hand to shake hers.

Meg took his hand, shook it uneasily and said, "Oh wow, that's a big area. How do you get around such a big area?" She stared at him and tried to figure out why he seemed so familiar.

"I've got an RV," he said, "and I stay in the parks while I make calls on the area businesses. It works out really well."

"So is this your vacation?" she asked.

"Not really," he said, smiling, "I'm just here for the weekend. I have been living in Montana for most of the year. It's beautiful country here. Hard to leave once you've been here for a while. Here's my card. Are you here on vacation with the family?"

Meg took the card and wondered why he had given it to her. She wasn't interested in buying computer hardware. Her heart was pounding, and she realized that something strange was going on. She gave him her card from her mediation business and said, "No, I'm here with my girlfriend from Chicago. But I was here once before with my former husband and my kids."

"Oh, so you're single?" he inquired as his eyes lit up.

"Um, yes. I'm sorry. I have to go. My friend is waiting to go to dinner. Bye," she said and moved on. That last question was too close for comfort.

Meg reached their tent and grabbed Helspeth by the arm. "Oh my God, you won't believe it. I just met a man."

"You did?" asked Helspeth. "Good work, Meg. You go to the bathroom and come back with a man. Not bad."

"Yes, and I swear I know him but I can't place him. He says he's from California, but I know I didn't meet him there. Where could I have met him?"

"Well, let's talk while we drive. I'm starving."

The two women got in the car and drove toward Mammoth Hot Springs. There was a dining room there in the building next to the hotel. Camping out was fun, but they both were city mice and eating out was a necessity. For two women who were scared of bears, cooking out was not an option.

Helspeth daydreamed as Meg harped on the fact that the man she'd met had seemed so familiar. "Oh, and I got his card," Meg said.

"You got his card?" Helspeth shrieked. "Let me see!" she said as she grabbed it.

"Huh, Geoffrey Dennis. What an aristocratic name. You told me how he looks. Now tell me what he's like. Is he well spoken? Educated? Does he seem to be comfortable around money, a white collar type or blue collar or what?" Helspeth grilled Meg as if she was her mother.

"Definitely white collar, sort of polished, courtly but not stuffy. Very California, you know, sophisticated but open-minded, loose."

"How long did you talk to the guy?" asked Helspeth.

"Not long. Only a few minutes. But I feel as if something important happened," said Meg. She was excited and felt very drawn to the man. There was none of the normal reserve that she felt when meeting someone new. The next day she found herself looking for him but didn't know where he was. She had given up on finding him when she and Helspeth walked into the restaurant at Old Faithful. He came from behind, followed them to their table and blazed another one of his flashy smiles.

"Oh, hi," said Meg as she took a chomp out of her ice cream cone. "This is my friend, Helspeth, Geoffrey. Helspeth, this is Geoffrey."

Helspeth looked up from her cone and took in Geoffrey. "Hi," she said and smiled as if she was unsure of whether she wanted to meet him or not.

"Hi," replied Geoffrey, who turned immediately to Meg.

"So what have you been up to?" he asked. Geoffrey had a natural ease and charm about him. He found comedy in every situation. After living with Nick for so many years, Meg was swept off her feet by Geoffrey's joyful demeanor. He had a stage presence that got him a lot of attention. Women honed in on Geoffrey as soon as he walked in the room, but he didn't seem to notice.

"Oh, we've been to Indian Creek, Sheepeater Cliffs, the geysers at Norris Junction and now we're taking in Old Faithful. We missed the last eruption, so we thought we'd take in a little lunch until the next one," she divulged. A feeling of total familiarity grew between Meg and Geoffrey. She felt as though she had met her oldest and dearest friend after being separated for hundreds of years. "So what have you been doing?" she asked.

"Oh, I just took in Artist's Point," he said. As he spoke, his eyes were riveted on Meg's. His aura was hypnotic as his voice deepened. He leaned forward to speak to her. The allure of Geoffrey enticed her and she sat, cone in hand, transfixed by a feeling that she had never had before.

"What's that?" she asked slowly as she checked him out. He was wearing jeans and a powder blue and white striped shirt that contrasted with his tan and accentuated his blue eyes.

"It's a great place over on the east side of the north loop. You look down on a fabulous waterfall that runs through the Grand Canyon of the Yellowstone. You've got to see it," he said intensely. The change in frequency was not lost on Meg as her energies plummeted into the lower chakras.

She blushed, turned to Helspeth, took a deep breath and said, "Well, what do you think? Do you want to see it?"

"Sure," said Helspeth as she turned to Geoffrey. It didn't take long for her to shift into high gear. Helspeth was being the true blue friend and started asking all the questions that Meg wanted to ask but couldn't. She found out where Geoffrey was born, where he grew up, where he went to college, if he owned a house, if he had been married before, if he had any children, if he had any siblings and when his birthday was.

Meg was grateful. Now she knew most of what she wanted to know at that point in time. When Geoffrey revealed that his birthday was in August, Meg began to talk about his astrology. To her surprise, he knew a little bit about it, unlike most people. He revealed that he had a Cancer Ascendant, which told Meg that his Leo Sun was probably in the second house of earning money.

"Oh," said Meg enthusiastically, "so your Sun is in the second house."

"O.K.," replied Geoffrey, "and that means what?"

"It means," began Helspeth with a smile, "that you probably are very good at earning money."

Geoffrey's reaction was interesting. Meg recalled it months later. He said sheepishly, "Well, I don't know...," then he smiled and laughed uneasily while he rolled his eyes.

It was hard to interpret his reaction. It could have meant that he was being humble, or it could have meant that he was a deadbeat. Meg wasn't sure.

Later that evening as they were bundled up in their sleeping bags, listening to the nearby creek, Helspeth said, "Meg, I think he's so endearing, so enjoyable, and he is very attracted to you."

For the rest of the time Meg spent in Yellowstone, she spent it with Geoffrey. Helspeth bowed out gracefully and took off each day with her friends in West Yellowstone, understanding perfectly the situation Meg was in. "Make the most of your time with him," she said. "You don't know when you'll see him again."

So Meg and Geoffrey spent each day wandering around Yellowstone pretending that they were enthralled with geysers and paint pots while they were really in a state of bliss over finding each other. Geoffrey gave out big belly laughs that Meg loved. They were tickled over the same things, and she hadn't felt such elation since she was a small child. Nick had never laughed at her jokes; he took himself too seriously. Teasing him was out of the question.

Geoffrey clearly enjoyed her company and wanted to know how she felt about everything. Meg marveled as she watched the man absorb her soul with a hunger. She was starved for male conversation, and Geoffrey gladly filled the void. He talked nonstop. He took her to Artist's Point on the last day they were together and suggested that they get married. He said he knew it was crazy but couldn't help himself.

The day Meg and Helspeth packed the car for their return trip, Meg took off for the ladies' room. Helspeth turned to Geoffrey to shake his hand goodbye. She found him staring after Meg as he said slowly, "This'll work. Yup, this'll work," and he shook his head in approval.

When Meg arrived back in Barnstable, she was greeted with umpteen phone messages from Geoffrey. The man had found the woman he wanted and was carrying out the full court press. Heather and Amy were questioning Meg about "the guy who keeps leaving messages." Meg tried to explain the insanity of her meeting a man on vacation who wanted to marry her. The girls stared in disbelief.

It would be so nice for them to live with a stepfather who was warm and funny, she thought. *Our lives would be so much better. We would be a family again, a real family.*

Having a warm and loving family had always been Meg's dream. She thought it would be good for the girls to see their mother with a nice man who treated her well. She was thinking in terms of being a role model for her daughters and wanted them to witness how a good man treats his wife. "Am I concentrating too much on what would be good for the kids and too little on my own vulnerability?" she whispered.

For weeks Geoffrey kept on calling and proposing. Over and over, Meg received a prompting that said, "Marry him. Get through it as fast as you can. You have things to do on the other side." A trip to Montanta was arranged, and Meg explained to Heather and Amy that the possibility of marriage was imminent.

"I'm not sure if this is going to happen. But it might. I know it seems crazy, but this would be good for us. We could be a family again, and it would be a fun family. Geoffrey is a nice man. You'll like him," she insisted.

Silence was the response. Meg had trouble interpreting their reaction. Heather was always silent. Amy didn't seem to know how to react. Meg thought, *They'll come around.* Bringing the girls with her was out of the question. Nick had announced during their divorce that he would never allow Meg to take the kids out of state for any reason. She had to handle this as peacefully as possible, and she was too excited and in love to worry. Finally, her chance for happiness was just around the corner.

Every summer a branch of the Walsh family vacationed in the Hamptons. Heather and Amy were invited and jumped at the chance to see their cousins. Meg took off for Montana not knowing for sure what would come of the trip.

Arriving at the Bozeman airport was, for Meg, like arriving on another planet. It had only two gates and the architecture was totally Montana with huge wood beams and stones. Metal sculptures hung from the ceiling, and an enormous bronze bear sat in the middle of the place. Every man she saw looked like a cowboy. The atmosphere was completely relaxed as fly fisherman swarmed around her on their way to the Madison, Gallatin and Yellowstone Rivers. Meg drank in the atmosphere and thought, *What a great place! A new world for a new life.*

Geoffrey met her at the gate with a tender kiss and swept her off to the minister's house where, as a surprise, he had the whole wedding planned. It was really happening, and Meg was ecstatic. She thought that things would be much better for her and the girls. Everything would work out in time, she assured herself. As they arrived at the minister's, Geoffrey stopped Meg and brushed a lock of her hair away from her cheek with his hand. "Listen, Meg," he said, "there's one thing I've got to tell you. I want you to know that I've got some debts, but I've got them covered."

"How much debt?" she asked with some apprehension.

There was the mortgage on his house in Cielo and debts to friends and his mother, he explained. "About six hundred thousand in all, but don't worry. I've got them covered. I was a top salesman in California and I can do that anywhere."

"Six hundred thousand dollars," she repeated in disbelief.

Geoffrey smiled and hugged her. "Don't worry," he said, "I've got them covered."

Meg looked closely at his face. She didn't want to be disappointed. After all, Geoffrey was the man of her dreams, warm, funny, affectionate, a good communicator. After twenty years with Nick, she really, really wanted the bad times to be behind her. To be loved was her most cherished hope. All those awful times in Barnstable would be put in the past, forgotten. The old wounds would heal fast because of the love and bliss of the new union. His eyes looked so sincere. His handsome face, so convincing, so imploring. Should she believe him or take a step back? If she questioned him further, she might destroy the lovely rapport between them. Or she might see something ugly, something that she couldn't bear or even tolerate. The dream might end. But her financial situation was not the best. Practicality was the need of the hour, or was it? Her mind raced back and forth.

The minister's house was so elegantly decorated. The streamers hung from the ceiling. The roses were creamy white with soft pink edges. The cake was flawless with sugared pearls around its edges. Everything was in its perfect place and everyone looked so happy for them. The photographer aimed his camera. Tasteful music played in the background. All was ready. She stood at the fork in her road and chose to believe him.

The ceremony was beautiful. The delighted couple looked downright incandescent. The engagement ring was small, but Geoffrey promised something better in the future. Meg didn't care. She was too full of hope.

Eleven

An Abrupt End

MINDY SPENT THE REST OF THE TRIP with James, and when the vacation was over and they were back in Houston, she moved out of Michael's townhouse and got her own place. She would have moved in with James right away, but he told Mindy he wanted to "do things right" and have a traditional courtship.

There were layoffs at NASA, and Michael's job was cut. When he wasn't out looking for another employer, he put his heart and soul into his cycling, because it was the only thing that made him feel good about himself. Michael continued to train relentlessly for the L150 ride, and when the weekend of the ride finally arrived, he was ready.

Michael's watch alarm went off that Saturday at 4:30 a.m., informing him that it was time to ride his bicycle from Houston to Austin. On the fifth beep, he was jumping into his bicycle shorts and pulling his jersey over his head. If his bicycle had been next to the bed, he would have jumped on it and pedaled down the stairs.

He had loaded the car the night before, but even so, he mentally went down the checklist one last time as he brushed his teeth. His bike was tuned; his wheels were trued; he had spare tubes; his saddle bag had all the emergency road tools he might need (including CO_2 cartridges to make pumping up flat tires easier); there were spare spokes in his top tube; he had a variety of energy bars and three bananas; one bike bottle had water and the other had fluid replacement drink; his cycling computer was calibrated; he had plenty of sun screen; his cycling shades were in his helmet along with his cycling gloves; the cleats on his cycling shoes were adjusted properly; his mini-pump was loaded; all his camping gear was loaded; he had extra cycling clothes for Sunday; and he had spare clothes to wear after the ride.

"What else?" he asked himself. "Arggghh! The L150 wrist band!" That way, they would know he was registered, and he could restock at the refueling stations along the route. He turned around to verify that his number was attached to the back of his jersey. An identical number was on his bike and on his duffel, which he had also packed the night before.

He started to pull out his razor, but upon inspecting the stubble adorning his face, decided to go for the gnarly look.

"What else?" he asked himself again. "Arggghh! Spare tights and gloves in case it gets cold tomorrow! My Core-Vex rain jacket! My thermal jersey and thermal undershirt!" He packed the thermal jersey, thermal undershirt, and gloves, and put the rain jacket in his rear middle pocket. If there was anything else, he was going to have to do without it, because he was on his way downstairs for some cereal and juice. He whipped up the cereal with his best chef technique, munched it down with unmatched fury, bolted out the door, cranked up the car, and tore off down the road.

He put down all the windows and felt the crisp, refreshing morning air pour in and greet him.

"This is great! This is great!" he shouted out loud as he accelerated onto the freeway. He glanced down at his Macho Man watch. It was only 4:45 a.m! He quickly calculated he would be at the ride site at 5:00 a.m, way ahead of the "pedestrians." He was glad his prized Alchemy titanium bicycle was in back and not riding up top on a rack, because he didn't want to run the risk, even if remote, of forgetting that it was up there and going under some low hanging barrier. Also, his precious cargo would arrive bug free, grit free, and totally pristine. It was the least he could do for his truest companion.

"Yes!" he confirmed to himself. "My truest companion!"

He immediately thought of Mindy and their torrid, short-lived romance. She was doing the L150 with James because, as she had told Michael, he turned her on. James was very much in love with Mindy and was doing everything he knew how to do to get her to marry him. What James didn't know was Mindy was still coming to Michael's place for the occasional surprise soirée. It was too soon for her to do the horizontal bop with James, so she was using Michael and biding her time. Michael knew that it would devastate James if he ever found out, so he was keeping mum.

Still, Michael's conscience was bothering him. He liked James, man to man. He admired his racing and cycling skill, and he had let a woman stir up a very troublesome brew. Michael was compromising his own integrity, and he had no one to blame but himself.

As he pulled into the L150 parking lot, the excitement of the impending event came over him again, and he promised himself that he would focus up.

He found a good parking spot and whipped it in, carefully centering the car between the white lines. He jumped out, walked calmly to the back of the car and opened up the hatch.

He swore he could hear a symphony playing. There was the Alchemy in all her glory. Even the name gave him the chills. The artistry was worthy of Merlin, the great alchemist himself. He remembered George telling him that when he crashed on his Alchemy, he hung it up in the garage and it resumed its original shape. Farfetched, perhaps, but Michael wanted to believe. He thought of his maiden voyage with her. He remembered sitting down after getting out of the saddle for a brief climb, and feeling the Alchemy pick up speed. The Alchemy glistened up at him, and it was all he could do to calm down and take care of some logistics before pedaling over to the starting line. There were several big tractor trailer rigs on the other side of the parking lot that were going to haul the riders' gear up to the fairgrounds in Two Feathers, where everyone would camp for the night.

"No valet service?" Michael said to himself in mock tones.

He double-checked his tags, and took the duffel and his tent out of the car. He locked it up tight, and waving a fond farewell at the Alchemy, promised that he would be right back. He dumped his stuff off in front of one of the big rigs, and true to his word, got back to the car in remarkable time. It wasn't long before he was off, spinning casually and taking in big gulps of the fresh spring morning air. Riders were everywhere, and the excitement was rampant. He felt strong and ready, but he wanted to hang back a little to make sure that Mindy and James started way ahead of him. They would be riding with the old group, so Michael decided to ride solo and avoid them all. There were at least 5,000 cyclists doing the ride, so he knew he wouldn't have any problem remaining anonymous.

He looked down at the Alchemy.

"Don't attract too much attention to yourself, big guy. We don't want to draw them to us!" he said, fully expecting the bike to understand him. "What's that? O.K., just so long as you do your best!"

The sun wasn't up yet, but there was plenty of light in the early dawn to point the way. He remembered the first time he had done this ride six years ago. He had learned so much since then. He was riding a red chrome moly TRECKER that day, which he thought was just about the best bike anywhere. He was so self-conscious and self-effacing, not knowing at all how he would do or even if he could finish. All he had was a burning desire to get to the finish, no matter what. It didn't matter how long it took, it was the principle of doing the ride that counted. He was doing it to raise money for leukemia, and that was all that mattered. He was innocent, deferring to everyone else's judgement and not daring to voice his opinion. That was the year that was most vivid in his memory, not only because it was his first L150, but because it turned cold that night in the camp ground and was below freezing the next morning. The wind was gusting at 50 m.p.h. right into his face when he got into the saddle and didn't let up the whole day. People were wearing anything they could find to keep warm. One guy even grabbed a big trash bag, cut a hole in the bottom for his head, and kept on cruisin'. There were many heroes that day, not because they were racing half way across Texas to see who could get to Austin first, but because they could laugh in the face of adversity and still make it through. They were forging a common bond, made with nothing more than their determination to find a cure for leukemia and help people who were less fortunate than themselves.

Michael knew he still valued those old virtues, but he had become so cocky all he wanted was to dust everyone on the road. His memory was piled high with every statistic in the books, and all that mattered was the delta, the difference in speed between him and the next guy. He looked down at his legs, pumping effortlessly along as he made his way up to the start. He could see a guy waving a flag up ahead, and eased himself into position. When he got up to the line, he stood up in the pedals and accelerated ahead of the group that had clustered around him. He was feeling much better.

"Dual speed quads," he whispered. "What an engine!" Hours of relentless training had turned him into a bulging dynamo, a far cry from the skinny kid who showed up for his first ride six years ago. Since then, he had logged over 40,000 miles on the bike. He could ride 200 miles in a day and had no patience or respect for anyone who couldn't keep up the torrid pace he set. Somewhere inside of him, though, he was struggling to define who he really was. He seemed to be doing more and more and enjoying it less and less. Where were his true emotions, his real feelings? What code was he living by? Was he trading these values in for a faster time, a bigger thrill? Was he living just to get high on a fast ride, ignoring what was really important?

"Not!" he said to himself, grinning as he started to get into a rhythm, stuffing his emotions. The fact was, though, that he knew all too well what was happening to him.

He just didn't know how to face it. Something or somebody was getting in the way, blocking his view a little more each day.

"Why don't you try talking to your cycling buddies about how you feel?" a voice from somewhere inside of him said, startling him.

"As if!" he shot back.

"What are we now, a valley girl?" the same voice replied.

Michael thought about that one. Even his conversation had become competitive. He wanted the right quip at the right time, and it had to be quick.

"Come on!" his ego countered. "What's with this lag time? Let's have a reply! What will people think?" He felt a slight irritation but didn't give in to it. He bolstered himself by thinking about how cool he looked in his new cycling jersey and matching shorts adorned with the name of the latest cycling great. Actually, Mindy had given them to him, but that didn't matter. He looked cool and in vogue.

Focus, Michael, focus! he thought. *Visualize!*

Visualization didn't sound all that bad. It even seemed like a very good idea. He felt calmer, and scenes of a recent commercial came to mind. That commercial had really motivated him, and he wished more than anything that he could have been the guy in it. In the opening scene, several people were huddled around a video monitor, watching a lone cyclist pedaling down a deserted country road that was lined with towering oak trees whose branches arched across the road to form a stunning sylvan canopy.

The people in the video room were all engineers, each adorned in a white smock and each looking very serious, attractive, and intelligent. The lead engineer, a gorgeous blonde, was panting into the monitor.

"He's doing it!" she said. "He's doing it!" The rest of the group nodded affirmatively and leaned in unison closer to the monitor. One of them was holding up a stop watch, and suddenly, with an emphatic click, he punched it. A roar went through the room, and all knew they had a winner. The guy on the bike had just come through in record time riding on their tires! It was a breakthrough of unprecedented proportion.

The net effect was that Michael wanted to be at the center of attention, just like the rider in the commercial. There was no way that "they" would have let Michael do that commercial. Those "other guys" were doing commercials, not him.

He bolstered himself again by flexing his biceps.

"Lookin' good, dude!" he shouted to himself.

He was getting into a pretty good groove, really starting to feel his oats. Next thing you know, he started thinking about his helmet. He was wondering what his hair would look like when he took the helmet off at the end of the day. Now, if he were Roger, every hair would be in place. But no. He had longer hair. He had wavier hair. It would be all frizzed when he pulled into the campground. He would have to spend several minutes fussing over it to get it to look right. Roger, on the other hand, would just walk off, looking perfectly coifed. Roger could get lost at sea for weeks on end and still look perfectly coifed.

"Your hair is beautiful!" a kind voice spoke into Michael's mind.

Michael was painfully aware a whole string of riders was sucking his wheel. He moved over to the left, and they moved over to the left with him. He moved back to the right, and they moved back to the right with him.

Bummer! he thought.

He started on a new strategy. He moved over to the left again, motioning the rider behind him to come around. Reluctantly, he agreed, and Michael moseyed back to the end of the line. That was fine for a while, but the pace of the whole group slowed way down. No one would look Michael in the eye, as if no one individual was actually the culprit. It was always the next guy over. They were all anonymous.

Michael waited for his opportunity, and suddenly it appeared. Another group of riders was coming up on the left, and when the last one passed him, Michael sprinted around to their left. That effectively blocked out the wheel suckers, and Michael was free once more.

"Ha!" he blurted out triumphantly.

The predominant wind was usually out of the northwest on this route, but this day, it was coming steadily out of the southeast. There would be a slight tailwind most of the way. Michael couldn't actually feel it, but there was no sound of wind in his ears, and he was blasting along at a good pace, expending very little energy in proportion to his speed. He went past the first rest stop, wondering if the people there noticed that he had no need to stop. He glanced at them out of the corner of his eye and was mildly disappointed to note that they were going about their tasks completely unaware of his passing.

Suddenly, an unwanted memory crossed his mind.

"No! Not Rainbow Glow and Dreary Dismal! Get out of here! This is kiddy stuff!"

"What would Rainbow Glow say about you passing up all these people and not even saying Hi?" a little voice in his head asked.

"She wouldn't say anything, because she knows that Dreary Dismal will get her back!" came the reply.

The conversation went back and forth automatically, as if it was being interjected into Michael's awareness without him consenting to it being there. The characters were from a kids' story he remembered from the early eighties, and they seemed innocent enough. In spite of this, though, there was something about the way that the conversation intruded upon him that was all wrong. If he didn't consciously put it there, if he didn't actually want it there, it had no business being there.

Michael checked his cycle computer. He was averaging 23 m.p.h. for the first fifteen miles, which he felt pretty good about in view of the slow start he'd had because of all the riders of various skill levels getting in his way.

He remembered how, on his first L150 ride, all the cyclists were so friendly, and he talked with everyone he rode by. This time, all that was communicated between him and his fellow riders was "On your left!" or "On your right!" The last guy he passed even had the words "Shut Up and Ride!" inscribed into his top tube. Conversation that didn't convey vital information was simply a waste of time. It was better to point at an obstacle in the road rather than make an attempt to describe it and its exact location.

Michael grinned to himself and imagined a conversation with a fellow rider.

"I say, I do admire the wonderful hues reflected from that broken bottle just three feet, three inches in front of your wheel!"

He was out here to soak up the countryside, but he had seen precious little of it so far. There was no time to take his eyes off the riders all around him. One slip, and 50 riders could go down in a very messy heap. He had to keep a constant vigil, and the tension of each moment narrowed the scope of what he could experience and feel as he sped down the road. He could not afford to lose focus, for to do so was to invite catastrophe.

"Don't dwell on crashing!" he told himself. "You'll draw it to you!"

He was covered with a respectable number of road rash scars from previous mishaps, and actually enjoyed showing them off and talking about them. He had learned that the real reason cyclists shave their legs is to avoid having to deal with all that hair that is left when your skin gets scraped off.

Memories of crash scenes started to fill his mind. Some of them struck so close to home, too. One of his closest friends had been killed by a dump truck, and another one had lost his leg when a car dragged him along an overpass fence. At least there were no cars allowed along the route this day, only cyclists. He thought about the pavement, and how unyielding and brutally hard it was. The natural instinct was to put your arms straight out to protect yourself. No wonder so many crashes resulted in broken collarbones.

It's the risk you have to take to achieve excellence! he thought. *Calm down, NOW!*

A quick glance at his cycle computer revealed that he was averaging 24 m.p.h.

"Good," he said out loud. "Good! I'm really making up for that slow start."

The whirl of his chain gliding over his rear cog sounded clean and crisp, without a lot of wasted up and down motion. He knew that his trusty Alchemy was translating most of the energy into forward motion, losing only the bare minimum to frame flex, wind resistance, and friction. He knew that most of his energy went toward fighting the wind, but he could accept that, because there didn't seem to be any way around it. He got down into a better tuck. The guy next to him was all the way down in his aero bars, which were so popular with triathletes. They attached to the handlebars and protruded forward in a giant "U", allowing the rider to stretch out and rest his forearms on them. Michael looked over at him with true disdain.

"Tri-geek!" he said to himself. "How is that guy going to react when someone in front of him changes speed?"

He had gotten the expression "Tri-geek" from Mike Dudley, of the infamous "Dudley corner" fame. Mike went around a corner at top speed in the park where they all trained, and his inside pedal caught the pavement. Why he was pedaling around a turn was a mystery to

Michael, but that was Dudley. He didn't even bounce or slide when he hit the pavement; he just came to an immediate halt. His hip took all the force, and the ball in his hip completely came out of its socket. He tried to get up, but his right foot was pointing in the wrong direction, and his leg was just hanging there. He spent several months in therapy, and to make himself feel better during the process, he took his Tri-geek aero bars off of his bicycle and put them on his walker. Some people called it false bravado, but Michael admired the fact that he could keep his sense of humor when he didn't know if he would be able to ever ride again.

Michael was determined not to draft behind anyone, because he wanted his time to be all his. A rider on his own might spend 85 percent of his energy fighting the wind, and the guy in back of him could practically get a free ride. Michael just didn't like the idea of riding in a pack all day, and if you rode behind a guy's wheel for awhile, you were obliged to return the favor. Someone was always getting in behind him, though, so he constantly had to shake them off. The riders would come in waves, and he had just gotten by a huge swell and was all on his own with no one around him. The tension disappeared in an instant.

His endorphins were starting to kick in, and he was feeling as if he never wanted to slow down. He was atop a chariot of fire, free of all earthly constraint. The air was crisp with just a hint of a chill, and as he breathed it in with rhythmic cycles, he knew this was why he was out there. You couldn't create moments like these, even if you spent all your time trying. When they happened, Michael cherished them, wishing they would go on and on. Everything felt perfectly in place, and he was intimately involved in every little process of the universe around him. To Michael, it was cyclic flow and harmony. It was perfect attunement, a resonance that sent reverberations throughout his entire being. He felt awe and wonder, and was overjoyed just to be alive and participating in this moment. He had earned the right to feel this way, not through artificial stimulation from who knows what source, but by putting every ounce of his being into his training and discipline. He felt a sense of pride and a sense of accomplishment that no one could take from him. He didn't even care what his cycle computer said, for he was speed and fury itself. He was unlimited motion, willing himself onward. No obstacle even dared to present itself before him.

He didn't know how long the moment lasted, because he felt as if there was no time with which to measure it. As he approached the next wave of riders, though, he could feel the wonderful high start to subside.

“Yo, dude!” a voice from the crowd greeted him, at least seeming to be filled with good will and intent.

Michael looked over at him, not really wanting to come back down just yet. He decided to do his foreigner imitation again, only this time he would be a Scotsman.

“What’s with this ‘Yo dude’ expression, mate, I’m totally knackered.”

The young Texan looked him over, choosing his next words carefully.

“You’re not from around here, are yuh?”

“Right you are, and I’m quite fussed!”

“Is that right?” the Texan had a perplexed, good-ole-boy look.

“Been pedalin’ all the way up here without so much as a tattie to eat. Here it is half-eight, and I’m dyin for some scran!”

“I’d love to help yuh, but I’m not quite sure what yer wantin. Just what is scran, anyway?”

“Don’t get yerself all fussed. We’re just cravin a bit to eat!”

“Well, why didn’t you say so! Here, try one of these!” That was the wonderful thing about cycling. You could be screamin’ down the road and still carry on an adult conversation. You could even ride and chew at the same time.

The Texan had stashed several pieces of several energy bars right on his handlebars. They just stuck there, and when he got hungry, he peeled one off. He handed one to Michael.

“Is it true then that the days are bigger in Texas?” Michael asked, using all his strength just to chew off a piece of the energy bar.

“You can count on it, my man! We don’t care where yer from, neither. Texas wants you anyway!”

Michael laughed to himself. The guy had the name “Hugh D. Mann” engraved on his top tube, and the words “Shut Up and Ride” tattooed on his forearm. One thing was for sure, though. He was all heart.

“It must also be true then that the sun is bigger here!”

“Well, yuh know what they say. A day without sunshine is like, night!”

“Thanks, Hugh. I’m off to see the wizard now!”

“Say hello to him for me, man!”

Michael stood up in his pedals and sprinted around a wave of riders. He was coming into the hills just before Belleville, and he was stoked.

"Climb and rhyme!" he shouted. He decided that he would remain in the saddle for the first climb. He knew this hill well, and he knew just when and where to shift to maintain his cadence. He sailed to the top, weaving in and out of riders, all grimacing with the strain.

"Definitely not poets!" he whispered.

He cruised through Belleville and headed on to Industry. Sure enough, the same ole cop was there at the four-way stop sign.

"Put yer foot on the line!" he admonished each rider. Michael shuddered to think what would happen if some hapless cyclist disobeyed orders. Would he be shot on sight?

Michael stopped, put his foot squarely on the line and took off again, somewhat peeved that he had to slow down. As he started to get back in the groove, he noticed a rest stop on his left. He was low on just about everything, and since he had slowed down anyway, he decided to nip in and grab everything he would need to get him to Two Feathers. As he was heading back to his bike, his eyes almost popped out. There was the Healthy Foods racing team, zipping by at full strength. He clenched his fist, and the banana he was holding shot right out of its peel and landed several feet away.

"I've got to catch them!" Michael exclaimed, jumping back on his steed. He charged out onto the road, accelerating with all the strength he could muster. He recognized Mike Dudley, of Dudley corner fame, at the rear of the Healthy Foods team. Mike was a big target, and Michael zeroed in on him.

"Hang on, big guy. He's getting closer," Michael told himself. He was closing in, and he could hear bits of conversations between the riders. Finally he caught them and came up next to Dudley.

"Morning, Dudley," he said, matter of factly. Dudley glanced over at him quite casually.

"Morning, Michael," he said, nonchalantly. It was an unspoken rule to leave your poker face on, and not exhibit any signs of strain, even though you were putting all your effort into every stroke.

"Nice day for a spin," Michael commented, not really seeming interested.

"Quite," Dudley said. "Why don't you hang in for awhile?"

"Why not?" Michael shrugged his shoulders, masking his excitement at riding with this elite team.

They rode on together for several miles, bantering amongst themselves, a collage of quick quips and snappy comebacks. A slower group of riders was coming up on the right, and everyone moved to the left as one unit.

"On your left!" Michael shouted to a rider in front of him who was clinging to the white line on the side of the road. The mystery rider was not on the Healthy Foods team, and he was riding extremely slowly.

All at once, inexplicably, the rider moved to his left, right into Michael's front wheel. Michael felt himself losing control, and a wave of horror surged through him. His rear wheel came up, sending him sprawling over the handlebars. Suddenly, his sense of time altered. He was flying through the air in slow motion, knowing he was in grave danger, yet feeling a strange sense of calm starting to envelope him. He felt suspended high above the Alchemy, looking down on it, and having the odd thought that the Alchemy would have to prove its magic and pull itself back together after this one. He watched himself come down on his front wheel, as if he was a somewhat disinterested spectator. The spinning rubber tore the flesh from his shoulder, leaving it raw and bleeding. He barely felt it. He saw himself slide down the front of the wheel and heard the crunching of his helmet as it whacked the pavement. He never knew that anything could be so hard and unforgiving, so indifferent and unyielding. The ground was merciless, and his tiny frame was no match for it. Gradually the light faded, and he was only vaguely aware that he was tumbling along the ground like a rag doll, arms and legs flailing wildly.

Twelve

Gigolo Mode

"Oh my God," Geoffrey said as he pulled over into the little triangle of shoulder between the main highway and the exit for the bridge. He looked panicked and pale, a crumbled version of his usual self. "I can't do this," he said. "You're going to have to drive. I...I can't drive over bridges." He bolted to the back of the RV and began fumbling around in one of the cabinets under the fridge.

As Meg undid her seatbelt and moved quickly toward the driver's seat, she said, "Why can't you drive over bridges?" He didn't respond. She jumped into his vacated seat and put the RV in drive.

Their destination was the north woods of Wisconsin. The plan was to combine their honeymoon with meeting Geoffrey's family at their summer home. She looked over her shoulder at the oncoming traffic and then into the mirror on the right side. In her peripheral vision, she noticed that Geoffrey was drinking something. Worry overcame her happy mood. *Strange,* she thought. For the time being she ignored him and concentrated on accelerating so that she could merge into the traffic that was exiting for the bridge.

Underneath, the navy blue water looked deep and choppy with an angry wind churning it up. At the end of the bridge, the wind sagged a bit. Meg relaxed, pulled over and checked the rear view mirror. There sat a dejected Geoffrey with a gallon jug of wine in front of him. She spun around and glared at him. “Where did that come from?” she asked, pointing at the booze.

“I needed a drink,” he said, looking guilty. “I can’t go over a bridge without having a drink.”

“Damn,” she said. After Nick, she vowed to herself that she would never live with another drinker again.

“I promise you,” he said, “the only time I drink is when I drive over bridges and when I fly. That’s all. Really. That’s all.”

“It was fortunate, I guess, that I was driving when we crossed the Mississippi. Have you ever been to AA?”

Geoffrey looked uneasy. “Yes, but I never finished the program.”

“Why not? It works.”

“Not really. It’s just a bunch of people who are replacing one addiction for another. Instead of being addicted to booze, they’re addicted to their stupid meetings”

“Sounds like denial to me.”

“Look, baby, I...”

“Don’t call me baby,” she snapped. “I’m not your baby. You’ve probably called a dozen women ‘baby.’ Call me something else, something that you’ve never called any other woman.”

“O.K.,” he agreed. “I’ll call you my ‘cosmic cupcake.’ Is that better? And I promise you that I will only drink on planes and when I’m crossing bridges. Truce?”

“You need to get to the bottom of it, Geoffrey. You need to figure out why bridges and planes scare you so much. Get into therapy and then...” She tried to keep eye contact, but Geoffrey was looking around at the scenery.

“Yeah, yeah. Great suggestion. I’ll look into it,” he said. “Look at this place, Meg. Isn’t it great? We’re almost there.”

Meeting Geoffrey’s relatives in Wisconsin was a positive experience for her. His recently remarried mother was there with her new husband. Geoffrey’s brothers were very accomplished men with Ph.D.s in multi-syllabic scientific subjects. One brother had taught in Harvard’s medical school for a number of years, and the other one worked successfully in the corporate world. Both men were not bad-looking, but it was obvious that in Geoffrey’s family his claim to fame was his looks while his brothers were appreciated more for their brains.

A week later, Meg arrived back in Barnstable, and told Heather and Amy that they had a stepfather. Their reaction was explosive.

"What," yelled Heather. "You got married? How could you do that? Why didn't you tell us?"

"But I did," responded Meg, a little disappointed with the reaction. "I told you that I wasn't sure, but that I knew that he wanted to marry me and that marriage was a distinct possibility when I went out there."

"I can't believe that you did this to me," fumed Heather, who retreated to her bedroom in a fury. Her dark eyes blazed at her mother. *She looks just like Nick*, thought Meg.

Amy's response was less angry but mournful.

Meg looked in her bedroom mirror and realized the enormity of her actions. It had been so foolish of her to expect that her daughters would be happy for her, that they would see the marriage as a good thing, a positive change in their lives and financial situation. Her wedding had cast another pall over their home and Meg could foresee that they would probably not forgive her no matter how many times she said, "I'm sorry."

Geoffrey was coming to live with her soon after he arranged a change in his territory. She was hoping that things would get better and that the girls would grow to like him. He was such a likable guy. It seemed impossible that they wouldn't accept him quickly.

Meg hoped that Bernard, the astrology teacher, would have soothing words. "Oh, my dear," he said. "You, unfortunately, are dealing with Uranus. It is quite a triple whammy. Your life is in such a state of upheaval that you hardly know what will happen next. Most people go through the 'middle age crazies' when they have only one aspect, but you've got three. Don't condemn yourself too much. Your daughters will do enough of that, I'm afraid. Here, I want you to read this book on Uranus. Concentrate on the section on Uranus square Ascendant."

Meg had married Geoffrey when Uranus was squaring her Ascendant in a retrograde motion. According to Bernard's book, the relationship would end. *No*, she thought. *That's not possible*.

That night Geoffrey called. He had accomplished a change of territory within his company. This was supposed to be a happy occasion, but he sounded upset. "What the matter?" Meg asked. "You sound strange."

"Do I?" Geoffrey asked. "I'm feeling as if I'm under siege here." He spoke with a slurred voice and a little giggle. "There's this woman who has just come over to my RV. She's hysterical, screaming, beating on the door and windows. All of the neighbors in the park have come out to look at what's going on. She's gone now but I'm afraid she'll come back."

"Do you know this woman or is she just some crazy?"

"Well, yes, I know her. I know her because when I first moved to Rowena she was my landlady."

Meg could feel that she was only getting half truths. She was familiar with the tactic. Nick had used it often. "What's her name?"

"Constance Rolando."

"Have you been drinking?"

"No, not at all," he responded, but his voice was still slurred. "Look, do we have to play twenty questions like this?"

"Well, no. You could tell me the whole truth up front."

Geoffrey was silent.

"O.K. Does she own an apartment building?" asked Meg.

"Uh, well, no," Geoffrey answered. Meg could feel him squirming. "She's a nurse and she owns a trailer on the lake and I rented one of the bedrooms in the trailer."

"Well, if your relationship was strictly business, then why is she so upset with you?"

"I can't help it if she fell in love with me. I guess she's angry because I married you. She's in love with me and she wanted me to marry her. But I told her many times that I didn't want to marry her. I even went to her therapist with her and told him that I didn't want to marry her."

"Did you ever tell her that you would marry her?"

"NO," Geoffrey yelled. "I never wanted to have anything to do with her."

"Then why didn't you get your own apartment?"

"Because when I first moved here I was low on money and she offered to let me stay with her until I got my own place. I got the RV in April and moved out."

"Wait a minute, Geoffrey. You told me that you were a top salesman in California. If you were a top salesman, why were you so short on money that you couldn't afford an apartment?" Meg demanded. She was feeling frightened.

"Oh my God," he said. "She's back!" Geoffrey's manner was the perfect blend of fear and guilt.

Meg could hear Constance screaming, begging and beating on the door. "How could you do this to me? How could you? I need closure. I need you to hold me one last time. Please, please."

It was an awful thing to hear, a mess that Meg didn't want to sort out.

"What do I do? She's crazy," asked Geoffrey.

"Well, I don't know. You're a married man now. Tell her you're sorry, but be firm. If she doesn't quiet down, one of your neighbors may call the police. She's disturbing the peace. Remind her of that."

Geoffrey covered the phone so that Meg couldn't hear what he said. His tone was soothing. "O.K.," he said. "She's gone."

"On a lighter note, when are you coming here?" Meg asked while her mind raced to sort through the scene with Constance. She could feel goose bumps all over her body.

"I'm bringing the RV down to Bozeman tomorrow. The RV guy said he'd sell it on consignment. Then I'm on the road to Barnstable. This place has gotten a little too crazy for me. I love you, Squeegy," he said. Geoffrey had taken to calling Meg 'Squeegy.' She didn't know why and didn't ask. There was too much else to think about.

That night, as she lay in bed, Meg reviewed their conversation. His voice sounded slurred. Was it her imagination? He swore that he only drank on planes and bridges. Was he lying? In his panic he never explained why he'd had no money for an apartment when he first moved to Montana. Did he lie about being a top salesman? Was the woman really crazy as he claimed or did she have reason to believe that he would marry her? Had he been honest with her, as he claimed? Meg's heart was pounding as she hashed and rehashed the scene over in her mind. She wanted to believe him, but the little voice inside of her kept saying, "You're in trouble, Meg. See the truth."

Two days later, Geoffrey arrived in Chicago. Amy seemed unsure of how to behave around him but was at least willing to make conversation. Heather, on the other hand, would not look at or talk to Geoffrey. Neither girl was willing to welcome Conor, Geoffrey's white German Shepherd, into the fold. He was a little too tall, a little too muscular and a little too scary.

Geoffrey began working his new territory with enthusiasm. He told Meg that he liked his new boss and the guys in his office, but he didn't feel as if he fit in. His sunny disposition was dampened by the purposeful and resolute personalities of his co-workers. Meg recalled that the West has a surplus of natural beauty and is relaxed in its ways. As the weeks passed she tuned into Geoffrey's mindset and knew that his living in a town precisely named "hog butcher of the world" was not a good fit. "These people in Chicago are a solemn bunch," he said after a month of being an Illinois resident. "They have no interest in anything but going to work. They work and work and work. A joyless lot. The lack of beautiful vegetation, mountains or even an ocean is probably the reason. There's nothing uplifting to look at, and that includes the women."

"Now there's a telling observation," sparred Meg. "I guess that means you've been looking."

Geoffrey ignored her jab. "You are an unfortunate transplant to the area. I see you as a fox from New York City who had the bad luck of emigrating to the area. This is the last place on earth I would choose to live. A tribute to how much I love you, my dear. For you are the only thing that is tying me here."

Meg knew that he truly was depressed by the location but even more so, he felt downhearted because of the almost daily dismissal he received from her kids. After living with Nick's rebuffs, she knew the sting of rejection and felt for Geoffrey. The girls had no idea of the sacrifice that he had made by giving up his western territory to come to Chicago. She mentioned it to them once, hoping that it would make a difference in their treatment of him, but neither one showed any concern for Geoffrey's plight.

Meg watched the melancholy around Geoffrey become more and more pronounced. He hardly noticed the fall, which is probably Chicago's most beautiful season. His enthusiasm for the job dropped, and he watched a lot of TV. The steel-gray skies that Chicago is famous for rarely broke, and Geoffrey parted the curtains each evening to gaze up at them. "It's so incredible," he said. "The radar on the weather channel shows that there aren't any clouds, but when I look out the window they're always there. Why is that?"

"It's always cloudy here, Geoffrey, from November 'till May," Meg said.

He quickly covered the length of the room and put his hand on her shoulders. "Meg, look," he said, with the tone of a man planning a jail break. "Let's get out of here. Your kids hate you. They hate me. Let's give them to their Dad and get out of here."

"Geoffrey, I can't do that. These are my kids. I love them. I can't leave Barnstable until Amy leaves for college. That's not for four years."

"But they hate you."

"That's a horrible thing to say. They don't hate me. Why are you saying that?"

"Look at the way they talk to you and treat you. Anyone can see that they hate you. Why are you wasting your money and energy on them? They don't appreciate it. They don't appreciate anything that you or I do."

"But all kids are like that."

"No, not really. Did you treat your mother like that?"

"Well, no. But we did have our disagreements. I can't deal with this, Geoffrey. Stop it."

By the holidays Geoffrey had all but stopped working. He arrived home at noon every day and slept all afternoon when he was supposed to be calling on clients. Things got even worse when Meg mentioned to him that she had a chunk of money in the bank from her divorce. He realized that the bills would be paid whether he worked or not. Geoffrey slipped into gigolo mode and began running up Meg's credit cards. She felt his desperation with every unnecessary purchase.

One morning Geoffrey called Meg from work. "Hey Squeegy, will you look for my business cards for me? They're in the vinyl case under the desk. They want to know if I need to have more printed. Let me know how many I've got left."

Meg scrounged around under the desk and pulled out three different vinyl cases. The first case she opened held Geoffrey's camera equipment. Stuffed in beside the camera she found a pair of navy blue lace panties. Because of the dark color, it was easy to notice that they were soiled. Whoever the owner was must have had a good time with Geoffrey.

"Damn," she said. "My life is turning into a stinking soap opera."

A number of cards fell out onto the bed when she pulled the panties out of the case. A valentine card, birthday cards and a thank you note, all from "Constance, your cosmic cupcake."

As expected, Geoffrey arrived home from work at noon. Loosening his tie, he approached the master bedroom with a relaxed gait. He glanced at the newly discovered booty on the bed and fixed his eyes on Meg, who stood up to greet him.

"O.K. Geoffrey," she asked as she grabbed the panties off the bed, "who is the sexually satiated lady who owns these panties?"

"Where did you find those?" he asked.

"In your camera case. Where else would you find a pair of lace panties? Who owns them?"

"I don't remember. They belong to someone in California, and I don't know which one."

"You don't remember? Which one? How many women have you had, Geoffrey?"

"When I turned 30 I stopped counting at 75. Since then, I don't know how many I've had."

"That was a rhetorical question." She put her hand on her forehead, took a deep breath and composed herself. "So you're saying that these panties came from an affair you had before we were married?"

"Exactly. It means nothing to me. You're the only woman I care about."

"Who is Constance?" she asked him as she picked up one of the birthday cards from the bed.

"My landlady in Montana."

"Oh, yes, now I remember. The nurse who was screaming and beating on the door of your RV? You told me that she was your landlady, and you couldn't help it if she fell in love with you."

Geoffrey looked uneasy.

"So why did she sign those cards 'your cosmic cupcake' if your relationship with her was strictly business?"

"Well, O.K., I did sleep with her. But she always forced me into it. She would cling to me in bed. I tried not to have sex with her but she was so damned aggressive."

"So she came into your bedroom..."

"No, uh, actually, I was in her bedroom."

"I thought you said you rented a room in her house."

"I did. There was only one bedroom in her house."

"So the bedroom you rented was her bedroom? Now I get the picture, Geoffrey. So the panties have been in the camera case since you left California?"

Geoffrey nodded.

"Well, I guess you don't take pictures too often," she whispered, arms crossed as she gazed out the window.

"Meg," asked Geoffrey, looking sheepish, "do you love me?"

"God, Geoffrey, don't ask me that now."

"Do you love me?"

"Yeah, yeah," she said, still looking out the window, "but you certainly don't make it easy."

He looked afraid.

"Geoffrey?" she asked.

"Yeah?"

"Don't ever call me your 'cosmic cupcake' again."

Each morning as Meg passed from the netherworld of sleep into another day she felt the unmistakable feeling of dread. "Dear God," she whispered, "what's going to happen today?" It was difficult for her to outline in her mind why living with Geoffrey made her feel so frightened. He was funny and entertaining. Most assuredly, he was a financial hardship on her, but it was more than that. She wasn't able to feel comfortable in his presence. There was a lack of trust and a dark feeling of dread.

His attitude toward sex and women really disturbed Meg, who felt that sex was a sacred act, something done only when love was present. Geoffrey regularly bragged about all of the women he had serviced over the years. Some of them were his mother's friends and neighbors. He had a list of women back in California who had willingly handed themselves over to him for his pleasure. He used them for sex without remorse. He balked when Meg protested that he'd been using them. "Hell, no," he said. "They were all consenting adults. They enjoyed the sex as much as I did." He believed that he had done them a favor. It was, according to Geoffrey, a privilege to have sex with him. With each retelling of his story, he dropped lower and lower in her estimation. The honeymoon was over.

The phone rang one afternoon in November, and Meg answered. Happy events had become rare events, so the message was greatly appreciated. "Your daughter, Heather, has been chosen to be this year's Homecoming Queen," the caller said. "Yes. She's very well thought of. Everyone likes her. Please bring your camera to tonight's football game, because the King and Queen and their Court will be announced after the game."

Meg could hardly believe it. Heather was pretty dour around the house and portrayed herself to Meg as being not very popular or well liked at school.

"Hey, I'll bring my video camera and tape the whole thing. She'll love it," said Geoffrey, eager to do something that would make Heather like him. "This is a big deal, Meg."

"O.K.," said Meg, but then that feeling of dread came over her. Would Geoffrey be able to do this without mucking it up?

When the announcement came, Meg and Geoffrey got as close as they could to the field and taped the whole event. Geoffrey approached Heather. She was surrounded by her friends and was smiling a radiant smile. Meg thought, *When was the last time I've seen her smile so beautifully?*

"Heather," he called. Heather looked at him and the smile left her face. She regarded him with a frozen disdain. Meg's heart sank. "Congratulations," he said as he reached to shake her hand.

Meg held her breath and thought, *Come on Heather, shake his hand. Come on, you can do this.*

Heather reluctantly reached up and took Geoffrey's hand. She stared defiantly at her Mom while she shook his hand. All of her friends stopped laughing and smiling. They looked at Geoffrey and Meg hesitantly, not knowing what to do. None of them said "Hi" to Meg, even though they knew her. It was time to leave.

She and Geoffrey drove home. Geoffrey was still excited about the evening and kept talking about how great it was. Meg was silent. It was going to take a long time for them to become a family. It was going to take years for everything to heal.

When they arrived home Geoffrey took the tape out of the camera and headed for the family room. Amy came home a few minutes after them. "Oh cool, are you gonna watch the tape of Heather?" she asked Geoffrey.

"Yes," he said, "right now."

"Let me change into my pajamas and I'll be right down."

A prompting told Meg to start the video before Amy came back. "Geoffrey," she said, "will you start it right now? Please, just humor me and start it now."

Geoffrey put the tape in the VCR and pressed "play." What came up on the screen for about three or four seconds took Meg's breath away. "Oh my God, Geoffrey. What is that?" she said, jumping up from the couch.

"Oh, I'm sorry. I didn't rewind the tape all of the way to the beginning before I started filming."

"Will you take that tape and erase it? But please don't erase the parts with Heather."

Geoffrey ran out to the backyard. When he came back he said, "I think it's gone." He looked stressed out.

"Geoffrey, that was a video of someone masturbating." said Meg as she tried to whisper, but wanted to scream.

"Haven't you ever wanted someone to video you while you're making love?"

"No," she yelled in a whisper. "I have never had any desire for anyone to film me while I was making love and I don't think I ever will. It's a private act." She felt frustrated and then it struck her. "Wait a minute," she said slowly, "Are you telling me that you were the person in that video? You held the camera on your shoulder and pointed the camera down into your pants?"

"You're a little uptight, Meg," he said. Geoffrey showed no signs of apologizing.

"I swear to God, if my kids had been in this room and seen that video, Geoffrey, you would be very dead right now," she hissed. Her body was stiff from anger.

"Oh come on, Meg. For God sakes, they're in high school."

"I don't give a damn how old they are. Are you saying that it's O.K. for a Mother to give permission for her kids to watch their stepfather's passionate parts on TV?"

"Well...why do you have to be so conservative about it?"

"Because they're children, and the innocence of a child should always be protected. The environmentalists are always squealing about protecting the purity of the mountain streams, the oceans, the forests. What about the children? Am I the only person left on this planet who believes that the mind and body of a child needs as much protection?"

Just then Amy came in the room. "Hi," she said with a smile. "Are we gonna watch it?"

"Oh, sure," said Meg, while she took a deep breath.

That night she lay in bed, looking up at the moon. She wasn't happy about living with a gigolo. If he had tried to earn money for them, he would have gotten her total support. But from all appearances, Geoffrey liked living off Meg, and that turned her off. She was no longer flattered by his very frequent sexual needs, nor was she interested in his constant chatter about old concubines. Meg felt stuck.

Thirteen

What Next

A FEW DAYS BEFORE THANKSGIVING OF '96, Meg and Geoffrey sat in the kitchen eating dinner. The phone rang, and Geoffrey began a nervous conversation with a man named Gilberto. Meg noted Geoffrey's unease. He was speaking too loudly and being too friendly as he shifted back and forth from one foot to the other. She watched him during the entire conversation. He was not being himself at all. The dialogue made no sense to her. He was talking about people whom she had never heard of before. It seemed that something was wrong with his house in California.

When Geoffrey got off the phone, Meg peppered him with questions. It turned out that since his departure for Montana, Geoffrey had been renting his house in California to a man named Gilberto. When Gilberto originally signed his lease, he asked for a lease option to buy, which required that he put $10,000 down and pay Geoffrey's monthly mortgage payment of $3,300 in rent. The down payment was never paid, but he had been reliable in covering the monthly payment.

Despite the failure to pay the down payment, Geoffrey intended to sell the house to Gilberto, but Gilberto couldn't get a mortgage. He did not report all of his income on his tax return and couldn't find a bank that would give him a mortgage with the low income that his 1040 reflected.

"Why don't you tell him the deal's off and find a buyer who can get a mortgage? Then you're rid of the place," Meg asked.

"Because if I lose Gilberto, then I have to come up with the money to pay the mortgage and I can't do that right now," Geoffrey said, looking uneasy. "I'd have to pay the mortgage each month while I looked for a new buyer. What if it took a year or more to find a buyer? The market in California isn't that great right now."

The subject of paying Geoffrey's mortgage hadn't come up until now. Meg really didn't want to have to make two mortgage payments each month. "Is he still trying to get a loan? Does he want to keep renting?" she asked.

"I think, at this point, he's all but given up on the loan and yes, he wants to keep renting. He really loves the house, but a small problem has developed."

Meg froze. With Geoffrey there were no small problems, only nightmares. "What's the problem?" she asked slowly.

"Well, Gilberto is having a problem with his business, and he can't pay the $3,300 a month, so he has sublet the upstairs to a man and his wife."

"Does he have the power to sublet according to the terms of the lease?"

"Well, no. As long as the $3,300 is paid each month, I don't mind. But the man, he's an Armenian, has accused Gilberto of coming on to his wife and he's thrown Gilberto out of the house." Geoffrey looked weary.

"What?!!!" yelled Meg. "This is like the Wild West. They're living in your house. You've never met them. You have no signed lease with them and you don't know if they can afford the rent?"

"Well, Gilberto had them sign a lease with him before they moved in."

"Yeah, but Gilberto didn't have the authority to do that, so the lease isn't valid. Oh God, call your attorney. He'll write them a letter and tell them to move out. If they don't, you can have them evicted."

"No, Meg. It's not like that in California. The tenant is king in California. The law is in their favor. There are professional squatters everywhere. Landlords are helpless to do anything about it. I'm telling you it's not like Illinois. Look, let's see if these people pay the $3,300 each month before we react."

"But what about Gilberto?"

"I guess he loses. How can he have a lease option to buy when he's paid no down payment, he can't afford the rent and he's no longer living in the place?" Geoffrey concluded. "I'll call Kousan tomorrow and feel him out. Hopefully, he'll pay the $3,300 each month."

Geoffrey called Kousan Hibamian, his new tenant, and schmoozed him big time. For the next two months the Hibamians paid the $3,300 a month in rent even though they had signed a lease with Gilberto for a lot less.

But Kousan was not stupid and his wife, Kristy, an American, was as crafty and shrewd a golddigger as had ever graced the California coast. Meg spoke with Kristy one morning and reported to Geoffrey that night. “You know, she sounded as dumb as a stump, but she kept referring to her lease with Gilberto. I’m a little concerned that she intends to find an excuse to not pay the whole $3,300. In other words, the stump’s not so dumb.”

Within a week, Kristy had her justification for not paying the rent. A small earthquake hit the Cielo area and the plumbing in Geoffrey’s house broke. There was water everywhere, and the drywall and woodwork were damaged. Kousan called Geoffrey and demanded that the repairs be made. He refused to pay any rent until that time.

Of course, Geoffrey had no earthquake insurance. It seemed a little unbelievable to Meg that the bank allowed him not to have earthquake insurance in an earthquake zone, but that’s the way it was.

The total bill for the repair of the earthquake damages was $10,000. Meg’s heart broke as she took the money out of her divorce settlement to pay for Geoffrey’s mess. She remembered his words to her before the wedding: “I’ve got some debts, but I’ve got them covered.”

The repairman kept calling. Apparently he couldn’t make the repairs according to his schedule because Kristy kept coming on to him. She was aggressive enough that he had to run out to his truck to get away from her. “She walks around the house with no clothes on!!” he said. Wily Kristy had figured out a way to delay the repairs.

The neighbors kept calling with complaints about Kristy. Mothers were concerned about their sons’ virtue. Kristy had purchased a basketball net and attached it to the top of the garage. *It was so kind of her to do this free of charge,* Meg thought. The boys were invited over to play basketball and then enjoyed the pleasures of Kristy with a little marijuana to boot.

Geoffrey called the police to have the Hibamians arrested for possession of marijuana, but the police refused to get involved. He called several different attorneys, and the advice was always the same. “There’s nothing you can do.” One of the attorneys was a former judge. He said, “If I were you, I’d pay them to move out. It’s the only real option that you have if you want them out fast. If you offer them $15,000 to get out, you’d probably save money.”

The repairs were finally done in mid-December. The Hibamians refused to pay the rent because the repairs weren't done to their liking. They complained about picayune details, such as the toilet paper holder being too high for Kristy's reach. "If the toilet paper holder is too tall for her, then she's got to be as big as a chihuahua," Meg said. "Why don't you just allow the bank to foreclose?"

"I don't want to call attention to the loan," said Geoffrey. "I'm afraid that it will be audited."

"Why are you afraid of an audit?"

"Well, you see, I had to refinance the original mortgage note," he said, "because interest rates went down and I wanted to take advantage of that, but also I needed some cash to pay the monthly mortgage payments. I just wasn't able to earn enough."

"When you built that house, didn't you know what your monthly payment was going to be?"

"Well, yes, but I figured I'd get my inheritance and pay off the loan."

"You mean you thought your mother was going to die?"

"No, not my mother, my grandfather. I figured that he'd be dying pretty soon and I'd use my inheritance to pay off the loan. So I didn't worry about the payments."

Meg absorbed his comments. It was as if Geoffrey couldn't wait for the old guy to leave the planet so he could grab the money and run. She felt butterflies in her solar plexus.

"So how would refinancing give you more cash? Were the payments going to be lower?" she asked.

"No, the payments were higher, but I got the cash by taking out a bigger loan."

"So, you're saying that you borrowed more than the principal due and owing, and used the excess to make the monthly payments?" Her voice squeaked as it rose up an octave.

"Yes," said Geoffrey. "What's wrong with that?"

"Because it's a tactic that spells disaster. Because you have to keep taking out bigger and bigger loans that you can't pay back. Why didn't you sell the place?"

"Because I wanted to live in it," he said.

"Geoffrey, don't you see how financially irresponsible that is?"

"No," he said. "It all worked out fine."

"Fine for you, but I'm getting bled dry!"

Geoffrey didn't respond. Meg was beginning to see the picture. It had all worked out fine because she was there to pay the bill while

Geoffrey sat around and watched the weather channel. He didn't care that he was going through her money. He was pretty happy with himself. Marrying Meg had been a very smart move.

"So you still haven't explained about why you're afraid of an audit," she said, stuffing her anger.

"Well, when I refinanced they needed more collateral, so I used my interest in my Grandfather's testamentary trust. My brother, Charles, is the trustee. He refused to sign the papers for the bank. He said he wouldn't allow me to use my interest in the trust as collateral.

"I gave the loan officer my copies of the trust agreement, and she thought that it would be fine as collateral. So I think she forged Charles' signature. The loan went through, but I'm afraid that if it gets audited I'll get thrown in jail."

"Why would you get thrown in jail if she forged the papers?"

"Because I think she'd blame me to save her job."

"Geoffrey, why would a loan officer forge Charles' name? What was in it for her?"

"Because she wanted the loan to go through. She felt sorry for me, I guess, or maybe she wanted her commission."

"She'd risk going to jail for such a small commission?"

Geoffrey said nothing. Meg watched him closely. His eyes were cast down as he tapped his fingers on the table.

"O.K., look, we need to get rid of your house. The Hibamians aren't paying the rent, so we may as well have it on the market," Meg said. "I'll call the realtor tomorrow and tell her to list it."

She resigned herself to paying both mortgages each month. Geoffrey had no savings whatsoever. The house went on the market the next day, and the Hibamians moved into action.

The phone rang the next weekend and it was Marnie, the realtor. "Hi, Meg," she said without drawing a breath. "It's Marnie. Look, I can't sell this house with Kristy in there. At first, she was scaring off all of the buyers. The place was a mess, and when they walked through, she told them about everything that was wrong with the place. Now, she's refusing to even let them in. Also, they've made friends with Gilberto again and they're encouraging him to move back in so that you can't sell the house to a different buyer because of his option to buy."

When Geoffrey came home from work at noon as usual, Meg confronted him. "Geoffrey, you've got to start bringing in some money. The Hibamians are sabotaging the sale of the house, and we can't afford two mortgages. Until my house sells, we're in big trouble." She explained what Marnie had told her, and Geoffrey listened without a lot of emotion. He seemed really preoccupied.

The next morning Geoffrey didn't get up to go to work. He said he was sick. "I frequently get a strep throat," he said. "I need to go to the doctor and get some antibiotics." That afternoon he returned home with the prescription that he wanted. "Well," he said, "he's not a very good doctor. He told me that the test was negative and that I didn't have strep. I told him I did. I told him that I've had strep dozens of times and that only certain drugs work any more. I just kept talking until he gave me the prescription."

Geoffrey went back to bed and stayed there for days. He really did look bad. Meg left him alone while he was sick. She didn't bring up the subject of work again until the next week when he arose from the bed.

"Geoffrey, when you got your transfer, didn't they agree to pay you $2,000 a month for three months?" she asked.

"Yeah," he said.

"Well, don't they expect you to make some sales during those months so that during the fourth month you're in a position to earn on your own?"

"Yeah."

"Well, I'm sure they're not just giving away $6,000 because they're generous. They expect some kind of progress. Next month is the third month. What are you going to do after that?"

"I don't know."

"Geoffrey, if you don't make any sales, they're gonna fire you at the end of next month!"

"No, they won't. They don't care."

Exhaustion was setting in. Life with Geoffrey was tense, and her kids were not much help. Heather was still refusing to speak to her. Amy was better, but going through a tough time making friends during her freshman year. The cliques were forming fast and she was worried that she wouldn't fit into any of them.

The next day Geoffrey ended up in bed again. "I don't think the antibiotics got rid of all of the strep," he said.

From that point on, every time Meg mentioned that Geoffrey needed to earn money he came down with strep and went to bed. At the end of November, he got fired.

A few weeks before Christmas, Meg was drafting a divorce mediation agreement in her office out in her coach house. She realized that she had forgotten to bring her briefcase out to her office and had to run back to the main house to get it. On her way out the back door with the retrieved briefcase, she miscounted the number of steps on the stairway. It was dark. There was no moon that night and it was very, very cold. The ice on the stairs crunched under her boots. She reached for the last step and it wasn't there. After what seemed like an unusually long drop she landed on the outside of her left foot. At the same time, a loud popping noise went off inside her head. The next morning she awoke to a swollen and darkened ankle.

"That's gonna take six weeks," said Geoffrey as he surveyed the injury.

"Don't say that," said Meg.

"Look, Squeege, I've had several sprained ankles over the years, and they always take six weeks."

"I can't have a sprained ankle. I've got Christmas shopping to do, and we promised the girls that we'd take them shopping in Chicago. I haven't even begun to decorate. I can't have a sprained ankle. It's not on my 'to do' list."

"I'll do the Christmas shopping, Squeegy. Just make me a list." He spoke boyishly, as if he was excited to help and to please her.

The list was compiled promptly by Meg, who was grateful that Geoffrey was finally going to do something to justify his existence. "I'll order my brothers' gifts from catalogues but these gifts have to come from the mall and ..."

"I'll take care of it all today," he said and with a dramatic gesture, he swept up his coat and sailed out the door. As she watched his truck pull out of the driveway, she was relieved to be spared the fun of Christmas shopping on crutches.

There were a lot of Christmas festivities going on at school that afternoon and night, so Heather and Amy weren't due home until 10:00. Geoffrey didn't arrive home for dinner, which was good since she didn't feel like standing in front of the stove on one leg.

After spending the better part of her day with her ankle elevated and iced, she decided to hop up to the attic to resurrect her old crutches. Their attic was crammed with stuff and junk, but she uncovered them at the bottom of an old church pew left by the former owners. Thumping noises downstairs drew her attention away from the crutches. They fit easily under her pits and she swung herself to the top of the stairs. She listened. Someone was fumbling with the keys. She could hear them hit the concrete floor of the back porch once, twice, then three times.

"Who's there?" she yelled.

"It's me," said Geoffrey, but it didn't sound like him.

The shopping bags rustled as he entered their bedroom. There was a familiar odor. His body was rolling like a wave.

"Well, I see you're wearing those circular shoes again," said Meg.

Geoffrey was stinking drunk and acting very pious. "Now, Squeege, don't get upset. I have every right to get drunk now and then."

"No, you don't, Geoffrey. You said you only drink when you drive over bridges and fly in planes. Did you take a 747 to the mall?"

"Oh, ha ha. You're very clever. I can drink whenever I want."

"Oh really? I already told you I've lived with one drinker and I won't live with another."

"So what are you gonna do about it?"

"I'll divorce you, Geoffrey. I swear to God I'll get rid of you," she slowly hissed.

"Oh, right," he mocked.

"Don't tempt me, Geoffrey. I never make a threat that I'm not willing to carry out. It's only a matter of timing."

Geoffrey started to rage. He threw things around the room and luckily, only hit Meg with a pillow. Disgusted, she turned her back on him, got into her nightgown and went to bed while he continued to rant about how he was a grown man and could get drunk any time he wanted.

The next morning he got up early, looked at Meg sitting in the lazy boy chair with her ankle up, crossed the room and kneeled in front of her. He put his head on her lap and said, "Please, please forgive me. I'm so sorry. I'll never do that again."

"Do you remember last night?" she asked.

"Yes, and you have every right to be furious with me. Please forgive me. I swear I'll never do it again. I really hate living in Barnstable, and it grieves me to see your kids treating us the way they do. Heather hasn't spoken or looked at either one of us in weeks. Amy's a little better, but not by much. I've really been trying to make us a family, Meg, but they won't cooperate. I'm not used to rejection." Part of Meg was relieved. *Maybe he won't drink again,* she thought. But her promptings told her that he was merely trying to hang onto a damn good meal ticket.

During the first week of January '97, Meg got a phone call from Dick, her cousin Sally's husband. "Well," he said, "we did it. Our buyers sold their house. We'd like to close on March 3rd."

The listing agreement on Meg's house had run out at the end of

August. She didn't renew it because she was tired of cleaning for the constant parade of recreational lookers.

Meg remembered that Sally had always loved her house. She jumped at the opportunity to buy it after Meg dropped the selling price by the amount of Fran's commission. Since Sally had a more affordable house, her realtor had found a buyer within a few weeks, but the contract with her buyers stipulated that she could not close on her house until her buyers closed on their house back East. So Meg's house was locked up in a selling chain for four months.

The sale meant that Meg would have to find another place to live quickly and clean out twenty-two years worth of stuff from her house, all in less than two months.

Meg tapped on Heather's door and hopped into her room on her crutches when she heard the words, "Yeah, come in." She told her that their house had sold. Heather's eyes dropped and she said, "O.K." Her stoic expression didn't change. She continued to read at her desk.

Amy's door was open, and Meg hovered in the doorway. "Amy, Uncle Dick called and their house has sold. We'll be closing on our house on March 3rd," said Meg. She saw Amy's face drop. It meant she was losing her home. Meg's heart sank. She didn't want to hurt her kids. She loved them, but the mortgage was killing her financially. She had explained this to them many times, but it didn't matter. They were still angry with their Mom.

The next day Meg visited several different realtors on the north shore. There were few homes or apartments for rent in Barnstable. So she began her search in the Kingston area, close to Heather and Amy's school. Within 48 hours she had located a house with an affordable rent that had room enough for all of them. It was only a mile or so from school. She didn't want to buy another house while Geoffrey still had his mortgage. As she drove home, she thought that Heather and Amy would be relieved to know that they would be living close to school and their friends.

After dinner, Meg called for a powwow in Amy's room. Geoffrey stayed in the sitting room and let Meg handle this alone. "I've got good news," Meg said with an upbeat voice. "I've found a house for us to live in. It's right in Kingston, only a mile or two from school. The monthly payment is definitely affordable, and we'll all have plenty of room. We can move in on March 1st."

Heather stood up and began to yell, "I can't handle this any more. All of these changes are too much. Just yesterday three kids from school died in a car crash and now you want me to move? I don't want my friends to see that I'm living in some run-down rental. I won't go. It isn't fair. And I don't want to leave my friends."

"Heather, your friends aren't around here any more. Your school is near Kingston and that's where your friends are. And it's not a run-down rental. It's new construction," Meg said meekly. She was in shock. Heather's reaction was so sudden and so completely illogical that she was unable to follow the conversation.

"I can't handle this either. When will we see Dad? He's part of the picture too, you know," yelled Amy.

"I know he is. I'm going to call him tonight and tell him. I expect him to be fine about it. Kingston's only twenty minutes away."

Heather and Amy took turns crying and screaming in protest at their mother. Meg sat there in a state of helpless confusion. "I don't understand why you are so upset about Kingston. We have to go somewhere. Where would you like to go?" she asked. There was no answer. Just screaming and verbal abuse. A defeated Meg got up from the chair and slowly walked out of the room. She went into the sitting room and looked at Geoffrey. His eyes were full of pity. Meg sat next to him and said, "Did you hear that?"

"Yes I did, and I think it was the most ridiculous conversation I've ever listened to," he said. "Listen Meg, they hate you. No matter what you do, they will criticize you. Let's go somewhere else. Let them live with their father."

"I can't do that. They're my children. Why do you keep saying they hate me?"

"Because they do. I've never heard any children talk to their mother as they talk to you. It's shameful. Look, Meg, I've given your kids a chance. They're spoiled little rich girls. I left a job out West with lots of potential. I hate Chicago. I'm looking for a job now, but not just in Chicago. I'm going to look at out-of-state locations too. I don't know if I'll get anything, but I've got contacts. Don't sign that lease just yet."

"No, Geoffrey. If you get an out-of-state job, they might not come with me and I'll lose them. How can this be? I've always loved them and taken care of them. I've always been there for them."

"Because Nick's been disrespecting you with his words and attitude ever since you filed the divorce papers and probably before. He spoils them with his money and lets them get away with murder. He doesn't discipline them, and you do. So you're the bad guy. To him, this is just a big competition and he's Superdad, their good buddy. They aren't going to figure this all out, Meg, until they're much older, if ever. Maybe when they have kids they'll see the whole picture, but for now, my dear, you are the quintessential fall guy."

That night, Nick answered the phone, and Meg explained that they were going to live in Kingston. Nick's reaction was exactly like the kids. He began to yell, "I'll never see them if you move to Kingston. This is unacceptable!" Meg got off the phone and wondered whether the three of them were in a conspiracy of insanity.

There was little conversation in their home for the next few days. The realtor was pressing Meg to sign the lease, and Geoffrey came down to the kitchen the following morning with his "good" news. He had been offered a job by a communications company in Denver to start on March 10th. Never in his entire life had Geoffrey been so fast to find employment. Meg was shocked but elated that Geoffrey was once again excited about working. She thought that maybe Denver would be a good idea for all of them. Heather would leave for college, but Amy could go to school in Denver. She found a Catholic girls' high school in Denver, the sister school to the local Jesuit school, and got ready to give the news to Amy. Meg hoped that the girls would be happy that Geoffrey had a new job in an area where they could go skiing often.

That night Meg asked Amy to come into the sitting room. She and Geoffrey looked at Amy, who was sitting on the radiator cover across the room from them.

"Amy, I've got good news. Geoffrey has found a job and it's in Denver. There's a great school there and we can go skiing every..."

Meg didn't get a chance to finish. Amy rose up from the radiator cover and yelled, "I'm not going to Denver. I'm staying here. All of my friends are here. It's taken me a year to make new friends in a new school and I'm not going through that again in a strange city."

"But Amy, the child always goes with the mother," Meg said, almost begging.

"Not this child," said Amy.

Geoffrey tried to reason with Amy. "Look, why don't you give it a few days. Think it over. Denver's a beautiful city and..."

"No," said Amy. "I'm not going there."

Meg held up her hand to Geoffrey and said, "No, don't push her. She's made up her mind. We have to respect that."

"Why don't you just tell her that she's coming with you? I moved to Cleveland with my mother when I was in high school. I hated every minute of it, but I went with her. She was my Mom."

"That was a different situation. Your father wasn't a prick like Nick," explained Meg. "Nick thinks it's O.K. to separate a mother from her child, even when he has no intention of giving Amy love or attention. It saves him child support and alimony. He'll marry Barbie so he has a free housekeeper to do his dirty work, and he won't look back."

"But you've been a good mother."

"It doesn't matter when the child is older," explained Meg. "She turns fifteen in a few weeks. Nick will drag us into court and the Judge will ask Amy what she wants to do, and Amy will say she wants to stay, and the Judge will rule that Amy stays, and that's that. Meg loses. I'm not going to waste money going to court when I know I'll lose."

Weeks went by, and against all of Meg's hopes, Amy didn't change her mind. She would live with her Dad so that she could stay in the same school with her friends. "Amy," said Meg, gingerly, "if you stay with your Dad I don't think you're gonna get much in the way of love."

"I'll be fine, Mom. Don't worry. I can handle it," Amy said. To her Mother she looked taller, close to five foot nine or ten and very confident. Meg looked up at her daughter. The wavy, auburn hair had grown longer and thicker. Her blue eyes had lost their innocence. There was a grit that Meg had never felt before.

There was nothing more that Meg could do. *I could put a real guilt trip on her,* she thought. *I could tell her about how she's broken my heart. That wouldn't be a lie.* But it didn't seem honorable to be manipulative. After all, she hated being manipulated by Nick. To manipulate Amy would mean that she was a hypocrite.

Things were not so clear cut from Heather's point of view. She picked at her Mom daily for the decision to move to Denver. Her scornful jabs were carefully placed so as to guarantee the most pain. Meg finally turned to her and said, "What do you want from me, Heather? No matter how right or wrong my decisions are, you criticize them all the same. Geoffrey is my husband. If your father had been transferred to a different city during our marriage, I would have moved with him too. What is it that you want?"

"This is hard on Amy."

"Of course it is. But it's also hard on me, or haven't you bothered to notice? Amy should come with me. I want her to come with me. The child always goes with the mother."

"Her friends are here."

"In twenty years, she won't remember most of their names. What's more important? Your friends or your Mom?"

Heather stood up and walked out of the room.

Fourteen

Inner Work

AS THE LIGHT STARTED TO FADE BACK in, Michael found himself sitting in a ditch, turned completely around from the direction in which he had been going on his bike. He didn't recall how he had gotten there, but the wet and the mud covered him. The pain in his left shoulder was almost unbearable, and at first he dared not move, thinking that the collarbone was surely cracked. Gingerly, he tried to move his left arm.

To his surprise, it obeyed, moving through a circular trajectory without any strange sounds or resistance. He looked up then and the sight of his left hand sickened him.

The knuckle of his left index finger was separated, and the upper and lower parts of his finger were held together only by his flesh. His shoulder hurt so badly that he didn't even know his finger was separated until he saw it. He first reaction was to grab it and put it back together, and he reached his right arm around. Suddenly, a soothing voice was telling him not to touch it.

"Easy, big guy." It was the sports doctor who always rode with the Healthy Foods team.

"A rodeo clown would have rolled better," Michael half mumbled.

"You didn't do too badly! That was actually quite awesome!"

"Oh, yeah?"

"I'd give it a 10," the doctor said. He was carefully checking Michael over for any signs of broken bones.

"I think we can lift you over to the van now."

Michael was in a state of semi-shock, breathing very fast, and feeling very scared. The calming presence of the doctor soothed him. Several huge guys lifted him out of the ditch and carried him toward the van. Someone was placing some hefty trash bags down in the back so that Michael wouldn't get blood all over the back. He was covered with the stuff, especially around his knees. He couldn't reconstruct the series of crash events in his mind, but he remembered the moment both his knees hit the pavement. Not only did he remember it, he felt it most intensely. Even so, he thought of his bike.

"Is the Alchemy O.K.?"

"Miraculously, yes," said the tallest guy. It was Dudley. "I saw it pop back into shape after it was a tangled mess!" Dudley loved to exaggerate.

"Is that you, Dudley?"

"Yep!"

"How are ya doin', man?"

"Better than you!"

The guys put Michael gently down in the van, but it was on a slight incline, and Michael kept sliding on the trash bags. The driver moved slowly up to more level ground, much to the relief of all. The doctor gently took Michael's left hand, and with several downward strokes on Michael's left index finger, applied enough pressure to get the joint back in place. Michael tried to move it.

"Don't move it!" the doctor cautioned. Michael obeyed. The thought of not being able to play his guitar again sickened him.

The driver was talking to an aid station in Two Feathers on his two-way radio, describing the accident and telling them to get ready for the injured rider. They were amazed that only one rider had gone down. Usually when one falls in the middle of the pack, it brings everyone who is behind down, too. Somehow, all the riders had managed to avoid running over Michael and grinding him into the road.

"We're ready to roll as soon as we get some bandages on him," the driver said.

"Hey, I'm going to beat you guys to Two Feathers!" Michael said.

The guys laughed, telling him not to gloat too much. Michael was starting to calm down a little. He knew it could have been much worse, and his main concern was his finger. He remembered the really serious accidents that had happened to guys he knew and considered himself fortunate. The problem, though, was that this was a triple whammy. In the space of one week, he had lost his job, his girlfriend, and now this. He could have handled any two of these, but three of them were too much. The impact just hadn't sunk in yet.

Dudley went over and got the Alchemy, placing it behind Michael in the van.

"Thanks, Mike!"

"I thought you could use the inspiration!" Mike grinned. "See if you can resume your original shape!"

As the van doors shut, the camaraderie ended, and Michael was suddenly alone with his pain. His thoughts were jumbled and confused, and a helpless feeling started to press in upon him. His independence was gone. The van paused for a group of riders, and as Michael looked out the van window, he recognized Mindy and James and the entire group. They were laughing and joking together, unaware of what had just transpired.

Don't you do it! he thought. *Don't you spiral down and get depressed!*

When Michael got to Two Feathers, he managed to get out of the back of the van on his own, testing his limits. He could walk O.K, but his knees hurt with every step. The driver had stopped in front of a little cabin on the Two Feathers Fairgrounds that was serving as an Infirmary. There was a long line of walking wounded waiting for treatment, and it reminded Michael of Atlanta after Sherman's invasion. The driver got Michael's Alchemy out of the van for him, and politely offered to take it over to the "corral" where all the other bikes were being stored for the night. Michael politely refused and told him he was going to sleep with his bike. The driver gave him a confused look, wished him well, got back into the van and drove away.

Michael slowly walked to the rear of the line, clutching his Alchemy for support as he guided it along next to him. Gone was the festive atmosphere of the ride, and in its place loomed a murky, dismal, hopeless air that permeated the Infirmary and all the hapless victims of the morning. They had all started out with great hopes, only to have them dashed in an instant of clashing metal and asphalt.

Michael could feel a sense of depression gnawing at him. Gone was his air of dignity, his first line of defense. He didn't want to look at anyone, and he steadfastly eyed the ground as he waited in the back of the line.

"Odd," he whispered. "People are coming in here to get attention, to get healed, but the feel of the place is enough to make a person worse!"

Two hours later, Michael finally got to the front of the line. The volunteers bandaged him up as best they could, and when they were done, Michael praised their handiwork and hobbled away.

There was a big tent on the fairgrounds where the cyclists could just lay down a sleeping bag, and that seemed like the way to go. The tent looked big enough to sleep several hundred people, and some of the cyclists who had made the 100 miles in good time were already laying out their bags. Long rows were starting to form, with a narrow walk space in between each one. Nobody was hanging around in the tent yet, because the thing to do was to hang around at the front gate and look superior. It was a subtle way of bragging to your fellow cyclists that you had gotten there first. These guys wanted to be seen relaxing in a lawn chair, not even remotely fazed by the 100 miles they had just ridden.

Normally, guys in lawn chairs wouldn't have bothered Michael, but today it was just one more extra weight upon him, putting him that much closer to his limit. He looked down at his bandaged knees, feeling like a complete dork. Actually, "dork" was not the word he really wanted to use, but it fit the mold that his public image was forcing him into.

Don, though, probably wouldn't call him a dork. Don would more likely call him a loser. Don would say that his genes were inferior, and that he had come out on the short end of the survival of the fittest. To Don, it was the way nature eliminated the lesser specimens and improved on the next generation.

As Michael pondered this, it added just a little more weight on the pile, which was almost about to topple him. He felt a cross between anger, resentment, helplessness, depression, and outrage. It was obvious to him that Don's real fear was that Don was not good enough, and underneath it all, Don was terrified of being a loser. It was a merry-go-round that kept coming back to the same old spot, never really getting anywhere. Michael knew that there had to be a way out, but he didn't know just where it was. Every once in a while he would discuss his ideas with Don, but he was never sure whether Don was just being polite or was genuinely interested. Don probably thought that Michael was just creating a buffer between himself and reality, because Michael could not accept the way things were. Michael not only wanted alternatives, he wanted to demonstrate their truth. He wanted to find the power from somewhere within himself, not from out there. He was looking for his own internal kernel of perfection, and from that tiny seed, he would produce a giant.

"Right!" came the nagging voice again. "You can't even ride your bike. You might not even play the guitar again! You can forget about that little seed! It's not there! Look around at the guys that are already here. They beat you and they will ride again tomorrow. You're going home on the bus with all the other losers!"

Michael was feeling more and more alone, as if he had no connection with all the other people in the fairgrounds. He looked outside of the tent, and noticed a happy couple setting up camp a few yards away.

"Oh, great!" he said to himself. "It's James and Mindy! They're going to spend the night right next to me!"

Now the stage was complete. He had no job, no girl and a whole bevy of very painful injuries. On another day, he might have said, "So what! I'll get over it!" He would have told himself to count all the many blessings that God had showered upon him. This day, though, something had snapped, and he couldn't shake it off. He was embarrassed to walk around outside, so he receded into the shadows and lay down on his sleeping bag.

In only a few days time Michael was deeply depressed. He had never felt so helpless, so totally without hope. By some miracle, he managed to get to a psychologist for help.

"Hello, Michael," the psychologist said. "I'm Francis. How do you feel?"

"I just can't, I just can't...," Michael tried to explain, trailing off, fighting to hold back the tears. They came anyway, first in little trickles, and then in great torrents.

"Please help me!" Michael pleaded. He had hit rock bottom, and he was scared.

"I can help you," Francis assured him, "but you must promise me that you won't harm yourself before our next visit."

Michael shook his head in agreement.

"A colleague of mine will prescribe some pills for you, and it's extremely important that you take them as prescribed and that you take them on time."

"O.K.," Michael said softly, almost inaudibly. He barely had the energy to speak.

"Do you have a ride home?"

A ride home was a luxury that Michael didn't have. The truth was that no one was available. His riding buddies were out training, his siblings had families of their own, and his parents weren't taking an active interest.

"I drove myself," Michael explained.

Francis looked concerned, but said nothing. Michael picked his prescription up at the local drugstore, and drove home in silence. He leaned forward as he drove, almost resting his head on the steering wheel. When he got to his house, he walked unsteadily up the stairs. Mustering all his strength and will, he walked over to the bathroom and managed to get his first pill down before he collapsed on the floor next to the bed. He just sat there, staring blankly at the wall. He had heard people describe despair before, but this was the real thing. There was knowing about despair, and there was experiencing despair. It had taken him by surprise, coming over him all at once. If he had seen it coming, he would not have succumbed to it. He would not have agreed to it. He could feel the fear gripping him, paralyzing him. He felt catatonic as he saw the depth of the darkness that surrounded him. How could he escape this dungeon, this blackest of prisons? He drew his knees up to his chest and wrapped his arms around his legs, shaking with fright. A cold sweat emerged from his brow.

"End it, end it now!" a voice urged.

He leaned forward, supporting himself with one arm, his head dangling down loosely.

"Why go on? You can't go on. It will never change! You fought all those years to recover from the LSD, and for what? Look at you!" the voice continued from out of nowhere.

He couldn't move. If there had been a pill next to him that would save his life, his hand would not have moved forward even an inch to pick it up. What happened to the superb athlete who was pushing back all the boundaries? It had all happened so quickly. The sweat dripped from his face, soaking the floor in front of him. Finally, he fell forward, and a merciful sleep came over him.

Michael awakened exactly at midnight, as if the denizens of that hour had prodded him from his restless slumber. A new fear took hold of him as he wondered how in the world he could pay his mortgage without a job. Memories of the old days taunted him. He remembered the desperate times when he had to work for the temporary labor pool, and the time he almost got his head sliced off by a wild wino with a shovel. There was always danger then, and complete uncertainty. He could see himself hitchhiking in his old tattered coat and dirty jeans, and he remembered how his old girlfriend Amelie had come cruising by in her father's luxury sedan. Maybe she recognized him, and maybe she didn't, but she kept on driving.

He realized how close he was to being on the street again. *No!* he thought, *Please God, no!* The scenes kept coming, depriving him of sleep.

In the morning the darkness still enveloped him, but somehow, he kept his promise to Francis and took his pill on schedule, even though he didn't believe it could possibly work. Time had slowed down for Michael. He walked down the stairs to make a meager breakfast, and at the bottom of the stairs he just stopped, not feeling motivated to take the few extra steps into the kitchen. He collapsed on the floor, not moving for hours. Miraculously, though, he got his next pill down, and then the next. It was harder for him to take a pill than it had been for him to pedal his bike a hundred miles. Time didn't mean anything to him, and nothing seemed to matter to him, yet the power of the simple promise he made to take his pills moved him into compliance, because somewhere inside he still wanted to believe in the integrity of the human bond. Gradually, more slowly at first, the pills began to work. The excruciating anxiety he felt started to subside, and in its place a glimmer of hope appeared. The fear, so furious in previous days, was being pushed back.

After several weeks and several sessions with Francis, he slowly got back to stable ground. Occasionally his riding buddies would drop over and say hello, but they wouldn't stay for long, and Michael realized that cycling had been the only tie that held them together.

Michael wanted desperately to understand what had happened to him, and how the depression was able to envelope him so quickly. He told Francis about the LSD, and he and Francis explored Michael's early years to find out why he was hanging out with a group who was doing drugs. Michael had had a horrible childhood. He was the youngest of three. His older sister was six years older. His brother, four years older. His parents divorced when he was two, and his mother raised the kids while pursuing a Ph.D. in French. She was a very beautiful woman, but she was vain and self-absorbed, incapable of caring about the world outside of herself. She had married Michael's father at seventeen because she was pregnant. Her entire life was out of kilter at an early age, just like Michael's, and she went back to school to get educated and get her life back on track. She went through man after man, looking for one who had more money than Michael's millionaire father. She never had enough time for Michael, so his domineering oldest sister took over the job of raising him. The other sister was intellectually arrogant and discounted Michael's intelligence. Michael's older brother beat him on a daily basis, and Michael almost died from one such beating when he was only four years old. He grew up poor while his father played golf at the country club, and when Michael was old enough, his father put him to work in his warehouse. Indeed, Michael had gotten into cycling because he wanted to overcome the LSD experience, but he also wanted to prove to himself that he was masculine, not in the brutal way of his brother, not in the "look out for number one" way of his father, but in his own way.

"What did Mindy look like?" Francis asked. It was Saturday, and Francis and Michael always met on Saturday.

"She was not a bad looking girl. I think the first thing I noticed about her was that she had very long hair. It was all the way down to her waist."

"Did she remind you of anyone?"

"I never dated anyone with hair that long before. The only person I ever knew with hair that long was my mother."

"Did your mother come by and see you during your depression?"

"Yes, she came by once, but just briefly. She acted as if she was being greatly inconvenienced. I had some laundry that wasn't folded, and she said she would come by and help me. When she got to my place, she kind of flitted around, looking very agitated. She folded one tee shirt for me, and then she said that she had to go meet her boyfriend and that she couldn't be late."

"I see. What about your father. Did he ever come by?"

"He phoned up and said he was coming over, and I met him out on the driveway. It was the first time he had ever seen my townhouse, and the first thing he told me was that it was the worst looking one on the block. He didn't ask to come in, and I didn't ask him to either, because I could tell he was feeling awkward and that he wanted to leave. His Labrador Retriever was in the backseat of the SUV, and he was looking forward to getting out into the country with her."

"Did any of your cycling buddies come over to help cheer you up?"

"Occasionally, but they wouldn't stay for long. Cycling was all we had in common, and the visits felt awkward. Besides, they all had very strict training schedules."

Francis looked pensive. "I want to pass an idea by you, Michael. I know the LSD was devastating to you, but it may not be at the root of what we are looking for here. You got over the LSD physiologically a long time ago, but not emotionally. I want to emphasize that the goal here is not to get you to listen to my advice. I want to get you to listen to the advice of your own spiritual guidance. I want to raise your vibration high enough so that you can tune into your Higher Self, and then you can see if what I say is congruent with what your guidance is telling you. You raise your vibration by getting in touch with your heart. These are the powerful frequencies, the frequencies of love, compassion, joy, and peace. This is true power, much higher than any mere brute force."

Francis had Michael's attention. Francis wasn't coming from his ego, he was coming from his heart.

"Go on," Michael asked politely.

"What are some of your earliest memories of your father and mother?"

Michael sat back in his chair and closed his eyes. "I remember my father coming over to our house just after the divorce. It was the only time I remember seeing him at our house. He was angry, incredibly angry. It was terrifying for me to see it. I remember how he pushed my mother into the wall in the upstairs hallway. Her head went inside the wall, making a huge hole. She slumped down on the floor, and we didn't know if she was dead or alive. We jumped on my father, trying to keep him away from her. We ripped his shirt up as he peeled us off of him. He headed out the front door, cursing, shouting and shaking his fist in the air. He never came back."

"I know we have talked about your sister, but I need to know what bothers you most about her."

"My sister, who actually raised me, is the type who always looks perfect. She was an actress, a very pretty lady. You can only get along with her by going along with her. She can be incredibly bossy and covertly controlling. She has the need to mother me, to take care of me. Behind my back, though, she tells people that I'm weak and can't take care of myself. She thinks she can control me by appealing to the little boy within me, by making me remember subconsciously when I really needed her. When I was little, she used to scare me so that I would come sleep with her. She would tell me there were ghosts in my closet and that they were going to come out and get me."

"Was there any sexual activity between the two of you?"

"No, believe it or not, although she is obsessed with me somehow. There may be a sexual aspect to it, but nothing sexual has ever happened."

"I think she has some real hooks in you," Francis said. "She was able to put them there because your mother was never around. There is a stage of development in early childhood when the mother mirrors the child so that the child can get a sense of self. I don't think that happened for you. Your sister was able to come in and tell you who she wanted you to be, and you kept jumping through hoops, because you desperately needed to have a sense of self. She probably didn't want you to have one, either, because her wounded self needed to keep this unsavory relationship going. All this at your expense, of course. If you had a strong sense of self, she wouldn't be able to keep it going."

"I'm not really sure who I am," he said, so softly that Francis leaned forward to hear him. "I don't know what I'm doing here, or where I fit in, or if I count."

Francis gave him a look of true compassion. "You most assuredly do count, Michael."

Michael knew this, but he didn't feel it. "How can I figure out who I am?" Michael almost pleaded.

"We need to start with some basic definitions," Francis offered. "I believe our problems arise because we have lost the connection to the Divine and the God flame within ourselves. We need to bring Divine Light in, we need to connect with Light, and we need to let Light work within us. You have to remember who you are. You have a core soul, and this is your essence. This is the child of God within, your healthy self. Believe it or not, he is in there, right alongside the wounded parts of you, the parts of you that have developed all kinds of false beliefs and protective behaviors to keep you safe. This is your false self, your critic, your ego who is trying to run the show. What we want to do is replace this false self with a loving, healthy self. This loving self sees you as you really are, he sees your essence. This loving self is connected to your Higher Self, and surrounds you with a wonderful loving radiance. The loving self loves you and all of your parts unconditionally. He doesn't judge the wounded parts of you. Judgement is a lower frequency, and it separates you from God. By offering unconditional love, your heart opens up, you get in touch with your Higher Self, and you learn why you became the way you are now. You find out from your Higher Self what loving action you should take on your behalf, and you take it. You keep doing this, and keep doing this, and keep doing this. You want to find every wounded part of you and heal each wounded part until you are completely whole, until nothing about you is wounded.

At that point you are whole, and you are at one with your Higher Self. We don't want to act from fear and control. We want to act from love. This is how we will find our natural joy and peace, which is our birthright."

"Let's not ignore the females by using all these masculine pronouns," Michael warned.

"I use them not to denote sex, but to denote the doer, the part of a person that takes action. We all have it; it's not relegated to a particular sex."

"I like that," Michael said.

"Now, Michael, your parents and older siblings were never healthy models for you. I mean, they were wounded, too. You never got unconditional love and approval from your family. I submit that you have the false belief that you are basically flawed, that you are bad. You criticize yourself relentlessly, thinking that if you get it right, your father will like you, your brother will like you, and your mother will love you the way she should have. The fact is that none of this is true. You go to incredible lengths to get approval, to win the affection and admiration of your biking friends. You took that LSD so that you could fit in with the hip crowd, and it almost ruined your life. All the while, you are neglecting your soul, your inner boy child. He is screaming out for you to listen to him, to take care of him. He is probably terrified and feels completely helpless and alone. That pain you felt when Mindy fell for James was how you felt as a little child, how you felt when your mother ignored you as a little baby, and you cover it up with this false façade. You couldn't handle the pain of that aloneness when you were little, but you can now. You just don't realize it. You have developed all these addictive behaviors so that you don't have to feel it, but you need to feel it so that you can heal it. That depression you experienced was the end result of your trying to define your worth externally instead of internally. You just couldn't do it anymore. It takes all your time and energy."

"How can I get healthy when I have no clue what it feels like? Where do we start?" Michael asked. He understood that Francis wasn't criticizing him, that he was modeling what it was like to lovingly heal your wounded parts and connect to your Higher Self.

"Your frequency will automatically rise when you have the intent to learn and to love. Intent is the key here."

"I definitely want to learn," Michael confirmed.

"Now, imagination, creativity and joy come from God. They flow into you from God. You can't create them. When you took that LSD, the high you felt before your face melted off was actually an experience of your own inner self. It's not something out there that does it. It's in here. Drugs and alcohol can deaden you to the low frequencies and allow you to feel only the higher frequencies. But it's a false high. The kingdom of heaven is within you, and you don't want to take it by force with drugs or alcohol. You want to raise yourself up by opening your heart to unconditional love."

"What's the first step, Francis?"

"You have to be willing to feel your real pain, to get in touch with what you are really feeling, and then you want to ask your Higher Self what loving action you can take on your behalf. In the past, your inner dialogues have been taking place between various wounded parts. This is a vicious circle, because all these wounded parts don't have the power to raise you up. They are not offering you unconditional love. They are just warring with each other, never getting anywhere. Only Light and love can heal your wounds."

"The problem is that I don't have a loving adult on board with me that I can talk to," Michael said.

"That's where your imagination comes into play. I think of imagination as image creation," Francis explained. "Remember, imagination is not something you are making up. It is God coming through to you. When you let your imagination take over, you are raising your frequency. You are coming into those higher realms and matching your frequency with theirs. Eventually, with practice, you will find that you are becoming congruent with your Higher Self."

Gradually, Francis guided Michael toward that part of himself that was so alone and hurting. Michael started crying, little rivulets at first, followed by great, racking sobs. Gently, he asked Michael to give way to his imagination, and he took Michael through a guided meditation so that he could get in touch with his Higher Self. Michael's favorite character was Merlin, and he imagined that he was back in the days of the Knights of the Round Table, in a beautiful cave of hieroglyphs and symbols, among dazzling crystals of light and power.

He was sitting comfortably, talking with Merlin. Merlin was explaining the power of the Maltese Cross to him, training him to be a master alchemist, instructing him in the fine art of precipitation. Hues of brilliant color filled the cave, and as violet light surrounded him, he felt it holding a little wounded boy inside of him. It talked to this little boy in a language all its own, and the little boy was gurgling and laughing as the violet light took on various shapes that delighted the little one. Merlin lifted his hand and pointed the crystal ring on his middle finger toward a far wall of the room. The wall was made of amethyst, and on this wall, scenes from Michael's childhood began to appear. Merlin smiled deftly at Michael, and incandescent violet and pink light poured forth from Merlin's heart, bathing each scene on the screen before him, transmuting it and returning it to Michael's healthy core self in a pristine state.

Michael's pain started to subside, and in its place a wonderful peace bubbled up. Merlin told him the need of the hour was for Michael to realize that this was his universe, his native universe. He showed Michael his essence, a jewel of perpetual elegance, set in a mounting that would be the envy of Guinevere herself. He explained that this jewel was right there in the deepest part of his heart, it was the trinity itself, a three in one, a throne, worthy even of King Arthur. He showed Michael how to rise on the gradations of consciousness ranging from the human to the divine, how to merge with the universal consciousness, how to work the miracle works of the ages. He told him that as the trinity burned above him in the heart of the universe, so it burned below in his own heart. It was God's choicest gift to him, and with it he could work wonders. He told Michael that the true alchemical secret was, "Try!" Merlin told Michael that when he tried, Merlin would always be with him, guiding him up to the heights, transmuting the lead of his human consciousness into pure golden radiance.

Michael slowly came back down, opened his eyes, and smiled at Francis. They discussed his meditation for a while, and then there was another point that Francis wanted to make.

"Many therapists today agree that what we experience in our outer world is a reflection of what is in our inner world. That bicycle crash, for example, was not an accident."

Michael gave him his full attention.

"You are the center of your universe, and just as the planets of our solar system had their origin in the sun, so the planets in your universe had their origin in the sun of your inner consciousness."

"Which planet are you?" Michael asked, half serious. "Wait a minute, you're Pluto, because you are way out there."

Both men chuckled, and Michael was glad that Francis had a sense of humor.

"What I'm getting at is that your psychology attracts these circumstances into your life. Remember, psyche means soul. This is actually a good thing, because it gives you a chance to work out your stuff and come up higher. Your soul could be scattered across the cosmos, and you need to reclaim all of it," Francis continued.

"What we need is a soul round up, pardner!" Michael said, getting enthusiastic. "Rollin, rollin, rollin, keep those soul parts rollin!"

"Decorum, Michael, decorum," Francis admonished.

"Right," Michael said.

"The fact is," Francis explained, "that we are responsible for what is in our worlds, and for the situations in our lives, and when we fail because of them, we must realize we did it to ourselves."

"So what you're saying is that our very consciousness is creative; it's just that we've abused it somewhat," Michael said, seeking confirmation.

"That's right. Where we put our attention is where our energy goes. If you take any good motivational course, they will all tell you if you can visualize your goal, it will have to come into reality eventually. It's a very exciting thing," Francis said.

"My mind is a mess," Michael confessed. "It's a very Western kind of a mind. It's all over the map, wandering all over the place. It's very hard to rein it in."

"Rein it in is exactly what you have to do, and that will happen naturally as you do your work," Francis emphasized.

"Yes. I have to create a new version of myself, you know, release 1.1. I'll lose all this baggage, and they'll start calling me Michael Lite."

"I like that," Francis grinned.

"I have a question for you, Francis," Michael said. "What do you think about that vision that I had of the Moonlight Lady? Right after Mindy called me to ask me if she could come over, I had this vision. What timing! I need to speak to the vision people!"

"As I think about it, I'm getting that it was a girl who hasn't come into your life yet, simply because you need to work out some things first. She's up there, and you're down here. What's above is not quite congruent with what's below. She could be part of your higher inner feminine nature. If you get together with her on the inner level, things will work out on the outer."

Now this did strike a chord with Michael, but it was a deep inner chord, and he needed time for it to sink in. Francis had just given more meaning to his quest, "As above, so below".

"Oscar Wilde said that experience is the name we give to our mistakes," Michael said.

Francis laughed. "I never heard that one!"

"I certainly have a lot of experience!" Michael confirmed. "I'm learning, but it takes time."

"Yes," Francis agreed.

"One more question," Michael said. "Remember that angel I told you about in our earlier sessions, the one that stood in the middle of the road?"

"Yes."

"Why do you think he appeared to me?"

"I think he was there to help you. He knew you were going to face a very challenging time. I think he came to help you through a very difficult transition, to give you strength and hope."

"I see," Michael said. He liked the idea of being helped by an angel.

"For our next session, I'd like to discuss the problem of glamour with you," Francis said. "I'm not talking about glamour in the sense of getting dressed up and looking good. That's fine. I'm talking about illusion. I'm talking about all of the malevolent energy forms created by human desires throughout the history of our planet, and they keep us in a fog. There are any number of them, but in your case there is one which we especially need to work on; the glamour of the outer which conceals the real you. As a start, I'd like you to become a Heart Warrior. It's a men's movement that started around the Steel Man story. Are you game?"

"Tell me when," Michael said enthusiastically.

"There's an opening next weekend," Francis said, giving him the details. He also told Michael that he wanted to follow up with a session on the kind of glamour Michael was struggling with. The session was over, and the two men went their separate ways.

Michael spent the following week studying the Steel Man story. He was eager, and as a result it seemed to him as if the work week would last forever. At last Friday night arrived, and Michael drove out into the Texas countryside, following the directions Francis had given him. When he reached his destination, he spotted a group of men who appeared to be new recruits like himself, and he pulled over and parked. He got his gear together, locked up the car, and sauntered over to the other men. Just as he was about to introduce himself, a booming voice rang out.

"Maintain essential silence!" The warrior in charge of the recruits spoke with authority. It was a command, not a favor. About twenty recruits were all gathered for the Heart Warrior training weekend somewhere in the Texas hill country, and none of them knew what to expect or what was coming. Michael didn't make a sound, and neither did any of the other men.

"Follow me!"

The men gathered up their gear and headed off down a trail into the woods. The sun had set about an hour earlier, and darkness shrouded the forest. They came to a brook, and each man was stopped and asked an essential question by another warrior standing at the bridge that led to the other side. Eventually it was Michael's turn to cross.

"Do you know your life will never be the same if you cross this bridge?"

"Yes," Michael replied.

"Are you ready to cross this bridge?"

"Yes," Michael replied.

"You may enter now."

Michael took an oath that night never to reveal the details of what happened that weekend, and indeed, it was a transforming experience. He became a warrior of the heart, a man intent on having integrity. Heart Warriors were both fierce and harmless, as well as determined to discover the truth about themselves and others. That weekend, Michael learned how to combine his hard driving male energy with his beautiful, feminine, intuitive side. He was aware of the Light and the shadow within himself, and he took on a Heart Warrior name. From that point on, he was known among his new brothers as "Creative Eagle."

Fifteen

The Ultimatum

THE NEXT SEVERAL WEEKS WERE A whirlwind of cleaning, moving, sorting stuff for charity, stuff to be taken and stuff to be thrown out. Twenty-two years' worth of clothes, children's clothes, games, books and puzzles had to be organized. Meg felt pretty defeated as she hopped around on her crutches. Geoffrey was her right hand man as he happily boxed up things that needed to be moved, called the charities to make donations and ordered dumpsters to haul away the leftovers.

Things were going relatively smoothly until a week before the closing. During the mediation sessions that led up to their divorce, Meg and Nick agreed never to let a member of the opposite sex of romantic interest sleep overnight while their daughters were staying under the same roof. As far as Meg knew, both she and Nick were following the agreement until the week before the closing on her house. Meg called Nick's recently built Tudor in Indigo Falls to leave a message. Instead of getting his machine, Barbie Dufo answered. There was lots of noise in the background. Men were talking to each other. Meg wondered what was going on. Rather than try to converse with the always uncooperative Barbie, Meg called Nick and found out that Barbie was moving into his house that afternoon.

Recently Nick had announced their engagement. He claimed that he and Barbie had began dating during the summer of '94, while he and Meg were divorcing. They had not yet chosen a wedding date, and neither showed any enthusiasm for choosing one. Amy had been giving Barbie a hard time. She wondered how long her Dad had been "seeing" Barbie; she wondered when the relationship had really begun. Anyway, when Meg reported to Amy that Barbie had moved into Nick's house, Amy was angry. She refused to move in with Nick unless Barbie moved out or Nick married her.

Since Nick was clearly violating their agreement, Meg called him that night and gave him the message, "Move her out, or marry her." She also informed him that Geoffrey would leave for Denver as scheduled on the third of March, but that she would stay in a hotel with the kids until he moved Barbie out or married her. Knowing that Nick responded only to raw power, she threatened to send the hotel bill to him. He didn't act concerned, so she dug in the trenches for a fight. She spent several days calling around to friends who had coach houses on their property to see if she could rent a coach house, and she began calling hotels and motels for long-term rates.

When Meg reached Julia Reynolds, the mother of one of Amy's friends, she got more information than she had planned on. After Meg asked about the status of her coach house, Julia replied, "Oh Meg, I'm so sorry that I haven't called you. Your divorce sounded like such a mess that I just couldn't confuse my life with it. I can't believe he's claiming that he began dating her during your divorce. We all watched her wiggling her tush around the school in those tight skirts, especially on those nights when Nick had his school board meetings. You knew about the affair, didn't you?"

The next night Nick came over to the house. Meg had invited him to come and take whatever he wanted from the stuff that was left in their basement. Meg heard Geoffrey speaking cordially as he let Nick in the front door, and the two men walked down the basement stairs. Empty boxes were all around the kitchen as Meg packed the pots and pans. After a few minutes it occurred to her that things were too quiet downstairs. She hopped to the top of the stairs and listened. She heard a scuffle, shuffling feet and then a thump. A voice whispering through gritted teeth said, "Handle it. I want her with me when I go." A shadow of the two struggling men wiggled up the stairs. One had the other by the collar, or was it by the neck? She heard a grunt and then saw Nick run up the bottom stairs to the landing and out the side door.

Meg hopped down onto the landing and looked down at Geoffrey. He was in the final stages of straightening out his clothes. "What happened?" she said. "Nick left empty-handed. That's not like him."

"Uh, nothing. Well, I did tell him that he should marry Barbie or move her out. I told him that I wanted you to come with me when I leave. That's all."

By the end of that week, Nick and Barbie were married. Heather reported that Barbie was furious. She had really wanted a big, fancy wedding. The inconvenience of the sudden ceremony was blamed on Meg. The fact that Nick had breached his mediation agreement with Meg was completely overlooked, a conveniently forgotten bit of information. Meg found out about the wedding from Nick's secretary, who said when Meg called her, "Gee, I'm so sorry that you've been left out of the loop. It must have been an oversight."

That night, Meg walked into Heather's room. Amy was sitting on the floor. Heather's chair and dressers were gone. Nick had taken them when he moved out. He was earning $275,000 a year, $40,000 of which went to Meg as child support, but he told Heather that he didn't have the money to buy new furniture. So now the kid had all of her blouses, slacks, nightgowns and underwear folded up in piles on the floor.

"Hi guys," Meg said cheerfully, "Your Dad got married today, so you can move in with him on Monday night. The movers are coming on Monday morning and..."

"We know he got married. He told us," said Heather. "I don't know why you made such a big deal about getting married. It's just a piece of paper."

"It's a lot more than a piece of paper, Heather. When did he tell you he was getting married?"

"Sunday."

Meg paused to absorb Heather's words. She said, "You mean you knew that he was marrying her and you didn't tell me?" She looked at Amy and said, "Amy, I backed you, and you didn't tell me either?"

Heather didn't respond. Amy looked at Heather uneasily but was silent.

"You let me make all of those phone calls to hotels and people with coach houses while knowing that it wasn't necessary?"

Once again, Heather was silent. She looked directly into her mother's eyes and said nothing. There was an ever-so-tiny smile on her lips.

Meg walked into the master bedroom as if in a trance. She went into the master bathroom, closed the door, ran the water in the sink, sat on the floor and cried.

Geoffrey opened the bathroom door and said, "What's the matter, Squeege?"

Meg said while looking up at him in tears, "Here I am calling around to hotels, motels, trying to rent a coach house, and they don't even tell me that their father has arranged to get married.

"Nick and I taught them that abstinence is a good choice for the days of AIDS. Now that Barbie's in the picture, none of that matters. Isn't a father supposed to be a good example for his daughters?

"The bastard promised in mediation that he wouldn't do this. He just blames me and the kids go along with him. They were laughing at me, Geoffrey."

Geoffrey put his hand on her back. "Squeege," he said softly.

"And Barbie, she's more concerned about not having a big, fancy wedding than she is about being a good example to my kids. If I were dealing with someone else's kids, I'd at least try to be a decent role model. Turn on the ten o'clock news. Aren't they telling us that AIDS can kill?"

"Meg," Geoffrey said softly, "your kids are ungrateful and spoiled. Their behavior towards you is totally unacceptable. They get away with it because Nick supports it. He demands it. He never taught them to respect you, so they imitate his treatment of you. Let them live at his level. Let go and move on."

The movers, Jill and Sam, a husband-and-wife team from Indiana, arrived on the morning of March 3rd with the biggest moving van Meg had ever seen. When they first pulled up in front, they were cheerful and introduced themselves politely, but after a "once through" of the house, the husband looked stressed and the wife looked concerned.

Sam was one of those amazing movers who can walk through a house once and know where every stick of furniture and every box will fit on the truck. He stayed out in the truck all day long, directing two boys to retrieve specific pieces of furniture. It was Jill's job to label everything with a number and record the numbers on her clipboard, which she dutifully clung to all day long and into the night. She put it down only to pack a box here and there.

Meg was feeling pretty overwhelmed. She had numbed herself to the grief over the loss of her children. The girls were there packing with their Mom and spent a lot of time carrying things out to the dumpster. They were nice and cooperative and actually seemed sad that Meg was leaving. Geoffrey had ordered two of the largest dumpsters that he could order for a residence. They were filled up by late afternoon. Meg had given away boxes and boxes of toys, clothes, flatware, dishes, books and more to charity, but there was still too much left. It was too cold to have a garage sale, and the truth was that Meg didn't want to have a garage sale. She would have had to greet her neighbors and endure their endless questioning at a time when she simply wanted to cry and have everything be over with.

The day started out with a difficulty that proved to be an omen for the rest of the day. The girls' bathtub was stopped up with black goo that morning as Heather took a shower.

Geoffrey called a plumber who came that morning and added to the chaos. He was a bit odd. He wore a black fedora with soiled jeans, a pink tee shirt and black wingtips. He kept talking to himself as he looked down at his wingtips. Geoffrey, who was trying to pack, acted as if he didn't know what to make of him. He led him upstairs to the bathroom. The plumber looked at the goo.

"Now, how do I do this?" the plumber said.

"I dunno," said Geoffrey in disbelief.

"I'm not talking to you."

"Oh."

"Do you have the right parts?" asked the plumber.

"I don't have any parts," said Geoffrey.

"I'm not talking to you."

"Oh."

"You'll have to rod it out," said the plumber.

"I can't," said Geoffrey impatiently, "I don't have a rodder. That's why I called you."

"Hey, man," said the plumber with a raised voice. "I'm not talking to you. All right?"

"Well, if you're not talking to me, then who are you talking to?" asked Geoffrey.

The plumber ignored Geoffrey, and Geoffrey went downstairs to Meg. "I think the plumber is nuts," he said.

"Oh, uh huh, that's nice," she said as she threw stuff into boxes. Meg was loading three boxes at a time by tossing stuff into the air in the direction of the boxes. Some of it landed in the boxes and some of it didn't. Amy walked by periodically, picked the stuff up off the floor and put it into the boxes.

Heather approached Meg next and said, "Mom, I think there's something wrong with Jill."

Meg stopped chucking stuff into boxes, looked up at Heather and said, "What do you mean?"

"Well, I was upstairs in Amy's room helping her pack, and I heard Jill say to someone, 'Stop following me.' I looked up and saw her turning around as if she was talking to someone in your bedroom."

"Well, maybe one of the moving guys was in my bedroom," suggested Meg.

"No, Mom. I went into your room after she went downstairs and no one was there. I think that she sees things."

Just then, Geoffrey came down the stairs with the plumber, who still had the fedora on.

"Well, thanks a lot for coming so quickly, man," said Geoffrey with a forced smile as he slapped the plumber on the shoulder.

"You have to load the tools in the car," said the plumber.

"No. I don't think so," said Geoffrey and the plumber shot him an impatient look. "Oh, right, never mind. I know, I know, you're not talking to me."

The plumber didn't laugh, but looked back down at his wingtips as he approached the door sill. He came to an abrupt halt, looked up at Meg, lifted his fedora and said, "ma'am" with a nod of his head.

Jill came into the living room and eyeballed everything that was left. "You know," she said, "Sam and I move people every day. They always look stressed. But with you, it's more than that. Do you want to talk about it?"

"Oh," said Meg, hiding the dull pain in her chest. "It's just that my kids aren't going with me. They're staying behind with their father."

"Yeah," she said, "but they're old enough. They'll be fine. It's not as if they're little ones. Don't be so hard on yourself. You'll have plenty to deal with when you get to Denver, so lighten up now." Meg briefly wondered what she meant by "plenty to deal with when you get to Denver."

"Their father's financially responsible, and he's got a wife. They'll be O.K. I'd look out for myself if I were you," continued Jill.

"How do you know all of this?" asked Meg.

"Honey, I'm a little worried about you. When you get to Denver, you need to sit down with Geoffrey. Talk about why you got together in the first place. Light a purple candle and say some prayers. It'll help."

Meg heard Heather open a can of pop in the kitchen and yelled from the living room, "Heather, will you do me a favor and go to

Frederick's? Pick up the cold meat tray I ordered so that we all can make some sandwiches for lunch."

"Sure," said Heather as she went out the side door. One of the movers had taken the door off its hinges and leaned it against the driveway side of the house. As Heather walked by the door, it fell over and hit the driveway, smashing the window and damaging the paint job.

Meg looked out the kitchen window and saw Heather sitting on the curb of the driveway, crying. Geoffrey had gone outside to check on the damage. When he came back into the kitchen he said, "Heather walked by the door and it fell over. She thinks you're gonna be mad at her."

"Geoffrey, I'm not mad at her. I'm just frustrated with this entire situation. I feel as if something is holding us back. I pack and pack and pack, and I'm not getting anywhere."

Geoffrey got on the phone, called the glazier, and Meg paid to have the window repaired. Heather finally came inside the house and Meg asked her if she was O.K.

"Yeah," she sniffed. "Mom, I know you're probably mad at me, but I didn't do anything. I swear I didn't touch that door. I was shocked to hear it hit the ground behind me. It almost hit me and I never touched it. I swear!"

"O.K., O.K. I'm glad you're not hurt. Do you feel good enough to go get the food? We all have to eat, and there's a lot more to do," said Meg wearily. Heather dried her eyes and pulled the car out on the driveway. Just then the phone rang, and Meg answered it.

It was her attorney, Ruth, who had just finished the closing on the house. She gave Meg her report from the closing.

"Meg, I tried to talk Sally out of demanding the money for the roof, but she would not budge. It wasn't her husband who was greedy. It was her. I sat there and talked to the two of them and their attorney. I said, 'Now let's do what's fair. You're getting a great house for an incredibly low price. I think it's only fair that you give Meg a break and swallow the money for the roof.' But your cousin refused."

Meg remembered the scene that happened ten days before the closing. A fierce storm blew out of the northwest, and the flat roof on the back porch leaked. It had never happened before, and she was really surprised because it was a relatively new roof. To be honest, she reported it to her attorney and had the repair appraised for $1,500. She told Ruth that she'd give her cousin the money at the closing if she wanted it. Ruth had said, "Well, she's getting this house at such an incredible discount, I can't imagine that she'd expect you to give her money as well."

Meg listened to Ruth's report, got off the phone, went into the bathroom, turned on the water in the sink, sat on the floor and cried. *If Jane were here,* she thought, *she'd say, 'Girl, what do you expect? She's a white person.'*

"Mom, Mom!" she heard from downstairs. She dried her eyes and ran out of the bathroom. The tone of voice was scary. Meg ran down the stairs and Geoffrey met her at the bottom. Amy had hit her head on the chandelier. She was vacuuming the dining room. With the furniture gone, the chandelier was too low. She ran into the chandelier when Heather arrived home with the food. Meg walked into the dining room and saw Amy sitting on the floor with a nasty blue bump on her forehead. "Are you O.K., Amy?" she asked, wondering if she was going to have to squeeze a trip to the emergency room into her day.

"I don't know. I feel a little funny. I forgot that the lamp was there as I flew at the food."

The house was starting to look pretty empty, so Meg, Geoffrey and Heather started to clean. Meg went up to the master bedroom to vacuum. "We've got to work fast," she said. "They may want to start moving in this evening." Sally hadn't said specifically when they were moving in. Meg thought that most of the move would happen the next day.

She turned around, and standing behind her with clipboard in hand was Jill. "We're all loaded and we're ready to start," she said, looking cheerful. "I didn't think that we'd make it, but it all worked out."

"Oh my God," said Meg, "it's dark outside. What time is it?"

"It's 7:30. We've got to hit the road," said Jill.

"Well, thanks so much, Jill. Thanks for helping us pack when Sam didn't want you to."

"Oh yeah, well, he gets like that. We'll see you in Denver," she said as she walked out the front door. Meg heard the diesel engine fire up, and the semi pulled away. All that was left in the house were odds and ends that she and Geoffrey were bringing in their cars.

"Well, let's clean the kitchen and get out of here," said Meg. Geoffrey was loading the cars. Heather and Amy were helping Geoffrey and looking tired. Meg was cleaning the kitchen sink when her cousin Sally and Dick walked in the front door and straight back into the kitchen.

Sally stood there with an angry face and lashed out, "What are you doing? What's taking you so long? Get out!"

Meg glanced over at Heather and Amy and saw their faces drop with disappointment. "We're cleaning the house for you, Sally," said Meg. "We didn't want you to have to move into a dirty house."

"Just get out," said Sally.

Dick looked down at the floor in embarrassment. Meg turned around and began to ignore Sally. "Heather, will you please take the TV out to the back porch?"

Sally turned and stomped out the front door. Meg and Amy heard people storming around on the front porch. They were carrying boxes and piling them up next to the screens.

"Mom," said Amy, "they're moving in their stuff and we're not even out of here yet."

Meg was more disappointed than she could say. "O.K. guys, no more cleaning. If she wants the house dirty, then she'll get it dirty. Just load the cars, please, and walk through one last time."

The girls walked through the house in which they had spent most of their years. They came out the back door and walked up to Geoffrey and Meg.

"Goodbye, Mom, I love you," said Heather. She put her arms around Meg's neck. "Have a safe trip." Meg thought she heard a small sniffle.

"Goodbye, Heather," said Meg, "I love you too. I'll see you soon. We'll go skiing, O.K.?"

"O.K., Mom," Heather said as she turned to say goodbye to Geoffrey.

"Goodbye, Mom," said Amy, who had tears in her eyes. "I love you. I'll miss you."

"I'll miss you too, honey. I love you. Is your head O.K.?"

"Yeah, I'm fine," she said.

They actually look sad to see us go, thought Meg.

There really wasn't anything else to say. All four of them knew that the months they had spent together had been less than enjoyable. Meg wished that Heather and Amy had behaved this nicely to Geoffrey and her while they had lived together. *Maybe this is for the best,* she thought. *Absence makes the heart grow fonder, or at least, grateful for the absence.*

They waved goodbye as the car backed out of the driveway. Meg felt a giant sense of relief, as well as sorrow that she hid in order to keep on keeping on.

As she watched the car pull down the driveway, she was struck by how mature Heather looked and was reminded of a prompting that she had had when Heather was four days old. Coming home from the hospital with the new baby was an unforgettable event. The labor and birth had been hard. Meg had had some problems with hemorrhaging and was tired. She brought Heather into the baby's room and lay her on the changing table for the first time. As most infants do, Heather began to scream and kick her skinny little legs. Meg's mind wandered away as she changed the diaper. "What a major responsibility this is going to be! How am I going to carry out this role for twenty-one years?" she whispered. Then she got a prompting as she looked down into Heather's eyes. "For only eighteen years, for only eighteen years."

Heather's eighteenth birthday had been on March 1st, and Meg left for Denver on March 3rd. Her life with Heather had indeed been "for only eighteen years."

The car had reached the street and paused. The girls waved one last time and then drove on. Meg had a lump in her throat and an ache in her chest, but she didn't cry. She knew right then that she would never live with them again. The nest was gone as well as the chicks. It was time for her to move on to the next segment of her life, the long tenure of motherhood behind her.

She looked around. The house was empty except for Sally's boxes. The yard was empty. The sky was full of stars. The air was cool and brushed Meg's hair into her eyes. A strange sense of calm came over her, and she decided to go through the house one last time.

She walked up the stairs to the attic and recalled the thousands of nights that she had turned out the downstairs lights and scaled those stairs to go to bed. She had felt a chill as if there was someone behind her, following her up to bed. Most nights she had turned around to look, but no one was ever there. A woman had died in their house years before, but Meg shook that thought away.

The attic was hard to revisit. She saw in her mind's eye little girls with bouncy curls playing with Breezy Bears, Rainbow Glow and Susie dolls. She saw herself sewing Halloween costumes, and don't forget those Easter dresses. She saw the birthday parties and the closets lined with toys. She saw it all through a veil of sadness because Nick didn't love her.

While moving down to the second floor, Meg called to the angels to remove the Light from her home so that she could bring it with her.

"Always do that," Jane had advised. "When you pray in your home you bring Divine Light into it. So when you leave you have the right to bring that Light with you to your new home. Ask the angels to do it for you."

To the left of the stairs was Heather's room. Meg remembered that Heather had shared a room with Amy when they first moved into the house. She was five years old and said, "Mommy, can I have my own room?"

"Well sure, peanut, but you can't move Amy out of this room. That wouldn't be fair to Amy. You have to pick a different room," said Meg.

Meg remembered how she had decorated the room with Heather. Curtains and a matching bedspread were chosen from a catalogue that Heather liked. Meg painted the walls first and then stenciled little pictures of Heather's choosing. She saw school projects all over the floor and the messy bookshelves of a schoolgirl. Meg lingered in the doorway wishing that she could have gotten along better with Heather, but there was a wall between them that she could never scale.

Amy's room was the largest, and Meg saw herself reading to them before bed. Each night she said as she tucked them in, "Goodnight, I love you. See you tomorrow."

The guest room was pretty, but held few good memories. She saw Nick's mother in there laboring for breath. She had died in the early nineties of lung cancer, a few months after visiting them. She saw Nick living in that room during the divorce. There had been a peculiar odor in there during that time. Meg knew it as the stink of treachery.

The master bedroom was the coldest room. The feeling of love was never there. She saw Nick admiring himself in the mirror before they left for one of his firm's parties. Ready to leave, she stood next to him in a new evening dress and shoes, her hair and makeup carefully arranged. She had said, "You look nice, Nick."

"Thanks," he said while he primped, turned and walked down the stairs. Meg left that room quickly, glad to be out of it forever.

The stairs creaked one last time, and she walked down them to the living room. It had been a beautiful room. With dark woodwork, light walls, Chinese rugs and Queen Anne furniture, had Thomas Jefferson walked in the front door he would have felt quite at home. She stared at where the piano had been and heard the girls playing. Their music had brought joy into the unhappy home.

She saw the fireplace where she had sat alone after begging Nick to sit in front of it with her. "Please, just talk to me, sit with me, look me in the eye," she had begged. "Just tell me what I've done to make you hate me and I'll apologize." He had walked up the stairs as he loosened his tie.

The front porch looked pretty ugly now with all of Sally's boxes, but Meg remembered the white whicker furniture with striped cushions. Her plants hung from the tongue-and-groove ceiling. She had paid bills out there, run their home and planned their lives from that porch. The summers were beautiful. She watched the children play in the side yard and made Kool Punch for them and their friends.

Her mind's eye saw her brother and his family, her Mom and her cousin Sally and Dick in the dining room. She really hadn't done a lot of entertaining there. The house had needed a total renovation when they moved in. Most of Meg's time was spent dealing with workmen, but she saw the birthday parties, first Communion parties, holiday dinners and graduation dinners. They were happy times, but Meg had felt a shadow over each occasion. Nick didn't love her.

The family room had the best view in the house, and she saw the kids lying on the couch and watching TV when they were sick. Meg was almost happy when one of them was sick. She loved to take care of sick people. It gave her the chance to be extra loving. When Heather was sick, she didn't reject Meg. It was the only time when Meg was able to feel a little close to her.

The kitchen. Here were too many memories. She saw the girls as babies playing with the pots and pans while she cooked dinner. She saw them having cookies and milk after school and showing her their schoolwork. She had taught them that school was their job; everyone had a job, even them. She saw the dog banished to the kitchen because he had wee-ed on the rug too many times. She saw Nick coming in the back door, walking by her, head down, his real greeting reserved for the girls and the dog.

Meg decided to forego the basement. It had never looked good or smelled good, for that matter. Turning towards the back door to walk through it one last time, Meg heard Geoffrey running up the basement stairs and out the side door. "Hi," he said nervously, his face pale as he met her on the driveway. "Are you ready to go? Let's get out of here, Squeege. C'mon, let's go."

Meg looked at the garage and saw, in her mind's eye, Amy shooting baskets. She had given up the piano and the clarinet for basketball. Meg saw her cousins from Pittsburgh shooting with her as well as the neighborhood kids. She saw Nick washing the cars and changing the tires on Thanksgiving morning while he drank champagne. It gave him an excuse to avoid her.

"Squeege," Geoffrey said sharply to rouse Meg from her reverie.

"What?" she said, feeling edgy.

"We've gotta go. We have to keep up with the truck. We have to be there when it arrives."

Just then a car pulled into the driveway. Meg didn't recognize it. As it pulled forward towards the garage light she saw it was Jeanne, her astrology teacher.

"Jeanne," she said, "I can't believe you're here."

"Oh Lord, I'm so glad I didn't miss you. I need to talk to you before you go," she said breathlessly. "I've got all of these names for you. Astrologers in Denver. I have so many friends out there. I've thought of moving there so many times myself," she said. "But, more importantly..." Jeanne looked up and saw Geoffrey. Her face dropped.

Geoffrey stepped forward and held out his hand. "Hi," he said with his salesman's voice. "I'm Geoffrey."

"Yes, it's nice to meet you," Jeanne said with a voice that sounded as if it wasn't nice for her to meet him.

Jeanne reached over and gave Meg a hug. She whispered in Meg's ear, "Listen, lady, please take care of yourself. We'll be praying for you."

Jeanne stepped back and looked at Meg. "I'm sorry we missed you at class the last few weeks. We wanted to talk to you. But I know you've been busy. Keep in touch. Please?"

"Sure, Jeanne. Please say goodbye to Bernard for me. Give him my love."

"Oh, I will and Geoffrey, you take care of this special lady for me," she said as she winked.

"No problem," was Geoffrey's response. Jeanne did a double-take and got in her car.

She backed her car out of the driveway. Geoffrey pulled out next. Meg left last and paused to look at her house in the moonlight. "That house never did have any curb appeal," she mused.

She recalled the prompting received in Howard peak's office two years before, "You'll be leaving Chicago in two years, February, '97."

"*Almost to the day*," she thought. Her body relaxed as she accepted her new sense of freedom.

Something caught Meg's eye over to her right, over at her neighbor's house. It was the silhouette of her crazy neighbor, Nancy, standing in the window, still trapped by the suburbs, her marriage and motherhood. Another step forward and Meg saw her pale face in the moonlight. Her eyes were full of envy as Meg drove away.

Two and a half days of driving brought Meg and Geoffrey to Colorado. Great weather was a given, and the mountains were awesome, a gift to Meg's peace of mind. She pulled into a gas station to gawk at them, and Geoffrey followed. "I just had to stop so that I could take in that view," she said reverently.

"You're entitled," said Geoffrey, "after living in scenic Chicago for twenty-two years. I'll be shaking the dust from that town off my feet for a long time coming." He breathed deeply and smiled.

Meg felt lighter. Nick's heavy energy of hatred was gone. *After all,* she thought, *he's got custody and no maintenance and child support payments. He should be feeling pretty victorious about now.*

They met Jill and Sam at the house they were renting in Huntersville, a suburb north of Denver, unloaded one-third of the truck into the house and the other two-thirds into storage. When the job was done, they all sat in the dining area and Meg asked them if they'd like something to drink. "No thanks," said Jill. She turned to Sam. "Should I tell them now?" she asked Sam.

"Guess so," said Sam as he shrugged his considerable shoulders and smiled.

"I have psychic abilities," she said. "It's good that you guys left Barnstable because if you hadn't, you would have been separated and on the way to a divorce in three months."

"Oh no, no," said Geoffrey. "That wouldn't have happened. It will never happen."

"Well, I'm telling you that that is what I saw. I also saw a spirit in your house," she said, looking at Meg. "And she didn't want you to leave. She dearly loved you, Meg, as if you were her own daughter. She has seen all that you've gone through and clearly pitied you for it. She saw the love in you and knew that you were sincerely trying to make things work with your children. She was glad Nick was gone, but..."

Jill turned to Geoffrey and said, "She did not trust you or your motives and resented the fact that you were taking Meg away. That's why there were so many problems with the house on moving day. She was trying to prevent your departure. The tub, the side door, the chandelier, all of it was meant to prevent your leaving. She really didn't want Meg to go."

"What did the spirit look like?" asked Meg, who was totally engrossed.

"A little old lady. Gray hair in a bun. Long dress," said Jill. "She was following me around during the move and finally, I had to tell her to stop following me. She was drivin' me nuts. I was there to do a job, and she was trying to mess me up so that you couldn't go. She was very, very upset. Meg, she loved you. She was a mother once, too. That was the connection. She understood you and felt your sorrow."

"The lady who died in the house," Meg said. They all looked at her curiously. "Every night as I turned out the lights to go to bed I felt her presence. Her son stopped by one day to see the house. He was old, late seventies or early eighties, and it felt as if he was preparing to die. He wanted to see the place one last time.

"I spent the better part of a morning with him giving me touching stories about things that had taken place in each room of the house. It was all very poignant. He said his mother had died of a broken heart. His father had never really loved her, or so she believed."

Geoffrey looked embarrassed and said, "Before we left the house, I went back into the basement to go to the bathroom. I felt something cold around my neck. I got out of there as fast as I could. Why did she hate me so much?"

Jill was silent and closed her eyes. "All I'm getting is that she believed that your motives weren't pure. She hated you for what you were doing to Meg." Jill took a step back and changed the subject. "Anyway, I think you guys need to light a purple candle and think about what brought you together and say some prayers. You need to do this." She looked at Meg nervously.

"It's time to go, Jill," Sam said, impatient to get back on the road. Meg had given him their check for a job well done. They got into their truck and honked the horn.

The noise of the diesel engine almost drowned out her final warning. "Take care, Meg."

The next week, Meg started job hunting and Geoffrey began his new job. It didn't take long for frustration to set in. It all worked out as she had feared. Each night after work Geoffrey complained about his job, how he wasn't appreciated, the job was beneath him, they weren't doing things right. He had actually walked into the office of the President and told him that he wanted to buy the company.

"You did what?" asked Meg.

"I told him that I wanted to buy the company. He's not running it right. If I was in charge it would be a success," said Geoffrey, shoulders back and acting cocky.

"With what are you going to buy this company?"

"I thought that you would buy it for me."

"You're out of your mind."

Geoffrey shot her an angry look. "I'm serious."

"So am I," she said. "I guess it's safe to assume that you're no longer employed."

Geoffrey looked away.

Since her arrival in Denver, Meg had felt many promptings, each saying, "You're not going to use me any more. You're not going to use me again." Old resentments rose to the surface, feelings that she had never felt before. They were coming more and more frequently and with greater intensity each time. With this apprehension came an inner knowing that, with Heather and Amy out of the picture, it was time for her to wrangle with Geoffrey and their mutual karma. Her intuition told her that these feelings were a bit extreme, inexplicable. She felt more upset than she needed to, considering the circumstances. "This is old stuff," she mused, "from another life."

"Why can't you just have a job, Geoffrey? Why do you always have to be the big cheese? You want your wife to buy the company for you so that you can become the President overnight." She paused and turned slowly towards him saying, "Tell me, Geoffrey, what are you gonna do when my money runs out?"

Geoffrey looked uncomfortable, but Meg was on a roll. She was exasperated. Geoffrey didn't answer the question, so Meg continued. "I gave up my alimony to marry you and now I've given up my children and child support to come to a new town where you could have a new start and here you are as inert as you were in Chicago."

"Why don't you get a job?" he asked defiantly. In the past his arrogance had taken her aback, but not any more. She lunged back with everything she had.

"I'm working on it, Geoffrey, but you don't get it, do you? I'm carrying my own weight. I'm paying all of our bills from my divorce settlement, and I have a husband who's a gigolo. The spotlight is on you. You're the one who has to justify his existence. A marriage is a partnership and each person contributes. As I see it, Geoffrey, when the bills arrive, I'm the only one who steps up to the plate.

"Oh, and, by the way, I've looked at the online bank statements and noticed that you're paying your bills twice each month. How did you get my PIN number? I pay my credit cards once a month. How come you get to pay yours twice a month with MY money? And I'm not just talking about Visa. I'm talking about your mortgage. Why are you paying your mortgage two times each month with MY money?"

There was no response from Geoffrey. He had been exposed and looked uneasy.

"Get a job!" she yelled in frustration.

With that, Geoffrey shifted into the worst of his shadow self. He pitched his coffee mug against the tile floor and screamed, "I'm so goddam sick of people telling me to get a job. That's all they ever talk about. My mother does it. My brothers do it. My mother's accountant even does it. As if it's any of her business. Who does she think she is, anyway? I'm tired of taking their crap. She always got her husbands to throw me out of the house because she wanted me to get a job. 'Get a job,' they'd say. She was too much of a chicken to tell me herself. Why should I work? Someday I'll be a millionaire. When they're dead I'll get my share. I'll be a millionaire and then nobody can ever tell me to get a job again." Geoffrey was walking back and forth across the living room, nostrils flaring.

Another woman would have backed off. Another woman would have been scared out of her wits to see Mr. Hyde in her living room. Not Meg. She pushed things to the limit. "They wanted you to get a job because they're tired of being used. I know how they feel."

The shards of the broken mug were lying at Geoffrey's feet. It was all too convenient for him to bend over and pick up the sharpest one. Grabbing it tightly he moved towards her. His face was altered. A feeling of deja vu came to her. She had seen those eyes before and knew he could slit her throat without regret. She saw herself in her mind's eye, wearing a long white dress. Her hair was straight and black, reaching down to her waist. The sun was hot against her olive skin and she could smell the Mediterranean.

"No," she screamed as she blocked him with her arm.

He held the point of the shard to her neck and said with gritted teeth, "Don't tell me to get a job again. This is the last time we will ever discuss my getting a job."

Sixteen

Taylor Knows Best

MICHAEL FOLLOWED UP the Heart Warrior weekend with several group integration sessions, and he felt himself getting stronger. He went on an all-out job search, and landed a good position with a leading PC manufacturer in Houston. It was challenging, and there were long hours, but he was making it happen.

This is more like it, he thought to himself, enjoying a Sunday afternoon on the back porch of his townhouse. *I am movin' on up.*

The phone rang, and he reached over and answered it. "This is Michael."

"Hi Michael!" It was his big sister Taylor, calling from her home in Rocky Park.

"Taylor! I haven't heard from you in a while."

"I've been pretty busy helping Logan at the office. I have no social life to speak of," she explained, sounding exasperated.

"I bet being married to a tax accountant has its challenges," Michael said.

"I work harder than he does, I swear," Taylor said. "I don't know what he would do without me there to keep him organized. Next thing you know I'll be doing the 1040s with him."

"Right," Michael said, not wanting to sound too sarcastic. "Just make sure not to tell him how to do the returns." Logan was Taylor's third husband, and Michael was hoping she had learned to be a little less controlling after the first two debacles.

"He needs my advice," Taylor said, not sounding fazed by Michael's remarks.

"Taylor," Michael said, "he's the one with the tax degree."

"He never would have used it if it weren't for me," Taylor said with a chilling tone. "He'd still be helping all those bums who can't afford a good tax man."

"So what's up?" Michael said, realizing he was talking to a brick wall.

"Since I need a break, I'm going to host Camp Taylor at my house here in Rocky Park, and you are invited!"

"Camp Taylor?"

"A four-day fun and festive family get-together."

"When?"

"Next week, so you'll have to get time off from work. It'll be Thursday through Sunday. I've already talked to Arnold, and he wants to come. Logan's daughter and her friends will be there, and a friend of mine from Atlanta is coming. I met her at a spiritual retreat there."

"Wow, Taylor, this is short notice. I have my next session with Francis on that Saturday."

"Skip it. You've been going to him long enough already. What more can he tell you?"

"He wants to explain a few things about glamour to me that he thinks are very important," Michael said.

"Glamour? I can tell you all about glamour. I was an actress in New York, remember? Come on Michael, it'll be fun. Just reschedule Francis."

"I suppose I could reschedule," Michael said, yearning for the Rocky Mountains. "But I'll have to get approval at work for the time off, and I'll have to make sure there are still some available flights."

"I have faith in you. You can do it," Taylor said.

Michael asked Francis' secretary to reschedule, got the time off from work and the flights that he wanted, and on Thursday night of the following week he arrived just in time for dinner. Taylor escorted him in, and when all were assembled at the dining table, there was a blonde babe seated next to him. It began to dawn on him that this was the friend. There she was, looking somewhat lost and shy.

Taylor came over to make the introductions. "Michael, this is Misty Lee. We met in Atlanta at a spiritual retreat."

"Nice to meet you, Misty Lee," he gushed. "Are you from Atlanta?"

She looked at him innocently and somewhat helplessly, as if she needed him to help her out in these strange surroundings. "Yes, but when I got divorced I moved to New Orleans with my daughter," she said. Misty was about 5 feet 10 inches tall, with long, wavy, strawberry blond hair and deep green eyes, and she had a body that made Michael gawk.

"Is this your first trip to the Rockies?" Michael asked.

"Yes, and I just can't get over how beautiful they are. I can't stop staring! Taylor tells me you have actually ridden a bicycle to the top of them."

"Well, not to the top of all of them, but a few of them, yes. My last big ride was from Ouray to Durango, which included three mountain passes." Michael resisted telling her how high and difficult they were.

"Ouray?"

"The town of Ouray is named after an Indian chief. You can see some of the most beautiful alpine scenery in the world out there, and when you're on a bike, you can really get up close to it. Do you ride?"

"Oh, no. It's too scary for me! You don't even have fenders on your bike, and those tires are so skinny. My favorite sport is sailing."

Michael wasn't imagining how to get her off the boat and on the bike. It didn't faze him that she wasn't into cycling. He was dressing up the storefront, putting his best foot forward and trying not to let the other one follow.

"Well, it does get pretty hairy out there at times," he said, almost apologetically. He was already wishing that dinner was over, so that he could take Misty Lee for a walk. *Walking is not too scary,* he thought.

"I've seen how cyclists ride in single file, and I don't see how they keep from running over each other. I like being on the water where I can relax."

"What kind of sailing do you do?" Michael asked, steering the conversation in her direction. He felt compelled to be the gentleman.

Misty launched into a description of her sailing club back in New Orleans. As she talked on and on, Michael listened attentively, nodding politely at all the right moments.

After dinner, Camp Taylor started to get into full swing as all the siblings gathered in the den to reminisce. Michael was glad that they were all keeping it light and not getting into any memories that would reveal to Misty Lee how abusive his childhood had been. Still, he felt uncomfortable, and he felt the pain of his childhood as he watched his two siblings together. He was there in the den physically, but his soul was somewhere else. Finally, the evening wound down, and it was time to hit the hay.

"We're having a picnic at the lake tomorrow!" Taylor explained. "The girls are going to learn sailboarding, and we can swim, canoe or do whatever."

"Where should I sleep?" Michael asked.

"You can sleep on the living room sofa," Taylor directed. "Arnold already has dibs on the sleeper sofa in the den. The girls can sleep upstairs in the guest bedroom."

Michael retired to the living room as Taylor directed, but he didn't mind being relegated to the living room sofa, because he was somewhat Misty-fied.

He was awakened the next morning by a gentle tug on his big toe. He opened his eyes, and there was Misty Lee, looking back over her shoulder and smiling childishly at him as she walked out the front door. She and the other girls were in their swimsuits, heading over to the lake for a day of fun and frolic.

Wow! Michael thought. *She pulled my big toe. This is great. This is a sign! I'm in!*

He jumped off the sofa and got dressed quickly. When he arrived at the lake, the girls were out there sailboarding, all except for Misty Lee. She was paddling a little inflatable boat all by herself, and it looked to Michael as if it was a boat that was built for two.

O.K., Michael thought. *This is a tough one.*

"Ahoy Misty Lee! How about taking me for a tour of the lake?"

"Why, it would be my pleasure," she drawled.

She paddled over to the shore, and Michael got in carefully, not wanting to capsize their little nutshell. They had to pull their legs up so that they could both fit in, and they sat facing each other, their feet touching.

"Take me out, Scotty!" Michael said.

Misty paddled them away from shore, and then it was just the two of them, surrounded by the water and the craggy peaks of the Rockies.

"Do you like it out West?" Michael asked.

"Oh, yes," Misty said. "I've lived in the South all my life, and I feel free out here."

"Yeah, I know what you mean," Michael said. "I grew up in Texas, and this is worlds away from there."

"What's it like in Texas?"

"Texas is a unique kind of place. Ya might get ambushed outside the saloon, so ya gotta pack yer six shooter. Ya gotta look out for rustlers who wanna steal yer cattle. Ya..."

"What's it really like, Michael? What is it like for you?" Misty asked in a low, serious tone.

"It's stagnant," Michael said, meeting her gaze.

"That's how I feel in New Orleans," Misty said. "I moved there from Atlanta because everybody there knows my family tree and my history. I want to be somebody different than the person they think I'm supposed to be. I thought that New Orleans would be far enough away, but it isn't."

"Womb to tomb," Michael said.

"That's right," Misty said, smiling. "Just like South Side Story, accent on South. There's a place for me, but it's not down there anymore."

"Is that why you went to that spiritual retreat?" Michael asked.

"Yes, I was searching. I don't want to speak for the whole South, but religion is set in stone in my neck of the woods. People want you to think the way they do, and if you don't, look out."

"I know the type," Michael said. "And then there are those who go to church and pretend to be holy. The ones with the perfect public image and the secret agenda."

"I know the type," Misty concurred. "They are everywhere, and there is a lot more behind the façade than most people would believe."

"It's got to come out at some point," Michael went on. "But I try not to focus my attention on it too much. Religion means "re-tie," and I think that it came about because we lost our original contact with Spirit. That point of contact is the three-fold flame in our hearts. That's where the living church is. All those heart flames burning on the altar of everyone's hearts comprise the real church, and when we all get connected, the world will change."

"Yes," she said, excited that Michael was on the same spiritual page. "I've read that too. We are all one."

"Yeah, you don't need an organization to belong to or a building to go into, in order to talk to God. He's right in your heart. Since we lost the connection, we need lots of different religions because different people have different needs. I respect the good that these religions are doing for people to get them back to their hearts, whether it's Judaism, Buddhism or 'whatever-ism.' The problem is the original tenets of many religions have been tampered with, and false doctrines have been introduced."

"I know," said Misty. "I've heard the doctrine of reincarnation was taken out of Christianity, for example. Jesus taught reincarnation. He also taught what he did, you can do. The Christ he realized can be realized by you, too."

"Right. People are discovering the truth in this age, and they are climbing up the mountain on their own path. When they get to the top, nobody cares what path they took to get there. The view is the same. The main thing is to keep climbing and not stumble over too much dogma. You know, trail poop. Walk humble and don't stumble, and you'll make it up in spite of your dogma."

"Trail poop!" Misty laughed. "You do have a way with words, Michael."

"Two steps forward, one step back, and hot chow on the high ground," Michael said.

"Hot chow!" Misty laughed. "I like that part. There's a reward there, and that reminds me of abundance. Practicing spirituality can lead you to abundance, you know," Misty said.

"Good point," Michael said. "Spirituality is about being who you really are, and that means becoming empowered. As you become who you are, and as you discover the right use of spiritual law, abundance can flow to you. If you can visualize it, you can manifest it."

Misty looked out at the mountains and sighed. "I wish I had known that when I was growing up. You can sure get yourself into a tangle when you're starting out and you don't know much."

"How true," Michael said, thinking back to Aspen. "When I first came to Colorado, I had a bad LSD trip, and it took me years to recover. I'm still trying to get to where I would have been had I not done that."

Misty gave him a look of compassion. "Don't beat yourself up over it, Michael. Give yourself credit for climbing out of it and not giving up. Let me tell ya, I've made some pretty big bloopers myself!"

"Such as?" Michael asked.

"Ask me when I know you better," Misty said, giving him a sly grin.

Michael smiled back at her, knowing that he shouldn't pursue that one any further for now. "So tell me about your daughter," he asked.

"Ahh, my little snookums," Misty said affectionately. "Her name is Amanda. She's in high school back in New Orleans. I think she'd like to go to Tulane when she graduates, but I'd like her to see what the West is like before she makes that decision final. I asked her to come out to Camp Taylor with me, but she wanted to stay in town with her friends."

"At her age, fitting in with the right crowd is everything," Michael said. "I was the same way."

"Me too," Misty said. "I let my high school friends lead me down the wrong road, I'm afraid. I always wanted to be with the big man on campus."

Michael told her about some of his high school escapades, and as they compared notes, he began to feel a bond forming between them.

"What do you do back in New Orleans?" Michael asked.

"I started out as an actress, but lately I've become more interested in broadcast news. I think the ideal thing for me would be photography, and I've started taking courses back in New Orleans. I've even looked at some colleges out West. University of Colorado has a very good broadcast news program. It would be so wonderful to go to school out there."

"It's nice to have dreams," Michael said.

"How about you, Michael? How do you make your way in this world?"

"I started out my career at NASA, but after eight years, I hung up my spurs and got into the private sector with a leading PC manufacturer."

"Wow! NASA! I want to hear more about that when we have more time."

"More time?" Michael said, looking puzzled.

"Right now it's time for a swim," she shouted as she jumped out of the boat and turned it over.

Michael went into the water backwards, and when he came up for air, Misty was swimming as fast as she could for shore. Michael caught her as the water got shallow enough to stand up in, and he grabbed her around the waist.

"Take a deep breath, Misty!" he said, pushing her under.

She came up grinning, and promptly splashed water in Michael's face. Michael shook it off and an all-out water fight ensued. Misty ran for shore, and Michael bounded after her. When he caught up with her, he reached for her arm, spun her around, and drew her to him. He looked passionately into her eyes, and then softly, gently, he kissed her.

They spent the rest of Camp Taylor together, and when the weekend was over, Michael drove Misty to the Denver airport. Taylor had picked her up when she flew in, and since her flight was leaving two hours earlier than Michael's, the timing was good.

"Michael," Misty said as they waited by the gate. "Have you ever heard of Chastain Park?"

"No, I haven't."

"It's in Atlanta. I'm going to visit a friend there. I've got two tickets to a Van Cliburn concert there on Saturday, two weeks from now. Do you like classical music?"

"Yes, when I'm not cycling, I play classical guitar."

"Michael, that's wonderful! You didn't tell me that!"

"Yes, I love to play. After working with computers all day, I feel weary. It's all left-brain stuff. I need to get into my right brain. I need to put some rhythm into my life."

"Michael," Misty said, looking a little sheepish. "Would you like to go with me? Can you come out to Atlanta the weekend after next?"

"Yes, Misty, I'd like that. I'd like that very much."

Michael got home late that night, still feeling quite Misty-fied. When he checked his phone messages, there was one from Francis' secretary, telling him that they could squeeze him in on a Saturday, the same Saturday that he was supposed to be in Atlanta. Michael called back and left another message, telling her to cancel. He explained that his schedule was hectic, and that he would reschedule as soon as he could.

The following week Michael received a large packet in the mail, and inside he discovered a complete portfolio of Misty Lee's acting gigs.

"Whoa!" he shouted, pulling out a particular juicy shot of Misty on the beach. She was in her bikini, reclining gracefully on the deck of a sailboat that had been pulled up on the sand.

"Oh yes!" he shouted again, admiring a scene of her frolicking in a water fall.

He went through them all with gusto, and promptly went about framing them and putting them all around the house.

"I am Misty-fied!" he exclaimed. He let out a series of Simian ape grunts.

He continued walking all around the house, munching on his favorite frozen dinner, and gawking at all the photos. When the phone rang, he leaped across the room and caught it on the first ring.

"Hello?" he said, somehow managing to sound composed.

"Hey, big guy!"

"Hi Misty! I got your pictures! Very professional," Michael said, staying low key.

"The lady who shoots most of my sessions is a good friend of mine," Misty said. "She's invited us to stay with her when we're in Atlanta, and she wants to take some pictures of the both of us."

"Misty, I wish I could get on that plane tonight! How am I going to wait two weeks to see you?"

"I feel the same way, Michael!"

"I'm staring at the photo of you on the boat," Michael said, his pulse quickening.

"How do you feel when you look at me, Michael? I want to know how you feel!"

Thus began the long distance romance. All through the fall, it was Michael in Atlanta with Misty, Misty in Houston with Michael, Michael in New Orleans with Misty, Misty strolling on the beach in Galveston with Michael. As Christmas approached, Michael's big sister Taylor felt the need once more to bring the clan together. Michael was at his townhouse when Taylor called him with the news.

"Hello, this is Michael."

"Michael! What have you been doing all fall?" Taylor demanded. "I haven't heard from you since last August!"

"I've been somewhat preoccupied," Michael explained.

"You haven't even called me! Have you been spending all your time with Misty?"

"Taylor, don't get miffed. Sisters just naturally take a back seat to girlfriends."

"You could have at least called," Taylor insisted.

Michael held the phone away from his ear for a moment, feeling exasperated. He quickly regained his composure and replied as politely as he could. "Aren't you coming to town for Christmas?" he asked.

"That's why I'm calling. I want everybody, spouses, girlfriends, boyfriends or whatever to come skiing up here this Christmas. I've got a townhouse reserved at Beaver Creek. It's huge, and there's room for everyone, even you and Misty."

"Camp Taylor II, huh? How much is this going to cost?" Michael asked.

"Don't worry about the cost, I've got that all worked out. It's a package deal, and I'll be sending everyone their share of the bill. We can save money on meals by cooking at the townhouse. Each couple can have their night to cook for everyone else. That should help you and Misty recoup some of the money you've been spending traveling back and forth all the time."

"Taylor, this is a little presumptuous of you. Misty and I could already have made plans. Besides, I don't have any ski clothes, and I've only been skiing once in my life. That was when I broke my skis, remember?"

"I've got some skiing lessons lined up for you, and you can borrow some of Logan's ski clothes. All you have to do is rent your boots, skis and poles at a shop here in Rocky Park. Listen, Michael, if you're getting serious about Misty, then you guys should take some time for the rest of the family. Think about it."

"O.K., Taylor, don't have a meltdown. I'll talk to Misty."

"Now you sound like the Michael I've always known," Taylor said. "After all, you're the only baby brother I've got."

"O.K., Taylor," Michael said, trying not to let Taylor grate on his nerves. "Send me the details."

When it was time for Camp Taylor II, the clan arrived at Taylor's house to get organized. Taylor briefed everyone on "the plan." She decided who was taking which car, who was staying in which room, and who was cooking on which night. They all left on time for Beaver Creek, but a snow storm was blowing through Vail Valley that night, and Michael and Misty were the last to arrive. Michael was driving, and he had never seen a whiteout before. To compensate for his lack of experience driving on snow and ice, he crawled all the way from Rocky Park to Beaver Creek. He and Misty arrived late for dinner, and it was Taylor's night to cook.

"I saved you guys a couple of plates," she said as they walked in, staring daggers at Michael.

The next morning Misty and Michael were the last to arrive at breakfast, which Michael considered to be O.K., because everyone was on their own for breakfast.

"Misty," Michael whispered with a sly grin. "Has Taylor said hello to you this morning?"

"No," she replied, standing closer to him so that she wouldn't be overheard. "Has she said hello to you?"

"No!" he answered in mock despair.

"Oops!" they said in unison, laughing under their breath.

Michael spent the first day on the bunny slopes after a brief morning lesson, and Misty came along to give him encouragement and to videotape his spectacular falls. That night, they lingered in the hot tub, and once again, they were late for dinner. The pattern of "late for breakfast" and "late for dinner" continued throughout Camp Taylor

II, and even though Taylor looked miffed, she didn't say anything. When the fun and frolic was over, and everybody parted, she still didn't say anything. It wasn't until Michael arrived back home that he heard about it.

"Hello, this is Michael," he said, answering his phone late Sunday night.

"Michael, this is Taylor." She didn't sound the least bit pleasant.

"Hello, Taylor," Michael said amicably. "Are you calling to make sure I got home safely?"

"I've got something to tell you about Misty," she said.

"What might that be?"

"She sent me some pictures this fall," Taylor began.

"How nice," Michael said. "She sent me some, too. She is a fox."

"I have one of her walking arm in arm with another guy in Jackson Square in New Orleans, and another one of her with the same guy on Bourbon Street. Both of these are on the same day."

"Just when was that, Taylor?"

"The weekend after you were there."

"Then it was probably a photo shoot that she was doing."

"That was no photo shoot, Michael. And you want to know what else?"

"Do go on," Michael said sarcastically.

"Logan handled her divorce. You know why her husband divorced her? She was having affairs. She is violent. She has a temper that goes out of control. Her husband had to lock himself in the bathroom to get away from her, and she broke the door down. He wasn't her first husband, either. She got married the first time when she was only fifteen years old."

"Then why did you introduce me to her?" Michael demanded.

"I thought she had changed. But when I saw that picture of her..."

"You know what, Taylor? I don't want to hear it!" Michael said, slamming down the phone.

Seventeen

Jail Bird

THE SOUND OF Geoffrey's shower beating against the stall brought Meg back to reality. Seconds earlier, she had felt him pull the shard away from her throat. He strolled into the bathroom. *Breathe,* she thought. *Get the necessities. Hurry!*

Her backpack was rolled up on the top shelf of the closet. She began to stuff it with toiletries, clothes and her laptop. Her pea coat was the quickest thing to throw on as she ran out the door with pocketbook swinging from her elbow. The objective was to get out of there before his five-minute shower was up. She didn't relax until she heard the car doors lock in unison. It had snowed the night before, but the accumulation was already melting into ribbons of steam rising from the tarmac. Her frenzy blocked the realization that her bare toes were treading in slush.

Traffic was crazy, and Meg felt very much a part of the craziness. Jane's apartment was only a few miles away, but she was terrified that Geoffrey was following her. Constantly checking the rear-view mirror, her shaking hands gripped the wheel tightly, leaving marks in her palms from her fingernails. She pulled into the parking lot and ran up the three flights of stairs, believing the whole time that he was on her tail.

"Girl, what are you doing here?" asked Jane. She was in her terry robe and slippers and sat down at the table looking at Meg with concern. "My God, you don't have shoes on," she said. "Do you know that you don't have shoes on?"

"Oh," was all that Meg could say. She stared at her feet and realized that she was more upset than she knew. "I had to get out of there, or he was gonna kill me." Her voice cracked as her eyes grew moist. "I thought he was going to slit my throat. Can I stay here with you?"

"Sure," said Jane. "I've got an air mattress that you can use."

For the next three days Geoffrey kept calling Jane's asking for Meg, begging her to come back home. Meg refused. On the fourth day, he called and promised to get a job. "I've also got good news," he said. "The Armenians have moved out of my house!"

His news erased all memories of the shard at her throat. Before the day was over, at Meg's insistence, Geoffrey was on a plane to California to regain possession of his house. "Because if you don't go back out there," she said, "Gilberto will move back in and you'll have another squatter in there. We'll be back at the beginning of the game again." Her parting words to Geoffrey were, "Don't use my credit cards while you're in California. You're paying for this trip." There was no reaction on his face when he heard her words.

The next morning, Geoffrey called from his home in Cielo. His voice whined into the phone, "I can't even get groceries. I need a car. I've got to be able to buy groceries. And I need Conor. Last night I heard people outside walking around. I brought my gun and I've got a baseball bat, but I still would like to have the dog. He would keep Gilberto away."

"Geoffrey," Meg said excitedly. "Do you know what this means? It means that we've won. It's a victory. We have your house back. No more squatters. Now we can clean the place and really sell it without Kristy chasing away the buyers. I'm coming out. I can stay for three weeks until my kids come to Colorado to ski. I'll bring Conor."

"Great. You should see this house, Meg. It's a mess. The rugs are filthy, and there's black wax all over the bathrooms. I think Kristy was into burning black candles while she bathed. Oh, and all of the kitchen appliances have been pulled away from the walls. I think they were going to come back and take them with them or give them to Gilberto. And Meg, I really can't wait 'till you get here."

Meg wasn't worried about the trip ahead of her. She loved to drive alone. The hours sped by as she engaged in behind-the-wheel meditation. Driving through the Great Salt Lake Desert was as close to a spiritual experience as she had had in months. As far as the eye could see, there was nothing but dry, cracked ground and scruffy plants. She was too far north for the big cacti that she had seen in pictures, but this was truly a desert. Alone with her thoughts and the silence, she heard her still, small voice repeating, "For only a short time."

Conor slept in the back seat while Meg set up some short term goals. *I have to get rid of that house,* she thought. *Then my good credit will survive.*

Geoffrey's house was a disappointment. His description of it had been palatial, but Meg saw only a poor construction job with cheap windows and even cheaper stucco. The tile roof actually looked like plastic. The inside looked better than the outside, at least. As she toured it for the first time, she realized that every room had an entry door to the outside.

"Geoffrey," she said, perplexed. "Why does each room have an entry door?"

"So that I can leave in a hurry from any room," he said as he read his mail.

"Why are you concerned about leaving in a hurry?"

"Huh? Did I say 'in a hurry'?" he asked as he looked up. "Oh, Squeege, I misspoke. My mind was elsewhere. Uh, I just like the idea of being able to leave from any room."

"Yes, but now you have to worry about Gilberto breaking in through any room," she said.

"Now that Conor's here, he won't come near the place."

In spite of his cavalier attitude, each night Geoffrey went through every room of the house with his pistol and a baseball bat. He opened each closet and entry door and went around the outside with Conor before he could relax enough to go to sleep.

Marnie, the realtor, was thrilled that Geoffrey was in possession once again and was all set to dig in and pull the best buyer out of her hat. It didn't take her long, either. Geoffrey and Meg cleaned the house, and Marnie showed it the next day. A young entrepreneur, who could have showed Geoffrey a thing or two about working hard, fell in love with the place and was ready to close ASAP.

Geoffrey's Mom recommended the law firm that she had always dealt with, and a young Indian associate who went by the name of Raji, short for Rajalaxmi, was assigned to Geoffrey's case. A retainer of $1,000 was necessary to get the ball rolling. Meg was so happy to see the light at the end of the tunnel that she told Geoffrey to write the check on the spot.

Raji was friendly and competent. Best of all, she was young, energetic and determined to impress the partners in her firm. When Geoffrey told her about Gilberto and his claims to ownership, she was unimpressed. "If he didn't live up to the lease option agreement, then he doesn't have a prayer," she said.

"This is great," Geoffrey screamed with joy as he walked out of the law office. "One minority against another. I love it! If Gilberto starts to whine about discrimination, my Indian lawyer will nail him. After all, if I was the kind of creep who discriminates, why would I hire an Indian lawyer?"

The three weeks were up and it was time for Meg to go home to Huntersville. Heather and Amy were coming for their spring break ski trip. As she packed to go, Geoffrey brought up the subject of money. It seemed that he needed money for the closing. He was selling his house for less money than the principal due and owing and needed $20,000 to close.

Another prompting came as she looked into his eyes, "You're not going to use me again." Feeling the doors to the generous areas of her being closing tightly, Meg got serious. "Geoffrey," she said, "I've already lost $40,000 on you and your house. I can't afford to lend you any more."

"But Meg, I promise I'll pay you back when my Grandfather dies..."

"Well, you keep saying that, Geoffrey, but I have no guarantees that you'll actually do that. He doesn't seem ready to move on. I think he's trying to spite you. He wants you to get a job. I think I can hear him now, 'Get a job, Geoffrey.' Can you hear him?"

Geoffrey didn't laugh.

"You need to get the money from your mother," she said.

He didn't look concerned. "Don't worry about it," he said in a low, oily voice. "I know how to get money out of her." He threw on his jacket and left.

I bet you do, she thought darkly as she heard him start her car.

Hours later as Meg dragged her suitcases out of the house, Geoffrey returned.

"I got the money," he said. "No problem." Two checks waved up and down in the air between his thumb and index finger. "One is written out to me and one to you."

"Oh right, so she doesn't have to pay gift taxes."

"Yeah, yeah," he said as he strutted around. "So it's all in the bag, Meg. I'm rid of my house. I think I've done pretty well for myself. Listen, you need to sign your check and give it back to me."

Meg hesitated. There was a catch in his voice. She wondered if he was scared that she wouldn't do it, that she would keep the $10,000 for herself. She wouldn't have thought about it if she hadn't noticed his nervousness. She pretended that she was preoccupied with something in her pocketbook. She needed time to think. *Will he ever pay me back the money he owes me? This may be my only chance to get back at least $10,000 of it*, she thought as she held the check. The broken shard held to her throat flashed in her mind's eye. *He'd slit my throat if I did that. What about his mother? She'd think I was stealing from her.*

"Squeege, you need to sign the check," he repeated, this time with more urgency, his body moving closer to hers.

He's really sweating it, she thought. *I need more time to think.*

"I've got to go to the bathroom," she said cheerily. "I'll be right back."

Meg sat on the toilet and thought, *If I keep the check for myself, it might delay the closing. It's in my best interest to be rid of this house. I'd better sign it. But I'm so sick of doling money out to this gigolo and never getting a dime out of him. Yeah, but it's better to get rid of the house. There's no way his credit can seriously harm yours if you're rid of the house. Just give the user his money.*

Meg looked at herself in the mirror and saw a woman who was no longer in love. She spoke softly, "Meg, you don't love him at all."

She heard a loud bang on the bathroom door. "Squeege, I need the check."

"He knows what I'm thinking," she whispered, "and he's trying to intimidate me."

Meg calmly opened the door and looked Geoffrey right in the eye, "Don't worry, Geoffrey," she said with a grin. "I'm going to sign it." Her voice had an eerie, robotic ring to it.

She took the pen from his hand and signed the back of the check. He was standing over her, breathing quickly, watching every loop in her signature. She picked up the check at the same time as Geoffrey tried to grab it. His eyes were glued on the check, and he snatched it from her hand with such force that it sounded as if he had ripped it. Not a word was said by either of them as he turned and ran for the car.

That afternoon as Geoffrey drove Meg to the airport, he stopped for gas. She was rummaging around in her backpack, but in her peripheral vision she saw him whip out one of her credit cards. Her promptings were getting louder. "You're not going to use me any more!!" When Geoffrey got back in the car, she said, "I told you before you left Denver not to use my credit cards. You've got credit cards. Use your own."

"Well, I don't have a job, Meg, so I have to use yours."

"I don't have a job either, and I'm not your free lunch. Don't use my credit card again," she said sternly. There was no love in Meg's voice.

When she got to the airport she checked her bags, kissed Geoffrey goodbye and canceled all of her credit cards. When she was in love with him, she had shared her accounts and car keys as a kind of marital gesture of magnanimity. But Geoffrey never reciprocated. He always kept his credit cards to himself, as well as his car keys.

For three days, Meg skied with her girls in the Colorado mountains. She was really impressed with their skiing. The fact that they had always been flatlanders didn't make a difference. Heather was a natural. She had always been the less athletic one of the two girls, but skiing was her forte. Amy did well, but she held back more than Heather, who skied with abandon. Meg stuck to the green trails and was happy to be out in the middle of the fresh air and Douglas firs. She wasn't there for herself but for her girls. She had always wanted them to learn to ski, but Nick had put up his usual roadblocks. After the divorce, one of her first goals was to take the girls skiing.

In college, Meg had felt left out because most of the girls knew how to ski and she didn't. Mrs. Walsh couldn't afford to pay for ski trips, so Meg did without. The lack in Meg made her determined to fill the void in her children. They would learn to ski so that they never felt left out, as she had.

The trip was fun, but her intuition picked up the subtle and unspoken message that Heather and Amy didn't really want to visit her. They would never come just to visit Meg. They came only to ski. Once the skiing was over, they wanted to go home to Indigo Springs. She wondered if she was imagining it. As a Mom, this was hard to face. Did they love her? Was there any allegiance at all? They had turned into two people that she couldn't even recognize. The two little girls she had raised were gone.

They were back in Huntersville after the three days of skiing, and Meg answered the phone as it rang. Geoffrey needed help. Meg's car had been towed, and he needed her to fax a letter of direction telling the police to turn the car over to Geoffrey.

"Why did it get towed?" she asked.

"Well, I can't talk now, just trust me. O.K.? It's been towed and I need the fax," he said.

"I want to know why it's been towed."

"I can't talk now."

"Well, if you can't tell me why it's been towed, then I can't fax the letter of direction. Goodbye."

"Oh no, wait. O.K., O.K., I'll tell you. Look...I've been arrested for drunk driving. I went to buy a bottle of wine and they pulled me over. I had my pistol on the front seat and they were going to charge me with driving with a loaded weapon, but I talked my way out of it," he said, proudly.

"And what did you say to accomplish that?"

"I told them about Gilberto and the squatters and how I had the gun to protect my property. I talked about how white people in California have been castrated by the Hispanics. They were both white, so I knew I could get to them. Sure enough, they took the bullets, left the gun and I was only charged with drunk driving."

"So I guess I'll be paying larger insurance premiums in the future thanks to you."

"Oh, Squeege, I'm sorry. Please forgive me. I'll make it up to you. Look, remember when you were talking about buying an SUV because you car is old and hasn't been doing too well in the mountains? Well, we can go to the dealership that my Mom's stepson owns. Now that I'm family I can get you one for the dealer's cost. I bet that'll save you five or ten grand!" Geoffrey spoke charmingly. He really needed the letter of direction.

"If they arrested you, how did you get out of jail?" she asked.

After a long silence he said quietly, "My Mom bailed me out."

Meg thought of his mother, who was clearly an enabler. What can you do when you've got a kid like Geoffrey? She's stuck with him, but she could be tougher. If he didn't always have her to fall back on, maybe he'd shape up.

Meg got off the phone and faxed the letter of direction. Then she got down on her knees and prayed. Her tone was desperate. "Dear God, get me out of this marriage. I need a good reason to get out of it so that my family doesn't hold it against me. Catholics don't believe in divorce and this will be my second one. He's damaged every area of my life. Please, please help me." She wrote all of the above in a letter and burned it in the sink.

Jane had once said, "If you write a letter and burn it, the message goes right up into the ethers. It makes the request more powerful."

After her kids flew back to Barnstable, Meg returned to Cielo. She wanted to help Geoffrey get ready for the buyer's final walk-through of the house. She also looked forward to shopping for an SUV as Geoffrey had promised.

The night before the closing, Meg and Geoffrey were cleaning the kitchen appliances when the phone rang. Geoffrey answered. "Hi... Fanny," he said as he looked at Meg uneasily. "How are you?" He turned away from Meg and whispered, "Did you tell him about the golf cart?"

Meg walked closer to Geoffrey and watched him as he talked. His body stiffened, but he kept smiling and joking with Fanny.

When he hung up, Meg said cheerfully, "Fanny. That's an old-fashioned name. So who is she?" expecting her to be one of Geoffrey's old concubines.

"Well, Fanny is my neighbor, or I should say former neighbor. She's about 80 years old and is bedridden at this point," he responded. He continued the story of his friendship with Fanny and squirmed a bit as he admitted that Fanny had given him $10,000. Meg assumed that he had borrowed the money, but he explained that she had given him the money in exchange for a golf cart.

"A golf cart?" said Meg. "What would a bedridden woman want with a golf cart?"

"Well, she can't walk, so she can ride around in it."

"Who's gonna get her into it? And where is an 80-year-old bedridden woman gonna go in a golf cart? Is she gonna take the freeway to her doctor's office in a golf cart?" asked Meg.

"Well, I don't know."

"God, Geoffrey, don't you have a conscience at all?"

"Hey," he said, nostrils flaring, voice raised, "Watch your mouth. It was a good golf cart. They're expensive. I was her friend. I used to go over there and visit her and she enjoyed my company and she wanted to help me."

"Yes, and you poured out your financial troubles to her during your friendly visits. After a few visits she began to feel sorry for you. She thought that if she didn't help you that you might stop coming to see her. She was lonely, and then you moved in for the kill." Meg spoke quietly and slowly as she envisioned Geoffrey patiently stalking the old lady. "Did you visit Fanny because you wanted to be kind to a lonely old lady or did you visit her because you knew she had money?"

"I'm not listening to any more of this. You have no right to talk to me like this. It's not fair."

"Then why are you so scared?"

"Because her son wants me to pay her back. He's says it's not worth $10,000 and I don't have the money." Geoffrey pouted.

"Well, you're not getting it from me. Have you visited her since she gave you the money?"

Geoffrey was running around the house and yelling at the same time. "I'm not answering that question. You're supposed to be on my side."

"We both know you'll be leaving the state soon," she said. "Her son won't chase you to Colorado for such a small amount. It would cost him more than that to hire an out-of-state attorney. Isn't that what you usually do with your creditors? You leave the state?" Meg's contempt for Geoffrey was oozing over.

He glared at her over his shoulder and walked downstairs to the kitchen.

"Dear God," she whispered, "get me out of this marriage."

The buyer's walk-through and the closing happened the next morning. Geoffrey claimed that he didn't have enough money to pay the back taxes on the property, so the buyer agreed to pay them if Geoffrey would sign a note. He happily stuck the buyer with a note. Later that same day, as Geoffrey drove Meg to the car dealership, as promised, he told her about the note. "So you signed a note. Does that mean that the closing cost more than the $20,000 your Mom gave you?" she asked.

"Uh...yeah," he said.

Car dealerships were really difficult for Meg to deal with. Each one was like its own little kingdom of falsity. "Geoffrey, I hate buying cars. You always get ripped off," she said.

"No, no. Look, I know this guy. Remember, he's the son of my stepfather. You met him at the funeral. He'll give me a deal. I promise, Meg," Geoffrey swore. "I'll probably get this car for you for maybe $1,000 over the dealer's price, and that's how I can pay you back for all the financial trouble I've caused you."

"SOME of the financial trouble."

Meg tried to remember the stepbrother. Her mind drifted back to the day of his stepfather's funeral. The family had gathered after the service at a country club with a pleasing view of the ocean. When first arriving at the club, Meg had felt very comfortable. Geoffrey's mother, Angela, was the perfect lady, holding up well after the death of her fourth husband.

Soon enough the clouds rolled in. A man looking to be in his late 50's glared as his wife, Cherie, approached Geoffrey slowly and cautiously to exchange cordial words. She had been Geoffrey's stepsister during Angela's third marriage, and as Geoffrey later confided to Meg, he had "serviced" her. The husband watched ferociously from the sidelines with a look that Geoffrey was certain not to miss. The scene was awful. It seemed that Cherie still wanted Geoffrey, and her husband knew it. Like the snake that charms its prey before striking, Geoffrey had mesmerized this woman and the effect had stuck for years.

The episode was interrupted by Geoffrey's stepbrother, the car dealer, who was reserved, confident and well mannered. Meg noted the difference between the two men. It was Geoffrey who had taken the low road over the same 50 years.

They drove up in front of the dealership. It was enormous. Immaculate cars and trucks, blinding to the eye in the sunlight, were set in precisely arranged rows. Clearly, this was a lucrative business. Meg picked out the SUV that she could afford. The dealer suggested a price. Geoffrey complained that it wasn't low enough. The dealer protested that the offer was only $1,000 over his cost. Meg looked into his eyes and knew he was lying. The price was lower but not that low. She couldn't blame the guy. He knew Geoffrey was using him and was lying to protect himself. Geoffrey approved of the price and Meg wrote the check.

"So," said the stepbrother, "will the title be in joint tenancy?"

"Yes," said Geoffrey.

"Uh, no," interrupted Meg. "It will be in my name."

The stepbrother looked at Meg with a knowing glance. He understood her thinking. Geoffrey's face blackened. He recovered quickly. After all, he was on stage.

As they caravanned through the Great Salt Lake Desert Geoffrey's spirits were high, but after his arrival in Huntersville, the mysterious strain of strep struck again. "Oh Meg, please help me," he said. "I'm 50 years old and I don't know how to earn a living." There was panic in his voice. He held his head in his hands and breathed fast as he lay in bed. The Leo bravado was gone. He looked older than his years, and Meg was shocked into silence by his honesty. Geoffrey wasn't truthful very often. His life was filled with fallacy and delusion. It was a relief at last to see his façade gone, to hear the truth from his lips.

Meg said nothing. She couldn't help him because the only workable option he had was to start at the bottom and work his way up again. *Or perhaps, go back to school and start over,* she thought. She doubted that he would see that as an option that he could accept. His ego was way too big. He had spent his life drinking, womanizing, conning, using people and feeling pretty smug about it. Time was wearing him down. He was no longer dazzlingly handsome. The bright white smile against the tan skin and sky blue eyes didn't work as well as they used to. Sales wasn't an easy profession any more. Geoffrey's karma was descending.

Meg looked at his ashen face sticking out from under the covers. She served him his food in bed, which he was always happy to eat, and he really enjoyed watching TV. She no longer bothered to talk about his sending out resumes. It just made him angry and more determined to be sick.

It was April of '97 and time to get the 1040 information ready for the accountant. When she asked Geoffrey for his figures, he just made them up. When she realized he was pulling numbers out of the air she said, "Geoffrey, you're supposed to have records..."

"Oh, I don't keep track of that stuff."

The thought of going through an IRS audit with Geoffrey sent chills through her every cell. "God," she prayed, "please help me to get rid of this man."

Weeks went by and nothing changed. According to Geoffrey, he was still the bedridden victim of a vicious strain of strep not yet discovered by modern science. Exasperated, Meg called Howard Peak and explained the problem.

"Send me a photograph of him. Full length. It has to be current. No more than a year old," he said. "Then call me in a week."

After folding Geoffrey's laundry, Meg told him that Howard needed a recent photograph of him. "I don't have any that aren't in storage," he said. "We'll have to take some."

A gleeful Geoffrey jumped out of bed, showered, dressed, brushed his teeth and generally primped as if he had a modeling assignment.

He pulled out a Polaroid camera, handed it to Meg and started posing as a man on a stage. Meg snapped picture after picture. Reviewing the pictures was major. He spread them out over the dinette and ruminated over which one made him look the most handsome. "Come on, Geoffrey. Why is this such a big deal? Send him this one," she said, handing him a random picture, "I need to get to the post office."

"No, that one makes me look like a wimp."

"Hey, it's a picture. This isn't a beauty contest. He just wants to see your aura."

With a critical eye, Geoffrey dragged out the decision for an hour or so and finally agreed to two pictures that he felt were the most becoming. A look of indignation came over him as Meg unceremoniously shoved the acceptable pictures into an envelope and ran out the door. Her watch beeped 5:00 p.m. as she opened the door to the post office and popped the envelope into the "out of town" slot. When she arrived home, she saw that Geoffrey had slid back into bed.

Over the next four days Meg struggled inwardly over the question of disposing of Geoffrey. "I already have my out," she whispered, referring to the incident with the shard. "No," she concluded as an unhealthy part of her soul quietly quelled the memory, not wanting to relive her anguish. "Most of the time he's nice to me and he is entertaining. I should just stay with him and support him. That man is never going to work. If I go back to school, I can get an LL.M. at one of the local law schools. Then I can get a good job here, and I'll just support him. It's easier that way. I won't have to go through another divorce, another split-up and more scenes."

As the hours went on each day she continued to go back and forth, one minute visualizing herself filing for divorce and the next minute, accepting the fact that staying married and supporting Geoffrey was her lot in life. Shilly shallying to the max, Meg finally decided to go to school. "No matter what I do, I'll have to support myself with a full-time job," she concluded. Mediation offered no more than part-time earnings.

She contacted all of the local universities and found one that offered the program she wanted. The paperwork and the tuition were daunting but Meg sent off the oversized manilla envelope, and Geoffrey's bliss was immediate.

When Meg told him that she was going back to school so that she could get a job in a tax law firm Geoffrey jumped out of bed and smiling, ran toward her. "Oh Squeege, that's great," he exulted. He smiled, he laughed, he beamed, he gyrated and said, "I feel good enough to eat at the table today instead of in bed."

The sun made no impression as it rose the next day. The clouds were thick, and the rains came heavily. Meg answered the phone when it rang, and she heard Howard Peak's voice. "Meg, Hi. It's Howard," he said. "I'm calling to talk to Geoffrey, but first I have to tell you something. Look, after seeing his pictures I had a dream about him last night and I think you might be in danger." Meg was silent and Howard continued, "I saw him as a soldier, overzealous in battle during one of the World Wars. He was in a frenzy of anger, bayoneting a dead soldier in the abdomen over and over. I think it might have been you. He has a violent temper. I think it would be best if you got away from him. I don't think you'll be safe if you stay with him. You must do what you want, but this is a warning."

A rush of energy flowed through her as she placed the receiver on the table. She walked into the bedroom and woke Geoffrey up, mechanically telling him that Howard was on the phone. Howard's words hung in her mind and sounded over and over, "Overzealous in battle...bayoneting a dead soldier...frenzy of anger." She looked at Geoffrey as he slowly left the bed and recalled the scene when he had struggled with Nick in her basement in Barnstable. And what about when he had held the shard to her throat? Gently closing the bathroom door behind her, she locked it and recalled the fuzzy memories, wondering if they had really happened as she had remembered.

"Hey Squeege," yelled Geoffrey after hanging up the phone. "Let's go out for some ice cream. I feel great. Howard's sending me the remedies and you're going back to school. Let's celebrate."

"Let's call Jane and ask her to go with us," said Meg. She didn't want to be alone with him.

An hour later Jane, Meg and Geoffrey drove around Henry Lake as they ate ice cream. "I came here last week for a walk. Look at the homes around here. Aren't they nice?" said Jane.

"Yeah. Let's buy a house here, Meg," Geoffrey said.

"No, I don't think so," Meg said. "Not until at least one of us has a job."

"Yeah," Jane said as she licked a dribble of ice cream working its way down the side of her cone. "A job always helps when you've got a mortgage."

Geoffrey was silent but he gripped the steering wheel a little harder. After dropping Jane off at her apartment, he started right in. "I told you that we were not going to discuss my getting a job again. So why did you make that comment about at least one of us having a job?"

"Because it's common sense. I'm not buying a house until I know we've got enough money coming in every month to pay the mortgage. Then there are repairs, decorating. The list goes on and on. It will take a year for me to finish school. The job I get will be entry level. If I get paid $50,000 a year, I'll be lucky...."

"Oh," he said, "I don't believe that. Lawyers get paid a lot more than that."

"I'll be earning what a kid first coming out of school earns. If you want a house in a fancy neighborhood, then you'd better get a job so that your salary can be added to mine."

"I told you that I will not discuss getting a job ever again. You have the money to make a monthly mortgage payment without your even having a job. You don't need a salary from me," he argued.

"And then what do you do when the money runs out? I don't have unlimited funds. If I keep spending my principal, the money will run out," Meg reasoned. "Then what happens?"

Geoffrey was silent. He carefully watched the road while he drove. Meg continued in a taunting whisper, "What are you gonna do when my money runs out, Geoffrey? I know what you'll do. You'll dump me and move on to the next woman you can find who's got some bucks. You've spent your life living off other people. If you can't find a rich woman, you'll mooch off your mother."

Geoffrey pulled into the driveway. "I don't even feel married," he said. "We don't have a joint checking account. Married people have a joint checking account. They share their money."

"Yes, Geoffrey," cooed Meg, "but you don't have any money to share. You're a six foot liability and you don't want to work to get money, do you?"

"No, I don't!" he yelled defiantly. "And what of it? I want to have a lot of money but I don't want to work for it. What's wrong with that? Isn't everybody like that?"

"No," she shouted. "Not everybody's like that. Some people have integrity or maybe 'honor' is the word. Look," she said while she held up the bank statement from the old Barnstable account. "I got our old bank statement today. I told you specifically that you could write a check to Raji for $1,000 and you made it $2,000. You stole that $1,000 from me, Geoffrey. Why did you do that? You're supposed to be my loving husband and yet, you steal from me.

"I know you're running out of money. You must have asked your mother for more money than you needed for the closing. You've been living off someone for the last several weeks and it hasn't been me. That tells me that you lied to the buyer and signed a note for the back taxes when you really did have the money to pay them. You kept that money that was meant for the taxes so that you'd have spending money for a while. Now you're hitting on me again. You're trying to make me feel guilty. Well, it's not working. Why would I choose to have a joint account with someone like you?"

"Look," said Geoffrey. "I told you that I won't discuss my getting a job any more. Some day my grandfather's inheritance will come in and I can pay you back for all the money you've given me. You married me for richer or for poorer."

"So if my money runs out and we have to live on the street you won't mind?"

"No. I've lived on the street before. I can live there again."

"I asked you once if you had ever lived on the street. Do you remember that?" she asked slowly. "You told me 'No.' Now I know that you lied to me."

Meg knew that if Geoffrey really loved her, he would do everything in his power to prevent her from ending up on the street. This lie was the final nail in the coffin. He didn't love her. He was simply using her. If her money were to run out he would dump her and move on to the next woman. He was out of chances. He had crossed the line.

"I am divorcing you, Geoffrey," she said.

"Oh right. Women always say that." He laughed as he sat down calmly in his vibrating recliner.

"Not this woman. I told you before that I don't make threats I am not prepared to carry out," she spoke firmly. "I'll help you move out, Geoffrey. You're leaving. Come on."

"No, I'm not leaving. You can't throw me out."

"Yes, I can. You are nothing but a con artist and a gigolo. You're the laziest man I've ever known, and I'm not living with you any more."

"I have nowhere to go. You can't throw me out."

"Yes, I can. I pay all of the bills and I don't want you to live here any more. So you're leaving. Come on into the bedroom, Geoffrey. We're packing your clothes. I'm helping you," she said with a sing-song voice as she lifted the hangers out of the closet and walked toward the front door. Meg didn't have a key to Geoffrey's truck. So she dumped his clothes on the front lawn and returned to the closet for a second load of his stuff.

"Geoffrey, I'm helping you. Your stuff's on the lawn. Give me the key to your truck so I can put the clothes inside it. Otherwise they'll be damp from the dew."

"I am not leaving. You married me for richer or for poorer."

Meg stopped by the front door and looked directly at Geoffrey. He was rocking his recliner. "That doesn't apply when one person deceives the other," she said. "You exaggerated when you told me that you were a top salesman in California. You hid the fact that you're an alcoholic AND a gigolo AND you lied about your debts. You said that you had them covered. You are a liar."

Geoffrey slammed his hands on the arms of the recliner. He rose out of the chair slowly and was breathing fast. It was all a blur in Meg's mind as she saw him walking tightly in her direction, nostrils flaring, his face getting redder by the second. Remembering the look in his eyes from the time he forced the shard to her throat, she shrank back from him. He grabbed her arm and twisted it. "Woman, I'm not putting up with your mouth any more. Do you understand? You better learn your place."

"Get your hands off me," she cried as she tried to untwist her arm. He was too strong for her and anger welled up inside of her. The pain in her elbow was sharp. Raising her foot she stomped down on his instep with all of her might. "You bastard, let go of me." His grip on her arm loosened and she pushed him away as he grimaced in pain. "You are outta here," she yelled.

Geoffrey regained his balance, moved forward and slapped her face. "I guess I have to teach you your place. I don't take this from anybody, especially not a woman."

No one had ever slapped Meg in the face. This was not an experience that she planned to tolerate. In a blind fury she reached down and grabbed the straps of his camera case. It had fallen to the floor as she carried his clothes out of the house. As her arm circled in a perfect arc she hissed, "How dare you slap me." He saw the blow coming and jerked back his head. The leather case grazed his jaw. "Get out of here," she hissed.

It took Geoffrey only a moment to recover from the glancing blow. He grabbed her shoulders and pinned her against the wall. His hands slipped firmly around her neck. His teeth gritted, he compressed her throat, moved his lips close to her ear and growled, "Nobody talks to me that way."

She stood in his shadow and felt the heat of his breath. She found that she couldn't breathe, talk or swallow. Panicking, she could hear the fierce pounding of her own heart. He held on with stony determination as she frantically slammed her fists against his chest, praying that he'd let go. *Knee him where it hurts,* she thought, almost out of air, but he stood with both feet between her legs. "Do something!" she shrieked inwardly. She knew she was running out of time and began to sweat coldly. She opened her mouth wider and tried to scream, but no sound came forth. Terrified, she raised a trembling knee and tried to force it between their bodies. Checking her move, he let the full weight of his body lean against her. Her hands shook as she reached around his arms and pushed his jaw back. Hysterical, she clawed at his hands, his eyes, his hair. His grip only got tighter.

Things were beginning to fade as she grew weaker. She submitted to her condition and thought, *If I'm gonna die, he won't see any more fear.*

With that, Meg looked up at Geoffrey and glared defiantly into his eyes. The hostile stare must have weakened his resolve. He loosened his grip and walked back to the recliner. His back was to her. A freed Meg stumbled into the bedroom, locked the door behind her and dialed 911.

A female voice answered. It was hard for Meg to respond. Her throat hurt and was making noises as she gasped for air. She forced out the words. "Please help me. My husband just tried to strangle me."

"Where are you?" the woman asked.

Her fear caused forgetfulness, but after a few seconds she managed to hammer out the address. Geoffrey was rattling the doorknob, and she was terrified that he was coming in to kill her.

"Please help me. He's coming into the room."

"Stay calm. Just keep talking to me," the woman said. "A car is right in your neighborhood. You're in luck. They'll be there in seconds."

Just then Geoffrey picked the lock and opened the door. "You're making a big deal out of nothing," he said.

"I don't think choking someone is 'nothing.'" Her voice quivered.

"Don't talk to him!" the woman yelled into the phone. "Don't talk to him! Just keep talking to me. Describe to me what happened. Say anything, but don't talk to him!"

The house exploded from a sudden pounding on the front door. Geoffrey turned white. He shot a look at Meg and said nervously, "Listen, I'll move out. Just don't press charges." He ran to the front door and stepped outside.

She heard Geoffrey tell the police that he had roughed her up only a little. "Hey man, it was no big deal. I just wanted to put her in her place," he said to the cop. In accordance with Colorado law, he was automatically arrested. Pressing charges wasn't necessary. One of the officers interviewed Meg. She insisted that Geoffrey had choked her. The cop look unimpressed as he examined her neck and explained to her that there would be a hearing the following week. Geoffrey would be required to stay away from her until then. The car door slammed and an unrepentant Geoffrey, in handcuffs, was hauled off to the local police station. As the police car pulled out into the street, Meg fell to her knees on the living room rug and thanked God that he was gone.

Eighteen

The Misty Mistake

MICHAEL CALLED MISTY THAT NIGHT, AND they had a long, long talk. True, Misty had been married when she was fifteen, but she had been a confused kid because of a rotten childhood, and she had done lots of therapy since then. She explained to Michael what her second husband was like, and that she was driven into an affair with another man because there was no love in her marriage. Yes, she had sent Taylor that picture, but it was from a photo shoot.

"Misty," he said, "it doesn't matter what Taylor thinks. I love you."

"I love you too, Michael. You're the only man I want in my life."

"I think that the only thing to do is to get married," Michael said.

"Why, you are absolutely right, Michael," Misty agreed.

They were secretly married in Austin that spring, and they honeymooned at Lake Travis and talked of an idyllic future. Misty Lee wanted to live in Colorado and complete her broadcast news degree at the University of Colorado, and Michael vowed to find a job up there before the summer so that Misty could begin classes in June.

When the honeymoon was over, they had a heartrending good-bye at the airport. Misty Lee flew back to New Orleans, and Michael began searching for a job in Colorado. He eventually landed a good one with a firm in Colorado Springs. He and Misty flew out to Colorado to find an apartment to live in while Misty finished school, and she coaxed

Michael into finding a place in Rocky Park close to the university. Michael would commute to Colorado Springs almost one hundred miles one way each day in his front-wheel-drive sports car, regardless of the weather. They signed the apartment lease and were scheduled for occupancy the first day of June. The plan was for Michael to move all his worldly possessions to Rocky Park from Houston the last week in May, get a shuttle to the Denver airport, fly to New Orleans, load Misty Lee's stuff onto a truck, load her station wagon onto a car tow, and then drive the truck across country to Rocky Park with Misty Lee and her cats.

When they told their families they had eloped, there was much surprise and shock, but when they saw how happy Michael and Misty looked together, everyone accepted them. Well, almost everyone. When Michael called Taylor to fill her in, she was not altogether amused.

Summer was a long time coming, but the nightly telephone calls between the newlyweds kept their nights lively. Finally the big day arrived, and Michael found himself driving out of his driveway waving good-bye to people he knew he would never see again. There was nothing to do but smile and wish everyone well, yet Michael was overwhelmed by the feeling that his life was just now starting, and that everything that had happened before had just been a prelude. Creative Eagle was flying north, intent on meeting the challenges ahead.

The journey went smoothly, and Michael hired a couple of guys to help him move in when he got to Rocky Park. He felt alive and full of expectation as he drove to the Denver airport to fly to New Orleans. Misty Lee was there to greet him, looking just as glad to see him as he was to see her. She couldn't wait to get out of New Orleans, and she got all the scoop from Michael about their new home. Michael responded patiently to her questions, all the time looking forward to a night with his new bride.

"How 'bout Amanda? Is she coming with?" asked Michael.

Misty's face dropped. "No. She wants to stay here with her friends. She'll live with her father."

They had everything ready to go by the next evening, and as they pulled out, Misty heaved a sigh of relief.

"Good riddance, New Orleans!" she shouted out of the window.

"I'd say you're relieved, Misty," Michael said.

"It's finally over, Michael. I feel like I've just escaped from a concentration camp."

"We're going to create all new memories now, Misty," Michael said.

"Yes!" Misty agreed. "Next week I'll be starting school in the West."

"What does your schedule look like for the summer?" Michael asked.

"Mostly prerequisites. I want to get them out of the way so that I can start on my core work during the fall."

After a few CDs and some light and gay conversation, Misty Lee drifted off into dreamland and Michael focused in on the road ahead. The miles drifted by, and he was pleased to encounter a gas station as the needle approached the big "E." He pulled in, gassed her up, and sauntered over to the cashier to settle up. As he headed back to the truck after paying his bill, he noticed a guy washing the windows of his rental truck. Misty Lee was still asleep, totally oblivious. Michael thought this was strange, because he was in the self-service lane, and as he got closer, the guy stepped down, got into his car, and drove away.

"That guy was just checking out Misty Lee's legs!" he realized. She was wearing a pair of shorts, and from the vantage point that guy had, he must have been quite pleased.

"Better get used to it," a tiny voice told him. "Guys will always be checking her out!"

"No problem!" he replied. "I'm the one she loves."

He decided to drive the next leg of the trip and let Misty Lee stack some more Z's.

Michael wasn't at all familiar with this part of the country, and he was glad that he had planned the route out the night before. He had drawn up a map, and he checked it to make sure he was where he thought he was. About that time, Misty Lee started to stir, and then she slowly sat up.

"Do you need any help with the directions?" she asked.

"We're cool," Michael explained. "I was just checking my map. I've got it all figured out. No problem."

"I like a man who is in control," Misty said, giving Michael one of her patented smiles.

For the first time since he had met her, Michael felt as if things were out of balance. Misty was telling him she liked a man who was in control, and it was flattering to him, but he was beginning to feel as if he was carrying a very big load for her, and that made him feel as if he was not in control. He felt as if Misty was in control, but in a covert way. For the first time, he wondered if all she thought she needed to do was smile just right and look beautiful. He felt as if he was doing the work she didn't want to do for herself. He was getting her to Colorado, getting her an apartment that was right next to her school, and he was going to drive two hundred miles every day to support her. *Relax,* he thought. *You're just imagining things. Misty is a very spiritual woman.*

"Are you anxious to start your core classes this fall?" Michael asked.

"I have to get accepted first," Misty explained.

"Hey, a girl like you won't have any trouble getting in!"

A concerned look came over Misty's face. "They only have a limited number of openings, way less than the number of students applying."

"Who do you know out there? Who can you put the squeeze on?"

"Just my counselor. She has all my transcripts and records, and after I get my prerequisites done this summer, all I have to do is write an essay and submit my application for admission. Would you help me write the essay, Michael?" She smiled seductively at him, laying her hand gently in his lap.

Watch the road! Michael thought. "I think I could handle that," he said cheerfully. "Consider yourself accepted."

They stayed in Dallas that night, and it was Misty's turn to drive the next leg. She was doing quite well handling the "big rig," with one minor detail. She started to nod off just two hours after getting on the highway. Michael came over and grabbed the wheel, very glad that he had decided to wait to take a nap.

He decided that he would take over Misty's shifts and drove most of the way into Rocky Park. They arrived late on a Saturday night, in time for Michael to crash and then get up early to meet the guys he had hired to unload the truck. They were students at C.U. and didn't complain in the least that they had to walk up two flights of stairs. As a matter of fact, they had plans for the afternoon, and they were in high gear.

The apartment had two bedrooms, and Michael was hoping to turn the front bedroom into an office that they could both share. When Michael went out to get lunch for everyone, he came back to find all of Misty Lee's office furniture in the front bedroom. She explained to him that it was going to be her office because she needed a private place to study. After all, she explained, she just knew it would be a good thing to do because Michael was out of school and didn't need a place to study. All he had to do was go to work.

The college boys gobbled down lunch and went back down to the truck, and Michael still had half a sandwich to go.

"Michael, get down there and help them. This is embarrassing!" Misty exclaimed. "These guys go to my school, and I don't want them to think I have a lazy husband."

Michael looked at her, not really knowing how to react to this. His sense of give and take was being overruled, and the problem was that there was no third party around for confirmation. He was in a new state, and he didn't know anyone outside of Misty and his sister. It was as if he was at the check-out stand and they wanted to know if he wanted plastic or paper. It was an innocent question, demanding an innocent answer. It didn't require much reflection, or at least it certainly shouldn't require any reflection. After all, everything was exactly the way it was supposed to be.

"O.K., Misty, just let me finish knocking down this sandwich," Michael said, giving himself a little room but at the same time not sounding too disagreeable.

Misty was miffed and went down to the truck and started carrying up anything she could grab. Michael felt that it was O.K. to relax, because he was paying the guys to unload. He didn't think that eating lunch was an act of laziness. It wasn't long before he was done, and he went down and helped move the rest of their furniture. Finally it was over, and the college boys went off for an afternoon of frolic.

"I was so embarrassed!" Misty Lee proclaimed. "Those boys were working their buns off, and you were just sitting around eating lunch!"

Now, this really gave Michael an uneasy feeling. He had done nothing but work his entire life. What's more, he had unloaded a lot more furniture than Misty, not to mention the fact that he was paying the college guys to unload. Michael was doing all the right things, and she was getting mad at him as if he was doing all the wrong things.

"Misty, did you notice that I was motoring at top speed up and down those stairs, heavy laden like a llama?" he said, smiling at her.

"Don't joke with me about this, Michael," she said sternly, her lips drawn together tightly. "Any other man could have done more."

Michael sat there in shock. He had never seen her angry like this.

"Don't worry, Misty Lee. I don't think those college boys were upset in the least. They were glad to be getting some help with the unloading. Besides, I gave them a great tip."

"You gave them a tip? Are you crazy? We are on a budget here!"

"Ya gotta spread that stuff around," Michael said, justifying his actions, attempting to defuse her anger with a relaxed approach. If there was one thing that Michael didn't like, it was anger. He had seen enough anger in his life, the violent and out-of-control variety. Misty's anger was way out of proportion to anything he had allegedly done. He felt that if he let her get to him, the situation would get out of control in a hurry.

"Money is not stuff, and we do not need to spread it around," she said, cranking up the vacuum cleaner and working it furiously around the living room. "We have to save every penny we get our hands on. We spent way too much money traveling around last fall."

"You always get back what you put out there. I was just priming the pump. The whole secret of prosperity is to give," he explained, appealing to Misty's spirituality.

Misty wouldn't even look up at him. She kept vacuuming wildly, almost frantically. Michael walked out of the room, and suddenly Misty clicked off the vacuum cleaner.

"You'd better not be going for a bike ride," she said, storming after him. "We have work to do. You have to wash these windows and clean the blinds."

Actually, a bike ride was exactly what he wanted to do. He wanted to ask her how she planned to stop him. He remembered his father telling him once that sometimes you had to slug a woman to keep her in her place. The idea repulsed him, but he could feel a rage gnawing at him, taunting him to hit her.

That's not my way, he thought. *Where is this coming from? Is that the kind of man she wants, one who will punch her lights out?* He pondered this horrible thought, and became even more determined to be a gentleman and somehow make her realize that this was how a strong man treated the woman he loved.

Michael sauntered over to the kitchen to get some cleaning rags and spray for the glass sliders, and got into a rhythm of spraying and rubbing, spraying and rubbing.

This is great fun, he thought. *I don't suppose I could talk Misty into taking a break and getting in a good toss in the hay?*

Eventually the new bride came over to inspect the progress. "I can't believe that you're a grown man and you can't even clean a window," she twanged out loudly. "My daughter could do a better job than this."

She grabbed the rag and started rubbing a missed spot furiously.

"I can't focus on this window because I want to take your clothes off," he confessed.

Misty leapt up on the kitchen counter, landing on her rear. In one deft move, she pulled off her shorts and panties and spread her legs apart. At first Michael thought it was an invitation, but something about the look in her eyes was not right. She was angry, very angry.

"Go ahead," she screamed. "Just do it. Just do it right here. Is this what you want?"

Michael was trying to go in so many directions at once that he just stood there idling. Never had he seen anything like this. What was this? Love was caring, giving, honest. Love's passion came from the heart. This was not love; this was not passion from the heart. This was coming from somewhere entirely different, and it was a place Michael did not want to go. He didn't even want to take a glimpse. Where was the Divine woman?

He remembered a quote from a comedian he was fond of. The man had said, "You can take the sting out of your enemy with humor, but you cannot defeat him." Had Misty Lee become his enemy? He turned around and walked out of room.

For a long time he heard Misty sobbing in the kitchen, great aching sobs that racked her entire body. He wanted to go to in and console her, but he didn't know how she would react to him.

Misty stayed in the kitchen for a very long time, and as the evening progressed, Michael went in and got ready for bed. Tomorrow was his first day on the new job, and he wanted to be fresh and ready. He found that he couldn't sleep, though, because he was trying to figure out what had happened.

Will the real Misty Lee please stand up? he thought. He searched his heart to understand what if anything he was doing wrong, because he knew that sometimes it was difficult to understand what your own role is in causing a given situation. He knew that it was true that people create their own reality, so how had he drawn this to himself? Was this an ancient karma, was this a reflection of something inside of himself, or was it both? Why had he married her? Was he lonely? Was it her looks? Was he avoiding analyzing his own psychology and looking at his own issues? Did he have it together, or was he looking to Misty Lee to help him get it together? Was he taking full responsibility for himself? He could hear the drone of the television coming from the living room, and eventually Misty turned it off and came to bed.

"I turned on the television," she said softly, "and what do you know, there was a couple making love right there on the screen. You never know what you're getting on cable. I just couldn't stop watching it. I know I wasn't supposed to watch it, but I couldn't help myself."

"Would you like to make love, Misty?"

"You've got to be kidding," she said, and rolled over to other side of the bed as far as she could.

He wanted to ask her if she was sure, but he didn't think she would appreciate the humor. Eventually he drifted off to sleep, and when he woke up he looked over to find Misty sleeping quite soundly. He chose not to wake her, and got ready for work as quietly as he could. She was still sleeping by the time he was ready to go, so off to work he went.

His new office was just about the most casual place he had ever been. Everybody was wearing shorts and tee shirts, with either sandals or hiking boots. He was way overdressed, and vowed to himself not to make that mistake again. He knew that he wouldn't miss the white cotton shirts and wool suits that were mandatory at the high-tech giant he had left back in Houston.

The little building that housed his new company had windows all around, and everyone had a view. Pike's Peak looked magnificent, and his new co-workers warmly welcomed him. He couldn't get over the fact that it took only 10 minutes to meet everyone in the entire company. They took him out for an early lunch at the Halston Hotel, and the president presented him with a picture book of Colorado. He realized that despite the casual appearance, these guys were some of the most talented "techies" he had ever met, and he knew he would be challenged. He couldn't contain the joy he felt over having such a wonderful work environment, and for the moment his domestic problems faded into the background. At least, until he got home that night.

"Why didn't you clean out the litter box before you left for work this morning?" Misty asked.

The joyful look on Michael's face faded abruptly. "Did the cats overflow their litter box today? They are really cranking out the poops," Michael said, not trying to be sarcastic.

"Come on, Michael. Maybe you wait that long where you come from, but that box needs to be scooped every day without fail," Misty said firmly.

"Does she want me to tell her to do it herself?" Michael asked himself. He had the feeling that Misty Lee wanted him to do just that, but it wasn't his way. He was gentle, but very strong. He was beginning to realize that Misty had a different notion of what a man should be like.

"Consider those poops history," he said enthusiastically.

Misty rolled her eyes. "You know, you lied to me," she said.

"I did?" Michael asked, somewhat surprised.

"You acted like you were somebody you were not before we got married," she said, her voice full of menace.

"I'm just me, Misty," Michael explained patiently. "I never deceived you about anything."

"You need therapy, Mister," Misty said, shaking her head and walking out of the room.

The next week Michael enrolled in a therapy class. Misty didn't go with him, because she explained that she had already worked on her psychology. Michael conceded that maybe there was something about himself that he could improve and thereby create harmony in his marriage.

He met with the group twice a week after work, which meant he didn't get home until after 10 p.m. He worked as hard as he could on his psychology, knowing that he was the creator of his own reality and his own world. If there were nothing but big nasty weeds in his subconscious, he would pull them all out and create a garden that would rival Versailles. His subconscious would be a mirror for his Divine Spark. It would be the Omega to his Alpha, existing in perfect harmony and allowing him to create like a master alchemist.

As part of his inner child work, the therapist recommended that he get a teddy bear and sleep with it at night. Michael thought it was a little strange, but then again he told himself that maybe this was what his inner child needed. He got the teddy bear on his way home.

"What is that?" Misty Lee asked as he got into bed with his new companion.

"It's my new girlfriend," he said, hoping for a laugh.

"That's about your speed," Misty said.

"Seriously, Misty Lee, the therapist said it was a good way to get in touch with my inner feelings, with my inner child," Michael explained.

"Do you have to do everything the therapist says," she asked incredulously. "Can't you think for yourself?"

Before Michael could reply, she walked out of the room.

"I hope you and your new girlfriend have a fun night," she yelled from the living room, getting comfortable on the sofa.

"Looks like it's you and me, big guy," he said to his little friend. "You're really not so bad looking, ya know."

The next morning, Michael went off to work, more than a little frustrated. The days and nights droned on in succession, and they didn't see much improvement in Michael's marriage. He completed all his counseling sessions, read countless books on healing the soul, and still his relationship with Misty wasn't improving. He asked her once more to go to therapy with him, and she reminded him that she had already done her work on herself. Michael was completely exasperated, but it somehow made him more determined to hang in there and find the answer. Michael decided it would help if they got out and met other couples, so they got active in a spiritual study center in Rocky Park. They met Horace and Jill there, and through them they had gotten involved politically in several state and national concerns. Horace was president of the study center, all pomp and ego, and his wife Jill was a sweet soul who doted on his every move. Horace didn't have an impressive job, but he acted as if the big one was just around the corner. Whenever Misty was around, he laid it on especially thick, and it wasn't long before Michael could sense that Misty preferred Horace's company.

August was coming to a close, and as Misty was wrapping up her summer classes. Michael helped her write the admissions essay, and they sent it off to the Dean. When they were driving home from dinner one Friday evening a short time later, Michael stopped to get the mail, which he started to sort through when he got back into the car.

"There it is," Misty said, looking nervous.

"Go ahead, Misty. Open it."

Misty took the letter and held to her heart. She looked over at Michael, and he nodded reassuringly. Slowly she opened the envelope and took out the letter. When she read the words, "We are pleased to inform you..," she burst into tears. "Oh, Michael, I did it! I did it! I'm in!" She took off her seat belt and showered Michael with kisses.

"This is so wonderful, Misty. I knew you would get in. I just knew it!" He held her tightly, cherishing their closeness.

That fall Misty was full of hope and optimism, and the relationship flourished. As winter approached, Michael realized he needed a winter coat. Misty was studying for an exam as Michael came down the hall and tapped on the door.

"Misty, tomorrow after work I need to take a trip to the mall and get a jacket with a goose down zip in. The winters here can be brutal."

"Michael," she replied, "you don't need a winter coat. You already have a windbreaker that is way too expensive. You can wear your fleece under it."

"Misty, I can afford to buy a decent winter coat."

"That's not the point, Michael. We need to save, save, save. You need to learn how to handle your money better."

"Misty, you have at least five different coats that I have seen you wear!"

"I got those before we were married, Michael. Please leave me alone now, this test is crucial. I need to make an 'A.'"

"Right, Misty," Michael said angrily, slamming the door.

When Michael was at work the next day, a heavy snowfall began blanketing Colorado Springs.

"You should have brought a heavier coat," his officemate said as he was walking out for the drive home.

"Next time!" Michael promised. "Besides, I shiver better in this one."

Michael slogged through the snow to his car, and he finally managed to get it dug out enough to drive away. He was wearing a pair of penny loafers, and his feet and pants became completely soaked.

No problem, he thought. *I'll get the blower going and I'll be toasty in no time.*

He fishtailed out of the parking lot, but he told himself he was in control. The ride home took him four hours, and it was more than a little scary for the rookie. He walked gingerly up the stairs, trying not to slip on the ice.

"Hi Misty," he said, opening up the door and spying her in the living room.

"We're a little late, aren't we?" Misty said.

"I'm late, I don't know about you!" he replied, attempting some humor.

"What took you so long?"

"It must have been the blizzard," he explained.

"You drive like an old man."

Michael was silent. *O.K.,* he thought. *That was definitely an unwarranted remark.* He walked silently to the kitchen and put together some leftovers. He had a quick dinner and started practicing his classical guitar. At least he could create his own harmony.

"You've been playing those same songs ever since I met you," Misty complained. "I thought you were going to compose some new music and make us some money."

"I play these songs not only because they are beautiful, but because they are also good exercises. I'm strengthening my fingers. It beats just playing scales," he explained. He had never told her that he would write songs and make them money.

"Right. By the time you get ready for a concert, you're going to have gray hair."

Michael was starting to catch that wave of rage now, but he was still managing to hold it in. Somebody had to keep a lid on it, because this was something that could really get out of control in a hurry. He continued to play.

"I hate you!" Misty screamed, and stormed out of the room.

Michael continued to play, but inside he was in complete turmoil. He knew that he had gotten involved with someone he truly didn't know. When he finally shut it down for the night and got into bed, it was with great trepidation. Misty was asleep, a fact which gave him great relief.

Michael managed to look cheerful at work the next day, joking about his misadventures in the snow and ice on the way home the night before. He dared not mention what had happened with Misty.

Whenever he appeared in public with Misty, her persona changed completely. She would showboat with everyone, but he could feel her utter contempt for him underneath it all. Once in a while they would meet someone from Misty's school, and even though Misty would introduce him, it was always an afterthought or something which she couldn't avoid doing. Later she would tell Michael how much he had embarrassed her, when in fact he had done nothing to merit that sentiment. He was a good looking man, tall and rugged, gentle and kind to the core. He couldn't understand why Misty despised him as much as she did. She wouldn't use his last name. Instead, she continued to use the name of her second husband.

In February, Misty and Michael's nine-month lease was up. A new luxury apartment complex in Rocky Park had just been completed, and Michael reserved a spacious three-bedroom. Misty had her objections, but Michael had just gotten a raise at work, and he explained to her that they could save as much as they had always saved. Besides, the complex was on the south side of town and was closer to Colorado Springs. The plan was to live there for the next two and a half years until Misty finished school. By that time, they would be able to build their dream house.

To celebrate their new digs, Michael planned a one-day ski trip to Vail, just the two of them. Michael hadn't been skiing since Beaver Creek and had to start all over again on the bunny slopes, whereas Misty had been skiing all her life and started right off on a black-diamond run. She didn't have much patience and didn't enjoy waiting for Michael to catch up, so they ended up skiing different parts of the mountain. Michael really didn't want to hold her back; he wanted her to ski terrain that was challenging for her. What hurt was Misty's obvious contempt for him. They agreed to meet at 4:00 p.m. and ski down the final run of the day together.

"Hey Misty!" Michael shouted, waving his arms to get her attention.

He was waiting at the designated spot and spied her getting off the lift.

"Hey Michael," she said, smiling brightly. It was just that kind of a smile that kept the hope alive in his heart. She looked radiant, but Michael felt a little bit embarrassed by the contrast in the way they were dressed. He was wearing a cheap pair of ski pants that weren't even waterproof, and she was wearing the latest ski fashions. He had a rented pair of ski boots and skis, and naturally she had her own. Of course, she had them before the marriage, and expenses for new skiing equipment weren't in the budget.

"I'll meet you at the bottom!" Misty shouted.

"O.K.," Michael replied.

Misty was off in a flash, and Michael awkwardly followed her tracks.

"Please don't let there be any moguls on this run!" Michael said to himself, pleading with the slope gods. He was fortunate and was able to get down with only two minor falls.

Misty was waiting at the bottom, and Michael skied up to her and tried to slide in gracefully.

"What happened to you?" she asked, half smiling.

"No biggie," he said. "When I really get going fast, I try to hold back, and that's when I lose my balance."

"Ya gotta pick out a line and stay with it," Misty explained. "Don't let the mountain tell you where to go. You decide where you want to go."

"Right," he said, taking off his goggles to clean off the fog and snow.

"Don't rub those goggles!" Misty shouted. "They're expensive, and you'll scratch them."

Something in the way she said it made Michael's emotions plummet. He wanted to sulk, but told himself that definitely was not the thing to do. He and Misty walked to the car in silence.

"I'll drive," she stated coldly, taking control. "I need to get home sometime in the near future. I've got a big exam coming up this week."

Misty had the hammer down all the way back, and Michael was about as nervous as a passenger could get. He knew it was useless to insist that she slow down, or even engage her in conversation. Michael heaved a sigh of relief when they finally pulled into the driveway, and he sat there in disbelief for a moment. Misty looked over at him and rolled her eyes. She went inside and left Michael sitting there.

Later that night, as Michael was lying in bed waiting for Misty to wrap it up in the bathroom, he felt the tears start streaming down his face. When Misty came in and noticed him crying, she stopped and stared at him.

"Do you want a divorce?" she asked indifferently.

Michael lay there silently, not wanting to look at her.

"I don't want to get a house with you," she said, walking down the hall to sleep in the other room.

Life droned on for the next couple of weeks, and the luxury apartment wasn't improving Misty's temperament. A group of college boys had moved in next door so that they could indulge their passion for rock music, beer and parties. There were at least six of them living in a three-bedroom on a permanent basis, and dozens more were in and out round the clock.

"Michael, get over there and tell them to turn that music down right now!" Misty shouted from her study. The new neighbors had been there for two weeks, and this had become a nightly ritual. This was Michael's third trip next door in as many hours. Each time the guys would apologize profusely, and each time the decibel level would creep back up into the red zone. When the noise became unbearable for the fourth time, Misty found a new gear and called the cops. In about 10 minutes, two officers sauntered up to the front door of the party apartment. The first officer knocked gently on the door and waited, but there was no reply. If anything, the music got louder.

"The Demon Screamers?" the first officer asked his partner.

"I believe so."

The first officer knocked again, this time with his night stick. Still no response. It wasn't that the boys were ignoring the front door, it was that the music was so loud they didn't know the police were there.

A few more moments passed, and the first officer pounded a little louder. When that didn't do it, he stepped back and kicked the door three times with his boot as hard as he could.

"Much better," he said calmly. "That should get their attention."

Sure enough, some kid swung the door open widely, and his big grin changed to a look of terror.

"Good evening," said the officers. "May we join you?"

The kid straightened up and rubbed the back of his head, actually wondering if they were in a party mood.

"Sure!" he said meekly.

They all went inside, the music went down to an acceptable level, and about thirty minutes later, the officers left amicably.

There was no more loud music for the next few weeks, but Misty and Michael were none too popular with the college crowd. Eventually Misty wanted to move, and given the situation, they were able to get out of their lease without a penalty and move into a townhouse that had a little more privacy. They rented it on a month to month basis while their "dream home" was being built. The college boys had pushed Misty over the edge, and she had relented and decided to get a house with Michael.

After they had been in the townhouse for a month, Misty noticed that a renowned family counselor was coming to Denver, and she insisted that Michael attend the lecture. She explained to him once more that she had already done her therapy and inner child work and that Michael had a lot of ground to make up. He recognized the lecturer as Francis, his old psychologist from Houston. The lecture was on a Saturday, which was a drag. Michael wanted to be outside doing something active and fun on Saturday, but nonetheless he drove into the city and attended the big event by himself. He took copious notes and when the lecture was finished, gave Francis a big smile and a wave as he exited quickly. He had always liked Francis, but was too embarrassed about his current life with Misty Lee to risk a conversation with the ever-intuitive Francis. He returned home hoping to impress Misty with his new insights..

"How was it?" Misty asked.

"He focused on dysfunctional families," Michael began. "More specifically, children of dysfunctional families. He talked about how it is never too late to have a happy childhood."

"You're talking my language!" Misty said.

"He said that if you want to get along in such family, you have to fulfill your assigned role."

"Exactly!" Misty said, riveted.

"He took us way back," Michael explained. "He asked us to write down the roles our inner child chose in order to be accepted in the family. Then he asked us what feelings we had to repress in order to fulfill our roles."

"What was the point?" Misty asked.

"Once we identified the roles, he asked us to give them up in order to reclaim our wounded inner child."

"Makes sense," Misty said.

"First, though, you have to discover what your repressed feelings about having played these roles are, and then discover what roles your real self would have liked to play."

Michael went on and on, relishing the attention. Time seemed to vanish.

"This is so great, Michael," Misty said warmly. "It's getting late, though. Let's go up to bed."

They rambled upstairs, and Michael went into the bathroom for a moment. He came back out into the bedroom to ask Misty a question, but he couldn't speak when he saw her.

"Do you want to be intimate with me?" she asked seductively, innocently. She was lying on her back, completely naked. She thrust her hips upward ever so slightly, and then turned out the light.

When Michael awoke the next morning, Misty was still sleeping.

This is wonderful! he thought. *She's in love with me!*

Misty started to stir, and as she opened her eyes, Michael looked down at her.

"Good morning, Misty. Did you have a good sleep?" he asked, a slight grin playing across his face.

"Don't let that go to your head," she replied coldly.

"I thought we made some progress last night," Michael said, already realizing that he was wrong.

"I've got to study, and you've got to mow the grass. We're getting a late start, so let's get a move on," she said, getting out of bed and walking toward the bathroom in the buff. "Stop staring at me," she said tersely, slamming the bathroom door.

Michael was reeling. He felt as if what he had seen last night was what Misty reserved for "real men" only, and that when she woke up and saw him in the morning, she had changed her mind and decided that he wasn't a "real man" after all. How long would he do cartwheels to try and qualify as a "real man" in her eyes? Would he stay in his "wounded self" and keep trying each combination, wondering if that was the one? What was puzzling Michael was he didn't know why she had changed her attitude toward him so quickly. He told himself this was wounded behavior on her part. Perhaps, if he could get her into therapy, the parts of Misty that were wounded could be healed, and then their relationship would heal. He wanted to believe that the real Misty was wonderful, that her anger was part of her wounded self, and that she was projecting her stuff out onto him. Yet, every time he mentioned they both needed to work on their psychology, she told him she had already done her work. A few more weeks passed, and the relationship kept doing a seesaw.

"What would you like to do today?" Michael asked, coming downstairs on a Saturday morning. It was a beautiful day, and he was hoping for a hike.

"Horace just called, and he wants us to meet him and the group at the mall today," Misty said.

"Misty, that's where they do shopping. You know, shopping?"

"That's where other people do shopping. We are going to set up a booth to push for a stronger military defense for America," Misty explained.

"Me and you, mostly you, right?" Michael said.

"I think you've got it a little turned around, Michael. If anyone can make this a success, it'll be Horace."

"We've got the gang all together, eh?" Michael asked, dreading the idea of spending a day with Horace and Jill and all the politically correct crowd. He didn't like the way Misty looked at Horace, the way she doted on him, the hours she spent on the phone with him while she was in her study doing everything but studying. He was the self-appointed president of this little group, and he had nominated Misty as the treasurer. All the nomination needed was a group vote.

"I suppose the mall is an improvement over driving down to Denver to have a meeting at Horace's house," Michael said. They had been meeting there regularly for the past couple of months. Michael never saw anything solid getting accomplished. It was all just pomp and circumstance with sanctimonious Horace on center stage and Misty googling over him. Horace kept a firm grip on the proceedings and minutes, and Robert's Rules of Order were rigorously enforced. It was enough to make a person barf.

"She's stepping out for hamburger when she's got steak at home!" Michael told himself.

The weekend dragged on, the work week dragged on, and Michael was becoming numb. He was going through the motions, yet he kept the hope alive that Misty would change when they moved into their new house in Crest Ridge, which he drove by each afternoon after work. He would get out of his car, walk all around the place, and look for each new addition, counting the days until they could finally move in. At last, after what seemed like countless days and nights, he and Misty Lee were walking out of the closing with their new keys.

They were all moved in by the next weekend, albeit on Sunday night of the next weekend. Michael was dog tired, but he was deeply satisfied with their new house. The ceilings were raised, there were skylights over the dining room, there was a roomy basement, a roomy garage, the floors were hardwood, and there was a custom home entertainment center over the fireplace that had speakers built into the walls in each corner of the living room. There were three bedrooms upstairs, a master bedroom downstairs and a master bathroom that was luxury itself. They were on a cul de sac in an upscale neighborhood, all snug and cozy. He and Misty sat on their new sofa together, looking out at the mountains. Michael hoped that at last Misty would be genuinely happy and at home.

The following week Michael started an intense job search campaign. The new house was expensive, and new bills were piling up at an alarming rate. Michael was determined, and it wasn't long before he landed the big one with a prestigious information technology company. He had negotiated the deal from his office in Colorado Springs, and it was all done remotely via email and telephone conversations. When the company mailed him an offer, he signed immediately and gave his boss the ole two-week notice. He had almost doubled his salary, and he couldn't wait to tell Misty the good news. They were going to meet Horace and Jill that night at a political debate in downtown Denver. Misty had to drive down separately from school, and they all planned to meet up out in front of the building where the debate was being held. Michael finally found the place, and the line was already a block long. He spied Horace and Misty and sauntered up.

"Misty, I've got great news," he said, dragging her out of earshot of Horace and his long distance ears.

"What, Michael?" she replied impatiently. "The debate is about to begin, and the line is moving."

"I got the job! I almost doubled my salary!"

"Let's have some exact figures," Misty demanded.

He whispered the exact amount in her ear.

"You could have gotten more, Michael. You have to learn how to negotiate!" She turned around to get back in line next to Horace.

Michael got in line behind Misty, feeling completely alone. He needed a friend, a confidant, and there was none. He had to dig down into his inner reserves of strength and be his own best friend.

When the debate was over, Michael and Misty walked to their separate cars and drove back to Crest Ridge. Misty got home first, having blasted down the freeway at 90 m.p.h. She was already in her nightgown as Michael came in, but something in the air made Michael's spine tingle.

"What kind of a man are you, Michael?" she shouted, her face turning bright red. She heaved a pillow at him as hard as she could.

"What did I do this time, Misty?" he asked.

"Don't get smart with me, Michael. You did everything you could to make me look like a complete idiot!"

"Like what, Misty?" Michael asked.

"You weren't the least bit interested in that debate. You couldn't have cared less about that debate. You had to humiliate me, didn't you!"

"I didn't try to humiliate you, Misty," Michael assured her.

"You are a liar, Michael. You are an old man. Your hair's gray. You need some Turkish formula. If this world collapses, I'll have to take care of you, because you can't do anything for yourself. You are so unprepared it's not even funny. You can't do anything right. You are nothing but a loser. You are so stupid you can't plan anything!" She started to wail and moan and a low snarl started to build into a scream that got louder and louder until Michael's ears were splitting. Michael thought about the rifle that Misty kept in the basement. "Don't let her go down there!" he told himself.

Misty started to pull wildly at her hair as she stamped her feet up and down furiously. Her upper lip was quivering with hatred, and she gritted her teeth as her anger mounted. Her face had become contorted with rage, her eyes were rolling up, and spittle drooled from the corner of her mouth. Both her fists were clenched tight. She bent completely over from the waist as her body writhed uncontrollably. She raised herself slowly, sobbing with deep, pathetic groans. She raised her head and stared at Michael, hurling psychic daggers into his heart.

My God, he thought. *She doesn't look human! Something has control of her! Stay calm. Don't let it take you over.*

She came over and started pulling Michael's hair, and then she beat on him with her fists.

"I hate you!" she shouted over and over. "I hate you!" She shoved Michael sideways, and he landed up against the bathroom door. Without thinking, he opened it, slammed it shut, and locked himself inside. The door was bulging inward from Misty's weight. She pounded on the door, cursing at the top of her lungs. He didn't know if she would break it down, or if she would get her gun and shoot him. Gradually, miraculously, her rage started subsiding, and she collapsed heavily on the bed, sobbing erratically. As the time passed, she became more and more quiet, and Michael prayed that she was sleeping.

He sat down on the bathroom floor and leaned back against the cabinet. "How did it deteriorate into this?" he asked himself. "How did it get to this?"

Nineteen

The Palace

JANE CALLED MEG LATER THAT NIGHT. "Meg, I just got back from the police station. Geoffrey called and asked me to bail him out. What happened with you two? You seemed fine when we went for ice cream."

"You bailed him out?" Meg cried. "Jane, he choked me. I thought I was gonna die. Why didn't you call me before you bailed him out?"

"I did but I got your machine. He said he just grabbed you by the shoulders and that you overreacted and called the cops."

"And you believed him? Where is he?"

"He's staying nearby in a hotel. He said he can't go near you until the hearing on Monday."

That night, Meg slept fitfully. At around 3:00 a.m. she thought about how she was paying a huge rent for a two-story house with a yard so that Conor would be comfortable. "The dog goes and so does the house," she vowed. The next day, she went to the rental office, told the women working there what had happened and found an apartment to move into at the end of May.

On Monday morning Meg went to the Huntersville Municipal Court, which handled minor domestic violence cases. Looking over her shoulder every few seconds, she nervously filled out the forms, hoping that she wouldn't have to see Geoffrey. Out of the corner of her eye she saw a woman in a tan and grey plaid skirt approach her.

Her hair was brown and long. No stylish "do" for this woman. From the waist up she wore a tan turtleneck. Out of the bottom of her skirt hung gray tights and penny loafers. "Are you Meg Dennis?" she asked, smiling warmly.

"Yes, I am," Meg replied.

"Would you please follow me?" the woman said as she motioned to a room on the right.

Meg walked behind her, grateful to be getting away from the door through which she knew Geoffrey would make his theatrical entrance. They walked into a smallish room with a big table in it. There were other women in there, some alone and some with a friend, a sister, a mom. The furniture was strictly government issue, but the woman's warmth made up for the cold decor.

"We have this room so that the victims don't have to see the perpetrator. Do you want to go into the court when he's in there? You don't have to, you know," she asked.

"No," said Meg, "I'd rather not see him. He choked me and I'm still afraid."

"I see," the woman said. "I'll be back to talk to you right before the judge calls him."

Two hours went by as Meg read a book that she was trying to be interested in. One of the other victims asked her what had brought her to the court. When Meg told her story about getting choked, the room went silent.

She remembered a conversation with Jane after Geoffrey had been bailed out. "My God," said Jane, "that's an attack on your power center. The throat chakra rules your personal power. Strangulation disempowers the victim — if she manages to survive."

The door opened suddenly and the woman approached Meg. "Quickly, tell me what you want. He's in front of the judge. Do you want a restraining order?" she asked.

"Yes, for at least six months."

"Good," she said and the plaid skirt disappeared through the door.

"Am I being too hard on him?" Meg wondered. "He's really going to be ticked off when he hears I want a restraining order."

"Who cares if he's ticked off," she countered with herself. "The guy's a con artist and a bully. Screw him."

Ten minutes later the door opened more slowly, and the woman returned. "Boy that guy is clueless," she said as she rolled her eyes. "Your husband doesn't have a clue. He was cocky and strutted around like a model on a runway. He was charged with assault and battery and harassment. He denied choking you, said he grabbed you by the shoulders and you overreacted. There were no witnesses, Mrs. Dennis; it was his word against yours. The charges for assault and battery were dropped. He's a mighty good talker, tugged on the judge's heartstrings. He was found guilty of harassment only. When the Judge issued the restraining order, he told the Judge that he had talked to you this morning and that you had told him that you didn't want any restraining order. Did you talk to him this morning?"

"No. I haven't talked to him at all. He lies a lot."

"Yes. They all do. I yelled over him and told the judge that I had just talked to you and that you did, in fact, want a restraining order."

"So what happened?"

"The judge told him that the court considered this particular act of harassment to be very serious and he set up a restraining order for one year."

"Oh, thank God," said Meg, collapsing against the wall.

"I think your husband should be in jail. Choking anyone is attempted murder as far as I'm concerned. He's getting off easy with a one-year restraining order. Listen, here's some information about compensation for the victim. You're covered if you want to see a therapist to help you get over the trauma. Please call me any time if you have questions about the restraining order. I can help you deal with the police or Geoffrey. Please stay in touch."

"Oh, my God," said Meg suddenly, her body stiff. "My keys. He's got them and I think he may steal one of my cars. Would you please get them from him before he leaves the building?"

The plaid skirt flew out the door one last time. She located Geoffrey as he was about to walk through the double-glass government-issue doors. Meg cracked the door a bit and watched the scene from the victims' room.

"Mr. Dennis," the woman yelled. "We need the keys to Meg's cars, as well as the home." Before he could speak, she said, "This is standing operating procedure for restraining orders, Mr. Dennis. The judge expects you to comply."

Geoffrey fumbled around in his pockets. "I don't think I have them," he said, looking confused.

"Oh lady, please don't fall for that one," whispered Meg. "Please."

"Wait," the woman said, "I think I heard a jangling noise in here." She grabbed the left pocket of his overcoat and felt the keys.

"Here they are," she said as she smiled a bigger than necessary smile. He joined her with the same smile. They laughed together to cover up his sham. He reluctantly twisted the keys off the ring.

"Thank you so much for your cooperation, Mr. Dennis," she said as she grabbed the keys.

Both women watched him turn and walk through the doors, every hair perfectly in place, a movie-star smile shining at all of the ladies entering the building. He wore his best and most expensive clothes, which Meg had paid for. "Dressed to please and already looking for my replacement," Meg whispered.

The next day, Meg was packing boxes for the move when the phone rang. She answered it reluctantly and was sorry she had.

"Hello," a very masculine voice said. "This is Officer Wallace with the Huntersville Police. I have been contacted by a Geoffrey Dennis, and he needs to come by to get his dog and his belongings. I am aware of the restraining order, ma'am. He will be accompanied by me or one of the other officers. When would a good time be for you?"

"Right now," said Meg. "I'd like Geoffrey to take his dog as soon as possible."

"I will come right over, ma'am. I'll tell him to meet me there right away."

Meg was surprised by Geoffrey's demeanor when he walked in the front door with Officer Wallace. "Glad to be back?" the cop asked him, trying to lighten up the grim job.

"Well," said Geoffrey as he removed his sunglasses with a casual wave of his hand, very California, "I still love her, but none of this was my fault."

He was impressively dressed and as he looked up the stairs, he saw Meg standing in front of the small bedroom. Any feelings of regret left her as she felt his lack of remorse. Meg went down the stairs and brought out his suitcase of clothes, which she had packed along with a box filled with odds and ends. As she pulled them into the living room, she was overcome with grief. She had prayed to be cut free from him, and yet a failed marriage is a defeat no matter how you cut it. *No,* she thought, *don't fall apart now, not in front of him.*

Geoffrey packed his computer, casually descended the stairs with his technological gear, suitcase and boxes, loaded it all along with the dog into his truck and was gone. It was all very final.

Officer Wallace stood for a minute right next to the front door to explain the ground rules for the restraining order once again. He was interrupted by the phone ringing.

"Would you please excuse me?" she said to Officer Wallace. "I'll make it short."

Meg walked into the bedroom to talk privately. "Hello," she said.

"Hello, Meg?" The voice was clearly Geoffrey's. "Look Meg, I want you to know that I've got a job. Please come away with me. It's in Salt Lake. It's a great sales opportunity, Meg. I can't do it without you," he pleaded.

"Why are you calling me? You know the rules...no contact of any kind for one year."

"Yeah, yeah, yeah. I want you to come with me."

"How come you never follow the rules? You never follow the rules!!" she said a little louder.

"Come with me," he repeated.

Meg stopped and thought about it. She wasn't looking forward to another divorce, but now that she had experienced the total package of Geoffrey, the decision came easily. "No. I won't. Why would I want to live with you? I thought I was gonna die." She spoke loudly at that point and Officer Wallace, hearing her, came into the bedroom.

"Is that him on the phone?" he asked. Meg shook her head "yes."

He grabbed the phone and spoke firmly into it. "I must inform you that you are violating the court's restraining order."

Geoffrey hung up, and Officer Wallace turned to Meg. "Look, if he calls you again don't talk to him. Just hang up. He can claim in Court that you violated the order by talking to him. He can get the order lifted that way. Do you understand?" he asked. He was clearly annoyed.

"Yes," said Meg. "I hear you." She felt like a little girl who had just been scolded by her Daddy.

She walked out to her car with Officer Wallace. "Tell me something," she said with a dramatic pause. "Why don't men ever listen? When a woman talks to a man, why doesn't he listen?"

Officer Wallace's eyes bugged out. His mouth hung open, unable to form words.

"Never mind," said Meg, shaking her head. "I guess it's just a rhetorical question." She turned and walked into the house to continue packing. As she entered the small bedroom she saw that her LaserJet printer was gone. Geoffrey had ripped it off.

It was June 1st and Meg was moving into her new apartment. In a strange way it really pleased her to be alone. She hadn't been alone since the early '70's before she married Nick. There was a funny-shaped living room with a little fireplace, a bedroom to the left of the fireplace and at the back of the living room was a little kitchen. Above it, reachable only by a spiral staircase, was a small loft. There was a little washer and dryer in the entryway hidden behind two bi-fold doors. Everything she needed was in this small space. This really pleased her. There was a simplicity to it that she craved. It was her own private space that no one could violate. Meg was home.

The following weekend, Jane called her and said that she and Meg were invited over to Taylor and Logan's house for pizza and a basketball game. The NBA finals were on. The Hulks were playing and it didn't matter who.

Meg had met Taylor and Logan through Jane when she had first moved to Huntersville with Geoffrey. They lived in Rocky Park, and Geoffrey was taken with the place. Before he fell in love with Henry Lake, he had fallen in love with Rocky Park. He wanted Meg to buy a house in Rocky Park.

Taylor and Logan had driven them around Rocky Park to show them the different neighborhoods. By the time Meg got out of the car, she was nauseous. The pressure of being with Geoffrey as he pushed her to buy a house was too much. As they drove home to Huntersville, she began to feel better. Now she was invited back to the same home that she had visited with Geoffrey. She wasn't sure that she wanted to deal with the memories.

"Come on. It'll be fun. It'll get you out of this apartment," Jane insisted.

So Meg relented and Jane showed up that evening at about 5:00. She took one look at Meg and said, "Is that what you're wearing?"

"Yup. This is it."

"You can't wear that," Jane said as she looked over the workout suit that Meg wore.

"What's wrong with this?" asked Meg, "It's cobalt blue, white, green. Shiny material. Not too hot. I like it."

"But don't you want to wear something that's a bit more feminine? After all, it's Saturday night."

"Nope. I don't care how I look. This is what I'm wearing."

"Do you have any makeup on?"

"Don't remember. Come on, let's go."

As they drove up to Rocky Park, Jane mentioned that Taylor's brother would be there to watch the game.

"Oh, no," said Meg. "Is this a fix-up? Is that why you wanted me to look nice?"

"No. He lives with his wife in Crest Ridge."

Meg didn't give it another thought. When she arrived at Taylor's house she complimented her on her beautiful decorating. Taylor had a Libran Ascendant, and her home had a decidedly Venusian touch. When they walked into the great room, Logan and Taylor's brother, Michael, stood up to greet Meg and Jane. The pre-game show was playing in the background. Introductions were carried out. Michael was pleasant but said little. He looked familiar but Meg couldn't put her finger on it.

They watched the game and ate pizza. Not a word was spoken about Geoffrey. Because of that, Meg knew that Taylor and Logan had probably been informed about the restraining order. Jane must have said something. She also assumed that Taylor's brother knew. How embarrassing!

It was now the second week in June, and Meg had to carry out the gloomy job of telling Heather and Amy about the restraining order. Heather answered the phone first and remained silent as Meg talked. While describing the scene with Geoffrey and the legalities that she had dealt with, Heather said nothing.

Amy was different. When Meg spoke with her, she felt some sympathy. Amy was outraged. "I hope you're not going to give him another chance, Mom. He's a dickhead."

Meg changed the subject. "What do you think about my returning to Barnstable?"

"Don't come back here, Mom. If you come back here, Dad won't give up custody and there will be a big court battle, and I don't want to get into the middle of it. Stay in Colorado," said Amy.

"Don't come back, Mom. I want to be able to go skiing at Vail," said Heather.

After a trip to the library and paging through a legal directory, Meg came away with the name of an attorney. She filed for divorce during the third week of June. The attorney was a woman in her late 50's. She had seen it all, and as Meg described Geoffrey, the attorney was able to finish her sentences.

The paralegal, Pam, was not as astute. Geoffrey regularly called her, begging for another chance, which he followed up with poetry written on bar napkins that were stained with wine. After passing the messages of love onto Meg, she went so far as to suggest that Meg stop the divorce.

Within a few weeks the attorney called. "I know that Pam has been feeding you a lot of messages from Geoffrey," she said. "I've put a stop to that. Sorry for the inconvenience. The truth is that yesterday he called and cried on Pam's shoulder for 30 minutes. He then asked to be transferred to me. He had a legal question. Wanna know what it was?"

"Sure," said Meg.

"He asked me whether or not, according to Colorado law, he was entitled to get half of your money."

"What did you tell him?"

"I told him to forget about your money because he was not entitled to any of it. Then I told him to stop calling here and concentrate on his job because he was going to need it to support himself."

Within a week Pam, the paralegal, notified Meg that Geoffrey had been fired from his job in Salt Lake because of drunkenness and had returned to California to live with his mother.

"Don't be so hard on yourself," Jane said as she and Meg ate at their favorite Indian restaurant. "When you have a lot of karma with a man, it blinds you. You can't see through him when others can. Haven't you ever seen a man with a woman who is clearly not his equal? People look at him and say, 'What's he doin' with her?' Well, she's his karma. You are drawn to people that you have karma with. When it's a member of the opposite sex there's a strong sexual attraction. It happens so that you are drawn to each other and the karma between you can be worked out. Then you can come up higher on the spiritual path."

"I don't think I worked out my karma with Geoffrey," Meg said. "I've thought about giving him another chance, but each time I mull it over, the little voice says, 'Nope. Don't do it.'"

"Follow that prompting, girl, or you may end up making mushrooms in the local cemetery. You can't say that you didn't balance your karma with him. The appearance is never the reality. You were good to him, and he used you. There's a good chance you did balance your karma with him. He may not have balanced his with you, but that's his problem. You had every right to stand up to him. He was stealing from you. You don't have to be anybody's doormat. Besides, there's more important stuff to be concerned with."

"Like what?"

"Look, the only reason that you're on this planet is to ascend. That's the only reason. Your job title doesn't matter. Living in a fancy neighborhood doesn't matter. Who you know doesn't matter. Who you're married to doesn't matter. How much money you have doesn't matter. Geoffrey was a great distraction for you from your path. A walking debit column, as well as a great distraction. Get back on your path."

The phone rang, and Meg heard an English accent on the other end. "Hallo Meg. How are you?" It was Becky, her old roommate from her summer retreat. "Listen, before you answer that, tell me quickly if you can go to a spiritual conference with me in Denver. I can't stay on long because Stan is worried about the bloody phone bill. From the brochure, it looks as if it's going to be a fabulous conference."

"When is it?"

"Over the July 4th weekend, and I need a place to stay. Can you deal with having a roommate for a week?"

That night, Meg was swept away by beautiful dreams. She saw herself walking with an incredible being of Light who was her guide. He was very tall and wore a long robe of white. They walked around a beautiful mansion with an ornately carved oak staircase. There was carved wooden trim and beamed ceilings everywhere. The ceilings must have been 20 feet high, and all of the walls were covered with portraits of happy couples from the ceiling down to the waist-high wainscotting. The portraits were all surrounded by golden rococo frames. Many happy people milled around the mansion, all looking at the portraits. The vibration of the place was one of complete serenity.

Her guide led her to a portrait in a little cove to the right of a massive staircase. In there she saw a portrait of herself with a man. She was seated on a chair and had a radiant smile. In that picture Meg was blissfully happy, released from all of her earthly burdens and worries. The man stood behind her with his hand on her shoulder. His vibration was soothing, but his face was not visible while her guide stood in the way. Meg kept jumping to the left and to the right, trying to see around the guide, but he was too quick for her. He lifted his hand slowly, making a smooth motion and a shadow came over the man's face. It was meant to be hidden from her.

"Oh, Meg, that's a great gift. You were taken to the Palace of Twin Flames. It wasn't a dream but a recall," Jane said.

"What's the Palace of Twin Flames?" asked Meg.

"Well, it's in an etheric retreat. All of the portraits of twin flames are hanging there. They are obviously trying to tell you something about your twin flame. It may be a warning that he's coming, or he's looking for you, or maybe that you need to pray for him. Do you remember your guide telling you anything like that?"

"No," said Meg. "But I woke up feeling really happy and relieved. What's a twin flame?"

"Oh, different people have different opinions about what a twin flame is, and I don't have a lot of time to get into it right now, but I'll just say that in the beginning when you were created you weren't created alone. Your spirit had a twin. You were both created from the same pattern of Light, from the same Tai Chi, cut from the same cloth so to speak. As you both made karma with each other, after coming to the earth, you were separated. Some twin flames have been separated for eons. When you are ready to live together in harmony, you'll be reunited, and now I need to run."

Meg was by no means an opera buff. She had gone to the opera only a few times in her life. So the constant interjection of the words "Madame Butterfly" into her thoughts during the last few days was puzzling to her.

Her friend Rhonda from Milwaukee was an opera buff. "So what's the story with Madame Butterfly? What's it about?" Meg asked her.

"Oh," said Rhonda, "whenever I experience that opera, I am so moved. It feels so allegorical...as if there is more to what's going on than just a simple love story...as if it's a story meant to impart cosmic truths to each one of us...as if the lesson is right out of the collective unconscious or something...something about a crucial reunion of souls and making sure that you're ready for it, that you don't blow it. I don't know. I can't put it into words. Anyway, Puccini himself is reported to have said that his operas came from the Divine. I don't know if that's true, but at the very least it's a stunning opera.

"Pinkerton is a Lieutenant in the U.S. Navy. He is stationed in Japan and agrees to marry Butterfly who takes big grief from her family when she marries him. Unfortunately for her, he never takes the marriage seriously. He is selfish, and uses her as he would a concubine. He leaves Japan and when he returns he brings an American wife with him. When Butterfly recognizes the betrayal, she kills herself.

"It seems to me it was a test for him. Could he love her and forego earthly success and prestige in America? Or would he go back to America and marry a woman who would bring him the approval of others? Needless to say, the universe brought the two souls together, but the guy flunked his test. He hadn't loved unselfishly. When he sees Butterfly's dying form, his soul understands the loss, and he is inconsolable."

Twenty

Take a Hike

The next morning, Michael got up early and put his hiking clothes on.

"Where are you going?" Misty asked.

"I'm going for a drive," Michael replied.

"Don't take too long. You have to get to the health-food store and fill up all the water bottles."

Michael headed North and ended up at Horsetooth Mountain. "I need a hike in a big way," he said. A few minutes later, he was heading up the trail. The morning was lingering on, and there was no one on the trail with him. The Rockies never failed to get him in the right frame of mind, even if it was only for a little while.

He knew that he couldn't hold on to the high, but it was all he had, and he was grateful for it. He started to breathe a little more heavily as the trail turned steeper.

Funny how you feel such a strain at first, he thought. He increased his gait just a little.

"Come on!" he said to no one in particular. "Let's have some of those endorphins!"

The reservoir was behind him, glistening in the day's new sunlight.

"You know she just used you to get to Colorado," a voice in the back of his mind came to the fore.

"How do you know?" came the reply.

"You are such a sap! If you go out of town for a week on business, she loves it. She's rid of you." Michael was climbing faster now, finding his rhythm.

"She's got problems. If she could get to the bottom of it, we could work this out. There's a root cause in there."

"Right, Michael. That's just what she wants you to think. She can tie you up forever with that one. Have you seen the way she looks at Horace? She never looks at you that way."

"Horace is a pudgy punk! He's a blowfish. He's got nothin' on me!"

"Just what is it about her that has you so Misty-fied?"

Michael had to think about that one. He was in his rhythm now, moving masterfully up the mountain.

"Can you repeat the question?" he joked, endorphins flying all over the place.

"What does she have under the hood? What is her true character?"

"I didn't marry her for her character!" Michael blurted out before thinking.

An internal silence ensued. There was just the wind blending with the cycles of his breathing. A few moments passed, and then the conversation started up again.

"Yep," the came the triumphant response. "You just wanted to get laid by a fox, and she is a fox."

"What's wrong with that?" Michael replied lamely. He knew that there wasn't anything necessarily wrong with it. It was just that he didn't look before he leaped.

"You got what you deserved. You wanted pretty on the outside, and you didn't care about the inside."

"Let me ask you a question for a change," Michael said. "Why do you think she married me? Oh wait!" Michael said before his alter ego could get in an answer. "It had to be that she wanted to get laid by a fox!"

"Not! It wasn't your athletic ability, either. She doesn't give a flip. She is not impressed."

"You're avoiding the question," Michael pointed out.

"You don't have to ask me, Michael. You already know."

Yes, Michael did know, but he didn't want to face it.

"She could have gotten to Colorado by herself," he said after a poignant pause. "She didn't need me to do it."

"Yes, she did. And you know what else?"

Michael was silent.

"Do you know what else?"

Still no reply.

"She's going to dump you as soon as she graduates. She's got it all figured out."

"Shut up!" Michael shouted.

"Ever wonder if she sees Horace when you're out of town?"

"He wouldn't. He's spiritual!"

"He would. He acts spiritual, but it's just a front!"

"We had Horace and Elizabeth over for a weekend. We all socialized together!"

"That was a real fun weekend, wasn't it? It was so much fun, that Misty even asked them to stay an extra day!"

The memories from their stay came flooding back.

"Remember how Horace took his shirt off and was flexing his muscles in front of Misty? Remember how she clapped and shouted her approval? Remember how Horace said that when Misty was president and he was her vice-president, he would make you their technical advisor?"

Yes, Michael definitely remembered that one.

"What about her constant insults? Calling you an old man, telling you that she will have to take care of you, telling you that you keep playing those same old classical guitar songs over and over? Telling you that you lied to her about who you were? Telling you that you embarrass her? Did she compliment you for doubling your salary? What about that insane tirade last night?"

Yes, it was all true.

"How about the time she had the Norwegian family stay for the weekend, and you carried their sick daughter all the way up to the top of a mountain on your shoulders because she wanted to go for a hike? Didn't Misty tell you that it was a stupid thing to do? That you could have gotten sick, too? Are we beginning to see a pattern here?"

Yes, a compliment would have been nice.

"When you got that prestigious assignment in Tokyo, was she impressed?"

No, she wasn't. She was only concerned that the Vienna leg of the journey got canceled, because she wanted to go to Vienna and take Amanda. Suddenly, there was money in the budget for that, even though there wasn't money in the budget for a new winter coat for Michael. They needed to save, save, save, and the mortgage was expensive.

"Didn't that trip to California teach you anything?"

It should have. She and Amanda had come out, and Michael had driven them all around the Monterey Peninsula and the 17-mile drive. Misty was rude to him the entire trip and argued with him over trivia in front of Amanda. After they left, Michael found a letter that Misty had written in the glove compartment of the rental car. It was addressed to her favorite saint, and she was pouring her heart out to him about how much Michael turned her off and how much she detested him.

"She left that note in the glove compartment so that you would find it. She knew that you would look in there for the rental receipt."

Michael was silent.

"Does she ever introduce you as her husband when you are in public? Doesn't she still use the last name of her former husband? Does she ever volunteer to tell anyone that you're married? Isn't she embarrassed to be seen with you in public? Didn't she insist that you work your way through that last spiritual conference you attended together? She arranged for you to work with the little kids while she worked in the bookstore and met a lot of guys?"

Michael was silent. He just let the "conversation" progress.

"What about her good friend in Orange County?"

Now, that was a roof rattler. One of Misty's friends had called a week ago, and Misty was out shopping. Michael answered the phone, and when the friend asked who he was, he said he was Misty's husband. The friend was astounded, and when Misty found out that Michael had told her, she almost took Michael's head off.

"I'm afraid you got me there, big guy. That was indeed weird."

"Now you're thinkin' with the big head!"

Michael was feeling so tense that he was making Uranus nervous.

"Oh! You're makin' me feel so bad. I'm always thinkin' with the little head," he said, as if it was not acceptable to be attracted to women. Michael was getting more than a little miffed now. He felt indignant, as he always did, when he was accused of letting the little guy think for the big guy. He felt that the entire male population was under attack for being male.

It was good for him that he was having a good aerobic climb, because he was getting it all out in the open. He wanted to understand and work out his psychology, but he had to work up a big determination to go head-to-head with this wild assortment of conscious and subconscious characters. Was there a main character? Were there more than one?

Were they all in cahoots? Was it his Higher Self or his lower self that he was having this conversation with? Was the motivation good or bad? He felt a sinister presence just below the level of his conscious awareness. It stayed down there and did its best to control things from behind the scenes. It didn't like being recognized, and it was extremely difficult for Michael to get a grip on it. Was it the sum total of all of his "misqualified actions" that had taken on a life of its own? A dweller on the threshold of his awareness? Was it blocking the sun of his own Higher Self? Was it a counter sun? A black sun? Was it trying to make him revolve around it instead of his Higher Self?

"It doesn't have to be so complicated!" he told himself. "It should just be my Higher Self and my inner child, waltzing together."

"Waltzing is for wusses!" he heard an inner voice complain.

"I don't think so!" Michael said through clenched teeth.

"You just want to blame me for everything, Michael!"

"Just who are you?" Michael asked calmly.

"You're on your own, there, bud."

"Let's get one thing straight. You are an impostor, and your days are numbered."

Michael had just taken a wrong turn, and wasn't even aware of it. He was heading downhill, and he knew that couldn't be right. He noticed someone further down the trail and decided to walk on a little further and meet up with him. As he got closer, he realized that the person walking up the trail toward him was an elderly Chinese gentleman. The old man paused and leaned on his walking stick as Michael approached.

"Is this the way to the Tooth?" Michael asked.

The old man shook his head and looked down for a moment. A sly grin played upon his lips, and then he looked squarely up at Michael.

"To get to Tooth, you must go higher!" he almost shouted, putting all his emphasis on the word "higher."

They stared into each other's eyes poignantly, and then Michael nodded politely, turned around, and headed back up the trail. Michael felt a calmness, interspersed with a giddiness that caused him to start laughing uncontrollably. It was as if God was speaking to him through that humble man, and God had an incredible sense of humor.

"To get to tooth, you must go high - ah!" he kept repeating to himself, grinning ear to ear. He could have sworn that the man said "truth" instead of "tooth." He thought back to his first trip to Aspen so many years ago. His angel guide was still with him.

Suddenly, he was aware of the mountain. He was outside of himself. He could hear the Aspen in the wind, the crunch of his boots along the trail, and the interplay of light and color on the mountain.

This is why I climb! he thought. He felt that the top of the mountain was pulling him up now, and the tooth was irresistibly near. He negotiated the few steep rocks just before the top, and then at last he was there. The calmness lingered, and he felt satisfied for the moment. He looked down at the houses below, each one looking quite nondescript among all the others in the neighborhood.

There they are, he thought. *Each one's little patch of earth. Their raison d'etre.* They looked so confining, and up on the Tooth his vision was unlimited.

As he pondered his world, he realized that even though he felt wonderful on top of the mountain, he couldn't go on fooling himself. Climbing would make him feel great for a time, but after a while, the reality of his life would come crashing in upon him. He knew that he had to make fundamental changes, changes that addressed the deepest levels of his psyche. If he ever wanted to be in true harmony with his Higher Self, he was going to have to understand his psychology totally, get rid of that dweller, the ego and work it all out completely. He was caught in a jumble, in a terrible tangle, and it was bringing his entire being down so low that he couldn't feel or contact his true self. This dual nature within him was causing his energies to vacillate back and forth, causing his attention to be divided among many masters. Where his attention went, his energy went. He had to become still, he had to become one pointed. He had to leave Misty.

He stayed on the mountain top for as long as he could, and as he began the long climb down, his resolve started to strengthen, and he started to formulate his plan.

As the school year was coming to a close and summer approached, Misty told Michael that she was flying out to New Orleans to visit Amanda. It would be Michael's opportunity.

The time passed slowly, but the day did finally arrive. Misty called Michael at work to let him know that she was taking her car to the airport so that he wouldn't have to pick her up Sunday night. They said a routine good-bye, and as Michael hung up the phone, he told himself not to feel sorry for Misty. *She has plenty of money from husband number two, and she's not going to miss me. She'll just cover her losses and play the part of the wronged and wounded one for her friends,* he thought.

On Saturday, as Michael walked out of the house, he felt a sense of courage and determination. "Good-bye, Misty," he said, closing the front door for the last time.

Michael found an apartment in Denver, and when he was settled in, he called Taylor to explain why he had left Misty.

"You don't have to explain it to me, Michael," Taylor said. "I just wish you'd done it sooner. My God it's been two years. As a matter of fact, I've been praying and decreeing that you'd leave her ever since you married her."

"Gee, Taylor, that was awfully nice of you," Michael said, somewhat sarcastically.

"I knew she wasn't right for you. I can't believe that you fell for that line about the guy in New Orleans. That was no photo shoot. When she sent me the picture of them walking in Jackson Square together, she told me that 'you can never have enough men around.' I couldn't believe it. Here she was about to marry my baby brother, and she sends me a picture of her with another guy! It really gives me the creeps just thinking about it."

"We've got a good friend who's a divorce lawyer. He does mediation too.Mediation is the way to go. You don't have to see her or talk to her. He can talk to her on the phone, and then he can talk to you on the phone. He'll do that until the two of you can agree on all the divorce terms. Oh, and whatever you do, don't tell her where you are."

"O.K.," Michael agreed.

The next thing Michael did was get in touch with Francis. They had several sessions by phone before Francis asked Michael to come down in person. Michael agreed, and shortly thereafter he was on his way to Houston.

"You're lookin' good!" Francis said as he greeted Michael.

"Ya know, Francis, I shouldn't have canceled that session with you about glamour," Michael said apologetically.

"Shoulda, coulda, woulda," Francis said. "That's all behind us. Let's just focus on the now."

"O.K.," Michael said. "Where do we start?"

"Why not touch on a few highlights about glamour?"

"Why not?" Michael agreed.

Francis leaned back in his chair and took a deep breath. When he was ready, he spoke firmly and powerfully.

"Those who are 'of the lie' cover up their lies with glamour, and the innocent ones, the good-hearted ones, can mistake that glamour for attainment. It's alluring, it draws you in. The glamorous ones are oftentimes not what they seem. Does this sound familiar?"

"Very."

"The wounded soul wants the approval of the glamorous ones. It wants their acknowledgment, their attention. In point of fact, though, it's the glamorous ones who need the attention. They not only need it, they live off of it. When they get it, they transfer all of their guilt onto the innocent ones. They weave a tangled web of deceit and treachery. Nothing is their fault. It's always someone else's."

"How true, Francis, how true."

"If a glamorous person accepts you, it makes you feel good. You think you are as good as they are. All the while, you are avoiding feeling your real feelings. Being in the presence of such glamour feels good. But as you are chasing this good feeling, your Light is being stolen in any number of ways. It may be your money that is stolen, or maybe your Light is taken through sex."

"Go on," Michael said.

"Wherever you put your attention, that is where your energy goes. You need to put your attention on yourself, but you're so wounded and scattered you don't feel like you have a self."

"Exactly!"

"When you withdraw your attention from the glamorous ones, be prepared to be condemned by them. But that is exactly what you have to do. You have to break the cycle that has been going on for lifetimes. Evil is inscrutable. It has no conscience. It constantly denies the truth about itself. Remember that intimacy means 'into me see,' and the glamorous ones don't want you to look inside, because there is no Light inside of them. They go strutting about pretending to be incredibly important, and we think that they must be important because of all the glitter. Arrogance and pride go with glamour. They think they are better."

"Yes," Michael said solemnly.

"A man is supposed to admire the qualities of the Divine woman. I'm talking about loving, nurturing, supporting others and disciplining the children in her care, as well as protecting their innocence. Men have come to see glamour as more important than these."

"How do I break the cycle?" Michael asked.

"Glamour vibrates at the astral level, and it lures you down. You have to raise your frequency. You have to put your attention on your Higher Self. Let's begin with a meditation."

"You have my undivided attention," Michael said.

Michael was silent, feeling himself merge into the stillness as Francis guided him. He found himself several hundred miles above the Earth. Even though he could see the planet in great detail, he was standing in a beautiful, translucent meadow, with waterfalls and nature spirits all around. As he looked at the trees along the streams, he realized that they were aware of him, that they were looking at him also. All of nature was aware of his presence, and a feeling of joy and peace was everywhere. He was standing in a circle with a band of spiritual beings, and he was one of them. There were 33 in all, including himself. Above each being was a wondrous sphere of light with smaller spheres of light inside of it, a beautiful multi-colored jewel. Crystal light was pouring into each being from the center of each one's sphere, their Divine source. Where it connected to their hearts, a trinity flame of blue, pink, and yellow was shining.

The light from each flame flowed into their chakras, causing them to spin and radiate their light. Each chakra glowed with the light of one of the concentric spheres. There were three chakras above their hearts, and three chakras below. There were other bands of spiritual beings in the meadow, one band for every color of the spheres. Each band was focusing on a specific color. On top of a hillside there stood Sanat Kumara, the Ancient of Days, and with him were Lord Maitreya, Gautama Buddha, Jesus, and Mother Mary. Sanat Kumara gave a signal, and a ring of light came forth above each band of beings. Michael's band was focusing on a hue of golden white. As each member of his band concentrated, light flowed from their chakras and formed a radiant golden white ring of light above their heads. They willed this to happen in unison, and as they all focused their attention, the light flowed where they willed it to flow. The ring of light intensified as it moved clockwise around the circle. It circulated slowly at first, then faster and faster, until the ring was dazzling in its glory.

When each band had completed their special ring, Sanat Kumara gave another signal, and the bands floated their rings to another part of the meadow. As the rings joined together, another signal went forth, and the bands hurled their rings as one giant spinning wheel toward the Earth. The wheel was directed to where it was needed most on the planet, with the intent to raise the vibration of that specific area. They made several more wheels, each with its own unique destination.

When the mighty labor was done, Michael disappeared from the meadow and came back to the present moment.

Francis allowed Michael a few more moments of silence, and then they discussed Michael's meditation. When the time for their session was up, Michael was glad he had made the trip.

"Thank you, Francis, thank you," Michael said, not at all embarrassed to give Francis a huge bear hug. As he walked toward the door and opened it, he turned and said, "There was one other very curious thing about that meditation that I didn't mention," Michael said.

"What was that?"

"When I was making the golden white rings, the beautiful angel next to me was wearing an amethyst necklace, just like the one I saw in the vision I had on the Midnight Ramble," Michael explained.

The two men looked at each other and smiled. Michael departed, satisfied that he had gotten more than enough bang for his buck. He would polish the mirror of his soul, he would become here below the reflection of what was above.

Twenty-One

I Don't

THREE WEEKS LATER, Becky and Meg arrived at the conference in downtown Denver. They went to as many lectures as they could on the ancient occult teachings as well as the more recent ones. The most important bit of information that Meg came away with was that the ancients believed in working on their psychology. Many of the mythological heroes at some point went down into the underworld. Like Virgil's hero, Aeneas, for example. Those heroes were allegorical spiritual seekers who pursued their chance to return to the Divine. Going down into the underworld means that they were facing their "stuff," psychological underbelly, dark side, or dweller. They explored the subconscious. After that, they were able to rise higher on their spiritual path.

She learned this was necessary because we all have self-defeating habits of behavior developed over many, if not all, of our lifetimes that cause us to fail the same test over and over. In order to pass the test, we have to get rid of the habit so we can react differently when tested. This was taught by the Kahunas on Hawaii, men who were spiritual Masters and could perform miracles as Jesus did. They believed that bad habits, anger, fear and so on, block the connection to your Higher Self. The initiation of going down into the underworld was also a part of the religion and mythology of the ancient Celts and Germans and performed in rituals by North Asian shamans.

"For instance," said the teacher, "If you have a bad temper, someone who's arrogant may ignore your needs and wants. This makes you angry. It's a denial of your worth. Until you work on your psychology, you will continue to explode in anger at that arrogant person for lifetimes. Once you learn to change your reaction, you can deal calmly with Mr. Arrogant, letting him know that you won't tolerate his neglect. If he insists on being arrogant and refuses to change his behavior, you can empower yourself by choosing to live separately from him. You can't force others to change. Until you change yourself, you'll never pass the test of handling anger appropriately. Once you do, then you can come up higher on the path."

"Well, that example really hit close to home," observed Meg.

The next day there were lectures on new methods of Psychotherapy and alternative healing. Meg went to two of them. "Well," she told Becky over lunch, "they have this new method where your eyes follow the therapist's hand as he makes figure eights or circles or whatever in the air. You can't move your head as you follow his hand, just your eyes. While you're doing this, you think about a trauma you've had, and it helps you to get the pain out and move on. Isn't that fabulous? So you don't have to suffer for years over this stuff. It's called EMDR. The acronym means Eye Movement Desensitization and Reprocessing. It's like rocket therapy."

"How amazing. So that would help you with all of that stuff with Geoffrey," said Becky.

"Yeah and you won't believe this," Meg continued, "The woman who gave the second lecture said at levels far below our consciousness, our body has knowledge of what is the truth. It knows about what is good or bad for it. It responds to stimuli depending upon whether the stimulus is good or bad, true or false. You just do something called 'muscle testing.' The cells in the muscle are weakened when faced with information that is bad for you or false, and they're strengthened when the information is good for you or true. It's amazing."

"I don't get it. How do they test the muscle? Is it bloody?" asked Becky.

"No, not at all. It's so simple. You stand with your arm held out straight and parallel to the floor. Then you get somebody else to press down on your arm. When presented with something true, the muscle in the arm is strong, it locks, and your arm can't be brought down. When presented with something false, the muscle becomes weak, and your arm will drop even when given the same amount of pressure."

"Well, couldn't a stronger person bring a weaker person's arm down?"

"It doesn't work that way. You're not squaring off. The person testing you uses just enough pressure to test the spring of the muscle."

"But what does this have to do with therapy?"

"The lecturer, who is a Health Kinesiology practitioner, said that therapists can use muscle testing to get information from your subconscious and perhaps even past lives by simply asking 'yes' or 'no' questions. They've never had access to the subconscious before, and he suggested that you can even access the 'collective unconscious' that Jung talked about."

The next day they attended a lecture on St. John of the Cross and his mystical teachings on the Dark Night of the Soul. At one point the lecturer discussed what it's like when you experience the Dark Night. He said that the person is stripped of all that is important to him, family, friends, possessions. His friends betray him, criticize him and turn on him. Everything that he tries to achieve, fails. Nothing works. It's meant to bring you to your knees. You can no longer depend on yourself. You must turn to God to survive. It brings about a stripping of the ego so that the soul can come up higher on its spiritual path.

"My God, Meg," whispered Becky. "That's what's happened to you."

"Do any of you recall the story of Job in the Old Testament?" the speaker continued.

Many hands went up. "Well," he said, "that story is the perfect example of someone going through the dark night. If you recall, while Job endured unimaginable suffering and testing, he never turned away from God. He loved God all the way through it. In fact, that's the key to surviving the dark night. Keep up your spiritual work, pray, decree, meditate, read those spiritual books, and having passed the test, God will come back into your life. Remember, 'This too shall pass.' It's just a test, and you can get through it, hard as it is. Suffer through it with dignity, not misery. Oh, and it helps to keep the vision of a future goal, too."

Meg never forgot that lecture. When you have bad times, just keep on keeping on. Don't get mad at God because he's testing your allegiance. Every parent wants to know his child loves him. At one point you chose to leave Him. In order to get back to Him, you have to pass many tests. If you get mad at God when misfortune strikes, you're missing the point.

At the week's end the two women hugged each other good-bye as Becky left for the airport. "You must ring me up weekly and tell me what's going on. You have the most amazing life!" Becky insisted.

"I think you mean horrific," responded Meg.

"Uh, well, yes. But remember, 'This too shall pass.'"

In July of '97, Meg was sitting at the dining table, with stacks of bank statements and bills piled high in front of her, figuring out how much of her money Geoffrey had taken. It tallied up to well over $40,000. Visa and Master Card wouldn't budge. Even though the divorce was in process, they refused to move Geoffrey's recent credit card charges from her accounts to his.

Since he had no money of his own, she was stuck with his debt. Her lawyer hammered away at him to get the $40,000 plus back. "I said everything I could think of to get the money out of him," she said. "But he insists that every nickel of it was a gift that you generously and voluntarily gave to him, and he swears that he never, ever promised to pay you back from his inheritances. He claims that the two of you never even discussed the subject. Because of that, he has refused to sign a note promising to pay you back from his share of his grandfather's and/or mother's estates."

"That's how he got the money out of me. He kept swearing that he'd pay me back from his inheritances. I wouldn't have given him the money otherwise," said Meg. "And I've got a witness."

"Well, that's great, but convincing the judge that he's lying will take time and money, and it's a risk."

Meg looked out the sliding door at the mountains. Some of them still had snow on the peaks. Their beauty soothed her, and her mind drifted. As the attorney talked, she recalled her grandmother's words. "Follow your heart, Meggie. If you follow your heart, you will always end up where your soul needs to be." Meg tuned into her heart and asked her Higher Self, "What's more important, money or freedom?"

The lawyer waited on the end of the line. A few seconds passed. "Forget the money," said Meg. "Cut me free from him as soon as you can."

As she hung up the phone, she saw that the squirrel was back. He came around often enough that she had named him "Henry." He stood on her balcony on his hind legs, with his belly exposed and his nose on the slider. Peanuts, routinely left on the deck, enticed him to visit often. She needed the company. Jane was visiting family in Louisiana, and

Meg was very much alone. Henry was never judgemental or critical. He chewed while she cried and whispered to him. "My God, Henry, I have screwed up my life so badly. I am so alone. I've lost my kids, my home, my friends and I only have myself to blame."

The next morning Meg looked at her calendar, and the day was a blank. Melancholia set in. She had friends to call, but pride prevented her from burdening them with the current state of her life.

"Your life is a mess. Why don't you end it?" she heard. The words entered her head as a prompting, but the frequency was different. She felt chilled.

She held her breath and thought about it. *It would be easier. I've lost everything. There's really no one who would care if I ended it.*

"Your kids hate you and so does your ex and his wife. Your family is mad because you left Amy behind. Everyone has lost respect for you."

"I didn't leave Amy. I wanted her to go with me. She refused," she argued.

"Nobody cares about that. Only an awful mother would leave her child behind. You may as well end it."

Meg cried silently as the room became darker and darker. The words continued. "None of them are calling you, are they? They know you're all alone, but they don't call. Your brothers, their wives, your niece and nephew, none of them call. They hate you. They feel sorry for your kids for having such an awful mother. Take the pills."

There was a malevolent feel to her apartment as if a dark fabric had been pulled from one side of it to the other. The mountain view through the slider was normally uplifting, but that morning Meg could barely see it.

"I've got to get out of here," she whispered. "God, please help me."

"Go down into your underworld," she felt a soothing voice say. A jolt of energy went through her.

Of course, she thought.

Tearing through her planner Meg found the name and number of the psychologist, Dr. Langdon, who had lectured at the conference in Denver. She set up an appointment for two days later.

As Meg sat in Dr. Langdon's waiting room, she read a metaphysical book about the Masters of the Far East. She remembered Jane's explanation. "The Masters are people who were in embodiment in the past as we are now, but they are different from us because they have already balanced their karma and ascended. They don't ever have to embody again. Some people refer to them as Saints and others as Masters. They come from both Eastern and Western spiritual paths. They operate at a higher frequency so that our eyes can't see them. Cosmic law requires that they can't interfere with or violate our free will. So they wait for us to ask them for help and then they are happy to assist the earth out of her darkest hour."

How amazing, she thought.

"Meg?" asked Dr. Langdon.

"Yes!" said Meg. She jumped as the doctor's voice disturbed her reverie.

"I'm ready for you now. Please come in."

"How is this going to work?" Meg asked as she walked into the office.

"Okay, I'll explain." Dr. Langdon began, "When we have a traumatic experience, our brain stores the memory and it stays with us mentally, emotionally and physically until we resolve it. In order to process the memory and relieve the pain, I use EMDR.

"What I'll ask you to do is move your eyes back and forth, following the movement of my hand, while you reflect on the hurtful experience. The left-right brain stimulation brings up the memory and whatever thoughts, emotions and physical actions are connected with it. And gradually, through the eye movements and discussion about what's happening, the memory, negative thoughts and hurtful emotions dissipate and the body relaxes. That's because everything we experience, remember, think or feel is energy. As we go along, you might also remember similar situations, even past lifetimes. And you begin to see the truth of the situation. All you have to do is be ready to face the truth."

"I'm ready," said Meg. Dr. Langdon asked Meg to give her a short synopsis of the trauma. Meg described her life and near death with Geoffrey as clearly as she could.

"Oh," said Dr. Langdon. "Sounds like you may have been living with a sociopath who's also an alcoholic. Am I right?" she asked. "Was he an alcoholic?"

"Well, yes. But would you tell me what a sociopath is?"

"Yes," said the doctor. "It's a person who thinks only of himself. He feels no guilt about his antisocial behaviors. He has no conscience.

When coupled with alcoholism, he is very good at being charming but usually has a hot button. When you bring up that particular subject, he detonates and things get nuclear. He'll blame everyone else for all of the problems that he himself has created. Things are never his fault. Until he's ready to face himself, it's almost impossible to live happily with someone like that."

"That fits," Meg replied.

"Would you like to get started?" Dr. Langdon asked.

"Absolutely," said Meg, enthusiastically. She made herself comfortable with several pillows, a box of tissues and a glass of water as she sat on the couch. Across from her sat the doctor.

After taking the initial measures, Dr Langdon instructed Meg, "Now focus on the scene you told me about and keep that in your mind's eye while your physical eyes follow my hand. Pay special attention to what you are remembering and feeling."

The doctor began to move her hand, left to right, back and forth, in front of Meg's eyes. "Keep your head steady, just move the eyes. Notice what you are thinking and feeling in that scene. Keep that in your mind's eye while your physical eyes follow my hand."

Meg followed the doctor's hand with her eyes. It felt very strange, moving her eyes without moving her head. She held in her mind's eye the scene of Geoffrey with his hands around her throat. She felt the terror all over again but there was little new to report. After several sets of eye movements, there still was nothing changing within Meg. And then the jitters began to go away.

Once she relaxed, it was almost as if she was entering another room. She no longer felt as if she was in the present. A cool, humid breeze brushed against her face and she began to feel fear and sadness at the same time.

"I feel frightened and sad," she reported.

"Do you see anything?" said the doctor as she changed the eye movement to a figure-eight pattern.

"No, I'm just afraid."

"O.K.," said the doctor, "Just keep going." She changed the shape to an horizontal line.

Slowly, the scene that Meg was holding in her mind's eye began to change. "Wait," she said. "He looks different now. He's getting bigger. He's really tall. He's all dressed in black, in a long black gown, black shoes and he's wearing a black hat with a wide, thin brim. He's hovering over me. Ohhh, he's so dark. I feel evil all around me."

"Where are you?" asked the doctor.

"I'm not in Denver anymore. I'm in Italy. It's raining. The cobblestones are shiny from the rain. He's walking toward me, and I'm scared."

"Are you male or female?"

"I'm a girl, a little girl. I'm five years old and he's smiling at me and coming towards me."

"How old is he?"

"I don't know. He's old like my parents."

"Why are you afraid of him?"

"Because he wants to use me for sex. He uses me for sex a lot and I don't like it. It hurts. I can't tell anybody about it because they wouldn't believe me. I can't tell my mama because she would beat me for saying bad things about the priest. I am powerless." Meg began to sob.

"The priest?"

"Yes, he's the parish priest for our town. It's a little town."

"O.K. Let it out. Just let it out."

Meg cried for quite a while, and the doctor said, "You're doing just fine. Can you stay with it a little longer?" Meg nodded.

The doctor continued the figure-eight pattern, and Meg settled into another scene.

"There he is again."

"O.K.," said the doctor. "Tell me about it. Are you still in Italy?"

"No. He's rich. He's my father. I'm wearing one of those Elizabethan type dresses. Very expensive material. My dress is white. My hair is long and black. We're standing in the courtyard of our home."

"What country are you in?"

"I don't know, but it's hot. I can smell the Mediterranean. Maybe Spain," said Meg shakily, "He's flirting with me. He wants me. My mother is standing behind him and she disapproves. She's mean to me because she's jealous. But I never wanted to have sex with him. I did it because I had to. He forced me."

As Meg paused, Dr. Langdon said gently, "So he's using you again."

"Yes, the bastard. And she takes it out on me when he's the one she should be angry with. Doesn't she know that? But it doesn't matter. She gets hers."

"What do you mean?"

"After a while I used his relationship with me to hurt her. She wasn't there for me. She was my Mom but she wasn't there for me. She didn't defend me. Her jealousy was so cruel. So I used it to hurt her. I got my revenge. I let her know that he didn't want her any more. He wanted me. That was the only way I could win."

"How did you feel about this?"

"It felt awful. I loved her and I wanted her to love me. But she wouldn't."

The session lasted two hours, and Meg left it understanding that she had a lot of karma with Geoffrey from those lifetimes. He had used her miserably. In this life she was finally able to stand up to him, and he didn't like that. He was used to getting what he wanted for nothing. Enraged, he tried to kill her. She had to understand that it wasn't her fault.

"Stop beating yourself up over this. This man is a dark soul that you need to get away from for good," said the doctor."

"I'm a little afraid to go home. Whenever I'm in my apartment I feel depressed and sometimes I have thoughts of suicide," Meg said. She felt embarrassed.

"I understand the pain, but suicide is not the answer," the doctor replied. "You don't want to let this man rob you of your life. Please call me if you have those thoughts again. Any time, night or day. I can talk you through it and get you a prescription too. Promise me you'll call," she insisted.

Meg promised. In her mind's eye, she could see an open doorway urging her to move forward into another life. As she walked out of the doctor's office, she breathed deeply and noticed the sun's light and warmth for the first time in many days.

The next day, Meg found the name and number of LuAnn Everly, the Health Kinesiology practitioner from the Conference in Denver. She made an appointment for the following day and LuAnn invited her into the office as soon as she arrived.

"Can you tell me how this is going to work?" Meg asked.

"Well, it's kind of a complicated story, but here goes. It's a blending of both Chinese medicine and its use of the Meridian System and a recent Western technique of muscle testing," LuAnn said. "The Meridian System is the energy pathway studied and used by Chinese doctors for thousands of years. Various doctors, chiropractors and scientists have studied that knowledge and a few have combined it with the practice of testing muscles. Muscle testing accesses the whole body/mind so the body's response to 'yes' and 'no' questions comes from many different factors and many levels of that person's being at the present moment. With muscle testing I can ask the body/mind to reveal what issue would be the priority for maximum healing at that time. This is not necessarily known to the client as he is tested. The healing in part depends on the client's sincere effort towards his own healing. Do you remember from the lecture how we do muscle testing?"

"Yes. I hold out my arm and..."

"Good. By asking various questions, we can discover what would be most beneficial for you at this time. This will start a process that can help you to help yourself towards greater health physically, emotionally—on all levels. It may be an allergy, a relationship, a job, an old hurt. We'll see once we get started.

"So tell me why you're here," LuAnn said softly.

"Well, I've recently had a very traumatic experience," Meg went on, getting to the heart of the matter and relaying the information about Geoffrey and her other experiences in therapy. "Can you help me to get these memories out of the cells in my body?"

"I believe that it's very possible if this is the issue your body/mind would like to deal with today," said LuAnne. "I've used muscle testing to help people with obsessions, addictions, self-destructive habits, allergies and food sensitivities—as many possibilities as there are clients. I am merely accessing the information, but your own body/mind is putting together the most amazing healing plan specifically designed for your maximum healing at this time. I follow the direction that your muscle testing provides along with my own intuitive and counseling abilities. It may take more than one session. We'll schedule as frequently as your body allows. We always get your body/mind's permission for any healing work, as well as its timing."

While Meg wanted to work on her experiences with Geoffrey, her body/mind wanted to deal with other issues first. LuAnn had asked if they needed to deal with the issues around Geoffrey, and the muscle testing gave a "no" response. So they worked on the other issues that gave them a "yes" response.

"This is so weird," Meg said to LuAnne. "My body is running the show. I can't work on what I want to work on."

"Well," LuAnne laughed, "you're thinking with your conscious mind and your body is responding from all levels. You may not be ready to deal with it just yet or other things need to be done first, but let's just see what happens the day after tomorrow."

"I can't come back tomorrow?"

"Your body says tomorrow's too soon. You always want to follow your body's wisdom which I have come to deeply respect."

In the car, Meg had a talk with her body. "Look, I need you to cooperate with me here. Do me a favor and agree to work on my experiences with Geoffrey. I want to get past that man so I can start a new life. O.K.?" Meg didn't hear any replies but let her body know in no uncertain terms that this was what she wanted, and she needed some cooperation.

During their next appointment LuAnn said, "Meg, during this session I'm going to whisper the questions that I ask, or sometimes I will be entirely silent and ask them inwardly. That way we are sure that your conscious mind isn't interfering with the body's response." Meg heard her whispering and felt the pressure on her arm. Her arm held firm, giving them a "yes" response. "We can now work on your issues with Geoffrey." She muscle-tested Meg over and over while she paged back and forth in her book of various 'corrections,' looking for exact phrases. She switched books a few times too but didn't say a word to Meg.

Sleep was overcoming Meg as she lay on LuAnne's table. It was too comfortable. Just as she was drifting away, LuAnne broke into her reverie. "I'd like to tell you about the correction your body/mind has come up with."

"What is it?" asked Meg.

"...I've muscle tested you three times, and the result is the same each time."

"What's the result?"

"O.K.," said LuAnne. "Do you have a spiritual side?"

"Yeah."

"Well, your body/mind says that it wants you to meditate on a picture of St. Germain. Do you know who he is?"

"Yeah. He's a Master. I just read about him a few days ago."

"And while meditating on St. Germain's picture, your body/mind would like to listen to Sibelius' Fifth Symphony, First Movement. "Then you are to repeat these words with utmost inner concentration: 'I am detached from selfish, put-upon, lazy Geoffrey Dennis.'" LuAnne watched Meg carefully as she said those words. "How do you feel about doing this?"

"Sounds O.K. to me. I'll do it."

The picture was set up and the music played. Several meridian points were lightly touched by LuAnn. At first Meg had a hard time saying the words. There was a part of her that was actually fighting the message. The words frightened her, and she felt ashamed, as if something bad would happen to her for saying them. Was she betraying someone whom she had been expected to idolize for lifetimes? Or was she, the brainwashed little girl, unlearning something she never should have mastered? LuAnne walked around a little bit and then after about five minutes came back and muscle-tested Meg. Her arm dropped.

"Oh," she said, "I wanted to see if the correction is complete. Not yet. Repeat those words on all levels of your being. Dig deep and trust your body's wisdom."

Meg kept repeating the words for about ten more minutes, and then a strange thing happened. She wasn't bothered by the words anymore. She had no more doubts and felt no more guilt. Geoffrey was selfish and lazy. He did act put-upon, especially when you told him to get a job. Her Higher Self was helping her to undo an ancient mind set.

LuAnne came back again to muscle test. Meg's arm held firm. "O.K., you're done."

"What was that about?" asked Meg.

"All I can tell you is that your body/mind gave you the keys to overcome and resolve this major issue in your life which may include other lifetimes. It's time to detach and see the truth about him and your relationship with him. By looking into the eyes of a Master and listening to specific classical music that your body/mind chose, you were able to undo the old patterns. And part of the correction included adjustments being made in your Meridian System so the energy is no longer blocked around this issue which can bring healing from an energy level that gradually moves through the body/mind to the physical level. Sometimes this is felt right away and sometimes it takes a little while to fully manifest."

"So, if I internalize the truth about him, I won't get hooked in again and I can move on," said Meg. "The correction brought to my awareness that I've idolized him for too many lifetimes and have let him use me. It's time to stop."

"Yes, you will notice that this whole issue will not elicit the same response as in the past and you can get on with the rest of your life without Geoffrey," LuAnne explained.

Meg felt very different, no longer unsure about whether she had done the right thing by filing for divorce. Geoffrey was out of her life. There was no longer an emotional attachment to him. Waffling whenever he wrote her a poem or left a message with the paralegal was no longer a part of her makeup. Finally, Meg was done with Geoffrey. She had cleaned him out of her underworld and was free to move on. From Bernard, the astrology guru, she remembered that another man would come along, and it was going to be soon.

Twenty-Two

Colorado Dreamin'

Good news awaited Meg as she opened her mailbox. Her letter of acceptance from the university had arrived, and if she was to get her LL.M. there instead of in Chicago, she would have to pay her tuition within a week. *I'll go to see the campus and talk to some of the people,* she thought. *I'll decide based upon that.*

Two days later, she packed a lunch and drove over there. She checked out the library and spoke with a few people in the administration. The grounds didn't really matter to her very much, but she was prompted to go out there to eat her lunch. There were several picnic tables out on the lawn and she picked up her pace so that she could grab one before they were all gone. As Meg opened one of the exits and walked outside, her pace slowed and she came to a stop.

I've been here before, she thought. *I know this place. When have I been here before?*

She recalled her first visit to Denver in the early '70's. *No,* she thought, *I didn't come here.*

One of the picnic tables was available in the center of the quadrangle. She decided to sit down and think about it while she ate. There was a beautiful brick building in front of her, and as she chewed she stared at its peaked roof. The other buildings had peaked roofs too, and the sidewalks were bright white, contrasting with the emerald green grass. The sidewalks went every whichway, straight up and down, across and diagonally. There were lots of trees, oaks, maples, pines and bushes as well. *This place is more etheric than earthly,* she thought, and then it came to her. She remembered that two years before, the night after her appointment with Howard Peak in Milwaukee, she had had a beautiful dream. It was all there in front of her to be absorbed. The dream wasn't a dream but a peek into the future, a little gift from her Higher Self meant to guide her two years hence when things would be very confusing.

Meg got the chills when she realized the enormity of the "dream." Now she knew that she belonged in Denver. She was meant to stay and go to school. Returning to Chicago was no longer an option. There was no sense in resenting Geoffrey for bringing her to Denver, because Denver was where she was supposed to be. He had unknowingly done her a favor. It was a role he had probably agreed to assume before they all had left the etheric to come down the birth canal. Maybe it was a karmic debt that he had to pay off. Geoffrey became a part of her path, brought her some major tests, moved her to Denver for the next chapter of her life and exited almost as quickly as he had entered. The only regret that remained was her incredible loss of innocence. Up until her experiences with him, she had thought that men like Geoffrey existed only in soap operas.

There was one part of the dream that she still didn't understand. There had been a man standing behind the bush just to the right of her. Two years ago she didn't know the face, but now she realized that his face was familiar. *Where do I know that man from?* she thought.

Meg was happy to be back in law school again. It had been sixteen years since she had graduated with a J.D. Going back to school in her late forties was no small undertaking. The other students were all in their early twenties, except for a few other hoary heads. The classes went at a furious pace, and she was having trouble with the accounting language that most of the professors used. Some of the classes required the reading of case law. Those classes were much more enjoyable because she could contribute to the discussion more easily than some of the accountants who weren't used to the language used by the judges. All in all, she felt good about the new life unfolding before her. The thoughts of suicide were totally gone now. She had goals and plans for her future.

At the start of October, Meg got a phone call from Taylor, Jane's friend. Meg hadn't seen or heard from her since June when they all had watched the NBA finals in her family room.

"Hi Taylor," said Meg. "How was your summer?"

"Oh fine, just fine," she said with a little twinge of a Texas accent. "Listen, I just got off the phone with Jane and I asked her if the two of you could do me a favor. Have you heard from Jane?"

"No," said Meg, "not today."

"Well," said Taylor, "my baby brother, Michael...You remember him, don't you? He was visiting when we watched the Hulks last spring?"

"Oh right," said Meg, "I remember him." Meg thought about how tall Michael was and how funny it seemed to hear him described as the "baby brother."

"Well, he's getting a divorce," Taylor said, "and..."

"Oh, I didn't know your brother was getting a divorce," said Meg, surprised. "That's too bad."

"Well, actually," said Taylor, "I'm very grateful that it's happening. His wife didn't really appreciate him too much. He's a very gifted computer programmer, he's writing a book, he plays the guitar, he rides a bike in those 200-mile races that they do. He's got a lot going for him. He made a six-figure income last year plus bonuses. He's had a reversible vasectomy so he can't have kids right now, but all of his apparatus works just fine, if you know what I mean..." Taylor rattled on and on, giving Meg a lot more personal details about Michael than she needed to know.

"Well, anyway," continued Taylor, "he just got a new SUV, and I think it would be good for him to get out and do something. He's kind of been stuck at home and as you do know, it's real depressing when you're going through a divorce. So do you think that you and Jane would take a trip in his new car out to Vail on Saturday, just for the day, of course?"

"Oh, of course."

"Oh, good," said Taylor. "I gave Jane his number, so she'll be in touch. I'll let him know that you're coming too." Meg was barely able to say "goodbye" before Taylor got off the phone.

A few days later Meg got a call from Jane, who didn't want to go to Vail. She told Meg that Taylor was being too domineering about the whole thing, and Jane didn't want to get pushed around. Meg was in the mood for a trip to Vail. She loved Vail. So Jane was getting coerced from both sides and finally agreed to go. "O.K., O.K. I'll go, but you have to call Michael and work out the details."

That night, Meg dialed Michael's number and heard his voice for the first time. At Taylor's house they had hardly spoken to each other. Meg had thought that he was happily married and so she had ignored him other than to say "hello" and "goodbye." Hearing his voice over the phone triggered a recall. She knew this man and his vibration. His voice was soothing, and she felt as if she had just come home. He was kind and seemed guileless. There was a natural humility there that she liked. In fact, it was a great relief after tangling with Nick and Geoffrey.

"Hi," she said, "this is Meg, uh, Dennis. Sorry, I'm in the process of a divorce, and so I am not quite sure what my name is any more."

"Oh yes," said Michael, laughing. "You're coming with me and Jane to Vail on Saturday."

"Yes," she said. "What time do you want to leave? I don't think I can go before eight. I know it's two hours to Vail, but I have a morning schedule that I can't do without." She was a little nervous. Her heart was beating faster and she didn't know why. This man made her feel very comfortable, so why was her heart rate speeding up?

"Eight'll work. It's not that far to Vail, but I want to take the scenic route. We'll be taking 285 to Conifer and on towards Fair Play on a jeep trail that'll connect us to Breckenridge and then around Dillon reservoir and up to Vail. It's beautiful."

"Oh, so you've done this before."

"Yes. Taylor said that Jane really wanted to do this route, and I've agreed to take her. I'm happy to get out of the city for a day."

Interesting, thought Meg. *So Taylor tells Michael that Jane wants to go, and then tells Jane that Michael wants to go. Neither one is dying to go to Vail, but Taylor gets her way.*

The conversation moved on as Meg talked about school and Michael about his job. They both talked about the difficulties of divorce. She brought up the subject of her spiritual path and he had read most, if not all, of the same books. His knowledge of mysticism was strong. Meg had found a kindred spirit.

The subject of astrology came up also. Michael had been waiting to have his natal chart read by an astrologer that Taylor had recommended, but it had been over six months since he had contacted her. He was getting impatient.

"Yeah," he said, "I sent her two hundred and fifty dollars six months ago and I still haven't heard from her."

"Get your money back," said Meg, "and I'll do your astrology."

"You do astrology?" he asked.

"Yes. I took the AFA test a year ago. I'd be happy to do your chart and your calls."

"What do you mean, calls?"

"You talk out loud to your favorite angel, saint, spirit guide or whomever you pray to, asking that he or she block the negative energies of the planets and their challenging aspects. You ask that the challenges be taken away and only the positives of the aspects happen to you. Then you pray, and the energies that you invoke are used to transmute the challenges."

"Meg, if I could even transmute half of the energy coming at me, I'd be happy."

"Well, I think it's more like eighty percent."

"Bring 'em on."

Meg got Michael's birth date, time and place and before she went to bed, pulled up his chart on her computer. Aries Sun, Sagittarian Moon and Libran Ascendant. His Moon was trine to her Sun, Moon and Ascendant. He would undoubtedly have a soothing effect on Meg's emotions. Her Mars was opposed to his Venus in Pisces, giving a strong sexual attraction. His Mercury was conjoined with her Venus, allowing for a loving manner of communication between them. In a year, his progressed Moon would cross over his natal Ascendant, indicating a possible marriage.

She put the charts down and took a deep breath.

Twenty-Three

Vail

ON THE MORNING of their trip to Vail, the mountains glistened with an icy violet hue. Each peak grew to a girlish pink as Michael waited for Jane and Meg to arrive at the central location. There was something about the mountains that was lofty, eminent. Perhaps "peerless" was the right word. Whenever Michael went to the mountains, he was aware of abandoning the effluvia of the planet, completely leaving it behind. It was as if any second he might bump into God.

Ahh, here they are, thought Michael as Meg and Jane pulled into the parking lot only a few seconds apart. He thought he could hear a Puccini CD blasting away in Meg's car before she turned the ignition off and hopped out. As Meg reached into the rear seat for her back pack, Michael gazed longingly toward her, not wanting her to notice how his eyes lingered on her. Her natural Irish beauty drew him toward her, and he hoped that she didn't notice him staring. She exuded her delicate femininity naturally, without pomp and fanfare, and the waves of her beautiful dark hair shimmered in the morning sun. The blue of her eyes rivaled the clear morning sky, and as she smiled in his direction he felt her radiance bathe his soul. Her jeans fit her just right, showing off her long legs and curvy hips. The backpack was old and worn, but he didn't notice.

"Get a load of those buns!" his inner child said, almost shouting out loud.

Jane was in protective mode and hurried to take the passenger's seat. Meg opened up the right rear door of Michael's car and looked in at his smiling face. "Hi," he said, tickled but nonchalant.

"Hi," said Meg. "Do you remember me from Taylor's? I hope I look better than I did that night."

"Oh, yes," said Michael, "I remember."

Yes, Michael did remember, although Meg hadn't said much at Taylor's house. Her distant demeanor had made him curious, and it made him want to make her smile. She had left so many impressions on him that he didn't even know where to begin remembering. He could still see the outline of her hips that he had managed to peek at through her workout suit.

That night as Meg and Jane were leaving Taylor's, he had strategically placed himself so that he could walk out to the car behind Meg. Her subtle female curves were enticing, and her carriage was elegant and noble. Madison Avenue and the twentieth century had so exploited the female form and forced so many millions of images into his subconscious that he found it hard to get to his true feelings, the secret garden of his romantic meandering with all its vivid and pure imagery. He sensed the spiritual side to Meg's nature, and as he looked at her, he felt as if he was gazing at a beautiful mountain lake. Something about her pulled him into the lovely garden of his inner world.

"We'll be taking a more scenic route to Vail than the usual I70 corridor," Michael explained. He was hoping that the scenic route would please Meg.

Meg was just thrilled to be in the back seat. She didn't give a hang about the scenic route. She got to gape at Michael without his knowing. Jane was carrying the conversation, so Meg was able to admire his profile and dark good looks, check out his clothes and listen to his soothing voice. She wondered what it was about his voice that she found so comforting. His hands gripped the steering wheel in a masculine but gentle way. After living with a man who thought it was no big deal to choke her, "gentle" was a quality that was high on her list.

The fingernails on his right hand were longer than those on his left. *I wonder why that is?* she thought. His hair was a little gray, grayer than hers. *This is good*, thought Meg. *Even though I color my hair, it's good to have less gray than your husband.*

Just then Jane said something funny, and Michael laughed. "Hmm," she muttered, "nice, melodious laugh and he's not afraid to show his teeth. I can live with that."

In all the years she had lived with Nick, she rarely saw his teeth. He wasn't big on smiling with teeth. A grin was all that he would give unless the heavy partners were around. Then he would force a smile so disingenuous that Meg had to turn away. Geoffrey smiled all of the time, but there was a crocodile vibration to it. She shuddered at the thought of it.

Michael breathed a sigh of relief as they started to leave the crowded city traffic behind. He felt elated as he thought about the distant mountains at Vail, an elation enhanced by the prospect of sharing the trip with Meg.

I hope that she doesn't think my fingernails are strange, he thought. *I can't just come out and tell her that I play classical guitar.* He imagined himself saying, "Hello there, Meg! I play classical guitar!"

Michael felt somewhat at a disadvantage. Meg could see him, but he couldn't see her. She was sitting behind Jane, and he could see only a slight portion of her left side in the rear view mirror. He adjusted the mirror for a better look.

Oh yeah, he thought, hoping he wasn't being too obvious.

"We're going to put the 'scene' back in 'scenic' today," he explained. "I thought it might be nice to take Highway 285 southwest toward Fairplay. We won't go all the way to Fairplay, though, because there's a forest road that cuts through from 285 to Breckenridge that I've been wanting to try out with my new jeep."

"A forest road?" Jane asked, looking somewhat concerned.

"No big deal," Michael explained. "A forest road is somewhere between a real jeep trail and a highway. Maybe a little dirt, maybe a few rocks, maybe a few bumps," he began with relish, trailing off as he realized Jane was a little less than enthusiastic. "Very tame, though, and nothing very difficult."

Jane relaxed, Meg relaxed and Michael relaxed.

"This is so unlike Chicago," Meg gushed. "I love the West!"

She started to talk about Chicago, the burbs, and the entire cast of characters that went with them, weaving a wonderful blend of wit and sarcasm into her tales, which she assured Michael she was not making up.

"Here's our forest road," Michael said, making a sharp right. True to his word, the road was not too rough, and the views were spectacular. He got them all the way through the mountain passes and safely down again into civilization. They skirted around beautiful lakes, took a quick ride through a scenic little mountain village, and headed on out highway 70.

At last they arrived at Vail, and Meg was elated. *Great,* she thought. *Now I get to check out his buns. He's wearing jeans so I'll get the real deal.* Michael stepped out of the car and Meg walked around. He was tall. *I'd say about six-two,* she thought approvingly, *about a 42 long.*

Michael's marriage to Misty Lee had made him "off limits" when she had met him back at the beginning of June. Meg never checked out married men. "They bring too much karma," she had once advised a friend. "You not only make karma with the man, but the wife and kids too. It's a total black magic attack on the wife's lifestream. Way, way too messy."

"Meg," interrupted Jane, "would you like to go on the gondola now or after lunch?"

"Oh," said a startled Meg, hoping that Jane hadn't noticed her scrutinizing Michael's buns. She took a deep breath and acted calm. "I'd rather skip the gondola. I've been on lots of gondola rides. Have you done it before?"

"Yeah," said Jane as she turned to Michael. "Is it O.K. with you if we skip the gondola?"

"Sure," he said. "That's fine. I've been on it in the winter and that's enough."

With a quick excuse, Jane suddenly bolted for the bathroom and left Meg alone with Michael. He was battling against the wind as he tried to unfold the map of Vail to locate the downtown area. Meg moved next to him to assist. The two of them looked at the map together and she felt the reward of standing in Michael's soothing aura. He reminded her of someone, but she could not remember who.

"Why do I feel so comfortable and at ease with this man?" she wondered.

Michael could feel his pulse quicken, and he did his best to control the tempo of his breath so that Meg would not be alarmed. It was obvious, though, that they were attracted to each other, because there they were just staring at the map, not having a clue about it and making no progress whatsoever. Finally, Michael started to pull it together and make a concerted effort to chart their course.

"Well," he said, "it looks as if the downtown is right over in that direction." Pointing over Meg's head, he began to refold the map.

"Do we know where we're going?" asked Jane as she walked closer.

"Yeah," said Michael as he took the lead. "It's this way."

The three of them strolled around the downtown area with Jane in the middle, talking to Michael about mystical subjects. Meg was quiet but listened intently. She felt a little out of it, but wanted to observe Michael and see how he reacted to others before she interacted with him. He seemed kind and calm and relaxed with women. There was no phony public personality as in the case of Nick. There was no calculated stage presence as in the case of Geoffrey. So far, he was just a genuine man with a lovely humility that served him well.

As the conversation went on, she learned he did have a good job, as Taylor had revealed. He had just returned from a trip to Cancun his company had awarded him for his contributions in the previous quarter. Meg was impressed that he was at the top of his game in spite of going through a messy divorce. He was also an accomplished cyclist and classical guitarist, and he had explained to Meg that the fingernails on his right hand had to be longer to make good contact with the strings as he plucked them, and the fingernails on his left hand had to be shorter to hold down the strings on each fret.

"Let's find a nice restaurant for lunch. I'm getting hungry," Meg begged. "If we walk around, I'm sure we'll find a really beautiful one." During the twenty years that she had been married to Nick, she had rarely eaten out, except, of course when his firm paid. Since her divorce from him, she made a point of eating in nice restaurants to make up for lost time.

"That sounds great," chimed Michael, who lit up at the mention of a nice restaurant. They strolled up and down the streets until they came upon the Alpenpine Hotel. At the sight of it, Meg slowed down to a crawl so she could soak up the atmosphere.

"All hotels should look like this one," she said. It had the style of a quaint little dwelling plucked from an Alpine slope, and on the main floor there was an outdoor café directly across from a modest little church.

"Here," said Michael as he looked down at Meg. "Is this good?"

"Yes," she nodded approvingly as he adjusted the table's umbrella so that the sun was no longer in her eyes. "Thank you." With that she took off her sunglasses and looked into Michael's eyes. "Do you hear the stream?" she asked.

"It reminds me of the first time I came to Colorado, when I was nineteen," he said. "A mountain stream has a sound all its own."

"Yes," said Jane, "that's great. We can listen to the rapids while we eat without getting ants in our food."

"Yeah," said Meg. "Ants really know how to ruin a meal." Meg looked over at Michael again to see if he had anything to add.

"I like the little bridge," he said. "It's European."

"Yes," said Jane, sitting in between Meg and Michael. "This is a great place to have lunch. I'm glad we came here."

A contented lull came over the three as they consumed their meal. Each one watched curiously as the church across the street began to come alive.

"Looks like this is turning into a wedding," said Michael calmly.

"Oh, I'm so excited," said Jane. "I love weddings. Look, there are the flower girls. Aren't they cute? And that little ringbearer keeps dropping the ring. He's driving that usher crazy." She threw her head back and laughed as she heard the "ping" each time the ring hit the sidewalk.

"That poor usher. He probably made the mistake of offering to help, and they gave him the job of watching the kids. He'll never volunteer again in this lifetime," said Meg.

A half an hour went by, and they watched the kids jump around in the grass while the usher held the flower baskets, the ring and the pillow. Florists came and went. The organist arrived with an armful of music scores. The minister came and opened the double front doors. He propped them open so that the three observers could see all of the way down the aisle to the altar. The church looked very plain inside. "I hope they dress it up a little bit before the bride shows up," Jane said with a worried voice.

After about ten more minutes, the guests began to arrive. It was a carefree group with lots of chatter and laughter. Most were definitely not slaves to fashion. The men wore sports jackets and slacks, but the women had donned flowered sundresses and straw hats that could have been worn in any decade since World War II. The summer months and the Colorado mountains brought a sense of fashion freedom to them all.

The bride's limo turned up next. The usher pushed the baskets, ring and pillow onto one of the bridesmaids and flew into the church. The bride looked lovely in an off-the-shoulder dress and short veil. The bridesmaids wore lavender and blue floral sun dresses with straw hats and matching espadrilles. It was a breezy and beautiful wedding that filled everyone present with joy.

The ushers closed the doors behind the last of the bridesmaids, and Jane, as if on cue, said, "Well, I'm gonna go for a walk."

"What do you mean?" asked Meg, not wanting Jane to leave. "Where are you going?"

"I'm just gonna walk around a little. I need the exercise." Jane left suddenly, and Meg and Michael were left with the uncomfortable feeling of being forced into a moment alone.

The sun was moving into the western sky and hovered right above the roof of the little church. As Meg squinted into the sun, she said, "So Taylor tells me that you're getting a divorce."

"Yes," offered Michael. "It should be final soon. I hope in a week or two."

"Oh, that is soon."

"Yeah, but not soon enough," he groaned. "I'm very anxious to sever the ties to this one."

"If you were to sum her up in two words, what would you say?"

"Manipulative, not what she seems," said Michael with a shudder. "Was that more than two?"

"Wow. That bad, huh? Is she a Scorpio?"

"I think so, maybe. Can we walk over by the stream?"

"Sure," said Meg, rising from her chair. "Well, when's her birthday?"

"Late October."

"Yeah, she's a Scorpio. Do you know what sign her Moon is in?"

"Libra."

"Ouch," said Meg. "It might be hard to get the truth out of that combination. But she's probably pretty and sexy."

"Very much so. She used to be an actress. But to her, sex was a vehicle to be used to get her way. It was never given with love. Games. There were nothing but power games. I never knew what she was thinking. I've never been so confused in all my life. I had to get out of there," he concluded.

"Sounds like my soon-to-be 'ex'. It took me several months to catch onto the game. By then, he had robbed me blind. To be guileless in this world is to be at a definite disadvantage."

Meg noticed that Michael had an innocence that she was partial to. He was guileless, a tad gullible, and this made her relax. There was an honorable feel to him. He seemed a little out of place in this world, which was exactly how Meg felt.

"So when will your divorce be final?" he asked.

"In a week or two," she said with a nervous laugh as she looked up at him.

"Uh huh," he said with a nod, looking down at her face as the sun shone upon it. *There's no such thing as a coincidence,* he thought. He was caught spellbound by Meg's eyes. He had seen that color in the Blue Grotto at Capri Island off the coast of Italy, but never had he seen it in a woman's eyes.

The sound of horses' hooves broke their gaze and they turned to see what was happening. A lovely old horse-drawn carriage was pulling up in front of the little church. The doors flew open and out came the bride and groom, running toward the carriage. The bridesmaids squealed as they hurled rice, and the bride stopped as she stood on the top step of the carriage. The bouquet soared backwards over her head as the groom grabbed her by the waist to steady her balance. Shrieks of joy arose from the circle of girls who surged upward to grab the prize.

A smile came over Michael's face as he watched the sweet innocence of the ritual. "No matter how horrible the world has become," he said wistfully, "we are always inspired by the ethereal beauty of a wedding."

"Why is that?" whispered Meg, enjoying his tenderness.

Michael paused and spoke carefully. "It renews our faith that the jewel is out there."

The carriage pulled away and the bliss waned. Meg and Michael walked slowly around Vail and each revealed a little about their past. He talked mostly about the marriage he was getting out of and what hell it had been. She tried to ease his confusion by explaining it astrologically.

The sculptures around Vail were of great interest to Meg, who was amazed at how some of them so easily seemed to defy gravity. Finally, after walking until her feet hurt, they found a bench outside of an ice cream parlor and sat down. She pulled out Michael's natal chart and asked, "Would you like me to give you a reading?"

"Yes," he said. "I love free advice."

Meg had a true grasp and a mastery of this divine science, and she was willing to share her knowledge with Michael. Of course, she was not yet going to share with him that she believed he was destined to be her next husband. She felt that such a conclusion was for Michael to come to on his own and in his own time. Before Meg could give Michael a full reading and completely delineate the chart, she noticed a relaxed Jane trekking towards them.

"Hey," Meg yelled. "Are you ready to go home?"

"I sure am," Jane responded. "I've done Vail. Let's get outta here!"

The three moved in fast forward toward the jeep and drove onto Highway 70 East towards Denver. Meg was glad that they had taken a different route out to Vail so that they were not merely retracing their steps.

"You wouldn't believe what the weather can do here in a winter storm," Michael said. "It's beautiful to watch, but it can be terrifying to drive through."

"Have you ever been through here in a storm?" Meg asked.

"Yes," he confirmed. "The first time was the worst. I was going on a ski trip to Beaver Creek, and it was a complete whiteout. You couldn't see the lanes, and you couldn't see the sides of the road. I was creeping along, because I didn't really know how to drive in snow and ice. It amazed me how cars would fly past me, almost at full highway speeds. I didn't know if they were nuts or great drivers."

"Neither. They were natives," said Meg.

Twenty-Four

Love is the Trunk

THAT NIGHT AS MICHAEL sat in his apartment on the south side of Denver, he reminisced about the day. He was wishing, hoping, yet knowing in his heart that this was more than a casual encounter. His mind was going round and round, but not from anxiety. He wasn't fretting over not having said this, or not having said that. He was thinking about Meg's wonderful serenity.

She must be wounded too, he thought. *Yet she hasn't closed her heart! It's amazing.*

Michael was gentle, and he could now tell when his gentleness clashed with the type of woman who wanted a man who would control her, who would push and push a man to see where the limit was.

"Perhaps I was a bit too polite, a bit too eager to please," he told himself.

"Maybe a little, but not too much!" he consoled himself. "She likes kindness. She sees it as a strength!"

"I can be a partner with her," he whispered. "As we get to know each other, these social norms will give way to a deeper rapport, and we can get to know each other heart to heart."

He liked the fact that they were about the same age, because they could share the same perspective on the past.

"Going through divorce, Meg and I are getting stronger," Michael realized. "We'll be stronger than we've ever been in our entire lives.

It doesn't matter what anyone else thinks. This is our time together at last."

This inner knowing brought a calmness over Michael, and he fell into a deep, relaxing sleep.

❦

When Meg arrived at home from Vail, she couldn't help but think about Michael. She began by having a conversation with herself.

"He's so soothing."

"Don't get excited. You need to really look at this one."

"I know. I know," she acknowledged.

"Remember, the signs are always there. You just have to look at them. Make yourself look at them whether you like them or not. Remember the first time you met Nick?"

"Do I have to?" she moaned.

"Well? Remember that party? Do you remember what he said to you when you dared to touch his stereo?"

"Yes. I remember," Meg said sadly, thinking back to the seventies, a time when her life had taken a turn for the worse. "I promise I will pay attention to the signs. But Michael's so guileless, and that's such a relief. The man doesn't seem to have an agenda. How long has it been since I was with an agendaless man?"

"You can't say that. You hardly know him. You have to really check him out. Did you think Geoffrey had an agenda?"

"O.K., O.K. You're right. But I have to say I am very attracted to him," she countered.

"That's nice but not enough."

"You're right. O.K., you're right," Meg agreed.

"Were there any signs today? Anything that made you go 'Uh Oh'?"

"Only that he kept telling me that every choice to be made was 'my decision,'" she said. "That made me nervous."

"Why?"

"Because I wondered why he kept abdicating his authority to me. I want a man I can make joint decisions with. I want a partnership. I don't want to dominate, and I don't want to be dominated."

"Then call him on it and find out why he's doing it. Maybe he was just being polite."

"I will, but I won't do it harshly. I don't want to confront the poor guy. That wife of his did her best to castrate him. I have to deal with this wounded bird carefully."

"You're a wounded bird yourself, Meg."

"Yeah, well, these two wounded birds will help each other heal." She put on her Puccini CD and fell asleep.

The next day, Meg was folding towels. Folding towels was Meg's greatest obsession. She thought there was only one way to do it. Fold it in thirds lengthwise and then fold it again in half. As a result, her linen closet had rows of towels folded perfectly in sixths. Any other way made her feel unsettled. Michael kept coming into her thoughts as she folded the towels. She liked him but knew she had to take her time. Wondering how long it would take him to call her, she turned to grab the sheets out of the laundry basket. Sheets didn't concern her as much, especially the fitted kind. It would have been nice for the sheets to look as good in her closet as they did when they first came out of the package, but Meg drew the line when she got to the sheets.

Making sure that the corners matched up exactly, she folded the flat sheets and pillow cases carefully. *I think it'll take a week,* she thought, recalling the opposition of her Mars to his Venus, one of the most powerful configurations for sexual attraction. *I'll be surprised if it takes longer.* She grabbed the fitted sheets, put the corners inside of each other and then rolled them up into little globs. *That's what they make doors for,* she thought as she shoved the sheets on the shelf and closed the bulging door to the linen closet, relieved that the sheets were out of sight.

When the phone rang, Meg jumped at the sound of it and grabbed the receiver right away. "God, I've got to turn that ringer down," she muttered. "Hello," she said, expecting the caller to be Jane.

"Hi," said a familiar, soothing male voice.

"Hi," said Meg in disbelief.

"Meg, this is Michael."

"Yes, I know. How are you?" she asked, realizing that her heart rate was going up.

"Did you have a good time at Vail?" he asked, sounding a little nervous.

"Oh, yeah. It was a good time. I especially enjoyed our front-row seats at the wedding."

"Yeah," he answered with a preoccupied voice. "Um, listen, would you like to go on a hike next weekend?"

"Oh, sure, yeah, that would be nice," she answered, "but I have to warn you. I'm a little out of shape. I haven't been able to exercise regularly. I can't do a really challenging hike." Meg could hear her voice rising to the pitch of Cinderella's mice. She was nervous and felt inferior to Michael, the elite cyclist. She had kept her health problems to herself, not wanting others to see her as powerless. School was taking a lot of her energy. She wanted to keep up with this man, but she had to tell him about her limits.

"Well, that's no problem," he said. "We'll just go to Bear Lake and Alberta Falls. It's a short hike. Then I thought we could catch some dinner in Rocky Park on the way back."

"Where's Bear Lake?"

"It's up in Rocky Mountain National Park, northwest of Rocky Park. The entrance is at Estes Park."

"O.K.," she said, wondering if this was a date or if he'd be inviting Jane also. "Will you be inviting Jane too?"

"Um, no," he said. "I'm rather attracted to you and not Jane." Meg felt as if Michael was speaking to her from his heart. The vibration was sincere. He wasn't hustling her.

"Oh," she said, taken aback by his frank approach. She heard herself say, "I am attracted to you too." Meg was blushing, but her heart raced as she spoke the words. She liked the man's ability to get to the heart of the matter without being coarse.

Meg got off the phone and turned on her Puccini CD. She hummed the arias as she made herself an omelet for dinner and looked at the mountains in the distance through her slider. A movement caught her eye as she realized that Henry, the squirrel, was on her deck waiting for nuts. Meg put aside the omelet and grabbed the bag of nuts from her cupboard. Slowly opening the slider so Henry wouldn't get spooked, Meg said, "Hi, Henry. I've got good news. I've met a nice man. He wants me to go on a hike with him next weekend. I've got good marriage astrology with him, but I have to wait for him to realize it. I'm in school, too. My life is better now, much better."

Henry looked at Meg sideways as he nervously chewed the nuts. When she finished talking, he ignored the rest of the nuts, backed away, ran to the edge of her deck, jumped onto the tree and raced down.

The nuts lay on the deck for the rest of the week and longer. Meg was so busy with her new life that it was a long time before she noticed that the nuts were still there. It seemed to her that Providence withdrew Henry when Michael entered her life, or maybe Henry just didn't like the competition. Whatever the reason, Meg never saw Henry again.

The following Saturday morning Michael picked Meg up at her apartment. "Hi," he said as he walked in the front door. "Are you ready? Oh, are those your hiking boots?" Michael was concerned, not critical.

"Yes," she said. "Is something wrong?"

"Well, they're O.K. for today, but if we do longer hikes, I don't think those will be very good."

"Oh? How come?"

"Well, they aren't...um...Where did you buy these?...I mean...Well, let's do the hike and you can decide how they feel. Look, I've got Bluff bars, apricot." He held up the granola concoction made for outdoor enthusiasts.

"Oh, I love apricot," she said. "I like all things sour."

"Do you have water?"

"No," she said. "Do I need it?"

"Nope," he said. "I brought enough for both of us."

"I've never really gone on a hike before. Years ago I did aerobics. I was pretty good at it, but then Amy, she's my younger daughter, refused to go to the sitter, so I had to give up the aerobics. I never got back into it again. I'd like to do yoga...," Meg trailed off, realizing that she was rambling. Michael was listening calmly and acting as if she was the only person in the world. His eyes were glued on hers. Meg wasn't used to this. Nick had avoided eye contact with her for the entire marriage, and Geoffrey was too busy looking at himself in the mirror to have eye contact with anyone.

She liked this man who cared about what she had to say. She felt like a little girl again talking to Kevin Nicklin. Kevin had been a friend of hers all during elementary school. Well, at least until Meg had reached puberty, when hormones cause a universal rift between the genders. He had always looked in her eyes and cared about her opinions. He'd even shared his two-wheeler with her so she could learn to ride. Meg felt as if she had found Kevin again.

"Do you have a fleece?" Michael asked.

"Oh, no," she said. "That's such awful material. It looks so cheap, but it's really expensive. I think that something that looks cheap ought to have the decency to be cheap."

Michael threw back his head and let out a large and loud laugh. Meg saw every tooth in his mouth. *I like this man,* she thought, wondering what was so funny.

"'Something that looks cheap ought to have the decency to be cheap.' That's a wonderful line. I need to write that down," he said.

"Why?" she asked, pleased that he enjoyed her mind. It had been a long time since anyone had enjoyed her mind. The role of suburban mother still hadn't worn off so that the old self-esteem could return.

"Well, I'm writing a book," he offered.

"Oh, how wonderful!" she said while thinking to herself, *What doesn't this man do? He's a cyclist, a computer programmer, a classical guitarist, and now he writes too.*

"What's it about?" she asked.

"Oh, well, it's about a man on a spiritual path. It's evolving. Anyway, are we off?"

"Yes, yes, I'm coming," she said, feeling flustered as she ran around and grabbed all of her stuff. "Why are we rushing?"

"Because we have to get there early."

"Why? Do they close the mountain at noon or something?"

"No, it's better to hike in the morning. It's good to be off the mountain by noon."

"Why?" she asked. "Oh wait, I know, in the afternoon they rent the mountain out to private groups?"

"No, I've heard that there's a greater chance of lightning in the afternoon, so it's probably safer to hike in the morning. Also, if you don't get there early you have to park a long way away, and that can add miles onto your hike. I'd rather hike up the mountain than hike from a distant parking lot. Mountain scenery's better than parking lot scenery."

"Ah, now there's a reason I can relate to," she said. "Let's get out of here."

On the very first date Michael was learning that Meg was a woman who would cooperate only if she understood why, and it had better be a good "why," or the cooperation would be less than enthusiastic. A "why" that was based upon fear or a need to impress others or a need to enhance one's public image didn't motivate her to shift into cooperative mode.

This was fine with Michael, because he was exactly like Meg. He didn't have a lot of patience with people's fears or their need to look good. In fact, if you had asked Michael to describe his public image, he would have said, "What image?" He was his own man and wanted a woman who vibed like him.

When they arrived at Michael's jeep, Meg saw it was filled with water bottles, fleeces and Bluff bars. He was clearly a hiking enthusiast and believed in being prepared. They headed east toward Highway 25

North, and about two hours later they arrived at the trailhead for the hike to Alberta Falls. Meg expected the hike to be hard work, with some natural beauty to balance out the equation. After all, she was only doing the hike so that she could be with Michael. But as she stepped from the car she realized that Rocky Mountain National Park was a very special place, a sylvan retreat with lots of prana to absorb.

"Do you need to go to the Ladies Room before we start?" Michael asked.

"There's a Ladies Room here?" she asked with surprise as her head periscoped around the trailhead. "Ah, yes, there it is. The obligatory hole-in-the-ground toilet that comes equipped with flies, spiders and, if the guy before you leaves the lid up, aromatherapy."

"Yes, make fun of it if you will. But ask yourself: 'Do I prefer the outhouse or squatting in poison oak out on the trail?'"

"O.K., O.K. I'll use the outhouse."

"Before you go, tell me, do you want to head towards Bear Lake or Alberta Falls? It's up to you," Michael asked as they looked at the map.

"No, Michael," she said. "It's up to us, not me. Can we turn this into a joint decision?"

Michael looked into Meg's eyes and saw a woman who was deeply concerned for him. She wanted to help him get over Misty Lee. He could see that Meg was fair, that Michael's opinions would rank right up there with Meg's and that she didn't want to take advantage of his gentle nature. Fear set in again, though, as he wondered how Meg would react if she didn't get her way. Would she get pissy as Misty always did? *No,* he thought as he continued to look into her eyes. *This woman has a strong sense of justice.*

"You're right," he said calmly. "I guess I'm used to avoiding an argument at all costs. But the truth is that I really don't care which way we go. I've been here before, and I'd like to know what you'd like to do."

Meg turned to go into the outhouse as it had just started to rain. She pulled up her hood and said, "Well, in that case, could we go to the falls? I love waterfalls."

"The falls it is," he said.

As they walked along the trail, it didn't take long for Meg to realize that Michael had been right about her hiking shoes. She could feel a blister forming after the first mile. *I'm not gonna be a pansy and complain about it,* she thought, trying not to limp. *I've got to keep up with this man.*

At last they came out of the trees, walked up a few more paces, and there it was. The roar of the falls was everywhere.

"Can we get closer?" Meg asked.

"Follow me," he said as he led them over to a cliff that allowed them to sit back against the rocks and take in the complete panorama. Michael sensed that Meg wanted to just sit and meditate by the water, so he didn't press her to explore further upstream.

"We can stay here and soak up the ambience," he assured her. "This is why we came."

He always had a tough time sitting still, but this was a very special occasion, and he loved watching Meg as much as the waterfall. She settled in, and he leaned back against a rock and "popped the cork "on his water bottle.

"Ahh, vintage!" he sighed. "Are you thirsty?"

"Very!" Meg said, holding out both hands to take the water that Michael offered her.

He loved the way she reached out both hands. It was an innocent gesture, and she was letting her happiness bubble up to the surface. She was feeling playful, she was feeling free. Michael sensed that other men in her life didn't let her express herself and probably weren't very interested in what she felt. *This is amazing!* he thought. *After all she's been through, she is still willing to trust. Her faith is still alive and vibrant.*

"The power of the water is in its softness," Meg said. "It shapes and smooths the hardest rocks."

They watched the falls together in silence, glancing over at each other sheepishly from time to time and breaking out into childish laughter. He thought about the cycling women he had been out with, how aggressive they were, and how he could almost see them going down their mental checklist of qualifications. Meg looked so serene, and he could feel her calmness splashing over him like the cascading water of Alberta Falls. He felt a lovely pink glow surround him, and he looked over at Meg. She had closed her eyes as she listened to the water, and he almost couldn't believe what he saw. She was surrounded by the glow of the most exquisite pink roses that seemed to grow from the air all around her. Their fragrance was wafting all around him. It was her gift to him, a bouquet from her heart. As Meg slowly opened her eyes, the roses vanished, but Michael could still feel their radiance.

"Thanks for the roses, Michael," she said peacefully. "I saw them all around you, and in my fancy, I plucked one for you and one for me."

"Perhaps the nature spirits brought them to us," Michael offered.

"Perhaps we made them just by being close to each other," Meg echoed back.

Michael smiled at her, and then looked back at the waterfall. Wherever he looked, she was there. The many hues of the sunlight played off the water and sang their lullaby to him, but it was coming from her.

"I like that song," she said. "You can play it for me anytime."

He felt himself soaring down the waterfall, gliding just above the surface of the water. Meg was right there with him.

"Let's dive into it," she said.

In their imagination they plunged into the silence, and even though the water was shallow to their outer senses, it was like the deepest ocean to the new lovers. They reached the river bottom, turned back toward the sunlight and burst back into the open air. They stood on opposite Rocky Mountain peaks, flooding the valley below with abundant love. The rapture gradually subsided, and they could feel their relationship blossoming. Eventually they hiked back to the parking lot, and Michael was glad that he hadn't pushed Meg into one of his famous "pedal to the metal" hikes.

Meg got in the car, looking happy that she had survived this little jaunt. Michael saw that she was dog tired and that she was trying not to show it. Prattling away about this and that, she began to fade. Michael enjoyed her conversation while it lasted, but it didn't last long. The combination of the car's movements and the warm afternoon sun overcame her resolve to be good company. She fell into a deep sleep as Michael drove on, feeling protective of her. She had many of the same qualities that he had. Their vibrations matched perfectly. Her company gave him such pleasure that he was grateful just to hear her breathing rhythmically next to him.

About thirty minutes later, Meg woke up. "Oh, I'm so sorry," she said.

"Sorry for what?" Michael asked.

"You must be thinking that I'm a great date," she said. "Here I fall asleep in the middle of the day."

"You've been through a lot, Meg. It's O.K. to sleep," he said gently.

What a great relief, she thought. Nick would have scorned her for taking a nap. Michael's relaxed attitude made her feel like crying joyful tears. Her long prison sentence was over. Maybe the second half of her life would allow for a return of self-esteem. She loved the way Michael listened to her. "Michael," she asked, "why don't men listen to women?"

"Now, that is a subject worthy of discussion," Michael said. "It reminds me of a joke I read on the Internet. A woman is talking to her husband, telling him that 'You and I have no clothes to wear because they are strewn all over the floor in this messy bedroom. We have to pick them up right now!' All the husband hears is, 'you and I...blah blah blah...no clothes...blah blah blah...bedroom...blah blah blah... right now.'"

Meg rolled her eyes.

"O.K., O.K.," said Michael and continued in a more serious vein. "I think the level of culture in a society can be gauged by how men treat women and how women treat men. If a man is not listening to a woman, there can be as many reasons for that behavior as there are instances, but generally speaking we have a patriarchal society. The man is elevated and the woman is devalued. The pendulum has swung too far in one direction. We have forgotten we are all one. No one person is more important than another in the eyes of the Divine. We are all one. A matriarchal society would be no better.

"If a man mistreats a woman, he may come back in another life as a woman and be mistreated by a man, and vice versa. The ruling elite on the earth stay in control by keeping the pendulum swinging from one extreme to the other. The only way out is balance, the middle way. A way that acknowledges we are all one. People need to maintain a balanced interchange of love and compassion for each other, and then they can come up higher on their spiritual paths to a universal harmony."

They talked quietly for the rest of the return trip, and then Michael pulled into the parking lot in front of a Middle Eastern restaurant. "Would you like to eat here?" he asked. "It's Logan's favorite restaurant."

"Oh," said Meg, trying to look excited. "Sure. I haven't eaten in a Middle Eastern restaurant since I left New York City twenty-two years ago," she said, remembering that there was a reason for that.

"They've got a belly dancer, and the food's good."

"Uh huh," she said, smiling.

She grabbed her backpack so that she could change into jeans in the ladies room. Michael approached the front door of the place while Meg looked it over. Dull stucco and gaudy lights gave the entrance a disappointing curb appeal. She wondered if the inside would be any better. Michael spoke with the maitre d' while Meg made her quick change. Walking out of the ladies room, she looked around to find Michael sitting at a table that was only slightly off the floor. Looking at her feet, he whispered, "You have to take your shoes off."

"Oh," she said as she turned around to leave them in a special room for everyone's shoes.

There was a big pillow for her to sit on. The room was dark, and their area was lit with a candle. Eventually the waitress ambled over and told them all about the specials for the night. Michael insisted that they should taste the delights, so he ordered a little bit of everything to be sure that they would not miss any special treats.

"This reminds me of Singapore!" Michael said. "I was in a restaurant there that was dimly lit, just like this one. Dimly lit was extremely important, because I didn't want to see what I was eating. I had ordered a dish called 'Assorted Meats,' and I had no idea what was in there. I didn't ask, either."

Somehow, this was not very reassuring to Meg, who was trying her best to be a good sport about all of this. They had to eat with their hands, and in between each course, the waitress brought by an ornate silver pitcher and poured cold water over their outstretched hands so that they wouldn't spoil the flavor of the next enticing culinary episode with the residue from the previous one.

At first, Meg felt fine sitting on the floor, but after the first half hour, her feet and hands felt icy. Their table wasn't too far from the front door, and as people came and went, the temperature of the room dropped too much. As she ate, her jeans started to feel too tight, so she was uncomfortable all over. Then the entertainment arrived.

A lady of ample size entered the room and began to wiggle around while she clanged a couple of brass Middle Eastern castanets. There was Middle Eastern music playing through a few hidden speakers. Meg could feel herself tensing up from the cold. Her knees were getting stiff, and she was all-around miserable. She wanted to make conversation with Michael, but the belly dancer was noisy and intrusive. The only thing to do was to pretend that she was enjoying the belly dancer. The woman was delighted with herself as she rolled quarters up, down and around her navel. Nobody in the room was enjoying the belly dancer more than the belly dancer.

Finally, Meg finished her dinner and they were able to leave. She couldn't wait to get out of the place. When she settled in the car she asked, "Do you mind if I turn the heat way up for a while?"

"Yeah, I guess it was cold in there," he said. "Did you like that restaurant?"

"Uh huh."

"If you had to choose a restaurant, would you have chosen that one?" he asked. Michael could feel that she was just being polite.

"Uh, no," she said.

"O.K., what kind of restaurants do you like?"

"French," she said with great relief. "And preferably one with a waiter with a Parisian accent."

"You know," he said, "I like French restaurants, too."

"Then why did you choose this one?"

"Oh, I don't know. Logan says it's one of his favorite restaurants, and I guess I thought you might like it too."

"How can he like that restaurant?" she said. "He must have had a past life as a tentmaker."

"How about we get a list of all of the French restaurants in Denver and we go to all of them?"

Meg lit up with joy. "Are you serious? You don't know how much I would love that."

"Good," he said. "Then that's what we'll do. I don't feel like going home yet, do you?"

"Nope!"

"How would you like to go up to Flagstaff mountain and watch the sunset? It's just past Chautauqua Park and the Flatirons. You can see Rocky Park, the Continental Divide and most of the Front Range."

She looked in his eyes and gave him a warm smile. He was romantic in a comfortable way, a way that made her sigh quietly and feel her heart unfolding. They headed west out Baseline Road, and when they got past Chautauqua they began their ascent.

"You should try climbing this on a bicycle!" Michael remarked.

"You climbed up here on a bicycle?"

"Yes. When you train for it, after a while you don't think it's any big deal."

"Do you still ride your bike up here?"

"Nope," he said. "I hung up my spurs."

"What made you decide to do it?"

Michael thought about giving her some line, but he knew he could trust her. "It was time," he said. "It served me well for so many years. It got me outside into the fresh air. It kept me out of the bars, and it kept me healthy and in great shape. I made a lot of friends, and I have a lot of good memories."

"Could you relate to those friends on a soul level?"

"At first I thought so," Michael said. "But we shared only that first room. There was no way to get past it into the second room. I spent so much time trying to be cool and performing daring feats of glory. The danger was always present, and it was mounting. The crashes started to get more serious and more frequent. Life went on so normally for everyone else after my last big encounter with the pavement. I was a replaceable part in the system, and they found another rider to take my place in the group. It made me reassess what I really wanted and what my life was all about. I decided to take all of the energy that I was putting into cycling and use it to follow the small, still voice."

"A wise decision," she whispered.

Michael was starting to feel giddy, because the more he talked with Meg, the more he wanted to kiss her. He was trying not to be too obvious as he looked for the right place to pull in. At last the scenic overview that he was looking for presented itself, and he turned in and parked.

"Let's walk over there," Michael suggested, getting out of the car, trying to look calm.

"O.K.," Meg said.

Just then, Michael's inner child started chattering silently to him in full gear. "Ya know what? I like her a bunch. Ya gotta tell her. Girls always like that stuff!"

"You are the expert here, right, little guy?" Michael asked, safe in his mental fortress where no one else could hear.

"Ya gotta listen to me. 'Love' is the trunk of the tree, and 'like' is the branches. It's simple! Ya gotta make your move and tell her. No more talkin' about bicycles. That's guy stuff. Stop hangin' out on the branches. Get over to the trunk where the love is. Plant one on her." Michael could feel how excited the little guy was. He was bouncing all over the place, begging for attention.

"How many girls have you kissed, anyway?" he retorted.

"As many as you have!" the little guy shot back. "I've been right here the whole time!"

Michael started to smile, and Meg looked over at him. "What are you smiling about, Michael?"

"Meg, do you know what the difference between like and love is?"

Meg's little girl started to kick into high gear. "Tell him that 'love' is the trunk of the tree, and 'like' is the branches!" she urged.

Meg didn't hesitate. "'Love' is the trunk of the tree, and 'like' is the branches," she said with authority.

"Way to go, Meg!" the little girl said, getting into full swing and bouncing all over the place. "He's gonna kiss ya now for sure!"

Michael was too shocked to speak for a moment. They had reached the lookout point, and there was actually a bench there for them to sit on. He took Meg's hand and pulled her down on the bench next to him.

"Are ya gonna keep yackin' or are ya gonna kiss her?" said the impatient boy within. "I'd have pulled her down on this bench and kissed her without any more goofin' around!"

Michael held Meg's hand with both of his and stared into her eyes, feeling the current flow between them in ever rising spirals.

"Where did you hear that, Meg?"

"The still, small voice within."

Michael could feel their worlds entwining, as if their roots were the same, as if the trunk had merely split in two to bring them both into this world. He didn't know where he began and where she left off.

"Better not tell her ya like her a bunch now!" said Michael's little one. "Ya gotta go for more gusto!"

"Not another word from you, understand?" Michael told him. The little boy was happy to comply. Michael was right where he wanted him.

Their passion was rising quickly, and Michael stood up and pulled Meg to him. He kissed her deeply, pouring his love into her without reserve.

Meg swooned backwards, feeling Michael's strong arms support her. The sun was setting over the continental divide as their first kiss ended. She looked up into his eyes, never wanting the moment to end.

Twenty-Five

The Necklace

On Monday morning, Meg was back in school. The difference between her weekends with Michael and her weekdays at school was unsettling. The tax program was becoming more and more stressful. She wasn't at all happy about this because she wanted to spend as much time as possible with Michael.

"How about we go to the next French restaurant on this list tomorrow night?" he asked.

"I'd love to, but I have to stay after class. There's some stuff I have to research in the library."

"Ahhhh, so you'll be skipping dinner?"

"No, I'll be doing a five-minute salad inhale at the cafeteria."

"And would you like some male company when you inhale that salad?"

"You mean you'd like to meet me at the cafeteria for dinner?"

"I most definitely would."

Meg smiled at this beautiful man who so wanted her company. The warm and cozy feeling in her solar plexus was a sure sign of a deep love that was growing more and more with each encounter. She felt respect for his comfortable and intelligent ways, and cherished his radiant smile. Lately, she made note of how safe she felt when he put his arm around her.

"Michael," she called as he walked into the cafeteria on the following night. "Over here."

Michael approached the table quickly, because he was hungry. "So do you want to get up to the salad bar pretty soon?" he asked, looking over his shoulder to check out the edibles.

"I have good news. I got a job," she whispered.

"This is wonderful," he said. "I didn't know that you were looking."

"I know. I kept it to myself. It was an alchemy."

"Ah, I understand. So no other human mind can interfere energetically with your plans."

"Yes, you know about alchemy?"

"To bring your ideas into the physical, you write out the plans, you visualize them each day and tell no man."

Meg smiled because she found that no matter what the subject, she and Michael were always on the same page.

"So when do you start?" he asked.

"Next fall."

"And where will you be working?"

"You won't believe this. I got a job in the Denver office of Nick's old firm. The one that fired him. I'll be doing estate planning"

It was a victory that comes maybe once in a lifetime. The betrayals and criticism had worn down her ability to love herself, but it was all coming back. With Michael's help, she was climbing out of the abyss. Having a job made her feel worthwhile again. It gave her life a purpose, but more and more, Michael was becoming the raison d'etre. He asked her if he could walk her to her class, and she gladly consented. As they went out into the quadrangle, her eyes skimmed over the campus buildings and trees that had been in her dream. She glanced at Michael and did a double take. He was standing near the bush where the man in her dream had been. Now her recall was complete. The man in her dream had been Michael himself.

For the better part of a year, Meg and Michael skied in the mountains and ate in Denver's best French restaurants. With Neptune in his first house, Michael loved to go to the movies, and Meg was happy to make it a joint experience. As they walked out of the theater in the local Mall, she noticed that Michael was shivering.

"Why aren't you wearing your winter coat?" she asked, looking at his windbreaker.

"I don't have one," he said.

"Why not?"

"You know, that's a good question. Why don't I have a winter coat?"

"Oh my God. Michael, you need a winter coat just like everyone else." Her words dropped into his brain as a stone slips into water.

"You know, Meg, I do. I do need a winter coat just like everyone else. I don't know what I've been waiting for!"

He grabbed her arm, turned her around, and headed back into the Mall. Her eyes dampened as she saw him choose the most expensive down jacket he could find. It was good to see Michael, with Meg's help, climbing out of his own abyss.

Michael's love for Meg was increasing each day, and when she told him about her promptings about "Madame Butterfly" and how much she wanted to see it, he decided to act. Even though the opera was not one of his favorite things, Michael surfed the net until he discovered a production by the Houston Opera. It was scheduled for the weekend before Valentine's Day, and he arranged the flights secretly.

"How about going to Houston with me?" he asked days later.

"Oh, sure. But what for?"

"It's a surprise," he said with a grin.

"Doesn't your family live there?"

"Some of them."

"When do we go?"

"The weekend before Valentine's."

A quiet peace of mind came over Meg. *I guess he's going to introduce me to his family,* she thought. *That's a good sign.*

As she slept that night, she found herself in a beautiful room. The walls were made of iridescent mother-of-pearl filled with a light that seemed to have no source. She wore a floor length white gown and saw Michael walking towards her. He, too, wore a robe of white and put his hands on her shoulders as he looked down gently into her eyes. The look on his face was serious as he began to speak. "Meg," he said, softly, "do you love me?"

She hesitated, thinking that a profession of love should come from a Texan first, especially if he's a man. "Do you love me?" she asked.

In that instant Michael disappeared...poof. Standing alone in the room, Meg felt sad that he was gone. She couldn't follow him because he had just disappeared, leaving no tracks. *Isn't that just like a man,* she thought. *Even on etheric levels, he can't commit.*

The next morning as Meg left for school she knew that secretly Michael loved her. Tucking the joy inside of her heart, she vowed to keep his love to herself as a quiet inner knowing.

It wasn't long before it was time to fly to Houston, and Michael called Meg with the details. "I'll pick you up at 10:00," he said. "The flight leaves at noon."

"Great," she said, "but can you tell me what kind of clothes to bring? Formal, casual or what?"

"February's the coldest month down there. It'll be in the 30's to 50's maybe. Bring whatever is comfortable, but bring one nice outfit. Well, actually, I think you should wear the nice outfit. We might be pressed for time."

"What's it for?" she asked, hoping he'd slip up and reveal the surprise.

"Nope, it's a surprise."

By the time they put their luggage in the rental car, it was close to the dinner hour. Michael drove to Memorial Park, refusing to answer any questions about the evening's activities. The car slowed down to a halt on the edge of the park, and Michael pulled in front of a lovely and large older home. Meg saw that its lush lawn and pond were a home for several swans. She watched them noiselessly glide across the water and began to relax. A valet sprinted to open her door, and she approached the elegant front steps and entrance. The gazebos on the lawn were not in use, the temperature being too cool, but upon entering what she now recognized as a fabulously romantic Italian restaurant, the violinist began to play. Meg took in a cleansing breath and relaxed some more.

"Name, sir?" asked the maitre d'.

"Michael Bedivere."

"Right this way."

As Meg walked behind the maitre d', she tried to see around him. Maybe Michael's family was already seated at a table. She looked for some people who resembled Michael. The other tables were filled with whispering people. Not one resembled Michael or looked up in anticipation as they approached. The maitre d's outstretched arm directed her to a table for two next to a large window with a view of the gazebo and the swans. "Señora," he said as he drew her chair out from the table.

"Oh, Michael, this is wonderful," she said, relaxing into her chair. A part of her was disappointed about Michael's family not being included in the surprise, but a bigger part of her was happy to be alone with Michael. Meeting the "fam" is always so stressful. "Will your family be meeting us later?"

"Nope. I don't want to be with them. I want to be with you."

The maitre d' winked at Michael as he handed Meg her menu. He assured them that their waiter would tend to them momentarily and returned to his station.

"Michael, this menu has no prices on it."

"I know. Just order what you want."

"Oh, I'm really liking this place," she said as she looked around. The decorating was beautiful, which meant a lot to Meg. Because she had a Taurus ascendant, her chart was ruled by Venus. No bare light bulbs for Meg. If her surroundings weren't beautiful, she had a hard time settling in. The lace curtains and crisp white linens with silver flatware met with her approval, and as she soaked up the frequency of the entire room, a radiant smile crept across her face.

"So what are you going to order?" she asked. She was in her element.

Michael didn't answer. He looked into her eyes and said slowly, "Oh, Meg, I love it when you smile. You have the most beautiful smile."

Meg lapped up his approval, and touching his hand, said, "Thank you." The compliment was wonderful to hear. She remembered her dream and his question, "Meg, do you love me?" She wondered if she should tell him that she loved him. It seemed like a good moment. *No,* she thought. *Don't be pushy.*

"You asked me about what I'm going to order. I don't know yet. How about you?"

"Well, as you know, I'm partial to salmon."

"Yeah, that sounds good. I'll do that too," he said nervously, looking around for the waiter.

"Michael, you seem nervous."

"Nervous? What's that?"

The waiter came and took their identical orders. "Excellent choice," he said as his notepad snapped shut.

"So you still can't tell me what's coming after dinner?" she asked gently.

"Nope," he said. "I told you. It's a surprise."

Meg was impressed with his one-pointedness and changed the subject. "O.K., so tell me about the book you're reading?"

"Are you familiar with the art of Nicholas Roerich?"

"Yes," she said. "It's very mystical. I love it."

They talked quietly about the book until the waiter brought their entrées. It had the kind of presentation that was so beautiful that you felt guilty eating it, but only for a moment. The pasta was delicate as well as the sauce, and the Caesar salad was supreme. The salmon was tender and moist, slightly speckled with herbs and tossed in with the pasta. All in all, it was a memorable dinner.

As Meg swallowed the last bite, the maitre d' approached her with a parcel in his hands. "UPS delivered this earlier today, Señora. It is for you."

Meg took the box and looked over at Michael. "Do you have anything to do with this?" she asked.

"You'll have to open it to know," he said.

She tore at the paper and pulled out a rectangular silver box wrapped in gold ribbon and crowned with a gold bow. There was no card. Her face lit up. "At this point," Michael said, "I'd like to take the credit for this."

Off came the bow, off came the ribbon, and then her fingers quickly removed the lid. She reached into a generous amount of tissue paper and pulled out a little model of a church. "This looks so familiar to me," she said. "Where have I seen this?"

"There's a much larger version of it in Vail," he coaxed.

"Oh my God. It's the little church in Vail. Our first date."

Meg held the little church tightly and the roof opened up. A team picture of the Hulks smiled up at her. "The Hulks? What are they doing in there?"

"The Hulks game at Taylor's, remember?"

"Oh yeah, the night we met." Meg pulled the picture out and underneath it rested a blue velvet ring box. She looked at Michael and gently picked up the box. He smiled in anticipation as she opened the box to reveal a beautiful sapphire and diamond ring. "Oh Michael," she said as she put the little church back on the table.

"There's something more to that little church. You're not done yet," he said.

Meg looked at it and turned it around and finally upside down. There was a little key on the bottom and she turned it. The little church was really a music box that began to play "Un Bel Di Vedremo" from Puccini's Madame Butterfly. She began to cry.

Suddenly, there was a ruckus out on the lawn. Looking to her left, she saw two waiters chasing some swans around the closest gazebo. They were laughing and looking in the window at Meg and Michael. "What are they doing?" she asked.

Michael didn't respond, but looked back at the scene. The waiters were still running around with the swans when Meg noticed a banner hanging from the gazebo. It read in large pink letters, "Meg, will you marry me?"

It took her a few seconds to absorb the moment. She looked over at Michael and saw him smiling. "You're asking me to marry you?"

"That's what the sign says." He touched her hand and assured her, "Meg, I love you."

The other people in the room were staring at her, grinning and giggling. As the maitre d' watched the happy couple, he motioned for the waiters to come inside.

It was Meg's moment. She had gotten her cue. "Michael," she said, "you are the kindest man I've ever known. I've loved you from the first moment I heard your voice. It would be a privilege to marry you."

As Michael turned and motioned to the waiter, he said, "Well, I'll take that to be a 'yes.'"

Meg put the sapphire and diamond ring on her finger, the waiter brought the champagne and the whole room broke out into applause and cheers. Tears moved down her cheeks and Michael said, "Don't cry, Meg. There's more to come." She shifted in her seat as she tried to relax. Being the center of attention always made her uneasy. As she made the movement, her blouse gently opened and Michael saw a slight sparkle of violet and gold.

"Mr. Bedivere," interrupted the waiter, "the violinist would like to know which aria you would like to hear." Michael turned to Meg and, again distracted by the glint of a necklace resting inside the folds of her blouse said, "Would you like to select an aria?"

"I would love to hear Musetta's Waltz from La Boheme, if that is part of his repertoire," was her reply, while Michael's mind raced to remember where he had seen that necklace before. The stone was rectangular with a flourished gold setting that reminded him of a doorway in a grand home.

The violinist performed beautifully, but the aria was lost on Michael. His heart beat wildly as he strained to remember the necklace.

Meg looked at him inquisitively. "Well," he said, suddenly changing gears and sounding in control once more, "we don't want to be late for the opera, do we?"

“The opera?” she whispered in reverence.

Unaware of Michael’s state of mind, Meg was thrilled.

As they drove downtown to the theater district, he was glad to be alone with her again. She was wearing an amethyst necklace, and as he looked into it, he felt drawn through its ethereal portal into another realm. It was an unmistakable sign that, with Meg, he was entering a higher world. What had, up until now, been a “not-to-be-believed” reverie was now a reality.

“Meg,” he said, “I’ve seen that necklace before.”

“This is the first time I’ve worn it since we met,” she said. “Do you know someone who has one like it?”

“When I lived in Houston, I did the Midnight Ramble every year in October when the moon was very full. We would ride our bicycles down this same road back into downtown on the last stretch of the ride. On the last ramble I did, shortly before I moved to Colorado, I had a vision.”

“A vision?” Meg asked, her interest piqued.

“It was a vision of a girl, a woman really. She was looking at me, but it was somewhat dreamy, and I couldn’t make out her features. One thing I could plainly see, though, was her necklace.”

“And it looked...?” Meg groped.

“Just like the one you are wearing.”

Twenty-Six

Reunion

THE WEDDING WAS PLANNED for the evening of the fourth of July, the astrology being perfect. The arrangements were confidently made to include the town home they purchased just prior to the wedding. Michael found their future home while driving through an area in Denver that was filled with galleries, shops and restaurants. The neighborhood was embraced immediately by his fiancée when she discovered that one of the best French bakeries in Denver was located about a half a block away from their future home.

The town home wrapped around a small atrium that Meg filled with terra cotta planters and hanging baskets overflowing with petunias, lobelia, geraniums, impatiens and begonias in pleasing pastels. "No fire engine red, please," she had told the florist. "Especially the geraniums."

Inside the town home she decorated with white and creamy pink roses that Heather and Amy picked up from the florist and arranged on end tables, the entry, cocktail and dining tables.

"Oh Meg, the house looks wonderful," offered Jane on the morning of the wedding.

Becky was visiting from England and was madly vacuuming the carpets with the "Hoover," as she referred to it. The furniture was polished, and the decorations looked beautiful. Becky offered to do the finishing touches to the house before the guests arrived. She was staying in the guest bedroom upstairs while Heather and Amy took the downstairs room. It felt good to have the house filled with people who would share in the joy.

"Doesn't the house have a beautiful feel to it?" asked Meg. "It feels so different."

"It's the wedding angels!" said Jane with a big smile. "They arrive before the wedding. Their presence guarantees that it's a sacred event. That's the special feeling that all weddings have. They make everyone present feel a precious bliss."

"You mean there are angels that only go to weddings?" asked Heather with a hint of sarcasm.

"Yes, girl, I'm telling you, and it's their job because a wedding is a sacred ceremony!" Jane responded with her hands on her hips.

"Just like the parking angels. Remember?" asked Meg.

"Oh Mom, you mean to tell me that there are angels that do nothing but help you park?"

"Yeah, and if you don't believe in them, call to them and ask for their help they're very..."

"I know, I know they're disappointed because they have nothing to do all day."

"That's right," said Jane.

"O.K., O.K., well, come on, Amy, let's go get the hors d'oeuvres," said Heather.

"You know, the only thing I forgot to do was hire a photographer," said Meg. "I can't believe I did that."

"Oh, no problem," said Becky. "I went to a small wedding in London last year and they handed out cardboard cameras and had the guests take pictures of each other, and then the bride had them all developed. It made for a lovely wedding album, and everyone had a wonderful time taking pictures. Don't you worry about it. I'll run to the store and get the cameras. It will be my wedding gift. You'd better get upstairs and get ready."

Meg went upstairs to fix her hair and get dressed. Her dress was Victorian, an off-white satin and lace street length dress with puffed sleeves, a matching imitation bustle on the back and a high lace collar. Her bouquet was filled with creamy pink roses and stephanotis draping down the front of her dress. She wore mini-roses and lace in her hair and a pair of off-white satin open-toed heels. For jewelry, she wore a pearl bracelet on one hand and a sapphire and diamond tennis bracelet on the other. "There's the 'blue,'" said Meg, "and the dress is 'old.' I've worn it once before, but the shoes are 'new.' Now I need something 'borrowed.'"

"How about I lend you one of my bobby pins to hold the mini-roses in place. They're sticking out and looking goofy," said Amy as she walked in the house with the hors d'oeuvres.

Heather and Amy went upstairs to get dressed as the doorbell rang. The guests were arriving early.

"I'll get the door," said Becky. "The bride shouldn't be answering the door." Becky opened the door and it was Michael, carrying his guitar case. "Oh look," she said, "the groom is here. Well, isn't it nice that we don't have to worry about him not showing up." Michael smiled, opened the case and began to play "Bianco Fiore." "Well, I must say, Meg, your life is, after all those ups and downs, quite idyllic, actually," concluded Becky.

"Mom," cried Heather from upstairs, "do I have to wear these stupid flowers in my hair?"

"Well," said Meg, "I thought they would look nice. See if you can make it work."

The doorbell rang again, and it was Taylor and Logan, Michael's Mom, and her boyfriend. As Michael had explained to Meg earlier, his father couldn't come because he was quite elderly, and his health prevented him from making the journey. Within a few seconds, Meg's brother Tim and his wife Annie arrived along with Meg's friends from school. The final guests to arrive were Michael's friends from work. Helspeth and Doug did not attend. Meg wasn't surprised. They had never repaid the $10,000 as promised when their big deal fell through.

All assembled, they began to get to know one another and chow down the shrimp. It didn't take long for Heather's flowers to end up in Taylor's hair. They really did look better on Taylor for some reason. She was a natural for the Hawaiian look of flowers in the hair. Heather and Amy wore pastel sun dresses and sandals and held their bouquets uncomfortably.

The noise level was pretty high when the time for the ceremony was announced. Logan, a minister as well as a tax man, herded everyone outside into the atrium and began with the ritual. It was a perfect Colorado day with sunshine and a few pudgy white clouds. Meg and Michael looked at each other warmly during the vows, and a hush fell over the little group as Michael put the ring on Meg's finger and kissed her tenderly. Meg turned around, showed everyone the ring, and shouted, “Now we can all eat! Follow me to the reception!”

They exited the front door en masse and walked the two blocks to the restaurant where the reception was to be celebrated. The food was great, and there was love all around. Meg and Michael said goodbye to their guests and left for their honeymoon.

That night, after a winding drive through the Rockies, Michael and Meg pulled in front of the cabin they had reserved.

“At last,” they said unison.

“I wanted to fly you here in my arms,” Michael said as he opened Meg’s door and took her hand. He carried her over the threshold and took her upstairs to the loft. The soft moonlight cascaded across Meg’s body as Michael lay her across the bed. He stood up and gazed longingly down at her. Meg lifted an outstretched leg in his direction, and as he removed her shoe, she lowered her leg back down and lifted up the other one. Michael tossed the shoe over his shoulder, and Meg deftly traced an arc down the front of his chest with the tip of her toe.

“Let me watch you undress,” he whispered, his breath quickening.

Meg stood up and undressed slowly, leaving only the mini-roses in her dark wavy hair. She lay back down on the bed, letting Michael survey the fullness of her sinewy curves.

“Take off your clothes and stand there in the moonlight,” she whispered. “I want to see my beautiful Michael.”

Michael was bursting as he complied with Meg’s wish, and as he stood naked before her, he felt the heat surging through him.

“Come to me, my beautiful Michael. I want you so much. I love you so much!”

Michael embraced her in the full fury of love’s passion, feeling their bodies and souls unite as one.

“I love you, my beautiful one. My beautiful wife.”

That same night, as they slept like two spoons tucked into each other, Meg had a dream. She was, once again, in the Palace of Twin Flames. Her long white robe trailed upon the floor. The being of Light, her guide, once again led her along the mahogany paneled walls. She was in awe of the heavy wooden beams that decorated the high ceilings. The floors were oak, arranged in an elaborate parquet pattern. She looked at the portraits of the elated couples and passed by the same carved stairway that she had passed during her first visit. Other visitors brushed by her as she rounded the stairway. Her guide raised his arm and pointed in the direction of a small cul-de-sac in the hallway, immediately past the stairs. "Look there," he said, but his lips did not move. There she saw her portrait, once again. Her face was flushed with joy, her partner's hand still pressing on her shoulder. She wore the same clothes in the portrait as last time, the same strand of pearls about her neck. The portrait was clearly unchanged but this time something was different. This time her guide pointed to the face of her twin flame sitting behind her and it quickly came into clarity.

Meg gazed on his face, then looked up contentedly at her guide. He smiled at her and spoke, once again with his mind. "You have passed your tests. You may, once again, be joined." Meg looked back at the portrait and witnessed the handsome face of Michael.

The next morning, Michael nudged Meg excitedly. "Meg, I just had the most incredible dream!"

"Yeah?"

"I was in an awesome palace. It had mahogany paneled walls, beautiful parquet floors, high ceilings, and there were portraits of smiling couples everywhere."

"Yeah?"

"I was escorted around by a being of Light, and he took me to a small cul-de-sac and showed me a portrait of us. There we were, smiling and radiant! He said we could once again be joined!"

"I had the same dream," Meg whispered, eyes wide.

Michael looked at her in disbelief for a moment and then hugged her tightly.

"It's been a long, long time, Meg!"

THANK YOU FOR PURCHASING THIS COPY OF

The Heart Chasers:
A Tale of Twin Flames.

We're so glad you enjoyed reading it.

To order more copies for family and friends,
please call 1-877-949-9336.

Don't forget to visit our website at:
http://www.heartchasers.com .
We would love to hear from you.
So email us and please don't forget to add
your review of our book on Amazon.com.

Our very best to you and yours,

William and Emma Moore
emma@emma-moore.com
william@emma-moore.com